D1515665

BODY COUNT

A Vietnam War Thriller

RICHTER WATKINS

BODY COUNT: A VIETNAM WAR THRILLER
Copyright © 2019 by Richter Watkins
Published by Pryde Multimedia, LLC

All rights reserved. Without limiting the rights under copyright reserved above, no part of this publication may be reproduced, stored in or introduced into a retrieval system, or transmitted, in any form, or by any means (electronic, mechanical, photocopying, recording, or otherwise) without the prior written permission of both the copyright owner and the above publisher of this book.

This is a work of fiction. The characters, events, and places portrayed in this book are products of the author's imagination and are either fictitious or used fictitiously. Any similarity to a real person, living or dead, is purely coincidental and not intended by the author.

Names, characters, places, brands, media and incidents are either the product of the author's imagination or are used fictitiously. The author acknowledges the trademarked status and trademark owners of various products referenced in this work of fiction, which have been used without permission. The publication/use of these trademarks is not authorized, associated with, or sponsored by the trademark owners.

This book is dedicated to the 58,000 American soldiers who died in Vietnam, America's greatest war disaster, and to those who came home to a vicious hostility such as no soldiers in American history had ever faced.

This war of attrition was fought in defiance of General MacArthur's warning after Korea to avoid ground wars in Asia. The failure to heed that warning tore this nation apart and left wounds from which America has not yet recovered

.

WITHDRAWN FROM
COLLECTION

DEAR READER

In 1968, the Tet Offensive changed the war in Vietnam and incited a massive resistance to that war across America, a resistance that radicalized politics in ways that still divide this nation.

This novel depicts events leading up to the Tet Offensive and centers on a war-within-the-war between the military and the CIA over the building of a revolutionary Third Force. This is a work of fiction and as such is not meant to depict the literal truth of characters and events, but rather the deeper meanings of what happened and why.

WITHDRAWN FROM
COLLECTION

PART ONE

The Nine Dragons

1

On an unusually hot Mekong Delta afternoon in the last week of 1967, CIA operative Frank Acosta walked up to the front doors of the Old Can Tho air tower where his partner, John Katt, a man everyone called JK, waited.

"Chandler's coming in now," Acosta said, putting his flight bag down next to JK's.

"About damn time, that problem out on the river is getting crazy. We need to get him there fast before it blows up. The chopper is waiting. Why in hell did it take him so long?"

"He couldn't get clearance at Tan Son Nhut. Place is a beehive of activity now that Westy is bringing troops back from the borders to protect Saigon."

They waited inside the air tower, not wanting to leave the shade for the midday sun until the plane landed.

Acosta was worried about the problem on the Bassac River; it had to be dealt with fast. If it went to hell, the whole Mekong

Delta might explode and the man they were waiting for was the one person who could calm things down in the dispute between river police and the boat people.

Acosta squinted into the harsh glare, a painful whiteness magnified by the mirror-like sheen on the surrounding stagnant paddies adding to the sharp glint from the runway's steel mesh plates.

"Chandler's not going to like this," JK said, a toothpick sliding pensively back and forth in his mouth. His tone of voice had that I-told-you-so whine that Acosta knew all too well.

"He's coming in now," a tower operator informed them.

Acosta donned his bush hat and his pilot's glasses, then picked up his flight bag, saying, "I'm sure he'll handle this." He pushed open the door and the unusual heat for this time of year swarmed over him, sucking out his breath and flushing his body as if he was a piece of dough shoved in an oven.

Acosta stopped. "Damn!"

He hesitated, like a reluctant swimmer testing the water temperature.

But then his attention was drawn to the jungle behind the rice paddy that circled much of the airfield as two shots penetrated the stillness.

"What the hell was that?" JK asked.

"Sounds a hell of a lot like a high-powered rifle," Acosta said, staring out at the jungle beyond the rice paddy beneath the pale, burnt-out sky. He searched above the feathered tops of the nipa palms into the lifeless pale sea, finding only the torn remnants of a cloud and two startled hawks flying off to less contested hunting grounds.

Finally, they heard an A1-E Skyraider's dull drone. The single prop plane appeared over the treetops. "That's our boy," Acosta said. In spite of self-disciplined calm, a small knot of tension lay heavy in his stomach because of the big problem developing out on the Bassac River that Chandler was coming in to deal with.

"Maybe that isn't him," JK suggested.

"You think?"

"He's coming in very rough. Who the hell is piloting? No slope comes in low like that. They drop from near vertical."

Acosta shook his head and stared pensively through squinting eyes at the plane making some strange, wobbly moves before touching down hard near a row of steel storage containers that housed massive ammo that was distributed when needed around the Delta. The plane lumbered past them, its single prop spinning like a big fan. Acosta and JK started toward it. But when the plane failed to brake, they stopped.

"What the hell's he doing?" JK asked.

Acosta stood with his flight bag dangling from his right hand as the Skyraider rolled on down the makeshift steel plate runway without slowing. He spotted two men in the cockpit, and they both had their heads bent as if they were looking for something on the floor and ignoring the landing altogether. The sun flashed off the Plexiglas and Acosta couldn't tell what the hell was happening. This old airport with a runway made of interlocking metal plates was short.

Suddenly the tower's emergency siren gave off a nerve-shattering wail that raced through his gut like a flock of flushed birds.

"Shit!" Acosta said, throwing his flight bag off to the side of the apron and breaking into a run.

The plane passed the Special Forces compound and a crash derrick parked along the runway and continued on toward the paddy field. But it was slowing and looked as if it might stop on the edge of the rice paddy. Sweat was already streaming down

Acosta's back and he had to take off his glasses for a second to wipe the sweat from his brow, flicking the water off his finger, the salt stinging his eyes.

Behind him JK said, "Those shots. Maybe they took rounds coming in."

The Skyraider reached the end of the steel mats and eased into the grass and on into the steamy, shimmering paddy field. Then, as if its wheels had hit a curb, the plane jolted to a halt, its heavy nose dropping to the water, tail swinging skyward until it was perfectly vertical. There it stood.

Running toward the plane, Acosta saw Chandler struggling to push the windshield up. He also saw two bullet holes visible in the underbelly.

American Special Force advisors and Vietnamese soldiers came out of the air tower and its annex, and from the heavily sandbagged compound, many of them half dressed, some in shorts, others struggling with their fatigue pants. These were men who fought at night and slept during the day.

One of the men from the compound was yelling for someone to get the crash derrick key. Others were lugging grappling hooks and steel cables.

The plane's canopy moved, but then fell shut again with a thud as the trapped pilot struggled to lift it. He was fighting its full weight against gravity. Single engine Skyraiders were built like tanks. Acosta slowed as he neared the place. Three hundred meters away, peasants had stopped their bikes and cyclos to watch the spectacle from the highway that led into town.

Then in slow motion, the plane began to topple over, but paused for a moment before continuing on until its tail slapped the water with a crack and lay like a stricken beetle on its back, with the men from the airfield surging around as it began to sink slowly into the water and mud.

When the two case officers reached the plane, Frank Acosta plunged into the paddy water, its cloying stench exploding into his nostrils. He yelled orders as he went. "Don't let it sink! Keep that goddamn canopy up!"

The men responded by grabbing for any leverage on both sides. The water was up to their chests as they threw their collective weight against the plane, grunting, shouting encouragement to one another. But the heavy plane sank into the water and mud in spite of the efforts of the men.

From the bank, a red-skinned sergeant uttered in a heavy fatalistic voice, "Never budge it! Only thing that'll pick one of those bastards out of the muck is a crane." Just then, as if in response to the ruddy sergeant's observations, the canopy slipped under water in a gurgle of bubbles leaving only the wheels sticking out of the paddy.

Acosta yelled, "Get the fucking crash derrick over here dammit, don't just stand there!"

"Can't move it without the key to turn it on and it ain't on the keyboard," one of the soldiers said. "I just checked."

JK turned to the sergeant. "Where the hell is it then?"

"Somebody got it in their pocket. We made a duplicate for the Viets, but they lost theirs a long time ago. We're looking for the guy who might have it. He's probably at the EM club bar."

"Is there a way to hotwire the damn thing? Jesus Christ who—"

"We're on it!" somebody near the crane yelled.

Furious, Acosta turned to a man who had a fire axe in his hand. "Give me that." He snatched it away, tossed his hat and glasses up on the bank and slipped down into the warm murky water. He felt his way alongside the canopy, his eyes struggling against the muddy water. He found a narrow opening in the canopy. His fingers touched Chandler's fingers. He pushed them back and wedged the axe into the slot and, digging in with his knees like a catcher digging in for a low pitch, he put his weight into it, but nothing moved.

Acosta stayed with it as long as he could then burst up for wild gulps of air before dropping back down again. But trying to both anchor himself and swing the axe in water proved utterly futile as it glanced impotently off the thick shield. A boot pounding out against the windshield from inside told him they had little time as the water was rising inside the plane and the men would drown.

When Acosta came up again for air, he saw JK helping with the attachment of hooks and cables. There looked to be at least thirty men now, among them half a dozen officers and a medic team. Some of the men had that spectator-at-a-fire look.

Suddenly all attention turned to the crash derrick as it coughed, died, then coughed and sputtered and came to life amid a wild burst of cheering. A triumphant face popped up from the derrick's cockpit.

The rusty machine moved with cranks and screeches to the edge of the rice paddy. The men holding the cables attached to the plane waited until the crane reached them and then they linked up.

"The cabin is filling with water. We need to get that goddamn plane up," Acosta yelled.

The winch turned, yanking the cables taut, and the plane started to move, but then the motor suddenly died and the Skyraider sank down amid moans of disgust and anger from the men on the bank and in the paddy.

Acosta stood helpless now, his wet cloths burning his skin, a sickening nausea of panic in his gut. Come on! Come on! He screamed in silent rage. The soldiers on the bank and in the water had no idea how important one of the drowning men was.

The crane motor started again, but only after the loss of another precious minute. Few cheers accompanied this renewed effort. Everything now depended on how much air was trapped in the cockpit and for how long. Otherwise they were on the verge of losing one of the most important CIA agents in South Vietnam, whose operation in the Mekong Delta was designed to change the entire course of the war.

The cables tightened and the plane began to rise. The nose popped free and suddenly the canopy fell back and Chandler's body slushed out in a rush of water over the side of the plane like a fish being poured out of a bucket and nobody could get him before he fell back into the water with a splash.

Acosta reached him first. He grabbed his arms and pulled him up and out of the water. Then a dozen hands assisted in getting Chandler onto the bank, where the medic team went to work to try and pump water from his lungs and bring him around.

The Viet co-pilot remained dangling in his harness, hanging in the air with his head and arms lolling loosely like a broken puppet until men finally pulled him down.

The medic team worked on Chandler for ten long agonizing minutes with the resuscitation pump before it was obvious he wasn't going to respond. He was dead. Acosta was in shock and for a time unable to react to what had happened.

Those who'd been working on the Vietnamese pilot with the pump got one last gush of water and weeds before giving up on him as well.

Acosta stepped forward and produced an ID card that identified him to the Special Forces officer. "He's one of ours," he said absently, staring down at the body, at the slime that lay on the dead man's neck after they had pumped it out of his lungs.

"Hell of a way to die," the captain said. "Who is he?"

"The best of the best," Acosta said.

JK dropped down on his knees and began riffling through the dead Chandler's pockets. He handed Acosta a slimy wallet, some keys and a few soggy ten pee notes of Vietnamese currency and a wet radio.

A jeep came down the road and when it reached them, a colonel got out.

Acosta identified himself and JK to the officer and then said, "I want this plane quarantined." He gave instructions for the disposition of the bodies until a team could come down from Saigon to investigate the plane. He spoke absently, his mind for the moment stuck in shock. Those bodies, exposed to the harsh sunlight, revealed the terrible vulnerability of life in a war zone.

"Nobody touches anything on the plane." Above them circled an AC 47 'Spooky' that were always prepared to go anywhere in the Mekong Delta. Another was circling the jungle area where the shots had come from. Special Forces soldiers would hunt for the shooters who, no doubt, were long gone.

Acosta went up to the plane and retrieved Chandler's flight bag, and then asked for transportation. The senior officer made his jeep and driver available to them.

"Tell air control not to respond to any messages about this crash, or the men involved, until we okay it," Acosta said.

Acosta turned once and looked back at Chandler, as if the dead man might suddenly jump up laughing, calling it all an elaborate joke. Then, a flight bag in each hand, his shoes squelching with each step, he and JK headed over and climbed into the jeep.

As they left, JK said, "We need to get hold of Teague. That problem on the river has to be dealt with."

"Not just yet," Acosta said. "We have a chopper out there watching over the problem. They'll keep us undated if it goes to hell, but first let's get into Chandler's place and make sure it's not been robbed, or being robbed."

The idea that this could be much bigger than just a couple of VC shooters wasn't something Acosta was ready to reject as their jeep rumbled down the feeder road to the crowd on the highway leading into the French-designed town of Can Tho on the banks of the Bassac River, one of the river branches that the vast river system the Viets called the Nine Dragons.

Acosta couldn't believe Chandler was dead. They just might be burying another program in the already overcrowded counterinsurgency graveyard. This was to be a last-ditch effort to get this war on the right track.

Out on the river, in the middle of the crisis, was former naval officer Michael Teague. He was Chandler's right-hand man in dealing with the alienated Buddhist sects. They had to let him know about Chandler, but not until they'd secured the dead agent's apartment.

The Buddhist Hoa Hao, Cao Dai, and Catholics were the sects that back in the fifties had defeated the communists driving them out of the western Mekong Delta. But Saigon had feared them and had disarmed the sects and rendered them irrelevant.

Chandler wanted to change that and had a big following in the CIA. But Saigon wasn't accepting of the idea of a resurgence of power in the Delta sects and neither were the Americans under General Westmoreland.

Acosta had some apprehension about what might be waiting for them at Chandler's pad located in the center of the city Chandler loved.

JK liked to joke that Acosta was full-on paranoid. But the way Acosta saw it, after seven failed coups, and a lot of death in the dark webs of this country, paranoia was, in his opinion, the only rational state of mind. He appreciated that the man taking them into town was a Special Forces sergeant with his Uzi on his lap.

Chandler's death, or murder at the moment when, out on the Bassac River, something was happening that involved Teague and the Buddhist leader Vinh Lac, scared the hell out of Acosta. He'd been touting the upcoming events in Long Xuyen as the beginning of something they'd been planning a long time. Now it could be a fast, ignominious end.

2

The crisis on the river had reached a critical moment. Former naval officer Michael Teague stood on the bow of his boat with his communications agent, former army Lieutenant Bruce Engler.

Teague's right hand was on a carbine resting on the gunwale as a message to the river police that they weren't going to get him or the Hoa Hao Buddhist leader to back down. Not this time.

The showdown on the river between police and angry river people backed by a radical sect leader had reached a critical stage with over fifty wide-beamed boats known as junks and sampans of the Buddhist Hoa Hao having been stopped and ordered searched by the river police.

Above this growing conflict on the Bassac River, the lower branch of the Mekong, a navy UH-1B chopper circled the growing conflict.

Teague turned to Engler. "Call the airfield in Can Tho again. Somebody has to know why Chandler's late. Where the hell is

he?" Something was very wrong. That nobody was responding
was not good. He glanced up at the circling gunship. The police
had to believe the chopper would sink them if they got stupid and
fired. The door gunners had their black visors down and looked
ready for action.

Teague turned to the police officer on a boat fifteen meters
away. "This is international water and traffic must be respected."
He shouted in Vietnamese, a language he'd studied for the last two
years. This was no regular police officer; he was a member of the
dreaded and hated Hoat Vu secret police, and he was pointing a
cocked forty-five at the man on the boat between them, Vinh Lac,
a Buddhist Hoa Hao leader and key element in Chandler's
operation.

Hundreds of sampans and junks lined up on both sides of a
steel cable that stretched across half of the river, stopping traffic
moving west toward Cambodia. Many of the boat people that lived
and worked on the river were crammed in along the banks, giving
as wide a berth as possible to the showdown.

The three boats at the center of this conflict now formed a
triangle almost nose to nose. It was the second time in a week the
Viet river police and Hoat Vu had stopped traffic for hours and
searched boats.

Teague was very upset that Chandler hadn't yet arrived as he
handled these river police better than anyone.

Ostensibly checking IDs and looking for contraband, the
National Maritime River Police made big hauls from these
shakedown operations. But now the Buddhist Hoa Hao were
involved and stopping it. This was an international waterway and
these mass searches were illegal and it was Teague's
responsibility, as he saw it, to put an end to the practice, but he
didn't want to call in any of America's forces. He'd commanded
one hundred and twenty fast patrol boats with their water jet

engines before being pulled into CIA operations by Chandler.

"He left CIA headquarters two hours ago and nobody seems to know where he is," Engler said.

"Call Acosta again, he's got to know."

Teague wanted this to end without trouble. The muscles around his sun-scorched neck and jaw felt tight. He studied the swarm of police and gunboats that surrounded his meager force of three PBRs and his boat on loan from Rivereign Assault Group, RAG 34. He wondered if the police were communicating with their superiors. This could not work out for them or for anyone else if it came to a firefight.

The police also wanted to board the Hoa Hao leader Vinh Lac's boat because they suspected he was armed and bringing weapons to his people, who'd been disarmed by Saigon over a decade ago. That was never going to happen. A lot of blood would be in the river before Vinh Lac would surrender to these crooks.

The officer running the show was Hoat Vu and ran much of the Special Branch. He looked very uneasy and his arm quivered a little from the weight of the forty-five aimed at the Hoa Hao Buddhist leader. "Khietan lenh khong toi ban!" the officer threatened again in a high, excited voice.

To Teague's right, one of his gunners reseated the belt of the thirty-caliber machine gun with a slap, yelling back at his adversary to get out—Didi mau-len! The tension was mounting dangerously.

From the bow of his very fast broad beamed junk, the Hoa Hao leader shouted, "You die here today, you make all your wife's lovers very happy."

That taunt brought a ripple of chuckles from Vinh Lac's men. The Buddhist leader held a carbine with one hand, the barrel resting on the gunwale. He wore a maroon headband and looked like an Apache Indian warrior. He took the radio phone and spoke in a low voice to the other boats in his fleet. His eyes never left the Special Branch officer, his enemy as much as were the Viet Cong, maybe in many ways more so.

Teague didn't like where this was headed. He was highly respected on the rivers, even by the most aggressive and corrupt Viet police and Province Recon Units, but the Hoat Vu secret police were a different breed and he wasn't sure why they would be out here unless it was to arrest or kill Vinh Lac.

The silence was broken by Vinh Lac's powerful voice. "You have two minutes to begin lowering that cable! Then I will open fire."

Vinh Lac was a good head taller than the average Viet male and when he moved, the lean, sinewy muscles under his taut skin rippled in the light of the late afternoon sun. Among the Vietnamese in the Mekong Delta, his exploits were legend. The Viet Cong had a high price on his head and Teague intended to protect him no matter the cost. He was a critical factor in the big changes Chandler and other CIA operatives were trying to create.

"Can't get hold of Chandler or Acosta," Engler said. "I'm getting a bad feeling about this. We'll end up in a shootout, coming down on the side of Resource Control's most wanted man that won't go well."

The real criminals here wore police uniforms. Vinh Lac ran convoys to Phnom Penh, especially rice, and got world market prices for his clients. Without him they'd be selling at Saigon's artificial prices. He was a hero to the boat people and the rice farmers and he was Teague and Chandler's greatest source of intelligence.

The Special Branch officer shouted at Teague in a mix of Vietnamese and some English, even though he was well aware of

Teague's fluency. "Lui Lai! Lui lai! You will be court-martialed for this. You are here to help us—not these river pirates."

Teague was sick and tired of having to deal with this ongoing exploitation. He studied the face of the Hoat Vu officer who had a round, soft face, but rumpled from abuse and dissipation, like an old couch pillow ready for the garbage. He had eyes as narrow and impersonal as coin slots.

"You can't block an international waterway. This is an illegal operation," Teague said calmly, the river beneath him gentle, the sky above still but for the circling chopper, a big asset that had stopped the police from getting too aggressive.

The officer's nostrils flared. "You don't tell me what kind of operation I'm running. You don't command here. Your purpose here is to assist my government!"

"You now have one minute," Vinh Lac stated.

"Lui Lai! Lui lai!" the officer screamed again.

When Vinh Lac changed his weight from one foot to another, the movement caused the officer to jerk the weapon up and extend his arm, his finger tightening around the trigger.

Teague needed this man to back off. But the officer had lost face and looked really crazy.

What happened here, a decade into this mess, would have major consequences. On the decks of the sampans and junks that had been stopped by the cables stretching from police boats, the women stood with the high oars in hand, the men squatted stolidly, and their children peered out from the cabins. Many of the sampans, and all of the broad-beamed junks had eyes painted on the front of them, a tradition on the rivers, and those eyes seemed to be watching. Who would the Americans support? That's what it all came down to. Either they supported the government and its thieves, or the Hoa Hao and the Mekong Delta people.

The police officer finally seemed to realize the American

wasn't going to get Vinh Lac to back off, so without warning, he extended his arm and it looked like he was actually going to shoot Vinh Lac. But he was a millisecond too slow and Vinh Lac shot him in the chest. The officer took two involuntary steps back and collapsed on the deck, his weapon skidding away.

Teague yelled at the other police to back down.

For a time, nobody moved, the stillness gripped the people on all sides of the river and in the boats. The only significant motion came from the chopper as it dropped down into a tighter circle with a good shooting range for its rockets and gave the door gunners an excellent view. That changed things fast.

The other officers on the police boat held some sort of impromptu conference. One of the men broke from the group and went over to his radio operator, stepping over the body of his fallen commander. Within a short time, the cable began coming down. Within minutes, the police boats were on their way down river.

Teague gave a thumbs-up to the chopper, but he knew this wasn't over, not with a Hoat Vu officer dead.

Teague watched the retreating police boats. "Chandler, dammit, where the hell are you?"

"What about Rivereign Command?"

Teague shook his head. "Keep them out of this. They have enough on their plates. Keep trying Acosta and JK."

He watched the sampans and junks, the river people, and on the banks, hundreds of villagers. He'd left his naval career at Chandler's behest and his vision of re-creating a serious Third Force in the Delta. The last thing they needed was a major conflict.

3

Frank Acosta and JK hadn't reached town when the airfield informed them that the chopper pilot circling the boat problem on the river reported that a police officer had been shot and the rest of the police boats were backing away and heading toward Can Tho.

Acosta said to JK who was on the radio, "Make sure the pilot understands we're sending another chopper and if it comes to some kind of counter-attack, they're to take whatever actions are necessary to stop it."

He thought again of calling Teague, but first had to see if Chandler's pad had been robbed. If it had, that would tell him the shooting of the plane had been a very deliberate act, maybe the beginning of something.

He told the driver to try and move faster. If the downing of Chandler's plane was an assassination, and that could be the case, he was very happy to have a hard core well-armed Special Forces trooper driving them into town.

The driver was taciturn and somber as he yanked the jeep with an almost ruthless finesse through the midday traffic of old, faded buses crammed with peasants and top heavy with baskets, cages and bikes, trucks, cyclos, and swarms of Solex motor bikes buzzing in every direction. Their driver had to avoid peasants crossing the road as they were considered the world's slowest walkers, yet he also had to deal with traffic as the Vietnamese were also very fast and aggressive drivers.

On both sides of the highway, flatfooted women without shoes shuffled along under the balanced weight of baskets at the end of shoulder poles. One peasant woman smiled mysteriously at Acosta, an apple-sized goiter bulged at the side of her neck.

He took a pack of Marlboros from his flight bag, the only dry item besides his bush hat, and lit a cigarette, his muddy shoe pointed out the door, his gaze skirting restlessly over the monotonous yellow stucco buildings.

They crossed the rickety bridge over the Doi Canal, the planks rattling under them. Below, along the fetid canal, spindly stilted shacks hung out over the water like festering sores, and naked children played in the mud while their mothers washed cloths.

They passed the thatched hamlets that made up the outer tier of the city and entered a street lined with tamarind trees, fenced in yards and small neat houses with red tile roofs. Acosta indicated where they wanted to go.

They continued along the central street of Can Tho. Unlike Saigon, or any of the cities where American ground forces were in big numbers, this city on the river's edge was still remarkably free of the assault of pimps, mini-skirted bar girls, or beggar kids hawking porno pictures of their sisters.

Definitely Chandler's kind of place with its French-designed wide streets, shops and bakeries, no bars in the center of town, and a great dike overlooking the river that was crowded every night with mahjong players, river boats and the young parading up and down the market side of the dike.

Slowed down at an intersection, a frustrated and anxious Acosta glanced at an old woman hunkered down on the curb, who glanced up at them from under her conical hat. Her blouse was pulled up, and a small girl was applying hot little suction cups to her naked back. The cups, used to ease arthritic pain, were about the size of shot glasses that left silver dollar-sized red welts. The old woman said something Acosta didn't understand and then she grunted and laughed raucously at her own joke, her mouth and teeth stained a reddish brown from betel juice.

Boys walked along the road holding hands, but never a boy holding hands with a girl, that was culturally taboo.

A truck load of ARVN troops rumbled by, the Vietnamese soldiers absurdly shrunken in their American helmets. One of them made a suggestive remark to a young girl on a bicycle. She turned and pedaled off, the panels of her ao-dai dress tied down so they wouldn't catch in the spokes. They billowed like small sails.

The driver pulled up and parked along the curb where Acosta suggested. They got out and walked into the complex through the outer gate, the driver carrying his Uzi. Acosta pulled the zipper of his flight suit back so he had quick access to his handgun as they entered the courtyard.

An older security officer in a neat white uniform studied Acosta suspiciously for a moment, displaying two gold teeth with his big smile. "Choi Obi!'yoste. You no come long time," the man said with his broken English as he scrambled to his feet and hurried over to shake hands—an American custom adopted by the Vietnamese military and police.

"Chandler no here. He go Saigon."

"He's dead, da chet." Acosta said.

The security officer's face clouded in shock. "Chandler fini?"

"Plane crash. Out at the airfield just a little while ago. Is there anyone in the apartment?"

"No. No one."

Acosta used the set of keys they'd gotten from Chandler's body to open the door to his apartment. He looked in and saw nothing out of place and no assassins waiting. He went out and told the Special Forces sergeant he could go back. "We're good, thanks."

As the soldier drove off, Acosta turned to the security officer and said, "Go find Von Khiet at the rivereign base and bring him here quick before those river police get back."

He flashed a smile of sorts, left and flagged down a cyclo driver.

The first thing Acosta did was get a Coors for each of them. Chandler had a quirk about 'in' items. Coors, having to be smuggled to Vietnam, was the 'in' beer. He handed one to JK and took one for himself.

They quickly and systematically packed Chandler's notebooks and records in a case they found in his closet.

From across the small courtyard, children peered at him through the window, their faces quiet and earnest. A woman came out on the second-floor balcony and scolded the children, but then she too couldn't help watching what these Americans were doing.

In a false bottom of the wardrobe, JK found more of Chandler's personal notebooks inside a fireproof box that he opened with one of Chandler's keys.

Acosta took the notebook diary and opened it. "Jesus!"

"What?"

"First damn sentence is about General Collins being outmaneuvered by Lansdale and the Catholic lobby in fifty-four."

"He's writing a book about that disaster?"

"He talked about that if things went wrong. He never got over being fooled."

Chandler had brought Acosta into the situation, and other agents. It was a moment when it looked like they had what they wanted with an independent anti-communist nationalist sect force joining the war with the new made-in-America regime. But they were betrayed, nearly destroyed and disarmed.

"Let's get this stuff packed up and out of here," JK said.

As he packed, something in the notebooks caused Acosta to reflect on the pamphlets dropped from planes, warning the North Vietnamese Catholics that atom bombs were coming. It drove a massive flow of refugees that provided Diem with what he lacked in the South, a legitimate power base. That alone had doomed the rise of Buddhist power. The northern Catholics were very different from the Catholics in the Delta, who were aligned with the Buddhists.

In those early days, Acosta was naive as a puppy, and he went with Chandler into the Delta to convince the Buddhists that now that they had cleared half of Vietnam of communists, they and the other sects could march gloriously into Saigon and take their rightful positions in the government. Chandler considered this his greatest error and guilt had consumed him.

That was one of the worst moments in the early stages of the war. Agents led those gullible Hoa Hao generals up Route 9, leading them not to glory and American alliance, but into a death trap that would destroy the only peasant-based political and military force in the South, severing completely the link between the peasants and Saigon in a betrayal that compromised the war and was a hard legacy to overcome. But one Chandler had become obsessed with.

To this day, Acosta couldn't remember exactly how he and Chandler had survived the ambush that had destroyed the cream of the Hoa Hao Buddhist army outside of Saigon. But he did remember later thinking that they had been used deliberately—not just because they were trusted by the Buddhists then, but because they were being punished for supporting anti-Saigon forces. Chandler hated that he'd been trapped in naiveté and it was a mistake he never recovered from but wanted to rectify.

They played the game year after year, crisis after crisis, coup after coup in hopes that a Third Force could be re-established. With the war becoming stalemated in bloody attrition, and the CIA being squeezed out everywhere in the country by MACV for control—the 'Old Hands' had decided it was now or never. They wanted to build a radical organization out of the wreckage from the networks in nationalist groups, especially in the Mekong Delta.

Teague was the only replacement they had for Chandler, if a replacement was possible.

"Nothing happening out on the river so far," JK said after making another call. "We need to tell Teague to move towards Long Xuyen. There he can figure out what he wants to do and what we want to do."

Khiet, another soldier Chandler had transitioned from Vietnamese Special Forces to CIA operative, finally arrived, looking very upset. "Who kill Chandler?" He was dressed like a Saigon punk: tight white pants, tight blue T-shirt, big Rolex watch, black hair down to his shoulders, which was very popular with the Hoa Hao. He looked devastated by the news.

"The plane was shot coming in. Who did the shooting we don't know. We're going to need a fast replacement for Chandler, and that would be Teague."

"Yes. Mister Gamewarden. Very popular along the rivers,"

Khiet said. "When the floods very bad he bring food to hamlets. Medicine. Many thousands have no home. Government steals the relief supplies."

"You go on up the river and see what's going on. I'll call Teague."

"He know about Chandler?"

"Not yet."

Khiet left. He had a very fast boat and could get upriver in a hurry.

Acosta finally made the call he hated to make.

4

When Teague got the radio call from Acosta about Chandler's death, he was stunned.

"Von Khiet is on his way," Acosta said. "You need to get out of the area, go on to Long Xuyen. Be safer there. I'll come up and we can figure this out." That city on the Bassac River was at the center of Hoa Hao country in An Giang Province.

It took Teague a moment to pull himself out of shock. Chandler had had the authority to change Teague's status from naval officer to advisor with operational independence from normal naval operations. Like Chandler, he had seen too much corruption and destruction to accept the idea of an all-powerful dictatorship in Saigon backed only by American power. He'd watched the suppression of peasant movements that were trying to become part of government and strategy and he'd looked at Chandler and the people backing him as someone who might change that.

Now, with Chandler suddenly gone and a dead river police officer, he faced the biggest crisis of his strange career. With Chandler's help, he'd become a separate force on the rivers. Now what?

"Gamewarden!" Vinh Lac shouted from his boat. He was leaning on the railing with the insouciance of a victorious pirate. He grinned, displaying perfect white teeth, the late sun glinting coppery on his skin. "You join Hoa Hao navy." His men laughed, as did most of Teague's Viets. "Gamewarden, we invite you and Chandler, when he come, to the big meeting tonight."

Game Warden was the operational name for the 116 U.S. Naval Task Force that Teague had once been a part of. He had somehow acquired it as his personal tag among the Vietnamese after he joined the CIA's Rivereign Operations that were separate from the Army/Navy Joint Task Force.

A speedboat coming upriver caught their attention. It bounded over the wake of the last of the retreating police boats.

Teague recognized the boat immediately as the Chaparral mini-cruiser owned by Chandler's close friend and counterpart, Khiet. The speed boat cut power and drifted toward the Hoa Hao junks until it stopped alongside the Hoa Hao leader's boat.

Khiet, the lone man in the Chaparral, took the line Vinh Lac's men tossed him, secured his boat, then took an outstretched hand and was jerked up onto the junk, where he disappeared with Vinh Lac into his cabin, no doubt to give him the bad news.

Engler, who'd worked with Teague in the joint army/navy operations, and who now was Teague's right hand man, said, "Sa Dec is on the horn?"

"I'll call them back, I have to deal with this," Teague said.

When Vinh Lac emerged, he didn't look happy. "Come over, Gamewarden. We talk." He eased his boat closer and Teague jumped onto his deck. Khiet came out of the cabin and joined them.

Vinh Lac said, "Chandler's death may be no accident. Khiet say bullets hit the plane as it was coming in and went out of control. VC?"

"We don't know," Teague said. This was bad news on many fronts.

Vinh Lac said, "You come to rally in Long Xuyen. We have much to discuss with you and you be safe there."

There was an urgency in Vinh Lac's voice that matched his expression in intensity and apprehension, something Teague hadn't seen in him before. He was usually as cool and collected as they come. This had him really bothered in a big way.

A sampan was passing close by, the man at the stand-up oars bowing repeatedly towards Teague and talking in a rapid singsong voice, his gleaming eyes visible in the shadow of his hat like fox's eyes peering out of a cave. He saluted Teague and Teague absent mindedly returned the salute and the peasant broke into a triumphant smile that spread to the face of his wife, his parents and the multitude of children on the over-packed boat.

Teague turned and stared west up river towards the city of Long Xuyen, the heart of the radical Buddhist Hoa Hao. He gripped the side of the junk and stared at the jungle wall and the river, the sampans and gunboats. It was decision time.

Vinh Lac, now using his English as he liked to practice from time to time, said, "Gamewarden! You meet my sister. She come Long Xuyen from Cambodia for big rally."

Teague felt the pull of Vinh Lac's offer. He stood on the threshold and he knew if he went to Long Xuyen it might well be an irrevocable step. The tension in him was palpable. For eighteen months, this moment had been building, incident by incident. With Chandler's death, it changed everything. It put him up front. His decisions would determine far more than just his future.

"Lieutenant," he said to Engler, "let's have dinner in Long Xuyen tonight with Vinh Lac's sister. You okay with that?"

"I don't see any better offer on the horizon. Let's do it."

Vinh Lac's sister, Thi Xam, according to Chandler, was a serious rising power. He likened her to past great female leaders in Southeast Asia. She was also elusive, spending time in Laos and Cambodia in areas occupied by rebel forces that had fled Saigon's attacks over the years.

Engler gave a sardonic shake of his head with a thin smile, as if believing this might be the beginning of the end, yet he was, like Teague, a free-floating advisor under control of CIA operatives.

Teague shrugged. "It had to come to this sooner or later."

"Maybe we're giving our enemies in MACV the rope to hang us with."

Teague nodded and said, "Xin loi, so be it."

Chandler's death and the confrontation with the river police changed everything. With his mentor dead, Teague knew he would face a major dilemma.

The decision to go to Long Xuyen and meet the mysterious and powerful Thi Xam was impossible to resist. The big question in his mind was, would the CIA continue the mission? The idea of walking away after all that had been done couldn't happen. But if it went forward what would his role be?

He felt a powerful need to fulfill the mission that Chandler had brought him into the program for. Something had to change and change radically.

Both he and Chandler had been big fans of the great scholar of Asia, Paul Mus who called the Hoa Hao founder, Huynh Phu So, the Martin Luther of Southeast Asia. But to his enemies, Phu

So was known as the 'Mad Bonze'.

When the Viet Minh killed the radical Buddhist leader, they cut up his body and got rid of it so there couldn't be a burial and grave that his followers could visit.

But the elements in the CIA that Phu So had started had to be continued. His followers had become the great fighters in South Vietnam and had driven the communists out of huge parts of the Mekong Delta. Because of that power that Saigon feared and helped destroy, many wanted it brought back and Chandler was a leader in that cause and had convinced Teague that it was the only strategy worth pursuing.

Teague saw no retreat, no escape, given what had happened on the river and the death of Chandler.

The Buddhist sect that fought for survival every day of its short twenty-eight-year revolutionary formation, and was betrayed time and time again, remained the mission Teague believed in.

5

Teague watched clouds sweep down on the river like billowing swells of white sails, blotting out the late afternoon sun for a moment. Halfway to Long Xuyen, and all the time expecting possible retaliation for the shooting of the river police officer, with a dozen junks around them, and choppers above, they were entering safer waters.

Engler was constantly monitoring a series of radio channels. The CIA operatives had given them a very advanced radio system, even superior to most of the navy and army equipment used in the Delta.

A short hard rain, very unusual as this was the dry season, blew in from the north and hit, engulfing the flotilla of boats, beating the river as if with a million-barreled Gatling gun, then passing and the sun burst back on them, bringing with it a rainbow from one end of the earth to the other.

The flotilla, now twice as big, entered the quay at dusk. The rebellious city was in the western Delta not far from the Cambodian border. People along the banks watched in seemingly grave silence and awe at the armed junks of Vinh Lac and Teague's military river boat.

Maroon-colored Hoa Hao banners and yellow flags hung from balconies and poles. Something big was happening in this beautiful river town in the western Delta.

Teague disembarked and joined Vinh Lac and Khiet, leaving Engler and his Viet crew to stay with the boat and monitor communications.

The mood in the city was exuberant. The market and streets were packed, teeming with humanity. The air was charged with excitement.

Walking between Vinh Lac and Khiet, trailed by a couple dozen Hoa Hao warriors, Teague felt a sense of historic purpose. It was a vague but powerful realization that he might just be crossing a boundary that he couldn't come back from. But he accepted for the moment that because he believed like Chandler and others that the war was headed in a very wrong direction, the loyalty of the most anti-communist peasants who could make a critical difference was at stake.

As they were making their way to the marketplace where the speeches were going on, an old man jumped out of the crowd with two young boys in tow. He ordered the boys to prostrate themselves on the ground, which they did, flopping down like a couple of fish, and then he kowtowed in the old fashion, dropping to his knees, lowering his conical hatted head all the way to the tarmac.

Vinh Lac scolded him for this outdated public obsequiousness. "Get up, old one. The Buddhist bows to the earth for no living man."

The old man stood and bowed, with hands clasped under his

chin. He told his sons to get up. They did so, but kept their heads bowed in respect.

Vinh Lac then bowed to the old man in the polite Buddhist fashion, a slight lowering of the upper body and with no sense of servility or submission. The old man, his wispy beard like corn silk, his face trenched as an ancient city under excavation, bowed back, hands clasped prayer-like in front of him. When he stood, he could not straighten out, his spine, calcified from a life time bent to the rice fields, allowed him only limited movement.

The historic submission and subservience of the peasant was anathema to the Hoa Hao and the lesson was delivered.

Teague, Vinh Lac and his entourage continued on, their numbers swollen by an army of children.

Long Xuyen was a tranquil town of tree-lined streets and yellow stucco buildings; a town of ease, under the sway of a perpetual tropic languor, but tonight in this electric surge of crowds, there was a different feel.

"A lot of people," Teague commented in understatement as they entered the market. The Delta had the most people with over nine million and a hell of a lot of them seemed to have come in for the big event.

"The Hoa Hao was two million strong in the Mekong Delta twenty years ago," Vinh Lac said as they made their way to positions near a crowded dais erected in the center of the market. "We have survived the Viet Minh, the French, and their boy Diem. And now, after much repression, we again grow. Very soon, we will once again be millions and we will be united under a single party, the Social Democratic Party of the Hoa Hao. And we will rearm our followers."

They took seats of honor in the public square.

The speakers came and went in rapid succession, each greeted with thunderous applause from the thousands of peasants. They had come to this rally from all over the western Delta. They had come by sampan, on foot, by bicycle and bus. Hoa Hao rallies were the only outlet for the frustration of these peasants trapped between forces they could neither control nor accept.

Caught up in the energy of it, Teague lost himself in the debate. It soon became apparent that there were two sides in a heated argument over policy.

The first group of speakers had called for maintenance of present policy of giving tacit support to the Saigon regime as long as the Hoa Hao and their Cao Dai were given the right to maintain their political and religious organizations.

The last of these moderates spoke. "The fate of Vietnam is in the hands of the Americans. Until the war is decided, it is better for us to stay out of it. We must build our strength slowly, without confrontation and challenging superior forces until we ourselves are strong. Now is not the time for us to enter a struggle we cannot win. We must turn away from confrontation."

That was met by booing and jeering.

"That is Trong Quy," Khiet said. "Quy hates Vinh Lac and Xam and is becoming a big problem."

A lone voice rose in defiance from the crowd, a female voice. "When a man is in the jaws of a tiger and lays still in hopes that his passiveness will save him, the navel he contemplates before he is eaten will not be his own."

The laughter that followed rocked the open market.

"That woman," Khiet said, "is Vinh Lac's sister."

Teague finally found the speaker in the crowd, but he could only make out her general features. He credited her with great poise and boldness to stand up in this excited crowd and challenge the speakers. "I still have two minutes, according to the agreement," the man on the platform said. "You will have your turn then."

Chandler had said that if Vinh Lac was the muscle of the coming revolution, she was the brains.

"Accept my most humble apologies," she shot back, "but either your watch is wrong or you have lured even the patience of Father Time to sleep."

Amid the roar and laughter, the speaker could no longer make himself heard. He held a conference with the dignitaries, mumbling something that apparently was derogatory and booed. He then relinquished the stage to Vinh Lac's sister.

There was a palpable change when she ascended the platform.

Teague thought at first he was seeing a very close resemblance to the Hoa Hao guerrilla leader, Madame Ba Cut, the beautiful wife of the general beheaded by Diem ten years ago. But then as this woman passed from the darkness into the light, he realized she was even more stunning and very young, maybe in her mid-twenties.

She strode across the platform as if she owned it and peered out over the open-air market at the mass of peasants and shopkeepers and cyclo drivers as if they were part of her personal entourage. She wore the black quons and white blouse of the simple peasant, but there was nothing simple in the effect. This wasn't sweet beauty; this was fierce beauty.

Xam addressed the crowd. "I am happy my opponent said bad things of me. In Asia, when a woman is called nasty names, it means a long life."

That was met by great applause and laughter.

She, like so many Hoa Hao, utterly lacked in past Vietnamese female virtues—shyness, demure deference, lowered eyes, perpetual smile.

"She speaks English?" Teague asked.

"Very good," Vinh Lac said. "And French and some Mandarin. She attended one year at University of Saigon before they threw her out for political activities. She finished her education in Paris before coming back home." The pride in Vinh Lac's voice was strong.

"Co dep wa," Teague said.

"Yes," Vinh Lac agreed, "My sister is very beautiful. She knows only politics. We call her Noi-tuong, the house minister."

The tropical darkness quickly enveloped the market in its thick, velvety richness, a single point of light on the stage centered upon this girl named Xam. When she spoke, she moved her head, punctuating her phrases with a nod and the people around Teague were nodding with her, and then yelling and clapping and the market was a thunderous deluge of emotion. Teague hadn't witnessed anything like this in his two years in Vietnam.

The slow, almost quiet, easy tempo of her talk grew stronger. "If your children perish in flames from bombs meant for the enemy, if your trees that grow your fruit and bring you shade wither and die, if by every victory, the South grows weaker, the cause of the enemy stronger...is it not time to question the wisdom, the sanity of the strategy? Is it not time to question the vision of the men who pursue such a strategy?" The power of her voice was in the depth of its passion and intelligence.

The men and women around him were on their feet yelling and shouting, fists waving in the air, faces distended. And it went on and on as she paced before the microphone excoriating Hanoi, Saigon, and the American military command. At one point, she stopped. Her flashing black eyes fixed on them. She made them wait. Even Teague found himself holding his breath.

"Between the Mekong Delta"—she spread her hands as if forming an invisible map—"where the Nine Dragons flow to nourish the rice fields that feed nine million people, we have been spared the catastrophe of the big war, but it is coming now and if a political solution is not soon found and this war of attrition continues to expand, the bombs will come, the tanks will come, the helicopters and artillery will come. The rivers of the Nine Dragons will fill with blood and tears."

She paused, her magnificent dark eyes admonishing her subjects to take heed, to bury this prediction deep into their souls. "For this madness to stop, we must stop those who shackle us with failed policies. We cannot do this with the lying down strategy of Trong Quy."

Teague felt a shiver through his body. He stared at her in a kind of trance-like amazement.

"What will stop it"—she fixed them with a fierce, hypnotic gaze, the headband of the Hoa Hao on her like a crown—"is fighting the political battles on our terms, not the Viet Cong's, not the Generals in Saigon, not Hanoi, not the Americans..."

When she finished and had left the platform amid thunderous applause, Vinh Lac turned to Teague, "Come. You meet our Noi-tuong."

For the former naval officer, one who grew up on structure and on order, this slippery political slope was taking him to a place he never in his life had imagined. He'd been known to challenge the thinking of political and military authority in his articles written at Annapolis, but this was on the battlefield, in the reality where everything changed. Still, without Chandler's intrusion, he would still be running the rivers hunting Viet Cong and trying to ignore the underlying politics.

Chandler was obsessed with moving very fast at what he thought was the last chance to bring the peasants into the war. He was so admired by the political element in the movement that Teague hoped he could step up and win them over.

<u>6</u>

Teague followed Vinh Lac and his crew through the clapping, cheering crowd. They made their way into an alley and through a door that took them to a private room at the rear of a restaurant.

There were about thirty people gathered there. Xam was on the other side of the room talking to Khiet and a bald-headed Theravada monk in a saffron robe. The three turned as Teague and Vinh Lac approached, and the monk, as if seeing something that disturbed him, hurriedly left by the side door.

"That is Nhu Bon," Vinh Lac said of the monk. "He is our secret link to nationalist groups in Saigon, Danang and Hue. He likes his anonymity where Americans are concerned. Especially now. He's been warning us about some new military intelligence operatives who have been watching us very closely."

They walked up to Xam. "I would like you to meet my sister, Thi Xam," Vinh Lac said.

"Chao co," Teague said with a slight bow, a bit shocked at

seeing her up close.

"Chao ong," she replied with a slight smile and reached out and they shook hands, something rarely done by Vietnamese women. But this, as he knew, was no ordinary woman.

Teague said something about her speech being powerful, but so lost in her look, he followed it up without any particulars.

She nodded and thanked him. She was taller and more full-bodied than most Vietnamese women, and had the most intense eyes and strong features. Vietnamese women were often very beautiful, but this young woman had something beyond simple beauty. Her features were strong and exuded intelligence.

"I am very sorry to hear about Chandler," she said. "He was a very good friend of the Hoa Hao Buddhist movement. Do you know what happened? I've heard his plane was shot as he was coming into the old Can Tho airfield."

"I know only what you know at this point."

Then she switched to English, saying, "Most Americans do not speak Vietnamese very well. They speak it the same way I speak English. But your Vietnamese is very good."

"Your English is excellent," he said. And so are you, he thought. "I studied your language intensely for over two years and it's still a struggle."

"Please, have dinner with us."

"Of course. My pleasure." Like there was any chance of refusing this incredible woman. Chandler had praised her, but he may well have understated what Teague was facing. Southeast Asia had a history of powerful women during their great wars. Some of the hill tribes were totally female-run matricides where women were the sole inheritors of land.

He settled with Xam, Vinh Lac, Khiet and half a dozen others on rugs and listened to their discussions. The Vietnamese were usually very cautious with opinions and it was extremely difficult to hear what their point of view was about anything, but there was no such restraint here.

Much of the talk centered on the introduction of massive American forces in the Mekong Delta well beyond the combined army and navy river forces that had come in a year ago.

Xam said, "The GVN cannot fight effectively here. They have no support from the people. The communist presence is growing. The Americans have no choice but to bring in many more troops or rearm and support the Hoa Hao as the real army. Saigon's ARVN are now little more than security guards for province chiefs."

Teague had the seat of honor between Xam and her brother. When the food was served on the low table around which they sat, it was uncooked and there were three large tureens, each filled with boiling soup with a hot charcoal center and a large snake of some sort wrapped around it.

Each person used their chopsticks to take pieces of raw fish or pork and then cook it in the soup and lay it on the table of the person to his right, which, in Teague's case, was Thi Xam.

At one point, she turned to him. "Please, you will make me fat."

"I've never seen a fat Vietnamese," he replied.

"Then you've never been to Saigon, where the government officials eat their elaborate meals," she replied, much to the amusement of the table.

He heard them speak of Saigon with as much contempt as they did of Hanoi.

Xam looked pointedly at Teague and said, "If American soldiers fight and die for our country, and we are not allowed to, what kind of Vietnam will Americans be dying for, a dictatorship of fat fools?" That brought laughter.

Xam studied him for a moment, then said, "When my brother told me the news about Chandler, I was very sad. He was one of our good friends. We need good friends with those Americans who understand the problems correctly."

Teague nodded. "He had a great vision of the future for this country and I share that." He got a powerful look from this brilliant young woman, a look he would think about. And he then promised her that he would do everything he and his associates could to change American policy and work to get the Buddhists in the Mekong Delta rearmed."

He was taken in by this young woman. And he realized that he'd lost any apprehensions about replacing Chandler.

When he and Khiet returned to the boat after dinner, he found Engler in the cabin monitoring his radios.

Seeing Teague, he took off his head phone. "How'd it go?"

"Very good. Anything going on?"

"The shooting of the river police officer is drawing a lot of reaction as he was a member of the dreaded Hoat Vu. I'm making all kinds of contacts and it doesn't look good. There's this colonel who runs some of MACV's 'dark force' operations with the secret police and some Viet Special Forces. Now he might just be heading to our world."

Teague didn't like the sound of that. "Get hold of Frank Acosta. We need to find out who this guy is."

If this military intel colonel was partnered up with the Hoat Vu secret police and hard-core Viet Special Force units, there could be very unpleasant consequences.

And he began to wonder exactly who was behind the shooting down of that plane and why a Hoat Vu officer had stopped the boat traffic that carried Vinh Lac.

7

An emergency military meeting was held in the new MACV headquarters in a metal building of heavy sheet steel on Ton Son Nhut airfield outside of Saigon.

Colonel Benjamin Stennride was now the senior MACV Intel officer with the charge of running covert operations in the Mekong Delta to stop the radical sect factions from rearming. The death on the river of a Hoat Vu police officer was seen as the beginning of a potential Buddhist revolt.

Colonel Benjamin Stennride listened to the concerns of three of the most powerful generals, who operated special counterinsurgency programs about his mission.

"The last thing we need," General Paulick said, "is a resurgence of radical Buddhists. Colonel Stennride is, in my humble opinion, the right man for the job. We've got a compound near Can Tho freed up for his use. A PRU unit and some secret police elements under Major Chien." He turned to Stennride. "You ready for a new assignment?"

"I'm always ready for a new assignment," Stennride said.

The idea that there were Americans once again involved with the anti-Saigon rebel Buddhists, who two days ago murdered a river police officer, had shocked the generals. But it had a very positive effect by giving Stennride immediate and wide-ranging authority to deal with the crisis.

He would have the assistance of Major Chien, the powerful and most effective operative in the Vietnamese secret police.

Paulick said, "The American who seems to be the replacement for the radical CIA operative Chandler, who died in that plane crash, is Michael Teague, a former hotshot commander on the rivers where he led over a hundred gunboats. He was pulled in by the CIA to become one of their agents. His former boss, Navy Captain Ferguson, can help Colonel Stennride locate Teague and talk to him about what's going on. Teague was with the radical Hoa Hao leader when the shooting happened."

"Will Ferguson cooperate?" Stennride asked.

"He has no choice. We're putting maximum pressure on him. His operation is joint army/navy. Do I hear any nahs?" Paulick asked.

"What the hell are nahs? That a Vietnamese term," General Mills asked, lightening the mood.

"Those rallies and political actions are spreading," Paulick said. "They can't be allowed to grow into the kind of force they were in the fifties when they took over the goddamn Delta. Colonel Stennride has his work cut out for him."

General Paulick came outside with Stennride. "Nothing will go on record and I want you to understand that we will support you in every way we can. This has to be stopped. Do whatever it takes. This Teague is a big potential problem. He was one of the best operators with Game Warden and its hundred and twenty boats on the river system. He's got the nickname Gamewarden from those operations."

"I'll get it done, sir."

"Good luck. Keep me informed." Paulick went back inside.

Stennride assumed his job would be much easier now that the renegade CIA operative Chandler was out of the way. But if the generals weren't pleased with the reports about the big Hoa Hao rally in Long Xuyen, Stennride was pleased because it gave him what he wanted, the power he needed to deal with the rebels and his career.

When the colonel walked to a waiting jeep that would take him to his chopper, his mood was aggressive, and happily so. He had the independence and authority he wanted.

The airfield was jammed. Saigon was rapidly moving troops back to protect the city and that was obvious in the three feeder strips angling to the 10,000-foot runway. Pipers, Beeches, Cessnas and Caribous were at the 5,000-foot drop-off, at the 7,500-mark C-54s, and 118s and then beyond them, the heavy fighters. He saw entire squadrons of choppers, crash trucks and mobile derricks as the war footing grew by leaps and bounds, the place humming with the rise of serious war with the coming of massive American troops.

Captain Keller, Stennride's chief assistant and pilot, was already on board and had the engine winding up.

"It's crazy. I've never seen anything like this. Got to be the busiest airport in the world," Keller said.

"I'm pretty sure right now it is," Stennride agreed.

"How'd it go?"

"Exactly the way I wanted. We're going to pay a visit to a naval commander and they're putting a lot of pressure on him.

He's the means to get at this replacement for Chandler. We're going to put an end to this insanity."

Minutes later, after getting the okay from the air tower, the chopper lifted off and headed towards the Delta, and a major river base.

Less than an hour later, they settled on the helipad of a command ship near the base at Dong Tam on the Bassac River. The base was expanding fast with the 2nd Brigade of the Army's 9th Infantry Division, five thousand sailors and soldiers who were trying to get control of the fluvial terrain of rivers and swampy rice paddies once controlled by the French Dinnassauts.

Stennride glanced upriver at the sampans, fishing junks and rice barges. The death of Chandler was a step in the right direction, but now they had to deal with the man who appeared to be taking over the CIA's support for a Buddhist movement. This was, in the colonel's mind, tantamount to treason.

It was time to clamp down and bring the countryside under absolute control. Politics were over. Now it was all about war and military power. Chandler's boy, if he didn't want to end up like Chandler, had to be brought on board or kicked the hell out of the country, but not before he provided the information they needed about the movement, its leaders and who was supporting it in Saigon.

As he crossed the ship's deck, an operation appeared to be in the making at the RAG base. An American SEAL team was boarding the shallow draft patrol boats, PBRs, and a sprinkling of Viet Special Forces joined them.

A lean, middle-sized officer broke from a group of men, snapped off a quick salute and said, "Colonel, the commander is expecting you."

Stennride followed the sailor down into the Navy Captain's office, then left.

"Colonel," Ferguson said. "What can I do for you?"

You know damn well what you can do for me, Stennride thought. He studied the naval officer for a moment. He had plenty of information about the man's tolerance of the rise of the sect rebels, and that had to end here and now.

Stennride said, "This growing problem with the Buddhists sects is back and I'm authorized to bring it to an end. One of your former officers is involved, as you well know."

"I'm aware of that," Ferguson said.

"Chandler's disciple and now apparently his replacement was under your command. The CIA agent who recruited him is way out of bounds and that's going to stop. There will not be a rearming of the sects. That isn't going to happen. You can help us put a stop to it."

"I'm not involved in any way. I doubt I can help you."

"I only want one thing from you and that is contact with Michael Teague."

"Teague is no longer under my command and what he's involved in is not my operation. You need to talk to the CIA. I don't think I can help you even if I wanted to."

"That's the problem. I'm not talking to the CIA, I'm talking to you and through you, I want to meet and talk to Teague, make him understand that things are changing and changing fast. If the Hoa Hao cause chaos they will then become the VC's greatest inadvertent ally by distracting government forces in the Delta. Soon we'll have hundreds of thousands of troops spread all over this country and there is no room for Third Force fantasies. Teague and his CIA mentors have to understand this new reality. I just want to explain things to him. Do you know where he is?"

"Last we heard he's up river near Long Xuyen. I don't

communicate with him."

"But you could if you wanted to."

"And tell him what?"

"You were his former commanding officer. I've heard he has a high regard for you. What I think might be a good idea is for you to bring him here and talk to him face-to-face."

"About?"

"About the death of that policeman on the river, for starters. Then about what is really going on. This can degenerate into something very ugly if he isn't cooperative. So, if you can set up a meeting with him I think we can work something out. He was a superior naval officer and I'd hate to see that talent lost. And I'm sure you don't want to see him and his once outstanding career go up in smoke."

"Just what are you authorized to do here, Colonel?"

"I can't tell you everything, obviously, but I can assure you this is in everyone's best interest, including his and yours. These rivers and swamps you're trying to secure are going to be up against something we've not seen before. This operation you are involved in, this navy and army combine is doing a very good job. I want to make Teague an offer that might bring him back on board."

"If he refuses?"

"Contact him and get him to come down and talk. I'll make him an offer he can't refuse. Call him, pick him up by chopper and get him down here and talk to him. Find out just what he is doing and see if you can get him to meet me. You won't be involved any further than that."

"I'll make an attempt. There are no guarantees."

"Captain, there may be no guarantees in this world, but there are always consequences."

8

Long Xuyen's markets were packed when Teague picked up some croissants and headed back to his boat at the main dock.

"Ferguson wants to talk to you," Keller said as Teague came on board with the pastries and Keller was happy to take one.

"About the river police incident?"

"He didn't say. But I'm sure that's what it is."

Teague made the call and didn't much like going for a visit but agreed to. "I need to get back this afternoon. Some important events going on. That work?"

"Yes. I can send a chopper for you right now," Ferguson said.

After he hung up he poured some coffee. "They'll be picking me up in about an hour. Let's go to the landing downstream."

"He didn't tell you what it's about?"

"No. But he's okay with getting me back. I want to be here when the Free Khmer and Yard leaders get here for talks with Vinh Lac and Xam."

Of the people who would see the rise of the Third Force as a positive, Captain Ferguson, though a straitlaced naval commander, was one of those who accepted a need for radical policy change, and he was admired by Chandler.

The chopper that picked up Teague an hour later was little more than an engine mounted on an open frame with a Plexiglas bubble on top and riding in it was like riding a loud, quick bumblebee.

They reached the command ship in less than forty minutes. The base just east of Can Tho was a beehive of activity from navy swift boats, airboats and SEALs boarding them while Seebees worked on the shore line. This was a world he did miss but left for good reasons.

Teague exited the chopper and went below in the Navy's half of this joint Army-Navy task force command ship.

Ferguson motioned for him to sit while he finished what he was doing on some paperwork. Teague sat in front of the desk of the man who had been his commanding officer for two years. On the walls around the desk was a gallery of photographs, the chain of command and in the center, President Johnson, resembling an old rumpled blood hound, on one side the Secretary of the Navy, on the other the Pacific commander.

Captain Ferguson said, "Mike, it's good to see you." He pushed some papers aside and reached over and shook hands with Teague. "Lots of things happening all at once. I'm sorry about the death of Chandler. He was a damn good man."

"He was brilliant and a great loss," Teague said.

Ferguson had a look of apprehension as he said, "I heard some Hoa Hao, Cao Dai, and Catholics are attending big rebel rallies all over the western Delta and in Cambodia and that they've made Long Xuyen virtually off limits to regular ARVN. How big is this?"

"We don't know yet. Why am I here?"

Ferguson had a pencil thin mustache and he played with it when he talked, running his fingers gently along it, as if the activity helped him focus his thoughts. "That river incident that got an officer killed is having repercussions. Celebrations in Long Xuyen aren't helping."

"What happened on the river was the result of illegal searches and it was the Hoat Vu officer who tried to kill Vinh Lac. It was just a case of the Hoa Hao leader defending himself. What's going on?"

Ferguson nodded. "But a dead police officer at the hands of a radical Buddhist won't be taken lightly. Vinh Lac was armed and that's part of the issue."

"Given the increase in VC forces, maybe being armed is the only way to go at this stage." That, of course, was the big debate.

Ferguson played with a cigar box and looked really stressed. "Look, Chandler's death and that of the Hoat Vu officer might look to some to be connected."

"How so?"

"One in retaliation for the other. I don't know. What I do know is that things are changing and changing fast. It might be a very bad time for some radical Buddhists to be violating the disarmament pact. Yes, the communists are moving to the villages and close to cities, but that is to avoid the massive bombing campaigns. Nobody knows what's next, but this is a bad time for any anti-government actions from the sects."

"Why am I here?"

"I need to understand what's going on. Chandler's dead. The idea he was sponsoring is where? Those agents supporting him are getting a lot of pressure to pull back, at least for now. I'm getting pressure because of my connection to you. I need to understand exactly what is going on."

"You know what Chandler was doing and I'm continuing that course because it's necessary. Maybe this is exactly the time to bring the greatest fighters on board."

"I don't think so." His former commander's face tightened. "Teague, things are changing fast. Dammit, you know on some levels I sympathize, but the reality is we're not configured to fight political battles in the midst of a military campaign that is growing by the hour."

Teague stared at him in stolid silence, offering no display of contrition or no commiseration. "Why am I really here?"

"I want you back on board."

"Abandon the most important police movement in the country to do what?"

"I went out on a limb to save Chandler's and your ass several times. I bent every rule in the book. Look, you achieved one hell of a lot by creating a new procedure for sending out artillery barges ahead of operations. It saved many lives. I was sorry to lose you, and for a time I believed in what Chandler was trying to do. But it's over."

"You don't know that."

"I know that this is no time for radical anti-government politics. I want you to consider backing away from this. I can get you reinstated in a new capacity."

"No. That's not going to happen."

Ferguson fumbled with a cigar. "What I need from you is to be sensible about the new reality. What happened out on the river the other day isn't good for anyone, but it can be resolved. But this course you're on can't continue."

"That's a decision for me to make."

"I need to know you understand what is going on, how big this is and how much CIA involvement there still is. Chandler's dead and things are going to change and you can't replace him. Is this rumor of re-arming true? And who is going to provide those arms, the CIA? That's not going to happen. You know exactly what's going on and I want you to tell me."

"You know I can't do that."

Ferguson stared at Teague for a time before saying, "You need to give me some information as to how big and how serious this sect movement is. You owe me that."

"I don't think so."

"In return, I'll help you back away from this."

"I'm sorry, but the answer is no."

Ferguson said angrily. "Dammit, I'm going out on a limb for you and you are now cutting that limb off. We have thousands of American kids out there fighting and dying in the fucking jungles and it's only going to get worse. It's not the time for a Buddhist revolution or the shooting of river police. I have no doubt that the incident was defensive, but those Hoa Hao junks are illegally armed. The war is changing fast."

Teague saw something in Ferguson's eyes, something small and narrow and mean that he hadn't seen before. "I don't know what's going on with you, but I need to get back." He got to his feet. "Maybe in a week or so we can talk again."

Ferguson said, "I want you to think damn hard about what you're getting involved in. You need to walk away while you still can."

"I'll think about it," Teague said. "Right now I need to get back. You should talk to those higher on the chain, like Acosta. I'm not in a position to reveal anything."

When Teague walked past the ship's war room, navel intel officer Jimmy Mawson came down the staircase. "I heard you were on board. How is it going?"

"Against the current, as usual."

"It's the nature of this war. Good luck with your new gig, whatever it is. Sorry to hear about Chandler."

They shook hands. Something felt wrong about the captain. He was under pressure because of that river incident.

Teague went on up to the deck and boarded the tiny bubble chopper and told the pilot to take him back to Long Xuyen.

In minutes, the pilot was shooting down the river at a thousand feet.

Teague stared morosely down at the wide tawny river with its fishing villages and boats. Ferguson had really disappointed him.

The pilot pulled the small bee-quick chopper up into the late afternoon sun and headed northwest, moving away from the river.

"Where are you going?"

"Avoiding some major bombing runs up river."

They skirted the edge of a rice field. South of them, there were grey plumes from a bombing run rolling across the tree tops like an avalanche of dirty snow. But when they were well clear, the pilot continued well off course.

The rice paddies below gleamed like endless glass windows in some fallen gothic cathedral.

After a few more miles, they moved out of the intricate patterns of intact rice fields into Long An and the operating TAOR of the American Ninth Division, the biggest American ground combat unit in the Mekong Delta and yet was not allowed full operating authority in the Transbassac where most of the population lived. They passed over a burned, cratered, scarred landscape, empty canals, hamlets that were black smudges, and paddies with broken bunds where no rice would be grown. Scorched earth and attrition was killing six to seven thousand VC a month, and was coming into the Delta where the majority of the people lived and it would be a disaster.

"This is a strange route," Teague said.

"I've got my orders."

"What the hell are you talking about? What orders? Where are you taking me?"

"Right here," the pilot said.

They passed over a large rubber plantation untouched by the surrounding devastation, its thousands of hectares of rubber trees in neat endless rows. Below, along a thin ribbon of canal stretched a hamlet of thatched roof houses half hidden in the trees.

They began to descend on the large, seemingly empty compound with a large villa and smaller buildings that appeared to have been abandoned, the grounds uncared for.

Teague had his hand on his sidearm, but the pilot shook his head. "My advice to you is to cooperate. Otherwise they'll hang you from the tallest tree in Indochina."

"What the hell is this?" Teague demanded as they were angling in behind the massive, colonnaded plantation house.

"Some people want to talk to you," the pilot said. He brought the chopper down near another larger chopper. He flicked off the power and his radio and started to get out.

A dozen red bereted carbine wielding Vietnamese Rangers, led by an officer brandishing a revolver, dashed toward the chopper, carbines at port arms.

"Di ra! Di ra!" the Vietnamese officer shouted, waving his revolver at Teague.

"Sorry about this," the pilot said. "Good luck."

The troops deployed, weapons drawn. Teague climbed out. He saw that there was an American sitting in the shade on the veranda reading a book. The man looked over at Teague, then went back to his reading.

The chopper powered up and lifted off as the commander of the squad of Viet soldiers removed Teague's .45 side arm.

9

Colonel Stennride smiled as he sat back in his bamboo deck chair on the porch of what was once a magnificent French estate. "Well, well, I got a visitor," he said as he looked up from the book he was reading and watched as Chandler's replacement was escorted up onto the veranda by the Province Recon Unit now under his control. Ferguson had come through. Not that the man had much choice with a group of powerful generals on his back.

Hopefully, this was the last rebel American leader in the Mekong Delta that he would have to waste time and resources to bring down. Chandler had created a mess that had to be cleaned up fast. The CIA lived in dream worlds of their own diseased imaginations, and meanwhile the VC and NVA were on the move.

"Sit down, make yourself comfortable, Teague," Stennride said. He nodded to the commander of the PRU unit and he and his soldiers backed off.

Teague sat down. "What the hell is this, Colonel?"

Stennride stirred his iced tea with a long spoon and with the other hand he replaced his bookmarker and closed the book. "'Witness' by Whittaker Chambers. It's a good read about Alger Hiss being a spy for the Soviets. Iced tea or coffee, or maybe a glass of excellent rice wine?"

"Iced tea is fine."

Stennride nodded to a servant at the door and he disappeared into the house.

Then a Vietnamese man came up the steps from around the side and walked to them in the middle of the Veranda and pulled up a chair and sat down.

"This is Major Chien, head of Hoat Vu operations in the Delta. He lost one of his men out on the river the other day and isn't happy about that."

"The man who shot him did so out of self-defense," Teague said.

"He was armed. Not appropriate for a Buddhist Hoa Hao leader."

The papasan hurried out with the tray of glasses, sugar cubes and lemon slices, a pot of tea and a pitcher of rice wine. He deposited the tray on the table with a flourish of bows and smiles and then quickly vanished back inside the house.

After they fixed their drinks, Stennride, who went for the rice wine, said, "Self-defense is often used as an excuse. Did you know that no great literature was ever produced without caffeine to aid in focusing the mind, just as no good dinner was ever consumed in this land without a little good rice wine? It would be a contradiction. Life is not art, it produces art. As the Latin phrase has it: ars longa, vita brevis. Art is long, life is short. There are few artists among us. They tell me that you"—he stared hard at Teague—"are somewhat above the rank of the dilettantism we usually deal with. There is, of course, evil art as well as the noble variety."

"I guess that often depends on who's looking at it," Teague said. "What is it you want from me?"

Following a moment of mutual observation, Stennride said, "The death of Chandler is, in my humble opinion, the end of yet another misguided CIA fantasy. The disaffected 'old hands' and their schemes and dreams are over. My job is to find out how many Americans are involved and who are the leaders in the radical Hoa Hao and what their plans are. That's why you're here. You know what's going on, who are those betraying the Saigon government's effort to stabilize this country with our help. You're a former naval officer and a very smart hardcore river warrior. You can be of great help. And the reward is getting back to your profession."

"I'm not interested. You have no authority."

After he studied the activities of geese out in the uncared-for garden pond, Stennride came back to Teague and said, "Let's be real. You come clean with us and we'll get you out of this mess. I'm making an offer you can't rationally refuse. You had an exemplary record and are much admired by many who operate with Rivereign Forces. And because I think you've become an unwitting associate of a small group of dangerously stupid malcontents whose only real contribution to this war will be to prolong it. I expect your cooperation in bringing this CIA conspiracy to an end. The days of wild schemes are over."

"Is this a threat, Colonel?"

Stennride grew increasingly aggravated by the insolence as he slid a thin case of cigars back and forth between his hands, flicking it with his fingers. He didn't like Teague's attitude. He opened the case and extracted one and lit it with a worn Zippo lighter that had a silver crest emblem on one side. "We don't always have good alternative choices in life. Chandler was old school and not somebody who could be called back out of the wilderness. Tell me something about how his operation works, who's involved and what is being planned by these radicals and who they are on all sides."

"I'm not your prisoner. And if I were, all you'd get is what any enemy would get: name, rank and serial number. Maybe not the rank, as I have no official rank."

Now he was really going in the wrong direction. Colonel Stennride frowned, shook his head at this ridiculous attitude. He glanced at Major Chien, who'd remained silent. "We have a tough guy on our hands. A once good soldier turned treasonous rebel infatuated with a lost cause. A man implicated in the death of a secret police officer."

"Look, if I'm in some kind of trouble you're going to have to do it the right way. I'm employed by the CIA and they will want to know what is going on. My advice—"

"I don't need your advice on anything, Teague. You're operating out of bounds and I have authority to deal with people like you."

"What authority? Whose authority? Let me see your orders."

Stennride stared at him for a long, intense moment. This guy was something else. He was throwing away his career and maybe much more for an illusion. "That's a ridiculous request by a man who'd abandoned his role and thought he was some kind of revolutionary. This is a dirty war. Our boys are dying every hour out there. Dying because this country is falling apart and you and your friends are not the solution, you're part of the problem."

"There are procedures even you have to follow, Colonel, your analysis aside."

"Your problem, Teague, like Chandler's, is that the CIA has been running all kinds of dark operations with no oversight by the people actually running this fucking war. That's changing. We're reducing the CIA's role everywhere. Bringing them back to running intel and not political action. It's over, Teague. Cooperate. You have no other choice. It so happens I have some dark force authority myself under MACV with the precise instructions to bring what you and your friends are doing out of the dark and end it."

"Colonel, this is bullshit. I need to make a call. I'm not helping you do anything."

Shaking his head in wry disgust, Stennride saw before him another goddamn Chandler. Maybe worse. He got up and nodded to Major Chien. "Take good care of our guest. He'll eventually get smart and cooperate, he just needs some incentive. I have to go to my new compound and settle in. Call me when you have something."

Before leaving the porch for the chopper, he turned back to Teague and said, "Two Vietnamese at a cafe table is a plot, three is a conspiracy, add a CIA agent and you have a coup. That is not going to happen again as it did with the murder of Diem. Those days are over. I want your full cooperation and, one way or another, I'll get it. You have a dead cop on your hands."

Teague said, "You're an officer in the United States Army. You can't do this."

Stennride couldn't believe the naiveté and arrogance of this former naval officer. "I can't do this, you say. Yet you and Chandler could do whatever you wanted, even if it meant betraying the government we built and support. Teague, I read some of your articles, especially the one about MacArthur's opinion that we should not be involved in ground wars in Asia. Well, that was then. This is a different time and we have different weapons. Communism has to be stopped right here and right now. You will cooperate because you have no choice. It's your duty and your only salvation. Right now, you're a rebel with a lost cause."

Stennride nodded to the secret police chief, and then he walked down the steps toward his chopper. He didn't understand Chandler and now had to deal with this guy. They violated every rule and regulation.

Once on board the chopper, as Keller began the liftoff, Stennride looked back as Teague was being dragged away. The would-be revolutionary had sealed his fate and it wasn't going to end well for him. The colonel had zero sympathy and a great deal of antipathy.

Against what he saw as the designated external enemy, he wasn't emotional. But dealing with the enemy within the American military and CIA was much different. The emotions of outrage and anger knew few limits. Teague was headed down the same path as Chandler and would end in the same graveyard, but only after he revealed the information Stennride wanted and needed.

10

Grabbed by Chien's men after a short, violent struggle, Teague was subdued and taken around the side of the main house to a small attached building and forced inside and then into a cage. They gave him a good beating in the process.

He couldn't believe what was happening, that an army colonel had this kind of authority, and that his former commander had apparently been part of this. What the hell was going on?

He lay scrunched up in the steel bar cage unable to fully extend his legs, with needle-like pain shooting through his battered body in a dozen places. After they left him, he pressed against the corners of the metal cage that imprisoned him, but soon realized that it wasn't going to give, so he tried to relax and think.

Later they came in and beat him, again, asking questions, a bright flashlight blinding him. He gave them nothing in the interrogation but lies. He gave up on the serial number and name as the foundation and went into creating stories that they would have to check out. He knew about the techniques in the infamous Saigon Chi Hoa prison where the interrogators used electric contacts on the fingers and toes, spilling water on the face and in the nose and mouth and sending electric jolts through the body. He wondered how long it would be before they brought that kind of torture equipment here for him and how he would respond.

They put a can in the corner of the cage and told him it was his toilet. They left him in misery and utter darkness. He was awakened by a horn every so often and sleep was driven into a wake/sleep nightmare.

They fed him nothing but water. They interrogated him over and over and he became an expert in spelling out lies and false names that they would have to check out.

They stripped him and he lay naked and had to exist with the heavy rancid stink of his own urine and sweat while being under assault from mosquitoes and bugs.

They continued to beat him at irregular intervals, dragged him out onto the concrete floor and asked questions and got nothing and pushed him back in the cage.

His sleep was always wiped out by a horn that went off at irregular times and he knew eventually that would drive him crazy.

He played elaborate mental games, attempting to recall everything he knew in one area, then in another. Sanity exercises. And he worked his muscles with isometric focus, one at a time throughout his body. Flexing and relaxing, flexing and relaxing. He played with his teeth when things got bad, when his hunger flared up, or when he thought he was going crazy.

The beatings, the lack of food and the stress of the horn had his number. After they blew the horn, he would lie in a state of desperation, hanging in exhausted limbo, dangling on the side of a cliff, feeling the adrenaline working like an acid in his bloodstream, eating him up.

He knew this would sooner or later drive him mad and now he believed that was exactly what they were trying to do and he wanted to fight them to the end.

Teague used his anger in a strange way to induce pain. It was something he'd learned from one of his Vietnamese counterparts. If you want to beat pain, you've got to practice it. A prisoner had to condition himself to ignore and endure pain and then almost welcome it. He drove his shoulder against the hard wood until he wanted to scream—then he laughed in a wild, maniacal way.

He played his games as a desperate quest to fight them and beat them. He wanted to fall into sleep, just let it come and pull him down into its warm soft arms. But when he began to give in, he remembered and stiffened and began his struggle. His lies just got him more and more serious beatings. He knew he'd never survive this for any significant period of time.

When fatigue, pain, hunger and weakness reached a certain point, even death began to look different, began to resemble sleep and that was what he had to fight with the fiercest determination. He had to reach down deep.

He relived all his firefights, the sudden eruption of machine guns and rockets from some river bank, the bloody wounds, Monitor flamethrowers shooting long tongues of fire into thatched huts on the banks. The looks on the stunned and grief-fixed expressions on the faces of men who had to put their friends in body bags. The constant pressure on regular soldiers to get stats, operate kill zones and think in terms of body counts as the defining strategy of this growing war of attrition.

In moments of icy fear, he knew the end. First, they wanted to break him down and then kill him. He had no intention of giving them anything. When negative thoughts snuck in, he beat them back with everything he could call up, but not always with success. He was much more afraid of being broken than of dying.

Maybe he had been here a lot longer. Days without night, nights without day. Time was lost. Maybe I'm already crazy, he thought. Yes, that was entirely possible. There were some strange moments when he was fantasizing about being somewhere else, like in front of his fireplace at home on Tilgeman Island in Chesapeake Bay and being a kid, the image so intense, the smells, sights, voices so real he was there and all the rest since was a bad dream.

But when struggling back to reality he knew he was actually dying. In his meddled mind a loud noise that wasn't the horn. A booming sound followed by another and another. A full-on attack.

He could feel the floor shudder. He was confused and disoriented for a moment. Some time went by and he wasn't sure what had happened, or even if what he had heard was out there or in his brain. Then he smelled smoke.

They were being bombed. The buildings would be burned to the ground. A horrific sense of dark irony came over him.

And now the fear he had so ruthlessly walled off broke through, and with it panic. Nothing, not drowning, falling to his death, being shot, even torture could produce such a desperation in him. When he was twelve he'd seen four people trapped in a burning car, the fire too hot for anyone to get near enough to pull anyone out. He'd seen a screaming, terrified girl in the backseat. That horror had never left him.

He exploded against the metal cage. He tried to leverage himself and find new angles, but the cage didn't budge. He lay still for a moment, sniffing the air like an animal. Yes, smoke. The building was definitely burning.

He heard the noises clearly now. Gunshots. Rockets. A VC attack? He gave it one last desperate attempt, and then he lay utterly spent. Not in a fire, he pleaded. But then he thought that the smoke would kill him first and that would be good, but he needed enough to breathe in to knock him out and kill him. He stared at the blackness and prayed for smoke and death. But that girl came back screaming.

Teague returned to fighting hard against the cage. He snarled and yelled. But then smoke began to filter into the room and it relaxed him even as he started choking.

The notion of his own death came to him like a revelation, bleak, startling, clear. This is it, he thought. He lay there for a moment focused on it. The fear receded in the acceptance of his end. He swore at his enemies and hoped they would get what they deserved.

He had wondered often about the moments leading to death, having seen too much of it, and now he would know. He had had choices all his life and now he had none, and that, more than anything, shook him to his core. To die fighting was acceptable. To die prostrated and imprisoned wasn't.

Then, after what seemed like an eternity, the walls crashed in. Men were out there and they were smashing it. They were going to shoot him and that was a better way to die than smoke or fire.

He braced himself. A flashlight blinded him. Then he felt the sides of the cage seemed to collapse and the pressure released and he knew he could stretch out and this realization overwhelmed him. For a moment, he forgot everything else as he tried to move his legs and feel some circulation before being killed, but they were locked. The voices yelling around him evolved into painful blurriness, then into human form, then specific faces. Hands were moving him out and onto a stretcher. He was rising in the air and being carried out!

These men were dressed in black cotton and they wore maroon headbands and he smelled an ointment he knew well: tiger balm!

He focused on a face with a perfect set of white teeth smiling at him and he was stunned. It couldn't be real.

"What you do, dai-uy? Get in your coffin before you dead, ah! No good. We take you to bac se. Fix you like new." Then the soft smile turned instantly combat hard. Khiet barked out orders and the men began to move out. Someone covered him with a light blanket.

"Khiet!" he mumbled.

But Khiet was already moving out into the night. Teague heard another familiar voice, a big voice and he knew somewhere out there was Hoa Hao leader Vinh Lac. Life flooded shockingly back into him as they carried him out into the night world, the fresh air.

And then facing his salvation, he was met by a very powerful, female voice ordering his liberators to give him water and get moving.

In his delirious state, he had a moment when he thought it was all a crazy dream. That passed. It was real. He was being rescued by people he admired and wanted to fight for.

11

Colonel Stennride was pleased with his offices in the new facility in the Mekong Delta outside of Can Tho. He had a lot of boxes shipped down and spent two days getting the servants to do things the way he wanted them.

He had a large contingent of Viet commandos at his disposal and he could enjoy watching their exercises and training from the window.

"I take it you really like this place," Keller said as he stirred his coffee.

"I do. But I'm not happy that Major Chien has offered no good interrogation results yet."

"They are taking a long time. Teague's a tough hombre."

"You try Lessing again?"

"Yeah. He's stuck on that island black site interrogating some high-level NVA they captured a week ago."

Stennride couldn't believe they were taking this long to break

Teague. He'd wanted to bring in the top American interrogator and considered stopping Chien until they could get the man. He was Captain Lester Manning and was nicknamed Cotton Mather after the 17th century witch trials. He as the man considered the future of interrogation techniques.

The colonel was clearing up his notes and thinking about getting some sleep after a late-night dinner when Captain Keller came bursting into the office. "Sir, big problems."

"What?"

"There's been a raid at the old plantation. Major Chien's interrogation team has been virtually wiped out."

"What!" Stennride jumped to his feet knocking over his beer.

"Just happened," Keller said. "Chien was in Saigon talking to his boss when he got a call from one of his men who'd fled into the jungle and was the only one from the team who'd escaped. The rebels are gone. So is Teague. Everyone who was there is dead except for the guy who hid in the jungle and the two servants who weren't killed by the attackers."

"Viet Cong?"

"Doesn't look like it. The raiders didn't kill Teague. It looks like he was rescued."

The colonel, shocked, couldn't believe what he was hearing. He grabbed his weapon and hat and they headed out to the chopper and took three heavily armed operators with them.

When, half an hour later, the chopper circled the old, unoccupied plantation he saw the burned-out ruins of the colonial house, its roof collapsed, only the walls standing. The grounds looked empty. After landing, he saw dead bodies.

In a near apoplectic state, Stennride demanded to talk to the one man who'd survived. But nobody could find him and he apparently thought getting out of there before Chien showed up was a good move.

"Definitely not VC," Stennride agreed. "They left behind some of weapons, and all the clothes."

That was confirmed ten minutes later when Stennride's PRUs found a servant hiding in the jungle. One of the men who spoke to the man said the attackers were Hoa Hao.

How had the rebels found out where they had Teague?

How big was the attack that it wiped out the secret police and PRUs?

Major Chien finally arrived, his chopper settling down in the clearing near Stennride's.

Keller went over to talk to him, but Chien wasn't listening to anything Keller was saying. Instead he stalked around, kicking debris like an angry child, came around the corner of the ruins trailed by two of his lieutenants who scrambled after him like eager hounds.

The Hoat Vu operations chief was in a state of an uncontrolled rage. There was a massive loss of face involved. He strode up to the bodies as if they were some sort of offending party and began denigrating them in a raucous, vile voice, calling them every filthy epithet he could summon, kicking dirt on them, accusing them of stupidity and cowardice. Then he spit on them and took out his forty-five and emptied it in the dead who'd failed him.

Having finished this madness to his apparent satisfaction, Chien then holstered his weapon like a man gratified that he had taken the vengeance he needed to recover his dignity in a manner that suited him.

"That man," Keller said, "is full-on nuts."

Colonel Stennride nodded, saying, "I want every asset we have hunting Teague and the rest of Chandler's dream team. This has gone way out of bounds."

Stennride had a lot to worry about if this mess in the Delta wasn't resolved soon. Historically there always were problems from one counterinsurgency hotspot to another, from Cuba to the Philippines and now here. But 'Nam was different and had potential to become a deepening disaster.

The last thing they needed was a serious growing rebellion among these crazy, fanatic Buddhists led by the new 'Mad Bonze' and his American advisor, who had given his interrogators nothing and appeared to have survived.

Stennride felt a combination of anger and apprehension. He had thought the death of Chandler would be the end to this. But now he began to think that Teague might be an even bigger problem if these rebels were willing to wipe out a contingent of secret police to rescue him. "I should have had the bastard shot. We need to track him and his friends down fast."

The colonel had been planning on going to Saigon in the morning to talk to the Mangs about moving back to the Delta where they'd once ruled. Now he had additional reasons.

Stennride had first met Madame Mang when he was on a mission to Hanoi in preparation for the movement of Catholic refugees. The spark of the first moment had lit a fire that still burned fourteen years later. He had helped her and her husband flee the North in 1954 aboard the USS Montrose, joining 700,000 others in that great exodus. What had helped get that great flood moving was the fear of a nuclear attack. This was a brilliant move by American agents and triggered the exodus that created the foundation for Diem.

The Mangs were once the second most powerful couple in Vietnam. It was their idea to scare the northern Catholics into fleeing for fear of the nuclear attack that was coming. These northern Catholics gave Diem the power base he needed to rule.

They had been a major help back then and could be a major help now. He feared this little operation that he'd expected to be over fast was going to be much bigger than anticipated.

Back in the day when the Mangs had power, they were known as the Domini Canes: The Hunting Dogs of God. They were instrumental in destroying the Buddhist Hoa Hao then and were again needed.

PART TWO

Domini Canes:
The Hunting Dogs of God

12

Colonel Stennride and Captain Keller flew to Saigon the next morning.

Stennride had worked closely with the Mangs during Diem's rule. His job, as he saw it then and saw it now, wasn't just to protect Saigon from rebel forces, but to transform Saigon into a real fighting machine and stop once and for all this Delta problem.

The Mangs had once been feared and admired for their efforts to bring the northern Catholics to power in the South. He knew now he needed a lot more authority to carry out the mission when the massive manhunt for the rebels who freed Teague and slaughtered the secret police unit turned up empty. For the second time in his long career, he was faced with the need to stop the Buddhists and their allies from becoming a major, disruptive power and he had to make the generals understand how serious it was becoming.

There was a growing sense that a significant part of the war, the political element, was once again on his shoulders. A driver took him from Tan Son Nhut to a narrow road in a middle-class section of Saigon's 3rd District where the politically defeated supporters of the Diem regime lived.

He needed much more power on all levels in the Delta and there was a couple that could help him and later maybe they would once again come back to power in the nation as a whole. He wanted them back to importance and power. He could help them and they could help him.

When the car pulled up to the gate of the Mangs', an old gardener hobbled to the iron entrance on legs like gnarled tree limbs. He opened the iron gate.

"How are you, papasan?" Stennride said, giving the old man a friendly tug on the shoulder.

"Me okay. You very good, ah?"

"I think I'll catch up to you one day."

The old man grinned with his few teeth and shuffled on back to his gardens, seeming very happy with himself.

Stennride walked toward the door of the villa where Colonel Mang lived with his wife in forced retirement. The pale villa was surrounded by twelve-foot walls topped with broken glass in a symbolic gesture of the Mangs' eclipse, their years of in-country exile.

The colonel had risked his position to save the Mangs from the massive purge of many northern Catholics who had made up Diem's ruling inner circle. It might just be time to bring them back. He pushed the buzzer. A wary old servant peered out at him through a window.

The maid opened the door, her face brightening, yet her eyes were clouded with concern. Was he coming to tell them to prepare to flee Vietnam, or was he the harbinger of good news?

"It is good to see you looking so well," he said, bowing

slightly. She smiled, mumbling her pleasure in her ironical way, with an old woman's hint of sarcasm. Then she waddled off to get her mistress.

He waited in the dimness of the alcove leading into the living room. His mind meandered through the thicket of a difficult relationship, one he had not wanted, but had not been able to resist. Madame Mang, far more than his past two wives, mirrored his soul in a powerful way and he missed her.

Wearing a shimmering red ao-dai, she appeared suddenly before him like a mirage, her magnificent eyes glad to see him, but full of questions and apprehension that maybe he'd come to tell them to leave the country.

"It is most pleasant to see you again, Colonel," she said, but with false formality for the sake of the servants. He detected both her hunger to see him and her anger at his having not come more often or come sooner. She moved over to the far side of the room by the three-foot-high flower pot.

"Is your husband home?"

"No. You have missed him." Her eyes fixed on him with the slowness of long intimacy and he thought he detected a slight quiver in her voice. "So long you not come."

"I know. I have been busy dealing with some major problems."

"As I heard. It is always good to discover what a person sees as important and what is not and then what they intend to do. Are we again in trouble?"

He smiled. "No, I am. I need some help." Her eyes flashed with beautiful mockery. "Please excuse me a moment."

He heard her speaking with her servants and then the sound of the back door.

She returned a few minutes later, followed by a servant with a silver tray. The coffee was served Vietnamese style—brewed into the cups from a slow drip brewer that took its time to produce a cup of coffee. The servant left them alone as the coffee dripped.

Now some of the Catholic children of those refugees were becoming linked up in the Delta with the radical Buddhists. No one could handle that situation better than the Mangs, if given power in the critical province where her husband was once province chief and from where their rise to power had started in the early fifties.

The Mangs had risen quickly in the new Diem regime and by the early sixties, they were second only to the Nhus in power. Behind the scenes clashes between Luc Mang and Madame Nhu had taken on almost epic proportions in the beginning stages of the Buddhist crisis. Now almost all of the victories on both sides lay in ruins.

"I'm going to press for complete control of special operations first in An Binh, then throughout the Mekong Delta," Stennride said. He lit a cigarette and stared at the slow drip of the coffee. "I will ask that your husband be once again selected as the new chief in your former province."

Excitement and a hint of shock and disbelief flickered across her elegant face. She waited eagerly, but patiently.

He told her about the CIA's current nefarious ambitions to bring the radical Hoa Hao to power and how various Catholic groups were also becoming radicalized to join them as they had a decade ago. That got her attention, not that she didn't already know this, but that he was here for a reason.

There were various levels to the conversation: they talked political shop, but they talked in a secret personal language as well. They had been very close for years and understood one another.

She was more animated than he'd seen her in a long time. It was as if he had touched her with a jolt of electricity. The fall from power had been a crushing blow to Madame Mang. Worse in many respects for her than for her husband. The loss of status had stripped her as painfully as if they had peeled the skin from her body. He hoped he was making a wise move, one that he could complete.

"How is this happening?"

"Certain important generals at MACV are not giving me the necessary power to put a stop to this insurgency, but I need to wake them up," Stennride said. "I am going to need you and your husband's help. We need the right people back in power." He knew they'd leave the isolated exile in a minute if given an opportunity to get back in the struggle.

A dazzling smile appeared on her face, and her eyes sparkled, and she laughed lightly like a young girl. It was a brief lapse, and she quickly returned to seriousness. "Will there be much opposition to our becoming province chief again?" she asked, always speaking of her husband's positions as 'our', but meant 'mine'.

"I think it can and will be accepted very quickly. But the generals who can make it happen need a little education as to what they're really dealing with. Your close friend, professor Huu Thuyet, has written about the threat and I was hoping he might be available to brief the generals."

"On something they are ignorant of," she said with her deep sarcasm.

"Unfortunately, the American generals know virtually nothing about the inner workings of Vietnamese society. But I have to get them educated in order to gain the kinds of advanced authority I'm going to need. They aren't aware of how serious the threat is from the radical Buddhist movement. They need to be educated. The one man who can do that is Huu Thuyet."

Madame Mang nodded. The ignorance of the military about the country's political culture, religions and inner workings was well known to her and her husband. Her eyes smiled at him now, softened to him and he reached out and took her hand. "It has been a long time," he said.

"Yes, it has."

His respect and appreciation of this woman had no limits. She was brilliant on many levels, and cunning. This woman was the help he needed on many levels, personally and politically.

But at the moment, he needed more power and if there was one man who could come to his aid to gain that power, it was Huu Thuyet, a genius.

13

At Madame Mang's request, professor Huu Thuyet agreed to talk to the generals the next day. Stennride left the hotel where he stayed that night and met the professor at the Mangs. After talking to Madame Mang's husband, who was as excited as his wife about the potential future, Stennride had the driver take them to the meeting at MACV headquarters on Tan Son Nhut.

The professor wore the black gown and cap of the traditional scholar. Stennride considered him one of Vietnam's premier historians who'd worked hard to get those half a million Catholic refugees from the north in 1954 to build the foundation on which this country was successfully governed for its first five years before being undermined.

Thuyet's English was fluid and natural, a result of his five years at Maryknoll in the States with Ngo Diem. Stennride had met him there briefly, then later when Thuyet returned to Vietnam for the Diem rule.

The old scholar entered the room, greeted the men there with a polite nod and sat down at the table, his hands folded on the table in front of him as he faced the generals. The nails on his index fingers were longer than normal—a sign of his distance from manual labor. He didn't waste time, getting right to the reason for his being there, for his very existence.

He spoke with authority as if they were his students, which on many levels they were. He got quickly to the heart of the Mekong Delta radicalism that threatened the provinces and ultimately, Saigon.

"Many Western scholars, such as Paul Mus, had a tendency to think of the Hoa Hao as being to the Buddhist church what the Protestants were when fighting the Catholic Church in Martin Luther's time. But the sect is a product of the delusions of its creator, Huynh Phu So, known by authorities of the time as the 'Mad Bonze' who began his preaching in the Delta towns in nineteen thirty-nine. His anti-colonial movement grew by thousands, then tens of thousands, and finally reached two million. Understandably, the French, being Catholic, were not happy with this political movement"—that got some smiles from the generals— "and they arrested Huynh Phu So and threw him into the psychiatric ward at Cho-Quan hospital. But he was very persuasive and converted the head of the psychiatric ward, Doctor Tam, to his visions and found himself once again a free man, and a very dangerous one."

The generals across the table shook their heads in amazement and now listened intently and very respectfully to the scholar who was teaching them the critical background for the war they were sent to win and knew so little about. Stennride loved what was happening here.

"While the French authorities were trying to round up the most fanatic followers, the Hoa Hao attacked communists' garrisons. One must remember that this part of Vietnam, known as the Mien-Tay, the New West, has always produced rebels. The anti-French rebellions as far back as eighteen seventy-five and nineteen thirties both came from here. In nineteen forty-five, fifteen thousand unarmed Hoa Hao peasants using hardly more than knives and clubs attacked a well-armed Viet Minh garrison outside of Can Tho. Thousands died. The Bassac, the lower branch of the Mekong, ran with blood. For weeks, fanatic Hoa Hao tied up bundles of communists and drowned them. They are crazy fanatics. They must be stopped before they get rearmed and started tying up bundles of Saigon supporters and drowning them. They cannot be underestimated."

Stennride smiled inside. He felt he'd made a brilliant decision in organizing this great awakening for the generals. He could see it in their expressions.

The old scholar's eyes flared. His interest in destroying the Hoa Hao went way back. He continued, "The communists were just as afraid of the Hoa Hao as were the French. The communist leaders invited Phu So to a meeting to discuss peace in the Delta. They lured him into a trap, hacked his body to pieces and it was never found. But they didn't kill the movement he created. He left behind a book of his sayings, predictions and prayers. It is called the Sam Gian and is the Hoa Hao bible. In the place where he wrote it—Nui Cam, Seven Mountains—there is still a rebel army holding out under the leadership of Madame Ba Cut. She is the widow of the last Hoa Hao general to be captured and beheaded by Diem. This was only ten years ago. The problem is arising once again with the followers of the 'Mad Bonze' and must be stopped." Now he had won their full attention.

"Why was this 'Mad Bonze' so popular?" General Paulick asked.

"He preached against all tradition. Much of Phu So's

popularity came from his opposition to feudal practices: match-making, elaborate funerals, the sale of child brides. He was also opposed to the use of alcohol and opium and other evils afflicting the peasants. But he did not stop there. He attacked traditional Buddhist shrines and Catholic churches. He knew no bounds. He preached the right of an individual's consciousness to take on responsibilities better left to family and community. The final result of his teaching, had he lived, would have been individualist anarchy and that is incompatible to the Asian mind and organization of Asian societies."

The room was stone quiet. The scholar spoke without moving anything but his thin lips. "With its leadership gone, and constantly under attack by whatever power was ruling in Saigon— the Japanese, then for a time the English General Garcy, then the return of the French—their movement is now divided into factions fighting among themselves while at the same time fighting off the constant attempt by the communists to destroy them. Still the Hoa Hao survived. They are not to be taken lightly. They still control much of the Delta, though they no longer have their private armies and cannot be considered true warlords as they were in the fifties. The Catholic Dioceses in An Giang, Vinh Long and Phong Dinh will suffer under this new rising tide of Hoa Hao radicalism. They are recruiting young Catholics once again and that must be stopped. If they gain power, they will destroy everything you are trying to do. They must be stopped, or this country will fall into chaos and the Americans, like the French and Japanese, will be defeated."

After his great educational speech to the generals, Stennride ushered him out to the driver and thanked him. "You may have changed the future for the better."

When Stennride rejoined the generals, he said, "The radicals now have a leader who has already proven himself to be very dangerous. Last year when Ky sent some troops to the Delta to take over rice warehouses in hopes of bringing the rice trade back under Saigon's control this new leader, Vinh Lac, sent Ky and his forces back with their tails between their legs. He's stronger than ever and has his own T.E. Lawrence to advise him and keep him connected to the rebels in the CIA."

"I assume you're talking about Michael Teague, the former naval officer?" General Mills asked.

"Yes, Michael Teague, a disciple of Chandler, the CIA operative who died in a plane crash. Teague is very dangerous and an expert on the river systems. Elements of the CIA are betraying everything we want to accomplish by supporting him. They seek to discredit General Westmoreland, General Thieu and the entire military directory in the pursuit of their holy grail of a Third Force. They will leave this country in chaos and anarchy. The communists will walk through here like a hot knife through butter unless we stop them and stop them fast. One of the CIA operatives behind this happens to be one of those behind the shooting of Diem and Nhu. This is serious. They're killing secret police and taking over the rivers. It's far worse than any of us thought."

This was met by a brief, powerful silence as it sank in. The generals, led by Paulick, collectively agreed to give Stennride what he needed to put a stop to the madness.

There were few objections. What kind of authority and how much power in the way of bases and manpower would have to be worked out. But at least these generals now understood what was happening and that it could destroy everything they wanted to do to win this war and stop the spread of global communism.

There were moments, and this was one he really appreciated. He had them seriously worried about something other than VC and NVA and that was the only way to get them to agree to what he had in mind.

While the world was focused on the battles in the north with VC and NVA units surrounding American bases, the war-within-the-war, the one that really mattered was being waged in the dark in the Mekong Delta.

14

In a small jungle compound near a canal that crossed into Cambodia, Teague, much to his amazement, recovered from his ordeal more quickly than he expected. He had extremely competent people around him and they knew how to handle wounds.

It was a couple of days before he could walk free of using bamboo canes, and the bruises weren't going away anytime soon, but the medical attention and muscle massaging helped him recover remarkably fast.

He'd been like a taut rubber band for a few days, but now, growing impatient and restless, anxious to get back into the battle. Crazy as it seemed, his anger gave him the energy, as it had also helped with his resistance and survival, and infused him with an even greater conviction, energized by a deep ambition for revenge.

But when he slept, the slightest sound jerked him awake, his heart pumping, the adrenaline triggered. He had to walk and walking made him think and thinking kept him awake. The compound sentries, oddly enough many Filipinos, had obvious orders not to engage in conversation.

When it was Frank Acosta who walked into the center of the compound rather than Vinh Lac, Teague was surprised.

The CIA operative greeted Teague with a challenge. "You have a big decision to make, my friend."

"Sounds dangerous."

"Oh, and yes, it's nice to see you alive and getting better. You are now at the top of the wanted list by the secret police and have a nice price on your head."

Teague said, "I survive to face one damn decision after another. What is this one?"

Acosta smiled. He looked a little bizarre in his new fatigue pants and a loose black shirt and bush hat. They walked away from the thatched roof building.

"We can make life easier for you. You get to go home with a good discharge and avoid getting hunted down and killed. But, I'm not so sure that's what you want, is it?"

"No."

"I didn't think so. You are afflicted with what German sociologist Max Weber called verstehen. Going native."

"I'm familiar with the concept. Maybe that's a part of it. In any case, I have zero interest in leaving."

"I figured as much. But if you stay, we will upgrade your status to Chandler's level and give you major dark force authority because something has to be done fast to consolidate peasants into a real movement or they're going to be destroyed politically. And the person who is the tip of that spear at the heart of the movement is the one who imprisoned you. Colonel Stennride and his associate, Hoat Vu's Major Chien. This secret little war-within-the-war is at a critical stage."

He sounded as stressed as he was after Chandler's death. Things couldn't be going well. "And what will this new authority you're offering give me?"

"The power to carry activities beyond any classification, or direct oversight. Not that it's that big of a change for you, but I want you to come with me to Saigon and meet some people who want to better understand what we face. You okay with that?"

"I have an alternative?"

"Other than going home . . . no. These men understand that if we can't get some kind of peasant base into this war soon, well, it's not going to go well. There are some operatives who really want to meet you."

"They going to trust me the way they did Chandler?"

"I think they already do and maybe more. You're famous among these guys, given you're the Annapolis grad who wrote a widely read and highly respected article comparing the French Expeditionary Corps operations here in the Mekong Delta with what we were trying to organize. You impressed those who needed to be impressed."

"I live to impress."

"Well, you've succeeded. Chandler loved that article you published that compared the Mississippi campaign during the Civil War, the river operations against the Seminole Indians in the Florida Everglades from eighteen thirty-seven to eighteen forty-two, and the American naval operations along the Yangtze River in China in nineteen twenty-eight to our current activities was something they reacted to. That had a lot to do with why Chandler wanted to work with you. We're in a very critical moment and you will be supported to carry out a mission, one that will not be on record, but one that needs to succeed."

Teague thought about all the displaced peasants, the endless devastation and what would be coming with America bringing in hundreds of thousands of troops and a massive bombing campaign.

"Did Westy really ask to get small nukes to use on the borders?"

"He did. Washington refused."

Acosta lit a cigarette and offered one to Teague, which Teague declined. "We have to show progress fast and you need to stay alive as there isn't another replacement."

"I'll try and stay above ground. I need to fulfill Chandler's belief in me."

"Chandler was big on using the Gittinger personality assessment system on all the military officers who had any real connection with the Buddhists."

"Then he chose me?"

Acosta laughed lightly. "He chose you because you were very aggressive across the Delta's rivers and swamps and you were also a bit of a rebel. He probably knew you better than you know yourself. Chandler could study a man for just a few days and make predictions of that man's behavior in certain future circumstances. He was right so much of the time he convinced me. Most psychological systems are based on similarities between people, but Gittinger's was based on differences. We now have a new computerized system of tens of thousands of attributes and traits in a master file, and when we get some information on a person, we run it against the master and get readable results. The CIA now uses it all over the world. It's the next great technological advance for war games. They're even used with cultural biases thrown in. You'll get a profile on your chief adversary."

"Just how powerful is this colonel?"

"He's the equivalent military intelligence officer that

Chandler was with the agency. A kind of one-man operational special task force and his power is growing by the day. Stennride was one of Diem's original power brokers. He is also the man who advised Loan and Nhu on how to deal with the dissident Buddhists. Stennride happens to be something of an expert on reducing the status and arms of the Buddhists. He fell out of favor after the fall of Diem, but now, with Thieu in power, he's back. He's MACV's political hatchet man and he'll get what he needs to stop any more coups or the return of any serious opposition to Saigon."

"Did he have anything to do with Chandler's death?"

"That we don't know. But he's best buddies with Major Chien and that man is a stone-cold killer. He may well be the one who orchestrated Chandler's death. After your escape, you are no doubt at the top of his hit list. You ready to meet your support system?"

Teague said, "It's a date I can't stand up."

The late day sun glinted off the buildings and runways at Tan Son Nhut airbase.

Teague and Acosta arrived at one of the airfields as planes of every type circled in designated or waiting for a chance to land. And on the way in, they passed over massive troop movements now being used to put a defensive wall around Saigon.

Three feeder strips angled to the main runway all very busy with every type of aircraft from small Pipers and Cessnas, to heavy bombers.

Teague hadn't been up here lately and was surprised at the increased activity of this busiest of airports.

Acosta pointed to black Skyraiders. "Those are Ky's." The planes were parked near a building that had insignias and Vietnamese markings. "They are always ready at a drop of a political crisis to go airborne."

Jets came down practically in the tails of the slower planes. Crash derricks and fire trucks lurking on the aprons for any disasters.

They were picked up in a sedan with heavily tinted windows and driven not directly to CIA headquarters that was in the Chancery Building Embassy compound but nearby to a small closed restaurant two blocks away.

A security officer led them inside and there at a table sat three case officers he'd known about but never met until now, two in suits like this was a business meeting.

"I'm glad to see you alive and in one piece," the apparent ranking officer said, shaking Teague's hand. "Have a seat. I'll get right to the point. We were devastated by Chandler's death, but we need to react fast to what is happening. I assume you're here because you want to continue the program and are willing to take his role."

"I have no better offers. But his role was created by him, mine will be by me. Circumstances have changed."

"The political action project you will be conducting won't be easy on any level for sure. But it has to happen. Chandler had great admiration for you and so does Frank. If you are willing, we will give you everything we can. You will be up against a serious move by MACV to shut us down."

"I'm here to carry out the goals of the project," Teague said. He knew his injuries and swollen parts of his face seemed a bit shocking to the men in the room.

"We've had enough goddamn coups, as you know," the man across the table from Teague said. "Musical chairs among the generals. What we need is what Chandler had been advocating for years and that is a non-communist style revolution. Colonel Stennride represents the opposite course. He's the principal advisor to a group of Saigon generals. He's a dangerous character."

"And he has the secret police as his right hand, as you obviously know," the officer at the end of the table said.

"With hundreds of thousands more American soldiers who will be drafted and sent here, we're in trouble," the third officer said. Teague was not introduced to their names and wouldn't be.

This agent continued, "Those draftees will not be trained-up for this kind of war. We need to stop it before it's out of control. Our own government has no interest in allowing a coalition of sects and nationalist groups under one political umbrella to come into power. We don't agree and we'll make sure you get all the support and assets you need. Cover, protection, money, you name it. As you saw coming in, the VC and NVA are running for cover near the cities to escape the expanding bombing campaign. If there is something bigger in mind, it will get ugly. Saigon is virtually surrounded and all our major forces along the borders are being pulled back here. It's getting a little crazy out there and we need something to change and change fast."

Teague spent three hours with this handful of operatives and he assured them, with backing, he'd do everything he could to create that coalition they wanted.

He saw these men as desperate political gamblers who were convinced they had only one more roll of the dice. It was all or nothing and he knew they saw him as that last roll.

15

In a village near Phnom Penh, Cambodia, three days after the big meeting with the CIA operatives, Teague saw Frank Acosta's chopper settle on a small clearing near the river.

Teague watched him as he ducked under the blades, nodded to stevedores and fisherman. In what looked like a new bush hat and jungle fatigues, Acosta looked like something out of a Joseph Conrad novel.

"Your recovery looks to be going well?" Acosta said.

"Slow, but sure."

"You scared the shit out of my colleagues, so at least those bruises and scars have a positive function."

Teague followed Acosta to the shade of a banyan tree.

"Because you and Vinh Lac are now the most hunted men in the Delta," Acosta said. "I have a surprise for you that you are going to like. Chandler's boat that he never got to enjoy, as it is only now just finished. It is designed to look like a junk but in fact that's all disguise. He named it the Wayward Angel. Captain Engler will be here with the boat shortly and he really likes it. This baby can outrun virtually anything on the rivers. Where is Vinh Lac?"

"He's dealing with the Corsican issue on the border."

Acosta frowned. "He needs to be careful. The last thing we need is conflict with the Corsican mobs and their friends and enemies in the Golden Triangle. We have enough problems. Colonel Stennride is bringing a once very powerful couple to take over one of the Delta provinces they controlled in the fifties. The Mangs. They were major factors in the Diem regime. What I don't want is to give them an excuse early on. Already Vinh Lac is being touted as a police killer and a crazy replacement for Huyen Phu So and resides at the top of their hunt and kill list. As are you. If this bastard colonel gets the power he wants, it'll not be fun and games. We need to slow him down and then put an end once again to the Mangs."

Acosta got a call. He walked off. When he returned, he said, "That was Engler. He's got a present for you. Your new boat. You'll pick Khiet up downriver. He's giving your boat to the Free Khmer forces."

They watched as the new boat came cruising down the river. It pulled into the dock of the small village whose houses were perched on stilts around the narrow inlet.

The boat did resemble the junks plying the river, but up close it had some distinctions that a boatman could see.

Engler emerged on the deck with his hands out to his sides and a smile on his face. "You're going to love this baby. It's one of a kind. It's also got the most sophisticated radios I've ever seen on a junk, for sure. The engines on this baby will give you a very fast and well-armed boat and its water jet engines are great for shallow water."

Acosta said, "You are now a stand-alone elite river force and you won't be easy to detect."

Engler swept his hand over the bow of the junk. "Nothin' like it that I've ever seen. Chandler spent a fortune and had some great builders."

He showed Teague the hidden twin jet engines, the teak cabin, instrument panel and the spring-mounted fifty-caliber machine guns that would rise up through openings with a push of a button on both sides and one that that rose in the front of the boat.

Acosta said, "Not bad."

"That's an understatement," Teague said. It was an amazing boat.

Acosta said, "I'll see you in Long Xuyen. I'm meeting JK there. We have certain arrangements—you don't operate in these environments anymore without the right arrangements, believe me. It costs a fortune every time you take a step. So, when one of our most important sources, the Corsicans, feel threatened we have to take steps."

Teague waited for the point that he knew was coming.

Acosta motioned him aside. "I know you admire Vinh Lac—he's a hell of a river warrior, and he saved your ass, but he's causing some problems. He's threatening an island that just happens to belong to people we do business with. Every now and then Vinh Lac's rice convoys get hassled from the island. The pirates there force him to pay a fee for transit. We'd gotten them to guarantee they won't harass Vinh Lac but you need to get him to back off and find out what he's up to."

"The Corsicans run the drug trade and shake down the boat people."

"Yes, but that's not the issue we are dealing with. Bring Vinh

Lac back on board. The Golden Triangle is off limits right now."

"If he refuses?"

"Then maybe he's out. We might end up with Quy. At least he's very cooperative."

Teague emitted a sardonic laugh, saying, "Quy couldn't clean Vinh Lac's shoes. They aren't friends. And Vinh Lac's sister, Xam, really doesn't like the guy, or trust him."

"Quy is cooperative, and—"

"In for the top dollar. No, never. He's a loser."

"Yes, but revenge against those on that island would be a mistake," Acosta said flatly, his voice hardening. "You need to stop that. What the hell is he doing?"

Teague said, "I'll talk to him and see what he's after and where he stands."

"Attacking, or even harassing, Quon Son Island is a bad idea. He's got enough problems without adding the Corsicans to the list of people who want him dead."

"Like I said, I'll talk to him," Teague said. "Quy isn't an alternative, so get that out of your head. I have a feeling that JK is the one really pushing for Quy and it's not going to happen."

An upset Acosta walked back to the small chopper, climbed on board and headed back toward Vietnam.

"He's pissed," Engler said. "What's the problem?"

"We need to find Vinh Lac. Acosta thinks he's going to take one of the islands the Corsicans use for their various criminal enterprises."

16

Teague was thrilled to feel the power of this high speed brilliantly designed and disguised river craft. They headed back toward the border away from the confluence of the Mekong and the Tonlé Sap tributary, two of the four intersecting waterways at Phnom Penh.

Two hours later, they picked up Khiet and joined three more boats. He thought he would miss his high-speed patrol boat, but realized very quickly that wouldn't be the case.

Khiet informed him that rebel Hoa Hao General Duyet and Vinh Lac were working together now.

"I want to meet the General Duyet as soon as it can be arranged," Teague said.

The boat seemed light on the swollen waters. He felt the pull of the current as the waters struggled against one another's opposing flows.

"This baby feels a little sluggish," Teague said sardonically, a big smile growing on his face as they hit the center of the river and he opened her up. It felt like a transition from a speedboat to a rocket.

Khiet let out that high trill laugh of his. "No, not the boat. That is the water. Wait until we are well away from the Tonlé Sap's effect."

Every year, because of the high water of the Mekong from the monsoons, the Tonlé Sap reversed its flow. It was called sweet water, as it fed the rice crops, but then in the post-monsoon, it reverted back to normal.

Teague turned southward away from the wide brown space leading to where the Mekong divided at the border where the lower branch, the Bassac, would take them to Long Xuyen. But first the island.

The silt-laden water glistened in the late day sun behind them. The sky was dotted with small creamy cloud tuffs, and the sun streaked through them with evangelical intensity.

"The Great River," Khiet said. "No dam slow her down, no bridge break the river's beauty. One day that change, but now she is virgin, always young."

Teague lost himself for the moment in the enforced solitude of the river. He, like Khiet and Engler, loved the world of the Nine Dragons. There was something about this world that was special.

The boats moved past stilted water hamlets and peaceful paddy fields of Cambodia, a world quiet as a fantasy, people with the easygoing gentle souls utterly lacking the intensity, aggressiveness and ingenuity of the predators around them.

Many Viets who'd been forced to flee Vietnam after their villages were destroyed lived in makeshift villages in huts, even pipes and on small junks.

"Go ahead and get the feel of this baby," Teague said.

Khiet gave Teague thumbs up with one hand and throttling

down with the other. The Wayward Angel surged forward, gathering her speed quickly, the nose lifting and driving over the water leaving the other boats behind. They hit twenty, then thirty knots almost as quickly as a PBR, but where a PBR reached its limit, this deceptive craft kept climbing.

"Number one!" Khiet yelled, breaking into an infectious grin as he handed controls back to Teague. They slowed to let the others catch up.

"Fiberglass is good for strength but makes noise," Engler said. "Plywood best for the hull. Lighter than planked hulls and faster. This has everything." He loved the switches that controlled the hydraulic trim tabs which allowed them to adjust the transom.

"See how she moves," Khiet suggested, waving his hands in and out to indicate he wanted Teague to test maneuverability.

Twenty minutes later, after having run her through every maneuver he knew, Teague shook his head in wonder. "Number one."

"You come from boat people," Khiet asked.

Teague nodded. "My great-grandfather was a Baltimore schooner captain. I grew up on the Chesapeake Bay in a place called Tilghman Island. My father worked with a famous builder of workboats and yachts. We built out of oak and pine. Fiberglass and plywood are what drove my father out of business."

"What does he do now?"

"Trains dogs. That business is from my mother's side of the family. Generations ago, they created a new breed called the Chesapeake Bay retriever."

"You sell them to eat?"

Teague chuckled. "Americans don't eat dog."

"Nor do South Vietnamese," Khiet said. "The northerners are

the dog eaters. So why you raise dogs?"

"For pets. Americans love cats and dogs. If nobody else loves you, your animals do. We have smaller families," Teague said. "So we make up for it with pets."

"Troi ohi!" Khiet laughed and nodded.

"What about your father, what does he do?"

Khiet's expression turned sour. "My father is dead. He was beheaded by Diem. He was accused of being an agent of Ba Cut's."

"That's terrible. Was he?"

"Yes."

And that's why we're here, Teague thought, glancing at Engler, who had great respect for Khiet.

An hour later, they pulled into a small village where Khiet said he had friends. It was a good place to spend the night as the Viet Cong were extremely active along the waterway at night and their presence on the stretch of river ahead invited trouble.

After the meeting with leaders, who were very positive about a coming revolution, they ate fish and rice, potent with nuoc manh sauce. Then they got down to the business at hand. Outside the cabin window, night brought a huge full moon over the treetops.

Everywhere they heard the laughter and playing of young kids, a dog barking. Life in the village.

Teague knew that Khiet was a link between the CIA and a group of Delta businessmen with headquarters in Can Tho who had supported General Duyet the last of the Hoa Hao generals of the fifties and the only one to survive the Diem period. Chandler had relied on Duyet and his contacts a lot.

"Any chance Vinh Lac will back off attacking the island? That seems to be something for later, after the Hoa Hao are back in power and rearmed."

"I think not," Khiet said. "Xam is very much pushing for this.

The Hoa Hao rice traders have problems with Quon Son Island being ruled by drug sellers and pirates and controlled by the Corsicans and protected by the corrupt river police. They control the flow of opium down the Mekong and Vinh Lac, like Phu So before him, opposes the selling and use of drugs. His rice convoys are paying a twenty-five-percent transit charge, so now he is going to attack the island and set up a different government. It may be happening very soon."

Teague studied the map he had laid out on the table but nowhere could he find the island. "Why isn't it on the government's map?"

"No, no," Khiet said with that rushing intensity of his. "No one can control the island because of its location. If one side claimed it then the other side would be forced to do the same and it would lead to a dispute between Vietnam and Cambodia. So, they leave it off the maps and therefore it doesn't exist. But there is another reason why Vinh Lac and Xam want to take control. The petty little warlord Trong Quy supports his operations with opium money and collusion with the Corsicans. That has to stop."

They finally closed down the discussion and went to mosquito protected hammocks on the boat that were the same as those commandoes took into the mountains.

"Gamewarden!" Khiet boomed, snapping Teague awake. "You sleep like the dead. Vinh Lac come to talk to you."

A brilliant morning light poured in through the open window frames diffusing through the mosquito netting around Teague's hammock. He broke out of a deep sleep, feeling like a marlin crashing up through the surface of a black sea into stunning light.

Teague rolled out, washed his face in the metal bowl and then sat down and accepted a cup of black coffee from Engler, who went back to the radios.

The village was all but empty except for the very old and some children, the rest out in the rice fields.

Vinh Lac pulled up alongside the Wayward Angel a few minutes later and he came aboard.

"How much do they offer me this time to become their puppet?" Vinh Lac asked as he adjusted his headband.

Teague took a couple swigs of coffee and tried to clear his brain. "Yet to be determined. They aren't happy with your ambition to take Quon Son Island. That should come later, after you regain control of the Delta. Why is it important now?"

"I'm not interested in Quon Son Island other than a means to an end. Weapons."

"I don't understand. Are there a lot of weapons on the island? Is that what you're after?"

"Not the kind we need," Vinh Lac said. "We have the island, maybe we have something to negotiate with."

"Negotiate with whom and for what?"

Vinh Lac smiled. "We need arms. Not a few rifles and pistols. We need serious arms. The men behind the opium trade in the Golden Triangle are also the biggest arms dealers in the world. Cholon is overwhelmed with incoming arms of all kinds from America. Even the Israelis came to Cholon for arms after the Six Day War and come back again and again. The shipments that come in from America are the best and we need them."

"See," Khiet said. "I told you he was our man. Chandler could never make up his mind. That—" he turned back to Teague and held his coffee mug up for a toast "—comes from seeing the truth. One learns to make decisions that have to be made in the name of survival and victory. Now we kill some pirates, rearm and take back our freedom to trade on the rivers that are the blood veins of our lives."

Teague said, "Pirates on the high seas were called hastas humani generas—enemies of all mankind."

"Maybe also on the rivers," Vinh Lac said. "Pirates are pirates wherever they are. You come help us."

Vinh Lac took a small hand-drawn map from his shirt pocket and laid it on the small fold up table. He explained the attack, how it was already in place. And that Xam had already placed supporters in Cholon near the warehouses and docks. He wanted Teague directly involved and then to bring the CIA in to put pressure on the arms merchants.

It was more than a little shocking to Teague. They had this worked out and at first it looked a little crazy, but then that began to change in his mind. The kind of arms they would need were serious combat weapons and a lot of them to bring in thousands of Hoa Hao and other sects and create an army that could once again defeat the Viet Cong, but also prevent Saigon from suppressing the movement.

"We go now," Vinh Lac said. "You come?"

Teague turned to Engler, who was now off the radios. "What do you think?"

"I think it will be the greatest heist ever. And I agree with Vinh Lac. Without rearming with real weapons equipped for major combat, there is no point to any of this. It's all or nothing."

Teague nodded. "Well, let's go steal an island and use it for the greatest arms heist in history."

It was utterly preposterous, insane, and yet in the crazy nature of this war, it had logic. America wasn't going to rearm the greatest fighters in the country for political reasons. So maybe the Hoa Hao would have to rearm themselves, one way or another.

17

As they made their way through the effluvial western Delta waters, the jungle was a glow of emerald jade. The boat traffic grew with the emergence of dawn. Teague stood on the foredeck in his flak jacket next to a gunner and Khiet.

Engler kept Teague updated on radio traffic from boats and aerial surveillance from one of Acosta's choppers.

Teague scanned the river with powerful binoculars.

Only five klicks out from Quon Son Island, word came that the attack was already in full swing.

The Wayward Angel, throaty and powerful, skated across the thick brown water, the river tapering off into a twisting ribbon ahead, the high green jungle arching out into a long funnel.

Khiet said, "Two pirate boats have broken through the cordon. Xam has closed off the other side. Vinh Lac is moving toward the lagoon. There are pirate boats coming to defend the island."

Teague nodded, Xam's presence a powerful incentive. He

studied the pirate boats with the binoculars. The island was still some distance away and it looked like these boys wanted to block their passage. He saw weapons in the hands of the men on the junks.

"Take them head on," Teague said. "Let them make their moves."

The unsuspecting pirate boats coming out of a canal were less than a hundred yards away when Khiet ordered the gunners to sink them. The big guns came up out of their holds.

The first burst of the fifty-caliber fire raked across the bow of the lead junk. It floundered and began to sink instantly, men leaping into the water on both sides.

Behind the first boat, a second junk opened fire as it turned and headed toward the leeward bank. Khiet's gunners, who'd come from the island with them, followed with steady bursts until they got her. A roar went up from the crew. Two quick kills.

They were investigating a half-sunk boat by the bank when a third pirate junk appeared out of nowhere like an apparition, making its presence known by a startled burst of machine gun fire.

The gunner closest to Teague took a bullet and jerked back. Teague caught him and eased him down against the cabin. He took the gunner's position and led the attacking boat with short bursts.

Incredibly, the junk kept on coming and was now only fifty yards out and closing fast.

Khiet yelled for rockets. Two of his men moved up with shoulder LAAWS. They fired simultaneously. The junk was there one moment and the next gone in fiery pieces.

What was left of it sank. Both rockets had made direct hits. Only a couple of wounded were spotted attempting to swim ashore and Khiet allowed them to go. Flanked by two other armed Hoa

Hao junks, they raced on toward the island. But soon they were alone again, their superior speed shooting them up the river ahead of the others. Teague stood in the spray of mist staring at the tendrils of black smoke curling up from the island.

Within a half mile of the island, they took fire from a fishing village on the north bank some eight or nine hundred yards away.

"Gamewarden, what do you think?" Khiet yelled, pointing in the direction of the village.

Teague shook his head, waving Khiet on. The shore parties had already landed at three points on the island and Vinh Lac had fought his way into the lagoon.

When the Wayward Angel passed down a narrow channel that was like a duct leading into the kidney-shaped lagoon in the belly of Quon Son Island, the sounds of battle drifted off, dwindling until only a smattering of occasional gun bursts indicated some resistance fighters were still alive. But in time, many surrendered.

Junks and sampans were everywhere, some half sunk, some burning. The distant sound of light weapon fire filtered down from the mangrove forests around the lagoon. Hoa Hao junks flying maroon flags were scattered along the shoreline, soldiers prowling through the trees.

The residents were coming out of their tunnels along the banks, some drifting down from the direction of the town, babies in women's arms, their bare bottoms perched on extended hips.

Soon it seemed liked the entire population of the island had gathered along the shoreline and they were waving Hoa Hao banners and cheering like it was a great liberation, the children surging back and forth, filled with that wild excitement that short, decisive battles create.

Teague found himself elated, yet irritated and saddened by the cost. But it still was the first real sense of triumph and post fire-fight satisfaction he could remember because it was the first time he'd seen peasants who actually looked happy that a battle had taken place in their territory.

"Pirates don't treat people very well," Khiet said.

They docked and went ashore. Teague stared at the various junks, looking for some sign of Xam. In some deep and unclear way, he knew he was linking his actions to her power and voice at the rallies, reaching to connect his ambition with her ambition as if, instinctively, he knew that the vision of Vinh Lac's sister was the one he had been seeking.

But she didn't appear at the gathering.

Vinh Lac, the conquering river warrior, spoke before an assemblage of the island's dignitaries, telling them that there would now be great changes on the island and their world. It was impossible to determine what they thought, yet Teague sensed a relief on their faces, a genuine thankfulness that the band of pirates that had ruled and milked them for so long had finally been ousted.

Then a night of feasting ensued. Fires dotted the shoreline all the way around the lagoon like the camp of some great nomadic army. There was much singing, prayers and laughing. The air wafted with the smells of sizzling pork, eel, and rice cooking in earthen pots. The troops consumed hundreds of huge ten-inch-long fresh water shrimp, and Pla Buk, a catfish that, according to Khiet, "Is bigger than a tiger. Ten feet long and weighs sometimes nearly a thousand pounds. Five will feed a battalion, ah!"

In the glow of the fire, Vinh Lac's angular face took on a mask-like quality, at once fierce and calm. He talked of the pirates, the drug traffic that spread like a spider web over the whole of Southeast Asia.

"It is the belief of the Hoa Hao," Vinh Lac said to Teague, "that one day an army must go into the Burma area and wipe out the KMT Chinese troops who run opium traffic."

Teague said, "That won't be an easy task as long as so many different powers benefit."

Vinh Lac was silent for some time, staring pensively at the fire. As if by prearrangement, all the men at the fire began to leave, one or two at a time until it was just Teague and Vinh Lac.

The fire flickered and danced on Vinh Lac's face as he spoke. "We have the means now to get the arms that we need. We will negotiate very quickly and we will be in a position to make the arms dealers want to cooperate."

Teague didn't know exactly what that meant, but he accepted that it involved the potential for action in Cholon itself. This was just the opening of an elaborate operation. It was crazy brilliant. If, that is, it could actually be pulled off.

"We have many good programs," Vinh Lac said. "Some of them are already operating in An Giang. At the root of all our activities is a single goal—to create a political movement whose purpose is the elimination of barriers that reduce every Vietnamese to a level of a beggar and servant. A man in Vietnam has no rights the way Americans do, he has only obligations. He cannot use his own intelligence and energy to improve his existence. He can only improve himself under the present way by kissing the asses above him. We want to change that. We will defeat the communists. Now you bring your CIA operatives in with us."

"I'll make the case and give no alternatives."

"Yes," Vinh Lac said. "For me to have to crawl on my hands and knees to get assistance from the CIA turns me into their tool. It is often said that one must embrace a lesser evil to defeat a greater evil. We took this island because it corrupts everything coming and going. The CIA needs to understand. You do as did Chandler. He was killed and you were nearly condemned to the same fate. And now the American military is trying to take over everything. Destroy the country and rebuild it according to their vision, not ours. A policy without the people cannot succeed."

At one of the other campfires about thirty meters away, one of the older men from the island was strumming a guitar and singing refrains from an old partisan song:

"Friend, do you hear the black flight of Ravens in the Plains, Friend do you hear the dull cry of your country in chains…"

Vinh Lac said, "My sister wishes to talk with you. Take the skiff at the end of the pier. Her boat is the one almost exactly in the center of the lagoon." When Teague got up to leave, Vinh Lac said, "I will work hard to have influence over you, but be warned, my friend, my sister will rule you."

18

Teague climbed into a small skiff piloted by one of Vinh Lac's men. The boat slid quietly toward a boat that sat in the middle of the lagoon. Fires were still burning on parts of the island, the cordite smells of war and sounds of celebration hung over the lagoon under a billion stars and a big bright moon.

Xam's boat was surrounded by a protective fleet of half a dozen other junks. The queen bee referred to as the Noi-tuong. He was strangely amused that he felt nervous and a little excited, like some teen on a second date.

He slipped into a circle of junks surrounding hers, aware of the eyes of her security watching his every move, even if well aware of who he was.

A rope landed with a thud in the skiff when it pulled alongside and a rough voice out of the dark told him to tie up. Teague grabbed hold and pulled himself on board. A Hoa Hao soldier motioned for him to go inside.

It was dark inside except for the dim, tiny light from a small oil lamp. Her cabin struck him immediately as austere. No feminine touches, no soft colors or frilly things. Fit for a monk. He didn't see her until she spoke.

"Please, sit down, Commander. It is nice to see you again."

He remembered their first meeting, her English so precise as if she had studied the guidebooks religiously and had worked to chisel the correct pronunciation until she was probably far more correct than most Americans would be. He imagined that's how his Vietnamese sounded to a native, overly exact.

Yet almost immediately she erred and caught herself. "We not . . . we did not expect you to come back," she said, correcting her stumble. He saw in the lamplight a little sparkle of triumph in those brilliant eyes.

He sat on a bench against the wall, put his weapon aside and removed his bush hat and stared at her for a moment before speaking. "It's a difficult country to leave," he said.

"The French disease," she said. "The pleasures of life are very cheap here for Europeans and Americans. One can have all the food, women, authority, servants one could possibly want. And for some, it is adventurous as well."

She's challenging me, he thought. He smiled. "You're probably right. There are many of what we used to call carpetbaggers." Christ, this woman is beautiful in a very strong way, he thought. No delicate prettiness here.

She hesitated, searching for something. "Carpetbag—excuse me, what is that term?"

"When the American Civil War was over—a hundred fifty years ago—men from the North stayed in the South and sometimes exploited the situation. The French have been defeated here, but many remain, owning hotels and restaurants. They are your carpetbaggers."

She picked up a pen and wrote it down. When she finished, she said, "You are a CIA agent now, like Chandler."

"I prefer to think of myself as an independent operator supported by CIA agents. It's a subtle but important difference."

She flashed a smile at that as she poured tea. He studied her movements in the tiny light, the deliberateness. She had a way of moving her head very slowly as if listening for something. "Why do you say that?" she asked.

"I like to think I have independence."

She looked directly at him for a long moment. "Do you?"

"I wouldn't be here if I didn't. The people who are seeking major change have very few options and time isn't on their side and they know it."

Teague was aware of her every move, her breath, the change of her gaze, the sliding of her hand along her arm, the way her blouse pulled taut across her chest. But he tried not to let her notice his awareness.

Xam said, "The CIA made many promises before, as they do now. But we have learned not to expect much. If you want to deal with us, you must keep in mind the history of that relationship."

"I'm sorry about what has happened in the past," Teague said. "I hope I can help change that."

She said, "The same people with the same motives and same incorrect view are still involved." She had reverted to Vietnamese to better express her indignation.

He stayed defensively in English. "I don't intend to be the beast of the CIA's burden. My actions will be based on my judgement, not that of some bureaucrat whose primary desire is to please his superiors."

"We shall see," Xam said, back to English. After a moment of silence, she went on. "My brother will one day be a great national leader, if fate and circumstance and the American military want success. There is an opportunity for us to seriously re-arm. But we can't do this alone. We need the persuasive power of the CIA associates to help convince the arms dealers in Cholon that if they want peace in the Golden Triangle and the island returned, things must change. And they must deal with us."

There was something ominous, accusatory in the way she said that. She looked directly at him and he waited, mired in his own feelings that he had no way to express. And the idea they would actually give up the island seemed unlikely to him.

And then she abruptly rose and announced that it was getting late.

When they reached the door, she said, "You must understand that nothing can be done until we are again fully re-armed and are able to withstand both the communists and Saigon's puppets."

"I understand and I will present it to my colleagues."

After a hesitation as she considered this, she said, "This Colonel Stennride is already gaining control of An Binh and bringing in supporters of former Saigon regimes. He has support of your MACV, but your Riverine forces are headquartered, Gamewarden. If they come under his control, it will not be good. He must be stopped."

"I'll find out everything about this from my CIA contacts. And we'll figure out the best way to deal with him."

They were really close and he saw that she was looking at the bruises and scars on his face as he was staring at the beautiful features of hers.

"Wait," she said. She went over to a small cabinet and when she came back she had a small round jar. "This is very good for healing small wounds and scars."

He thought she would hand him the jar, but instead she unscrewed the lid and then put two fingers in to get the cream and then she had him bend a little and she applied the cream, moving very gently with her fingers. When she finished, she screwed the lid on and handed the jar to him. "I have more. Use this at night before you go to sleep. It will help clear the wounds."

"Thank you," he said. "I will put some on every night."

"Yes. You will see the difference in just a few days." She opened the door. "Goodnight."

It had all become very awkward. He moved past her and went out on the deck. He looked back. "Thank you." Her brother was right about her.

Xam smiled as she watched the American climb into the small boat and return across the lagoon. She had trust in him, as she once had in Chandler, and she feared that he might end up the same way. Her people needed him and the CIA support. He had to be protected. And she liked him, his honesty and his strength. And she knew he liked her.

Xam couldn't afford to trust what the Americans were doing anymore. Their military and development cadres were breaking down the different political groups and trying to form a single base for Saigon's dictatorship. But there was no philosophy behind what they were doing. No support for business and the rising entrepreneurial class, for the rice farmers whose living costs were growing because of all the competition from the import of American foods and goods, and they owned very little land because the government was taking over. It was a not some funny joke among the Vietnamese that when the Americans were finished, the South would be more communist than the North.

Still, wishing to remain hopeful, she saw in Teague not just an operative like Chandler, but a serious warrior as well, and one very committed. She liked him and hoped he could bring others around.

But time was fast running out, with the Viet Cong forces moving closer to the cities and the NVA sending tens of thousands of troops from the north to confront this new American threat.

The underlying battle between the elements of the CIA that supported them, and the American military that wanted them to remain as irrelevant, would determine not only the future of the Buddhists, but of the country. Her people had been ruled not just by colonialists but by their own submissive philosophy and it was the mission of the Hoa Hao Buddhists to change that.

19

That they had to stay off the river at night to avoid VC strikes and bombing runs was almost an absolute now. The Delta was becoming a more dangerous zone.

They were worried about potential river raids, so they had boats well ahead and behind them tracking their moves as well as aerial surveillance by Acosta's operatives.

Teague slept little that night in the inlet near the island now in Vinh Lac's control. Thoughts of Xam and a strong restlessness combined with fear that the taking of the island might cause some disastrous consequences if Acosta didn't get on board fast.

He was happy once they got moving in the first light. Getting Acosta and the CIA operatives working with him on board might be a problem, but there was no alternative now.

Before they had gone very far, a group of fishermen waved

them over to the bank. First, two scout boats went in to make sure it wasn't some kind of ambush.

It was a small hamlet half a mile from the island. Most of the buildings were perched on stilts rising over the mud and water, except the little market where half a dozen two-story concrete buildings stood with their typical red tile roofs.

In front near the boats, a crowd of peasants had gathered around a sampan and there was a lot of yelling, arm waving and near hysteria among several women.

Teague, Khiet and three armed Hoa Hao soldiers went ashore. A young girl, maybe twelve years old, lay still on a straw mat with two frantic mamasans holding a pile of clothing as compresses to her bloody head.

Teague ran back to the boat and radioed Paddy Control at Binh Thuy airfield outside of Can Tho. He used his old 'Roadrunner' call sign. They patched him through to the hospital at Long Xuyen and the conversation was picked up by a Special Forces medic team operating in the area. He then had Engler let Vinh Lac and Xam know what was going on so they wouldn't mistake a chopper coming into the area as an attack.

Within minutes, Teague learned that a chopper on the way back from a mission was rerouted to the site. The hospital in Long Xuyen was alerted to an incoming 'scalped' case.

"They get their hair caught in the propellers of the fishing boats," Khiet explained. "It happens. Xin Loi!"

The girl was still alive when the chopper thwacked across the river and alighted on the hamlet clearing.

A black Special Forces medic jumped out before the chopper was settled, ducked under the blades and trotted toward them with his rucksack of supplies in his hand. The 'brother' as black soldiers referred to one another, ignored everyone and went to work on the girl with cool professional dispatch.

In what seemed like a minute, he had a perfect cap of bandages on the young girl's head, an IV in her arm, and was ordering them to get her on board the chopper.

"Appreciate your help, Sergeant—" Teague looked for a name tag.

"Moore," the big sergeant said as he packed away his gear. "I'm the only bac se for a hundred miles. And I work with the Yards as well." He looked toward Quon Son Island, where smoke tendrils were still rising from where the fires had been significant. "A VC attack?"

"Something like that," Teague said.

Moore looked at Teague, the men and their boats, but said nothing about the strangeness of this outfit. Working out of the mountains with the Yards, he no doubt saw many odd groups like SOG commandos moving around, never with rank or name.

Like a Saint Bernard, for all his size and obvious strength, he had a firm gentleness in the way he had dealt with the girl. Yet there was another, angry side to the man that came out. "This damn country has fifteen hundred trained doctors. Half of them are living the good life in Paris while jerks like me are humping the boonies taking care of their people. The doctors who stay in-country get forced into the army. We have about one Vietnamese doctor for every ten thousand peasants out in the paddies and bush. I don't just stick on a Band-Aid here and there and fuck it. That's not how I was trained. But you cover this much territory, it's getting like that."

"What's your base unit doing?" Teague asked. Something in the man's attitude, his frustration and anger, agreed with Teague.

The sergeant was moving toward the chopper and Teague fell in alongside. Moore said, "You going to report my bad attitude?"

"No. I have a very similar attitude, maybe even worse than yours. What is your biggest issue?"

"They change our mission constantly," Moore said. "We were training a CIDG force and then a night striker force and now my old unit is working with a special combination of PRU's and headhunters targeting VCI."

"You don't sound too happy."

Moore flashed a smile of amused anger. "You spook or lerp?"

"Maybe a little of each."

Then the big sergeant glanced back at the junks and their armed crew. He nodded wordlessly and turned toward the chopper where the men were hooking the stretcher on the wall rack.

Teague liked this bac se. He had a realistic attitude towards the mess that was the war. And he was one of the advisors who worked with Yards, a group the Buddhists wanted to recruit into the struggle. "Sergeant, you ever get sick of keeping the world safe for the wrong people, look me up."

"What phone book you in?" the sardonic sergeant asked as one of the men in the chopper gave Moore the thumbs up and the pilot began revving the engine.

"Those who sent you will know," Teague said.

Just as Moore turned to leave, Khiet came up toward them. "Okay, Gamewarden. We go? Bac se number one."

Moore stopped abruptly and turned back to Teague. "What did he call you?"

"Nickname."

"He called you Gamewarden," the sergeant said. "Wait a minute. That call sign you used on the radio: Roadrunner." Moore stared at Teague with an astonished expression, and then said, "Man, the strikers talk about you like you are the fucking Scarlet Pimpernel. You get an opening, I might very damn well be interested. I got to get this co-san to the skinners. Gamewarden, you look me up sometime. Check with your former associates at the C-Team at Binh Thuy. They'll know when I'm in the area."

He climbed on board and the chopper pulled up, angling against the tree line above the river. Moore leaned out the door and gave him a thumbs-up, which Teague returned.

"All right," Teague said, turning to Khiet, "Let's dede mau len."

What Teague had become aware of, Moore being a good example, was the rising tide of disgruntled American soldiers he'd run into over the past couple of months. There was a sense that there was no real strategy, no end game, just body count. The whole country was becoming a straight out kill zone whose strategy was attrition.

They headed down river. Khiet wanted to see his family later because of the mass arrests taking place.

Teague had big issues to deal with first. He knew Acosta would be unhappy with what happened on the island, but at this point he'd just have to adjust.

Saving the girl and meeting Sergeant Moore were two positives he took away from this. But the real issue before him right now was Acosta and his CIA backers. He had to bring them on board with Vinh Lac's operation and purpose. If he couldn't get Acosta to accept the Hoa Hao leader's ambition to get arms and change things in their part of the country, then it would be pretty much over.

20

An hour after the incident with the poor village girl, Teague steered his boat into a small dock just west of Long Xuyen. Several boats remained out on the river and two came in to provide a security team, even though this was probably the safest city in the Mekong Delta, but the death of that river policeman and the raid that killed at least five in his rescue took away any sense of security anywhere.

Teague was met by a CIA operative, JK, a man Chandler said had more college degrees than operational intelligence. He looked the part, very cerebral with big round glasses, bald and skinny and observed Teague and his crew with something close to disdain.

Teague climbed into a covered cyclo with JK and they headed into town, the security team following behind them.

"Acosta is at Vadot's," JK said. "He's not happy with what happened at Quon Son Island. It's not a brilliant move, for sure, especially with what is going on. This might just end things."

Teague ignored that. He had no desire to engage with this guy.

Jean-Paul Vadot's bar, Le Endroit, was another one of the CIA's watering holes in the Delta and in a part of the eastern edge of town where security was tighter.

They went into the bar, which was empty except for Acosta and the woman behind the bar. JK went on into a back room.

"You want something to drink?"

"Beer will work," Teague said. He recognized the woman behind the bar as an Eurasian, a gliding fantasy of sensuous curves and seductive smiles.

"That injured young girl going to make it?" Acosta asked.

Teague sat down across the small table from the operative. "Yeah, I think so. It was bad. Getting your hair ripped off by a boat's propeller is nasty, but the medic, a Special Forces Sergeant, did a great job. Name's Moore, says he's interested, at least for the moment, in getting a new assignment. Maybe with us."

"I know who he is. He's been working with the team that deals with the mountain tribes. The Yards love the guy. But, given where we're headed, he might be better off staying far away."

The beautiful young bartender brought them a pitcher of beer and glasses. She was her husband's third or maybe fourth wife. Vadot was a former captain in French intelligence and the agent responsible for the security of Saigon back in the day. He owned three bars, this one and another in Saigon and one in Can Tho, plus a rubber plantation, and various other 'investments' that made him one of Vietnam's major winners and one of Frank Acosta's long-time associates.

"Teague," Acosta said with a frown, "I don't know if we're going to survive much longer. What in the hell is Vinh Lac thinking? He's pissing off the biggest criminal enterprise in the country. It's their island. The guy who is the biggest drug and arms dealer this side of the fucking moon is going to be worse than getting hunted down by secret police. This guy owns the fucking police. Quon Son Island is at the heart of the Golden Triangle. It's important to many people we have no choice but to work with him. What the hell is going on with your boy? It's suicide."

"No, it's a step in the direction we need to go in. And that island is the first step to a deal."

"Goddammit, Teague." Acosta leaned across the table. "We have supported you in this just about every possible way. But this is crazy. What is this first step, if not off the cliff?"

"Vinh Lac thinks we need some help from this biggest gangster in Southeast Asia."

"What the hell are you talking about?"

"Pretty obvious, isn't it?" Teague shot back. "Anybody who isn't nervous about what's happening down here needs to wake up. It's not about one little island, Frank, this whole place is on the verge of falling apart and MACV has sent down this Stennride to get the job done. And with the VC on the move toward every major city, maybe a rearmed Hoa Hao in those cities will be important. It's a simple trade. You need to talk to the dealers in Cholon, especially one Konar Pappas, and make them understand what's at stake. The island is just the beginning and if they aren't willing to cooperate, they might lose a hell of a lot more. The forces that we need to rearm need serious weapons and a hell of a lot of them."

Acosta sat back. "Do you know how insane this sounds? Why in hell would the most powerful gangster, one who can crush pretty much anyone who causes a problem, cooperate? You think they'll actually surrender massive arms on the hope they'll get that island back?"

"There are big conflicts going on in the Golden Triangle

between rival gangs that might be leading to an all-out war and that isn't what they want. But some help from a well-armed Hoa Hao can help stop those problems and give them that island back with certain changes in how the people there are treated."

"You know how crazy this sounds?"

"Yes. Frank, this is the busiest time of the year for arms and drug dealers. The Israelis replenished their entire fucking army after the Six Day War and it hardly put a dent into the stockpile that grows by the day. Right now, Vinh Lac and Xam have enough of their people in Cholon awaiting orders."

Acosta shook his head as if he couldn't digest any of this. He stared at Teague. Then said, "For the privilege of security—the government certainly cannot provide any—we depend on the goodwill of those with the real power. We pay them off one way or another. It is a profitable arrangement."

"It's a trade, not an attack."

"Part of the secret of a long, successful life is having the brains to know who you can alienate, who you may not. The Corsicans, Greeks, and Chinese running that arms bazaar aren't going to like getting blackmailed."

JK had come in and sat quietly. He'd no doubt been listening from the room just off the end of the bar.

Teague said, "It's all going to be moot if what we think is going to happen does. In the end, all the bombs and bullets in the world aren't going to win if the people are ignored and that's what's happening and you know it. Re-arming the Hoa Hao and their friends, not with some old lightweight weapons but the top of the line is the only way to go."

JK butted in. "Teague has promoted himself to senior case officer and philosophical guru."

"I didn't invite you to the party," Teague said.

"I don't need an invitation. This is my job," JK snapped back.

"It's insane to think that criminal enterprise is ever going to re-arm a private army made up of radical Buddhists who oppose drugs, alcohol and criminal enterprises. You have to be kidding. These aren't your Arabs, Teague. Get that through your thick skull."

"They sure as hell aren't yours either." Teague forced himself to stay calm. "The only people who can do the job need the equipment for that job. AR fourteens, carbines and pistols aren't going to do the job. It's their world. We took it away from them in order to bring the likes of Diem into power. Now it's time to give it back. That was Chandler's dream and supposedly yours as well."

JK said, "Teague, I don't care if your boy is the Third Amnesty of God, there's no way this will happen. The Hoa Hao and Cai Dai are semi-feudal peasants and we were going to use them to spearhead a change of policy here and that's all. It's not in the book that they are going to end up the ruling class. Now even that minor change may never happen."

They both turned to Acosta. He took his time before saying, "Maybe we do need to think about this from a different perspective."

"You aren't buying this," JK said.

"JK, shut up and listen." He looked at Teague and said, "What's the plan?"

Teague said, "The last thing the gun dealers want is a street war that could shut them down, maybe even burn them down, and that can happen. So, you need to deal with Pappas and other big shots who run the warehouses. If that doesn't happen they might lose a hell of a lot more than just routes through the Golden Triangle."

"I don't know if I can get any agreement on this," Acosta said.

"Let me put it this way," Teague said. "The CIA is being shut out of a lot of programs. MACV is taking over. You failed over and over and over. This is maybe your last chance to reverse that. You know as well as I do that if the dealers in Cholon get real pressure from the CIA and see big trouble at their doorstep and want access into Cambodia they will make a rational calculation. Those docks and warehouses are overflowing. We won't put a dent into it. And we also need to arrange transportation. We can change things fast and give the Agency some credit it needs."

Teague pushed the beer glass aside and got to his feet. "America isn't here to replace France as a new colonial empire. Think about this and come up with an answer tonight. I have to pay a visit to Khiet's family. I'll be back later. If you won't cooperate it will come to a nasty end that nobody but the communists will appreciate."

"Teague, this is nuts," JK said.

Teague studied him for a moment, then said, "There's an old Viet proverb: 'The tongue has no bones and can be twisted in any direction.' You'd do better by keeping your mouth shut more often."

"Relax," Acosta said, "Let's not get carried away. I think we'll figure this out. I need to talk to some people."

"When I come back, you need to have an answer. It's going to happen, one way or another. This isn't a halfway house. You're either all in, or all out."

After Teague left, Acosta and JK sat in silence for a few minutes. Acosta nodded for more beers.

JK said, "This is nuts. Your river rat and his friends have us by the balls. What are we going to do? We muscle the goddamn dealers in Cholon, who happen to be connected to every gangster in Indochina."

"We can quit," Acosta said. "Forget the whole thing and go home. Or we can look back at all the mistakes we've made, all the failed coups, and take one last shot at getting things right. If you've seen the docks and warehouses lately, so much equipment and weapons have come in over the last two months there are piles of crates stacked up everywhere. They're overwhelmed. I think we can make a deal if we can get some of our associates on board."

"You have any idea what the consequences could be if it goes wrong?"

"It's already going wrong. Maybe it's time to get serious or get the hell out."

"Or maybe it's time to get rid of Vinh Lac."

"And replace him with Quy? You can't be serious. Wanting something major to happen, but afraid of what that something is won't cut it now."

21

This promised to be a very great day. Stennride was to meet the Roman Catholic priest, Reverend Augustine Nguyen Lac Hao. He was the leader of the famed Sea Swallow army in Binh Hung where he had settled a decade ago with only three hundred refugees during the great exodus from the north. He could be instrumental in reviving a new Catholic force in the Delta and preventing their young from being radicalization by the rebel Buddhists. This was a very big occasion. It was in a way like going back to '54 and '55 when they brought Diem to power.

Finally, things were starting to move in the right direction for Colonel Stennride and he was making progress with the province chiefs across the Mekong Delta.

He intended to end the rebellions fast and that meant taking out the major leaders and that bastard Teague. And, if it came to that, maybe some CIA operatives needed to get taken out. Send a big message. Already there were mass arrests filling the jails in

Can Tho and elsewhere. And Keller was getting calls about a
battle in the Golden Triangle that might involve the Hoa Hao.

The Mangs' new villa was a short flight from his compound.
Stennride said, as they circled the villa, "We need to set up a
meeting with the leaders of the Province Recon Units. They are
hardcore and the best against the VC. I want to bring them on
board and also get every Chinese Nung we can find down here.
That Ranger Battalion bivouacked near An Giang is working with
us and that's a big get. And we need additional security for the
Mangs. While I'm talking to her about that and other things, you
can make some calls. Find out more about that little battle on the
island."

Keller agreed. "If we can get the PRUs in the western
provinces on board they are the best trackers and ambushers out
there. The VC gave them a wide birth. I'll try and set up a meeting
with some of the commanders in the Western Provinces. And find
out what the fights going on out there are all about."

Keller sat the chopper on the lawn of the magnificent, white,
colonnaded, newly purchased villa on the outskirts of An Binh.

Seeing reality, the province chief had readily stepped down to
make way for the Mangs. Stennride left Keller to make calls and
went to the main house just as Madame Mang was coming out
across the veranda to greet him.

Stennride went for a walk with Madame Mang through the
gardens past the koi ponds, while birds chirped and sang in the
newly planted trees that surrounded them. Coming back to her
former province, and back in power, seemed to have done
wonders for her. Her husband was bogged down in Saigon and

wouldn't be back for a few days.

"We do not need an assault on the power structure of the province," she said. "They are proving very cooperative. We give much thanks to your presence here and the fear they have about both the rebels and the VC."

Stennride gave her assurances as they stood and looked at the beautiful sculptured fountain where her gardens came together in the backyard. Beyond that, the river frontage where she would now hold court each morning with various dignitaries from around the Delta.

Stennride said, "How soon is the Reverend coming?"

"He will be here shortly. In fact, he is coming in right now."

A three-car convoy drove down the feeder road and into the compound. The Reverend emerged and greeted his old friend Stennride, then he bowed politely to Madame Mang. They immediately went into the house walking through the plush living room and quickly got down to business out on the side terrace.

"I will have armies such as yours scattered strategically all over the Delta within a year," she assured the Reverend. "You have set an example for us all."

"As have you, Madame Mang. The people were very excited about the ceremonies."

Stennride and the Reverend had gotten authorities to allow her to officiate at recent ceremonies for the newly created women's paramilitary self-defense corps and it was a step in the direction of making her and her husband once again major powers in Vietnam.

When Major Chien's chopper dropped down next to Stennride's half an hour later, he brought four dignitaries with him. Stennride gathered with the men and Madame Mang on the main porch overlooking the river. This group would be at the very center of the new power base.

Madame Mang, both in English and Vietnamese, assured the dignitaries the bandits would be hunted down and destroyed. She got a very enthusiastic response from these visitors from the major cities along the Bassac and Mekong. They wanted to be with the force that was taking over the Delta

Finally, it was all coming together and fast.

22

Khiet's mother stepped back and stood before a small table covered with a red cloth, the cloth inscribed with the characters— BAO SON KY HUONG: A good scent from a strange mountain. This was an important prayer table of the religious Hoa Hao.

Teague watched with no small emotion as the smoke from the village's celebratory fire curled and vanished into the late afternoon sky.

Khiet wanted the family to move to Long Xuyen, but that wasn't going to happen, his mother assured him. The province chief had brought in a provincial recon team that was making people pay for protection. And like thousands of villagers, there was the fear that Khiet's mother, because she was his mother, would end up getting arrested.

As secret as the visit was, they still had security listening and watching in case they were discovered.

Khiet beseeched his mother again that it was time for her to consider moving. But she was having none of it. This was her ancestral home.

She turned to Teague, her face drawn, bittersweet. She forced a smile and said, "It is very kind of you to come. I like very much your ideas on flash freezing the shrimp that my son tells me."

"But you will need the right refrigeration. Once you make deals with the shipping industry, you will become queen of the world's shrimp business," Teague said with a smile. But in fact, he was only half joking, for Khiet's family's shrimp business could be on the verge of something big if the powers in their world permitted.

After a fine dinner and conversation, Teague said goodbye to this attractive woman of fifty, mother of three boys and two girls. She smiled, but beneath the smile she never let Khiet out of her sight, her eyes following him with an almost frantic apprehension which she would never give voice to, but the worry about what might happen to her son was obvious. He might have to come save her and the big family, but that wasn't her concern.

The entrance from the living quarters to the street passed through the family run beauty salon. Here, in a line, stood siblings and cousins waiting to say their goodbyes. Khiet was positively worshiped by his family and their friends.

Kheit was in a less than jovial mood as they quick-stepped down the street and headed for the river and the waiting boats.

"My mother is a businesswoman. She would be very successful if she could only get rid of her enemies." Khiet listed them on his fingers: "The VC, the French-trained civil servant class, the army, the ministry of the interior, the national police, the military Directory, the American economic planners, the American military, the American construction companies and industrial zones policy and now these new security forces in the province…"

"That's everybody."

Khiet shook his head, saying, "No. The Chinese merchants and the family who owns the bakery. Everybody else, yes." He laughed that shrill wild laugh of his.

Two attractive girls looked at Teague with wide-open, appreciative eyes. "Throi obi!" one of them exclaimed and they both giggled as they passed like beautiful bubbles on a rushing stream.

Khiet remarked, loud enough for them to hear, "The most beautiful girls in Vietnam are here."

For Teague that was just what they were—girls. His mind was on a young woman.

Curfew was in three hours, plenty of time to get back to An Binh to see if the agents had made up their minds. They could keep the Wayward Angel wide open all the way.

When they reached the river, Engler was there with the security team and three other boats.

Once on board and on the river, they joined a mass over river craft, the ultimate protection. Teague piloted while Engler monitored river traffic and Khiet was busy trying to pick up a song by his favorite singer, the white swallow: Bach Yen, Vietnam's most popular singer of love songs. "Number ten, number ten thousand!" Khiet yelled angrily in English when he could only get a static garble.

Teague said. "I like your family. This new oppression has to be confronted."

"My family is very good," Khiet agreed, giving up on the radio and digging out a cigarette as the Wayward Angel shot up the center of the Bassac, chasing the falling sun, the sky a fierce blaze of yellow and orange. "But this happens now everywhere.

The Saigon forces come not to fight VC but to run villages and rob them. The prison in Can Tho was built for five hundred and now has two thousand because of the protests against the government. Standing room only. I would like my family to move, but leaving my ancestral village is very difficult. But I am afraid my political actions will endanger my family at some point."

The Mekong Delta where over sixty percent of the population lived was at a critical crossroads and Teague hoped they could do something that would change what was happening.

Khiet said, "Everyone thinks life has become very difficult for the rice farmers, but for business people who want to create more product and open up in all the cities like Can Tho, Soc Trang, Vinh Long, My Tho, Saigon, Hue, life is not so wonderful. It was almost becoming a crime to want to be an independent businessman. The programs of the New Life Hamlets are not business friendly. All the laws are against people like my mother. She pays taxes to the VC, to the GVN, to every little official. You cannot buy and sell land, buildings, or products without special payment. Inflation is coming from the millions Americans bring in, the massive infrastructure your government builds to make it easier for your giant corporations to come here and do business at the expense of our little companies in the same way your military has come in here and taken over the fighting from the people. And the government is taking over all the land."

It was the first time Teague had ever heard his friend grow this passionate and hostile over policies. The visit to his mother changed Teague's understanding of the man and why this fight was all-consuming for him. A true Phu So revolutionary like Xam and Vinh Lac.

Khiet gave up on getting his music and it was now on a very dangerous part of the river so any radio communications were shut down.

They raced past a ship and on toward Long Xuyen and, hopefully, some good news for them about agreeing to a weapons deal.

23

Following a very good day and dinner at the Mangs, Colonel Stennride was in his new office looking at a 'forces' map of the Mekong Delta and reading some intel when Keller came in with that excited but anxious look on his face.

"What now?" Stennride said, a smile on his face at how eager Keller always was, especially now that raids were taking place in many places across the Delta, hunting Teague and his associates. Was there good news?

"There was a mistaken bombing of a village near the Cambodian border north of Long Xuyen."

"And?"

"The traffic we're intercepting is from several sources. One is a Special Forces medical team there and, if the reports are right, there is info that a Hoa Hao rescue team is evacuating wounded and taking them to the hospital in Long Xuyen. That the rescue is being led by Vinh Lac."

"Teague with him?"

"No info on Teague. Could be. The opposition leader, a guy named Quy, is the one who informed Chien. He wants to become the new leader of the Hoa Hao."

Stennride got to his feet. "This could be the break we've been waiting for. Make sure Chien informs everyone to keep this guy alive. It won't be Chien who interrogates him, it with be Major Manning. He's available now. Everyone in the area has to move to block off this area. Let's go."

When Stennride's chopper circled and then settled in a small field near the bombed village ninety minutes later, the sun was beginning to fall behind the mountains.

He and Keller and their four-man security team were met by a half-dozen commandos.

The world around them was in ruins, houses blown to pieces and burned.

In the dense rows of thatched-roof houses, many just bombed out, debris clustered in the growing darkness of the jungle. There were some small squares of yellow light here and there, smoke rising all along the waterway.

The Province Recon Units from the province chief were in place and Chien were there and a Special Forces medic team.

Opposite the PRUs along the road were Strikers brought in from the second district as backup. Chinese Nung mercenaries lurked in the caverns of buildings and alleys, ready to strike whatever target Stennride wanted.

Arriving from a nearby village center was an elite unit from the Ranger base. They came in a three jeep and one truck convoy, all the jeeps sporting mounted fifty-caliber machine guns manned by a soldier who looked as if he was itching to use it.

A two-and-a-half-ton truck full of Rangers stopped some distance away and the soldiers leaped out and deployed like a riot squad, forming a skirmish line directed at the now invisible strikers.

One of Chien's men informed them that Vinh Lac had been sighted in one of the still standing thatched homes on stilts near the water from where he'd directed rescue operations.

Keller checked things out and went to the Special Forces medic team to see what they knew.

Stennride spotted a massive figure of a Special Forces soldier behind him with a shotgun resting casually on his shoulder heading over to the jeep with Keller behind him. Somewhere in the cooling evening, a cat bawled.

Keller said, "He wants to know what is going on."

Stennride went up to the big, black medic. "This is police business, Sergeant. We'll be out of your way as soon as that business is taken care of. How many men are inside that house?"

"Not sure. Maybe only one. Most of the men who came in are all on boats taking wounded to Long Xuyen. He stayed behind we're told because a family that he knows, or maybe is related to, have lost two brothers and a father. The police are saying this guy is some kind of a major criminal."

"He is that."

Major Chien held a megaphone to his mouth and, in his high, grating voice, ordered Vinh Lac to come out of the surrounded house.

After only a moment, the door opened and a tall Vietnamese man appeared, framed in the flashlights on him.

Chien opened the little wooden gate, a megaphone in one hand and his revolver in the other. He yelled insultingly, in a gesture that, to a Vietnamese, was the equivalent of calling a dog. "Di ra!" Chien shouted. "Hien-binh. Toi muon hoik ong vai cau."

He handed the megaphone back to one of his lieutenants.

Women's voices flowed angrily from behind Vinh Lac, one young and one old. And then, suddenly, another young girl appeared in the doorway. Vinh Lac turned and yelled at her, motioning her to go back in the house. He turned and started down the path, shirtless, muscular and jaunty. Though he possessed no weapons, a dozen rifle bolts clicked as if their owners were in imminent danger for their lives.

Stennride was taken by surprise at the uncanny resemblance between this young man and the pictures he'd seen of the Hoa Hao general who had walked into that courtroom in Saigon over a decade ago to receive his sentence of death by beheading. If there was a difference it was that this rebel killer was taller, more powerfully built, but the face, the eyes were very similar, maybe a son who was given a different name for his protection.

Vinh Lac stopped a few feet from the secret police chief. There was a short exchange between the two men that Stennride couldn't understand, even though he heard them and understood many of the words. He knew they were insulting one another with abandon.

Chien produced handcuffs, used in Vietnam only on the most heinous of criminals, murderers, rapists.

Vinh Lac turned to Stennride and spoke in fair English. "Tell your boysan no." He pointed to the handcuffs.

Some insults are so effective there is no equal retort. Calling Chien Stennride's boysan, and acting toward him as if he was too low of a creature to talk to, destroyed face for the major in a way that seemed total and irrevocable. They were not equals. The best Chien could do was violence. He ordered his men to put the handcuffs on the prisoner.

Wolf-like, the Chinese Nungs closed in, their caution quickly justified. What happened was so fast in the dark it looked at first like a mass of confusion, falling bodies, grunts, rifle butts swinging, feet lashing out with thudding impact.

Vinh Lac was still on his feet after this initial assault. He was still standing in a relaxed position as the Nungs were closing again after having been beaten off. Two of them stayed back, one sitting where he had fallen, stunned, the other holding his ribs.

As graceful as a dancer in a pirouette, but with a scream that pierced the heart like that of a bobcat, the would-be prisoner spun, his body and leg extending out in a perfect plane, the heel connecting with the head of the man behind him. He took one more before they got to him. He took them all back, crashing through the fence. Two Viet Rangers joined the melee.

Stennride ran forward, yelling one of the few phrases he knew well, "Dung lai! Dung lai!" He tore one of the Rangers off Vinh Lac. "Get him to the chopper now!"

The Special Forces Sergeant looked very upset and wanted to know more about what was happening.

Stennride ignored him and then in the periphery of his vision he caught the movement as one might catch the leap of a cat on its prey.

The young woman who had gone back in the house after being ordered to do so by Vinh Lac, suddenly burst out of the house just as two soldiers were at the stoop. She broke past the Rangers and fired a pistol at Chien—but the Ranger to her right caught her with the butt of his rifle and the shot went astray, the gun flying to the ground. But she kept coming.

She almost reached Chien before a Nung intercepted her with a swing of his Ml carbine that caught her in the stomach. The air came out of her with a terrible moan.

A shotgun boomed. "Let her go. She's hurt bad," the Sergeant said.

A woman appeared in the door and shouted, "Dung ban!"

She came down the step. She walked with an aura of fatalistic pride as if all that happened was expected but intolerable nonetheless.

Stennride said, "Let's get the hell out of here. Now!" This damn place is on the verge of chaos.

The woman went to the younger woman and knelt in the mud. She looked up at Chien and said something that didn't sound nice.

"What is she saying?" Stennride demanded.

"That we're filthy pigs and she will see the day they cut out our hearts and feed them to the dogs."

She wiped the mud from her daughter's mouth and nose.

Sergeant Moore and his two men stood with weapons ready. The last thing Stennride wanted was a conflict with Special Forces.

As they were going toward the choppers, the Rangers began pulling out. Stennride holstered his .45 and glanced back. In the frosted glaze of the lights by the bridge, he saw Sergeant Moore with the mother and the young woman.

They were lucky something didn't happen that could have been a disaster. But they were successful. They had the leader of the radical movement. They had the main man, the wolf pack leader. They had to get the super interrogator, Major Lester Manning, down to the Delta to get the information they needed from Vinh Lac to find out who the secret leaders were and where they were.

24

With Teague at the helm and Engler and Khiet manning the radios, the boat surged up the Bassac River into the fiery horizon of a fallen sun through heavy walls of green jungle, passing slow sampans, junks and quiet fishing villages. They blew past an old French fort sitting like a decayed skeleton of an earlier time.

Their security lay in speed and the width of the river as they moved toward Long Xuyen. Not just from VC in this area, but from the raids directed at the rebel Buddhists.

The light on one of the radios prompted Engler to answer. It was on the emergency frequency coming from Acosta.

The message was as devastating as it was terse: "Vinh Lac has been arrested," Engler said. "Many people hurt or dead in a village area of the Mekong a mile from the border. Some Special Forces medics are there now."

Teague, shocked, said, "Check it out to make sure that's coming from Acosta and not some kind of set-up. And get directions." He jammed the throttles and the boat's water jet engines kicked them forward with such force the boat lifted nearly off the water. Glancing at the fuel and engine oil pressure gauges, his teeth clenched, his eyes shifting and fixing on the river ahead as the swift tropical night rose, he had to get to Vinh Lac as fast as possible regardless of the risk.

Khiet directed him to cut up a connecting river, the shortest route to the village area.

Engler called Acosta as he monitored traffic on the radios and updated them on the movement of forces in that village area. He got a callback that verified the report.

They left the Bassac and raced up a dangerous narrow waterway that forced them to ridiculously high, dangerous speeds until they finally reached the blown-out village as the last light of the evening faded away.

Radio traffic indicated the Special Forces medic team was still there. Engler was also picking up information about what happened after the attack about the arrival of the secret police and a military contingent of PRUs.

They came in very wary of a potential ambush, passing stilted houses that were still standing and many turned into piles of wood and bamboo, some out in the waterway.

Teague was surprised that they were getting a radio call from the medic who was still there. In the distance of a clearing stood a chopper and the man communicating with them became visible as they pulled into what was the center of the village.

It was Sergeant Moore standing on the porch of one of the still standing houses off a small dock, smoking a cigarette, surrounded by RF strikers in tiger suits.

"Small world," Moore said. "I was not far away when it

happened. They're calling it an accidental bombing."

"How bad?"

"Twenty-one dead, thirty-four on their way to the hospital in Long Xuyen. This colonel that showed up took one prisoner. Guy named Vinh Lac. He gave them a rough time but the colonel wanted him alive. And they left with him about an hour ago. What the hell's going on?"

Teague told Engler to get back to Acosta and let him know what happened and that they would be there as fast as they could. Set up a meeting. This whole thing looked bad and it could get really ugly once the news got out. Acosta had to get involved. They had to make the right decision.

While Khiet made calls and then spoke with the province commander of the striker force, Teague told Moore some of what this was all about.

As his people were getting ready to leave, Teague thanked Moore and the medic team.

Moore said, "Listen, Gamewarden, you said to look you up. Well, circumstances have made that call for me. Lot of folks sick of what's going on. You've got three thousand Yard rebels under Y Bham in Laos right now just waiting for the opportunity to finish what you're involved in. If your people can get me out of my current employment, as I know they have for others, like yourself, I think I can be of help."

"If you're serious, I'll see what I can do. I'll get in touch with you."

"No, actually I'm not interested in returning to my gig. The village was supposedly bombed by accident. Lot of supposed accidents lately. I'd like to go with you to Long Xuyen, learn more. I'm real tired of this shit happening. I need a change of direction and what I hear is you may be a big part of that. And this colonel, he's bad news. Thing with me, I'm old school. If I'm going to put my life on the line, that line better be for a cause I can believe in, and I'm losing that sense of cause. Who the hell is this colonel who can order PRUs and secret police around like they work for him?"

"He's been given power and authority to stop the sect re-emergence. But I don't have to warn you that things on our side are rocky, as you see for yourself. There's going to be a rocky ride and I can't get the right answers real quick, we may all suddenly become unemployed and unemployable."

Moore waved his hand at the blown-up village and said, "I'm not interested in this. If you can change things for me, I'm there."

Engler interrupted them. "Acosta wants us ASAP. Things are getting messy in Long Xuyen and Quy is making some kind of move."

Teague turned to Moore. "You might want to rethink this. It's gonna get ugly fast."

Moore asked Teague to hold a minute. He jogged over to one of the Viets who was part of the medical team and spoke with him.

Engler said, "The sergeant is really pissed."

Moore hustled back. "I'll probably be put on a desertion list if your boys don't intervene successfully on my behalf."

"We'll take care of it," Teague said. "One way or another. Let's dede mau len."

In the distant sky, he could see the red dot of a hunting chopper circling.

25

Engler and his team stayed with the Wayward Angle and half a dozen other junks when they reached Long Xuyen.

The city Xuyen was festive because of the big Hoa Hao meetings and the pre-Tet exuberance.

Acosta informed them that the news of Vinh Lac's capture hadn't reached the general population. That he wasn't sure Xam, who as at the Central Committee meeting, even knew.

Teague was obsessed with who had betrayed Vinh Lac's whereabouts and had gotten him captured.

Khiet went on ahead to the gymnasium that was being used for the meetings and was the Long Xuyen headquarters of the Social Democratic Party. He would let Xam know what was going on.

Teague and Moore, with two security operatives, headed to the small hotel next to Vadot's Bar where Acosta was waiting.

The hotel was close to the water and they went into an inner courtyard. Moore and the other two stayed outside. Teague went up to the door that was guarded by four men, and two police officers. One of the men said something and then opened the door.

Teague went in for his second meeting with the agents on this day that was going to hell fast. The door shut behind him. He looked at the two agents, who had the disposition of professional poker players on a losing streak.

"You find out where the colonel took Vinh Lac?"

"No. But we're doing everything we can to find him. It's obvious this Stennride has a hell of a lot more authority and resources than we anticipated. There's a secret police building in Can Tho near the prison. He could be there, or even, for that matter, at his compound," Acosta said.

Teague turned to JK. "You should be happy. You wanted Vinh Lac out of the way and you got your wish."

"Not like this," JK shot back defensively, nervously, as if he expected Teague to attack him.

"If you were involved in any way, you wouldn't be dumb enough to tell me, so don't assume I'm dumb enough to believe you'd lift a finger to get him out when getting rid of him is the whole point to your warped plan to put Quy in charge."

"That's not true."

"In any case, it's not going to happen. In the meantime, you'd better level with me. Right now, I'm in an unpleasant state of mind with Vinh Lac being captured, dead peasants and bombed-out villages. I'm near the edge."

Acosta said, "We didn't know a goddamn thing about Vinh Lac running around out there organizing rescue operations. We thought he'd be here at the big Central Committee meeting. Don't get all righteous, Teague. We had nothing to do with what happened."

Teague tried to restrain himself. He didn't know what to

believe. "Is there security at the big meeting?"

"Yes. This is still the most secure city in the most secure province, and it is so because of the Hoa Hao. But an internal struggle is the last thing we want and that may be what's going on."

"Just find out where Vinh Lac is."

They both looked over at JK, who was talking to someone on the radio phone. He hung up. "Things are heating up at the committee meeting. The police are getting nervous. That Vinh Lac hasn't shown up is getting rumors rolling. This could go south in a hurry. Quy's at the meeting and his men are causing problems."

"I'll deal with it," Teague said, getting ready to leave. "That medic, Special Forces Sergeant Moore, he's here and wants a major change. Get him free to work directly with me. I need him. That is, if you still have the power to do that. Or are you finished?"

Acosta said, "I'm still in the game. We can get him an emergency temporary transfer. No, we're not finished."

"Good. Do it. We'll talk about the other matter with arms after I deal with the situation. I need to get Xam and her team out."

He looked at JK. "Your boy isn't going to take down Xam and he's not going to run things in your version of the Great Game. And what we're talking about in Cholon, it'll happen with or without you. Best thing you can do is find out where they took Vinh Lac."

JK nodded wisely keeping his mouth shut.

Teague looked at Acosta and said, "You need to get fully in or the hell out. The Delta is about to blow up. And the communists are coming hard and massive and somebody is going to have to stop them. The last goddamn thing we need is some internal dispute."

Before leaving, he gave the two operatives a hard look. This should never have happened. It didn't smell right on any level that Quy was in town and with his people.

26

"How'd it go?" Moore asked as they moved out to the streets.

"That's a matter up for grabs. Those bastards should have seen this coming. We'll see. Right now, we need to get Xam and her team out of here. Maybe out of the country."

"Am I on board?"

"For better or worse, yes. I think. We'll see what those boys decide."

At this time of night, the streets of the city would normally be filled with the young, the lovers, people eating in the restaurants, and a sprinkling of American servicemen who worked in the support functions of the advisory structure. But it was obvious things were going downhill. Rumors no doubt were exploding all over the place.

Teague radioed Engler and told him to get ready. "We might have some trouble. I'm going to the committee meeting to get Xam. Send some of the boys there to help escort us out and get ready to go."

A serious internal struggle had to be avoided.

When they reached the building of the meeting, Teague and Moore left the security detail outside in the street. News of Vinh Lac's disappearance apparently had gotten to the streets. People were gathering around the committee headquarters and the atmosphere was tense.

Teague entered the headquarters of the Social Democratic Party and saw Khiet's men and those of Quy standing across from each other with only tables and local Hoa Hao between them.

Xam stood next to Khiet, talking to him and someone else Teague didn't recognize when Quy yelled something at them. The room erupted with shouts and everyone seemed to be on the verge of pandemonium.

Xam gave Teague a moment as he addressed the gathering of officials. He stopped abruptly, turned and faced Xam. "We cannot go the way of your brother. We need to change course."

A local police officer came over to Teague, one he'd met before and a friend of Vinh Lac's. He said, "There will be action in the streets to protest the arrest of Vinh Lac. That man," he pointed to Quy, "isn't helping matters. It might be good to get Xam and Khiet away. There's other problems. Secret police are in town."

"We'll get them out now," Teague said.

The officer headed up to where the argument was taking place and Teague motioned to Khiet to get ready to move out.

Quy said in a loud, demanding voice to the approaching police officer, "It is not always possible for the police to control everything."

"I have ordered my police into positions all over the city," the chief said. "I will break up any rioting with force. Government troops are at this moment breaking bivouac and preparing to come here if we demand their presence."

"What are they saying," Moore asked as he didn't speak the language.

"That we need to go," Teague said.

Khiet spoke to Xam and she glanced over at Teague and nodded.

Quy continued directing his anger at Khiet. "You are now a CIA stooge."

Xam and two of her security team joined Khiet, Teague and Moore and they left.

With the security detail, they moved carefully and quickly, anticipating the worst scenario, and found most of the dike empty of people when they got back.

Across the Bassac River, the jungle wall towered into the night sky like a tidal wave of blackness bearing down on the river and town.

Boat people squatted on the decks of the sampans and junks along the quay, their faces glowing in the sallow light of the oil lamps like prospectors at the bottom of a canyon.

Teague would have given a lot to know just what role Acosta had in all this.

They headed toward the backbone of the dike. Ahead of him he saw a silhouette break the line of the dikes narrow horizon.

Teague slowed, as did the others. A low, dark human shape was moving in a crouch, angling obliquely toward the far side of the dike, the top of his head visible.

"Watch that boy," Moore said.

Teague heard a little tic of a sound he knew too well and he quickly reached under the flap of his shirt and slipped his hand over the smooth wood handle of his revolver. He chose his steps carefully, warned by that ever alert inner alarm system that two years of irregular warfare had instilled in him like a sixth sense.

The figure vanished. The intensity of Teague's focus tightened on the spot.

But when what he feared came, it did not come from the man in front of him but from across the street to his right, up on the rooftop: a blip-blip of light, the crack of a rifle. He ducked behind some tables on the dike as Khiet returned fire.

The slugs twanged and spit around him.

Moore ripped off three rounds from his shotgun and that stopped the roof gunman.

They raced back across the quay. The firing continued and Teague kept himself between the gunfire and Xam as best he could. He couldn't believe Quy would actually have a sniper team trying to take out Xam. The secret police were the most likely source of this.

He anticipated the impact of the slugs. He realized he had a sharp pain in his side as he rolled over the edge on the quayside.

He had his weapon out, a snub nose .357 Colt. He was beyond the sight of the sniper down the quay. He lay sprawled on the bank of the dike with Xam and Khiet. Moore and the others were moving back up to find the shooters.

Over the radio, Engler said he was pulling in to get them.

Teague, elbows tri-podded in the soft earth, his right wrist cradled in his open left hand, focused his eyes just above the gun sights at the crest of the dike. A man came over almost exactly where Teague was looking. Teague squeezed the trigger in two quick smooth actions, the .357 boomed twice, the first stopping the man in the air, suspending him for a brief instant before the second slug spun him backwards, kicking his feet out from under him and slamming him into the dike.

There was a moment of silence, deep and total, as if the

universe had come to a complete stop, as if Teague's own heart and blood had stopped. He saw the blur of the hidden moon, spread in the clouds like a spilled liquid. He then heard voices, one, the booming voice of Sergeant Moore reverberating above the others.

The firing now was coming from two points.

From somewhere to his right, he heard a frantic voice. "Dai-uy! Dai-uy!"

"Here!" Teague replied.

Khiet moved with three others at the rim of the dike and Moore led his detail up the other side and Teague moved up the middle.

Khiet said, looking at the dead man, "Maybe one of Chien's secret police."

A moment later, they heard yelling from the other side of the dike and learned shortly that the other sniper had been killed.

The followers of Xam moved down the street and across the market to the waiting boats. The members of the Hoa Hao Central Committee climbed aboard the junks, moving silently and quickly, carrying boxes of pamphlets, political records and other documents on their heads and shoulders.

Teague prepared to board the Wayward Angel with Xam. Moore stood on the deck. They were still waiting for Khiet, who was out checking something.

Then Frank Acosta appeared with his security team. "Teague," Acosta yelled breathlessly as he made his way up the dike. "Don't go downriver."

"Why?"

"Just don't go where you can be hit from the air. We're getting all kinds of traffic." He realized Xam was there and nodded to her. "We're doing everything to find out where they took your brother."

"We have to go," Teague said. "We'll hide out to the west near the border. Keep us updated."

Two Hoa Hao hopped off the back of a motor scooter and came to join them as they went to the boats.

"Let's go!" Engler yelled.

Xam and two of her security team boarded, followed by Moore and Teague and two more of her team. The others went to other boats coming in.

Teague turned and glanced at Acosta, who stood forlornly on the quay. The boat's big engines rumbled to life and the powerful junk headed for open water.

"Bit of a mess," Moore said.

"Maybe you should rethink your plans."

"I got no problem with big messes, they are my life."

PART THREE

The Kill Zone

27

Colonel Stennride waited impatiently for news from Chien's operation in Long Xuyen that might well end this fast. But when Keller delivered the news, it was not good.

"All the leaders got out and two more of Chien's people ended up dead."

Stennride was once again shocked. "Chien can't do a fucking thing right. Jesus fucking Christ!"

That Teague had escaped once again was bad enough, but that sister of Vinh Lac was looking like a major problem.

"I'm getting sick of this." He'd considered telling Chien to go directly after the CIA agents who were in Long Xuyen and running the rebel operations with Chandler and now Teague. But that would trigger a direct and nasty battle with the CIA. It would bring the entire agency and maybe even the media into the mess.

That the core radical elements of the Hoa Hao were being rounded up and thrown into the jail in Can Tho and other Delta cities was a big step. But they had to get Teague and this Xam and then find and destroy the base camps in the forests and jungles around the Seven Mountains. That meant Vinh Lac had to be broken and soon.

The top dog super-interrogator was finishing up a project and would take another day to get to the Delta.

It had been a big mistake to allow the head of the secret police to try and break somebody like Teague. That mistake would be corrected when Manning finally showed up to take on Vinh Lac.

The thing everyone knew about Manning was that he could study and understand a prisoner in a short time and knew how to walk him down a nasty road designed by modern chemistry. Of course, he only worked in secret and off any record and used new chemicals. He had a reputation of success unlike any other interrogator. But his successes were not public record. Or, for that matter, on any record.

Stennride believed this man might give them the results needed to finally put an end to the CIA's plot by revealing who was involved and where the secret Hoa Hao bases were.

At some point Stennride understood the potential political disaster that could arise out of a thing like this if it just kept going. With no regular American ground forces south of Long An, the only units were Special Forces, Rangers and Riverine and the growing presence of the 9th Division focused only on operations against the Viet Cong.

That had to change and soon. "We need to get this sect madness under control fast," Stennride said. "We need to break this Vinh Lac and find out what we're really dealing with. Major Manning will get the answers we need."

Keller said, "I heard he's got some new chemicals that break any man's resistance."

"Just make damn sure Chien's men leave the prisoner alone

and alive. Their job is to stop any attempt to break him out of that Can Tho prison." Stennride shook his head. "I've been in this country too damn long."

28

Morning fell harsh and uninviting on Frank Acosta as he rolled off the tiny cot and pushed the mosquito netting back. He couldn't believe how fast things were moving and they were moving against everything he'd wanted.

It occurred to him now there was no chance without a real revolutionary change and that meant doing what Teague wanted.

That scared the hell out of Frank Acosta.

Fully rearming the Hoa Hao was something he'd resisted, but that was before a maniac like Colonel Stennride and his psychopathic secret police came into the Delta. Everything had changed for the worse. They were lucky it didn't all collapse last night.

He glanced over at JK who sat by the window of the old French-built hotel and stared out the window as he sipped his coffee and toyed with a cigarette.

Seeing that Acosta was awake, JK said, "Why isn't Teague

responding? Maybe they got him. Nothing but silence."

"What do you expect? Going dark and silent is what he has to do. I'm pretty sure he's in Cambodia or the U Minh. His people are good at escape and survival. This should trigger a reality check. We have big trouble coming. Teague warned us. This is a nightmare. Maybe it'll trigger the change we need."

"Don't bet on it," JK said. "Your boy has a lot of rogue in him and is maybe unrecoverable. This whole thing is going to hell and it fits into that colonel's handbasket. We lost Chandler and maybe it's over."

Acosta lit a cigarette. "Chandler didn't have a madman like Stennride running dark ops in the Delta. It's not over. It just needs to change. Teague has to make the right moves. I'm thinking Teague understands that rearming might well be the only way."

JK let smoke drain from his nostrils, then said, "Maybe we're finished here and you just don't want to admit it. Chandler was the only one who had the ability—if he even had it—to get these Delta factions on board without creating the nightmare of re-arming and the subsequent war. Maybe the program died with him. It's time we started thinking about an alternative scenario."

"Let me know when you have one because I don't see one on the horizon," Acosta said. He was sick and tired of JK's moaning and groaning. A very nasty idea had formed in Acosta's mind about JK and his contacts with Quy.

But he didn't bring it up. Instead he said, "I don't think we have a choice. I'm not ready to quit. We need a goddamn revolution here. We need to find a way to push Stennride out. He's brought the Mangs back. He's trying to redo the Diem disaster."

"He's getting the power and we're not in a position to stop him."

They could hear what sounded like artillery shells off in the distance and Acosta imagined the shells being fired out in the no-man's land of a free fire zone, imagining those shells arching out over unsuspecting hamlets, over rice paddies, canals, roads in search of the enemy. More than a decade into the war for the CIA and nothing had improved, it had gotten worse.

"We need a radical change and I'm beginning to think there's only one way to go."

"Come on, Frank, we need to get real. These peasants are trapped at the bottom and maybe there is no way out. Maybe the whole thing is over."

"Maybe you've been at this too long. You remember when, for the third time, State tried to have Lansdale sent over here to straighten things out and he was ignored, basically shot down? Remember what you told me about how the Douhet Theory had been resurrected? That sooner or later if the war didn't find another strategy, they would just bomb the VC and their northern brothers back to the Stone Age and create a nice totalitarian dictatorship here. Isn't that what we're trying to stop? Chandler had it right. One way or another, the peasants need to be brought into this war."

"He's dead and maybe so is his dream. Maybe there is no stopping it now," JK said, lighting another cigarette. "We got a serious rogue out there and he might bring the whole place down on top of us."

"I don't care about us. We have to figure something out. I can't accept another defeat. What worked to a large degree in Borneo under Walker, and the Philippines under Lansdale, we have to make work here, one way or another. Jesus Christ, please, rein in the defeatist mentality and start thinking about ways to deal with this crazy fucking colonel and stop this crackdown. There's already a big resistance building and one that, if properly led, can actually do something."

They were still smoking and arguing as morning seeped into the room like a yellowish paint spilling over the walls.

Acosta believed, had to believe, that Teague was in a very critical position to get something real going in the Delta. "We have to continue to mentor what we have, like it or not. And we have to find a way to get Vinh Lac free."

A tired looking JK laughed sardonically. "Not going to happen. They learned a big lesson in getting Teague free. Look, we have a very big problem in not just Stennride, but Saigon and the Hoat Vu and our own higher-ups. Right now, I'm thinking we need to beef up our own personal security. This Hoat Vu chief is a fucking psychopath."

Acosta didn't disagree.

A chain smoker, JK took a final drag from his cigarette and then immediately lit another, saying, "I always wondered what it must have been like playing music on the deck of the Titanic as it was going down."

"We're not there yet," Acosta said. He hated the idea of defeat of yet another political operation. "We need to throw everything into this. It's our last chance. You wanted Vinh Lac out of the way, you got that. But Quy isn't the answer, so maybe we need a new answer and fast or it will be over. General Duyet and all the other leaders out there in no-man's land are waiting for somebody to get this together. We need to support them or we need to get out. It starts with rearming. There are thousands of followers out there waiting for the opportunity. We need to give it to them, otherwise what the hell are we here for."

JK shook his head. "It may well be over already. If they break Vinh Lac, he'll give up the entire organization and its support bases. We have to be prepared for that. I heard a half hour ago from a contact in Saigon that this torture expert, Major Manning, might be headed to the Delta. That means that Vinh Lac is alive and going to face something really bad."

"I'm not ready for capitulation and some ignominious surrender. We've been in this goddamn war for a decade. It's degenerated into an insane strategy of attrition. I'm not willing to just walk away and neither are those who have been supporting us. The Hoa Hao and allies in the Free Khmer have taken control of much of the Golden Triangle and that's the coin of this corrupt realm, and maybe the means to re-arming. We can't walk away now. We still have support from above."

"Frank, this looks like it's going to blow up in our faces. If something positive doesn't happen fast, that support up top will dry up in a hurry."

That was true and depressing. Acosta began to wonder if he wasn't himself getting bit by Verstehen.

29

Since the interrogator wouldn't be there for another day, Stennride agreed to pay a visit to the latest of the New Life Hamlets under construction and deal with what the Mangs, his favorite couple, needed. They were complaining about a growing problem and wanted him to deal with it.

There would soon be few peasants still living in their traditional villages as forced draft urbanization would give government huge control. But the idea that the Viet Cong would take advantage of the program was not acceptable. Putting in a PRU unit and Hoat Vu operators would change things.

When they landed, RMK construction bulldozers were clearing the debris from the new construction. At the end of these rows of new houses under an open canopy he saw the skinny, boyish figure of Brian Vanderlin, the New Life Hamlet advisor, handing out the death payments to those who had lost family members in a refugee camp battle not far away.

Stennride waited until the process was done, then went over to greet the New Life advisor and administrator.

Vanderlin turned and faced the colonel with a less than friendly look, saying, "I came down here on the condition that I could build my prototype pacification program unhindered by provincial authorities. I don't want secret police in my hamlets."

Stennride stared coldly at Vanderlin for a moment. "They aren't yours. This province was on the verge of anarchy to some extent because of VC infiltration into the New Life Hamlets, your friend Hurwitz's brilliant economic theories not-withstanding."

"That's not the issue."

"Things are changing down here," Stennride said. "They are changing in a direction that you need to adjust to. The Mangs now control this province. They are worried that your social dreamlands are being infiltrated by Viet Cong. They aren't going to be recruiting grounds or hiding places."

"Colonel, you know what the Mangs are doing. They're reintroducing the reactionary Catholic Can Loa back into these new hamlets and that's not what our reformation is about." Vanderlin had that condescending, haughty tone of an anointed elitist.

"No one in history has reformed their way to victory in war," Stennride shot back. "Mao was right about one thing: victory comes out of the barrel of a gun, not out of the heart of a New Life Hamlet reformer. You cannot move forward without working with, and getting protection from, the new power structure. If you want to continue here building paradise, you will have no choice but to deal with those in power."

"I want to do my job and having secret police and Province Recon Units in the hamlets alienates the people."

"If the price is too high, maybe this isn't your future," Stennride said. He had a real disdain for the Vanderlins of the world. They thought they could beat communists by giving the peasants a communist-like lifestyle.

"Listen," Stennride said, "You have to understand that the war is changing and changing fast. By the end of next year, we'll have a half million troops, a massive air force and unlimited capacity. New Life Hamlets are a means of consolidating and protecting the peasants from the massive campaigns coming. To protect the hamlets from Viet Cong penetration, there is no group better suited for that than what you call the reactionary Can Loa. In the end, the only authority that will count is American military authority. But we can't have VC in the villages recruiting and being protected. That is a road we cannot afford to go down. I'm going to send in a team that will help keep the VC out of these villages. Attrition of the enemy demands the end to safe places. Get on board. You can't stop this, so don't waste your time. Security isn't in your playbook."

As Stennride and Keller were lifting off fifteen minutes later, Keller said, "I don't think that boy likes you."

"He'll adjust. That type always does. Maintaining their power is more important than risking it for policy or ideology. Let's have dinner with Madame Mang."

When they settled the chopper down only minutes later at the beautiful estate and new home of the Mangs, Keller remained on board to make some radio calls.

Madame Mang met Stennride as he approached the veranda and they walked out by the main gardens and pond. She snapped the head of a fat red rose from its stem and put it to her nose, appearing very pleased with the rich fragrance. He watched her turn to her nearby gardeners, who had stopped work to indulge in a little conversation.

In a moment, they seemed to feel the hot burn of her eyes and they hurried back to work.

"Colonel Stennride," her voice flowed with beautiful sarcasm and the promise that she was not one to take lightly, "did your visit with the architect of the new hamlets go well?"

"I think so."

"How is the hunt for Vinh Lac's sister and that American traitor going?"

"We'll know a lot about the secret camps and where they might be hiding from Vinh Lac. The man coming in can, I'm told, break anyone with the new methods and chemicals. We'll know a lot and very soon. We don't need a big problem with rebels and that has to be taken care of very fast. We have a growing problem that is partly due to the success of our attrition of the Viet Cong and NVA. Our forces are killing at a rate of four to eight thousand a month and they are looking for safe places to hide. So, it's a success, but with a cost. We need to take away all security from the communists. I'll make sure the Ap Doi Moi New Life Hamlets get more inside security."

Madame Mang placed the rose in the palm of her hand, as if it represented her enemies, and she began to pluck off the petals until she reached the palp center, which she crushed. She dumped the mess to the ground. "That little whore has an unjustified reputation among the people. Destroy that reputation. As the American saying puts it, there is more than one way to skin a cat whore."

Stennride smiled. He had a special relationship with this woman. They had very close views on the war and how it had to be run.

"I want to rebuild the aging Catholic Church and add a very good school, and my husband, when he returns from Saigon, wants that started soon."

"We'll help you in every way."

"The young Catholics in this province and others are again having a dangerous relationship with the Hoa Hao and Cao Dai and that must be stopped."

They had pre-dinner drinks on the veranda and talked about the coming campaigns.

When Keller finally came over from the chopper where he'd been making calls and came up on the veranda, it was with good news.

"Manning is leaving Interrogation Island and the tiger cages. He'll be here first thing in the morning."

"Good. Finally, we're going to get some serious information."

Interrogation Island, as some referred to Con Son, was fifty miles out in the South China Sea and held the most hardcore criminals and Viet Cong. That was where an interrogator like Manning could conduct experiments with new methods and chemicals and not have anyone looking over his shoulder.

The dinner included barbecued goat, whole tuna and toasted butterfly. Stennride avoided the butterflies but Keller devoured them as if they were potato chips.

"Tomorrow," Stennride assured Madame Mang, "everything will change."

<u>30</u>

Colonel Stennride had known about the mysterious U.S. Army Major Lester Manning for years. He had a reputation for having once been involved in trying to create a truth serum during the Manchurian Candidate hysteria in the intelligence community.

No truth serum was ever produced, but Manning was rumored to have developed a chemical aid to interrogation that was getting great results, even if it wasn't officially accepted. Vietnam provided him, as it provided so many other people, the perfect secret laboratory.

The morning of Manning's arrival in Can Tho, Stennride went to see the man at work. The interrogation room near police headquarters was a concrete, windowless box, a stink hole of old urine, sweat and mildew. A single, dirty, sixty-watt bulb dangled like a teardrop from a cord in the center of the room, suspended over Vinh Lac, who was strapped to a chair.

"Colonel, we have a tough case here."

"I figured he would be."

Two Vietnamese, including Colonel Chien and three Chinese Nungs and Manning faced the prisoner, who was strapped to a chair and wearing only shorts. Vinh Lac appeared to have weathered his isolation and his beatings with no loss of the defiant intransigence he'd had when they first brought him in.

That the prisoner's face was a mess, the lips broken and swollen, the nose scabbed, both eyes blackened and puffed, but still peering out with haughty, indomitable arrogance, hadn't made an effect. Chien's men weren't supposed to do anything to him. Maybe Chien, not liking that his role was being taken over by an American interrogator, had made an attempt to break down Vinh Lac, but he'd obviously failed.

Manning hovered over a small field table, fumbling with his syringes and little bottles of chemicals. He had a clipboard with notes scribbled in the hand of a child's over-large, awkward scrawl.

"I hear you have developed new chemicals."

"You are right, I have and they show great promise." Manning lit a cigarette, took a couple of quick drags, and then balanced it on the edge of the table. "This is history" —he held up a syringe to the light; it was a brownish fluid—"and, one day, chemicals will replace torture, electrodes, or shoving a man out at ten thousand feet to convince his buddy to talk as some of our Viet friends do from time to time."

Major Chien was watching Manning with a look of belligerent disdain as the American interrogator pressed the needle into an exposed vein in the prisoner's forearm, depressed the plunger and yanked it out. He dabbed the spot with a cotton swab—all very methodical and professional. Then he looked at Vinh Lac, reached up and cradled the prisoner's chin in his white hand and moved in close, almost as if he intended to kiss the man, and he said, "I know all you people just love B-twelve shots but this ain't no B-twelve shot, sweetpea, this is going to kick your ass with the force of a mule. And you won't be able to resist because it'll also block your ego."

Stennride doubted Vinh Lac understood much, given his limited English. But then he shocked everyone, especially Manning, when he spit in the interrogator's face.

Stennride's first impulse, which he checked, was to laugh at the stupidity of the major for leaning so close to the prisoner.

Manning stumbled backwards, as if the force of the spit had knocked him off balance. He reached for the table to catch himself, sending some of his paraphernalia skidding all over the floor. He swore and brushed the ashes and burn from the cigarette off his hand.

He regained his composure with some effort. He wiped the spit off with a washcloth he took from a case on the table. With deliberate, forced calm, he gathered up his things and placed them back in order on the table.

This can't go well, Stennride thought. It was very bizarre that Manning had gotten so close, like he maybe thought he was intimidating the guy.

"You're going to pay a big price for that," Manning said. "Stuff the bastard's mouth." He handed the washcloth to one of the Nungs.

Two men came forward. One pulled Vinh Lac's head back and the other forced the cloth in his mouth.

Manning stepped up to Vinh Lac and said, in a chilling voice so low as to be barely audible, "You're mine, sweetheart, all mine." The needle went in fast.

Manning turned to Stennride. "They say he speaks some English. We will have answers to your questions very soon. Interrogating for days and weeks is over. I'm changing that to hours."

Within seconds, the prisoner's stomach began to make strange spasmodic movements.

As soon as this started, the Nungs, superstitious, magical thinking mountain men from North Vietnam, began shifting their positions closer to the door, their eyes open wide like mesmerized children.

Manning glanced at his watch and then wrote something on his clipboard. Then he lit another cigarette. "Musculature disintegration will proceed up this fucker's right side first and then it will spread."

The muscular convulsions reached the upper part of Vinh Lac's body and he was looking down at himself in seeming astonishment at his uncontrolled convulsions. His arms and shoulders shook, the skin twitching the way a horse does when it was trying to ward off flies.

'Cotton Mather' continued with his triumphantly vengeful guided tour. "The brain has two sides, each performing at a different evolutionary stage, one operating on the basis of emotive patterns and images and the other operating on the basis of linear, sequential, logical structuring."

Vinh Lac's head began lolling back and forth as his neck lost its muscular rigidity. He was desperately seeking air through his nose and seeming to fail and looked really bad.

"How does it work?" Stennride asked.

"What I'm doing," Manning said, "is giving a chemical shock to the primitive brain stem where identity and ego have their base. It's like pulling him off the horse his sense of self rides on. It breaks the link."

The prisoner, who had a wild look on his face, now more resembled a drowning man struggling for air. The scabs on Vinh Lac's lips broke and blood mixed with saliva sprayed out as his head bobbed this way and that, tossed like a ball in a rough sea.

The musculature of his face broke down and in place of the hard, mask-like tenacity there was now a shifting jelly, the flaccid face of a madman in an asylum.

"Don't kill him before he talks," Stennride said. He'd seen many men die and this guy looked very close, his whole body under extreme distress.

Manning, apparently not all that concerned, said, "You have to be careful they don't choke, but a counter-injection brings them back."

The effect looked like a massive overdose that appeared to be tearing Vinh Lac apart in what was some kind of induced grand mal epileptic seizure that shook him violently.

In the man's eyes Stennride saw a wild, crazed battle to fight what was happening and losing to a force greater then himself.

Of all the things Stennride had seen over the years from those who'd been tortured or grotesquely wounded, this had something different about it. The fight, the defiance slipped away, replaced not by submission but vacantness. The prisoner appeared to have become nothing but a mass of protoplasm under the overwhelming power of the chemicals.

"I can do in twenty minutes what they can't do in the Hall of Photography and Pictures at Chi Hoa in twenty days," Manning said proudly, referring to the infamous torture room at the prison in Saigon. "Only thing you have to be careful of is you don't use too many CC's for the body weight or you can blow their circuits, fry their brains and they become vegetables. Let him calm down a little now. See his eyes? He doesn't know anything at the moment. Brain stem shock. He'll respond to questioning in a few minutes and it'll be effective for about an hour. Give all kinds of information before he understands what he's doing. That's the whole problem with so-called truth serums. They don't work because the inner self still can lie, still can protect its identity and integrity. All I've done is numb this inner sense of identity. Once they lose that sense of who they are, they lose resistance. Old school physical torture will be replaced by advanced chemicals."

Manning arranged his clipboard and pulled up a little stool off to the side of the prisoner, who now had the appearance of a retarded man with that dull, glassy look. He had the Nungs remove the cloth from Vinh Lac's mouth as he struggled to breathe.

"The brain is like a very sophisticatedcomputer each with its own program, its own code. You've got to get in there and short circuit certain aspects of the program. The Russians are working hard on this, but we're going to beat them. We have to beat them! Once you can control the mind, you can control the world."

Then the questioning began. Innocuous questions at first that just bounced off Vinh Lac's rubbery eyes without making any impression.

"Happens sometimes," Manning said, a little concern emerging in his voice. "When you want to do this fast, you take chances. There are variables in this we haven't been able to isolate." He went on with the questions and still there were no answers.

"If you overdosed him," Stennride said, "you said you had the antidote to bring him back."

"I do." Manning went on asking questions.

"Looks like you've cut his circulation off. Look at his hands?" They were bloated and bluish.

Manning asked Chien to have one of the Nungs loosen the bonds. There was something of a communication problem and the Nung, not too happy with having to get close to Vinh Lac, as if the whole thing might be contagious, leaped forward with the knife and cut the leather straps with two flicks of the blade in a motion so sudden it caught everyone by surprise. The Nung dashed back to his place on the wall close to the door.

"Jesus—" Manning yelled. "I didn't say cut them."

But suddenly, as if hit by an electric shock, Vinh Lac lunged forward, bringing the wooden chair strapped to his legs with him as he lunged at Manning and caught him in the head and throat with his forearm and sent him staggering back.

Chien already had his weapon out after the Nung cut the bonds and now, in spite of Stennride yelling at him not to, he fired point blank. He fired again and again, knocking Vinh Lac back with the chair against the wall.

And still Vinh Lac tried to regain some footing, tried to lunge forward again with the chair.

Chien shot him one more time. Blood spurted out of the chest and head wounds and Vinh Lac ended up sitting in the chair against the wall. His nostrils flared in a final gasp and then nothing. His head lolled forward, arms at his side. He was dead and no injection would bring him back.

Stennride glanced at the body of Vinh Lac and knew that when news of this man's death got out, there would be some big trouble. And, as with Teague, they'd learned nothing. I'm dealing with fanatics and fools, Stennride thought.

The Nung who'd cut the bonds had vanished out the door. Stennride figured he should not stop until he reached the mountains in Laos where the independent Nungs held out.

This was yet another disaster and he again blamed Chien, but said nothing because the man he shot had killed many of his secret police.

Manning gathered up his equipment and put everything back in the case. He said, "I've got to get back to Saigon. It wouldn't have taken all that long to bring that boy to where we could have gotten the answers you wanted. Sorry it didn't work out."

Stennride knew all hell could break loose and he and Chien

needed to warn their people across the Delta. If this exploded in violence in major cities, it would not be easy to stop and the conflict would draw a lot of unwanted attention.

31

Teague turned as he stood on the deck of the Wayward Angel and looked back at Engler who was on the radio. He came out and joined Teague and he didn't have a good look on his face.

"What's going on?"

"That was Acosta. He got a call from Can Tho from a Viet agent they work with. A big shot interrogator was brought down this morning."

"Then that is probably where Vinh Lac is."

"Yes, it is. Something went wrong in the interrogation and some kind of fight broke out. The report is that Vinh Lac was shot dead. Acosta wants a meeting."

Vinh Lac's capture had been bad news, but his death was a lot worse. Teague took a moment to digest this disaster. And he needed to talk to Xam.

Teague steered Wayward Angel toward Xam's boat near a village on the canal west of Long Xuyen.

Moore, standing next to Teague, said, "I wished I had known who he was when they came into the bombed-out village. I might have been able to get him out of there."

"You didn't know. Quy no doubt set him up. The day will come when we hunt that bastard down. Tell Engler to contact Acosta. We'll be a little late."

Teague pulled his boat up alongside Xam's. Her security chief nodded and it was obvious that they knew.

When he climbed on board her boat, the door opened and he went inside. He saw that her eyes were glazed with tears, and he could see the anger.

"I'm sorry. We'll get those bastards who killed your brother," Teague said, not sure how to deal with her. Or what was going to happen once the word got around.

Xam, struggling to get hold of this, said, "Yes. We will get those who betrayed him. And the body must be properly buried. You will tell your CIA people that if we don't get his body, the city of Can Tho will burn to the ground and the police will die in the ashes."

"Yes, I'm going to see the agents now. What happened to Phu So will not happen to your brother." He said it with a tone of confidence, but he didn't know the answer. The secret police might just hand the body over to people who would do what happened to Phu So.

"Yes." She stared out the small window, and then said. "I believe it was Quy who betrayed my brother. Go talk to the agents and make sure they help us. I don't want riots in the cities. I want a funeral and riots will prevent that."

When Teague returned to his boat and they headed for the docks at Long Xuyen, he contacted Acosta. "The body of Vinh Lac better not disappear as the founder of the Hoa Hao did, or this will be a disaster, Frank. Do what you can to make sure that doesn't happen. I'll be there in about an hour."

On their way, Khiet said, "I will contact the Digger. He will be very upset and he will help."

The Digger was the code name for the shadowy monk, Nhu Bon, Teague had seen at the dinner. He was, Khiet had told him, always there with a shovel when a regime was about to be buried as he hoped this in Saigon would soon be. He had been a political advisor to Thich Tri Quang, but when the big crunch came, he had vanished. No one was surprised to find him back in the Delta advising the Hoa Hao Buddhists.

32

At the end of what Frank Acosta thought was a very bad year, he figured it was about to get a hell of a lot worse with the death of Vinh Lac. He ordered another drink.

He'd been in Maria's Bar talking to four program operatives who were working on the new Phoenix Program. When he returned to the table, the agents were arguing about the Phoenix Program. He didn't tell them his problems. These guys were not part of his operation and knew very little about it. They had their own issues.

That got universal agreement from the men in Maria's bar, a popular CIA 'spook' watering hole.

He tried to look calm. He laughed at one of the jokes of the operatives in the bar, and said, "Being paranoid in this world is a sign of sanity." They were into the history of the misery and failure of programs.

Thinking about his upcoming meeting with Teague, he had no

idea how they would deal with this or what the reaction by the Hoa Hao would be. It could all end very fast with exploding violence across the Delta.

Waiting for Teague, a lot of bad memories popped up in his addled mind as he listened to the old hands tell crazy wild stories. Currently it was Upin on center stage. Upin was the code name for the pseudonymous Pat Gibbs. Everyone had a story about 'Upin'. He was the kind of paramilitary case officer that everybody loved to hate.

One advisor said, his voice laden with the sarcasm of someone who'd been in Vietnam too long, "What the hell does it matter if you're running around with the goddamn Hmong and chopping off the ears of Pathet Lao. It makes good copy, but does it make any damn difference?"

Then his associate argued that it depended on the relationship between the event and the media. He brought up the impact of that morning five years ago at an intersection of Le Van Duyet street in Saigon where an old monk surrounded by about three hundred followers and a pack of journalists hovering around like vultures. The old monk sat on a small square pillow he had gotten out of the trunk of a car and chanted, "Nam mo amita Buddha." Then he struck the match that set fire to Ngo Diem's regime.

"They could have stopped him," Mason said.

"It was his right to protest however he thought fit," Gruber countered.

The thing about that episode was that reporters knew what he was going to do and nobody tried to stop him. It was too good a story, too dramatic and it fit a narrative. So much circled back to Diem and the destruction of the Buddhists as a political force. And now it was happening again and at as bad a time, given the massive encroaching Viet Cong and NVA. That troops had been brought in from the borders and repositioned to create a defense perimeter around Saigon triggered all kinds of scenarios in Acosta's mind. This was the opposite situation, no media, no awareness, but the impact could be even worse.

They were talking about what it meant to bring all the troops from the borders. The man who had convinced the generals to do that was Ed Lansdale, America's most celebrated counterinsurgency expert who'd been reduced to the status of a sideshow.

Acosta had last seen Ed Lansdale at a graduation ceremony. They'd watched the cream of South Vietnam's urban youth, dressed to imitate VC, except for a few expensive adornments like Aussie hats, web belts, and canvas boots, marched up in neat battalion formations after graduation. That night, six thousand torches snapped at the night sky. And how were these graduates from the Vung Tau military academy's Revolutionary Development program after a few months' indoctrination supposed to know how to uproot and defeat a VC infrastructure that had been embedded for the past thirty years.

The four men still at the bar had cynically dramatized and laughed at the various disasters. The flamboyant Air Marshall Nguyen Cao Ky repeated the new vision of winning the hearts and minds of the peasants in a speech attended by no peasants, only the elite in the military and government and a handful of Americans.

Just being there and thinking about all of this ended when a man came in and told him that Teague's boat had arrived.

Acosta offered the next round on him. "I need to deal with a problem."

He went to the door as Teague was coming in. "Let's go to the back room." He asked Maria to bring some beers.

Teague said, "You contact people in Can Tho?"

"Yes. I sent JK to deal with the authorities and he's going to involve Lessing."

"What about the colonel and that crazy Chien."

"They know what will happen if that body goes missing. It won't serve their purposes. Lessing will deal with the colonel."

"Good. Hopefully he can handle it. You know anything about what actually happened?"

"Not much. Some big interrogator they brought in to break Vinh Lac failed and it ended in violence and the prisoner's death. We'll find out more."

Acosta called JK and was told the local authorities in Can Tho were willing to surrender the body. "This place is a powder keg," JK said. "I spoke with an Aussie doctor at the local medical clinic and he'll prepare the body. There are some Hoa Hao here who want to bring it up by boat in the morning."

"We'll get the body here tomorrow," he told Teague. "JK can handle this and you need to accept that he wasn't involved in betraying the location of Vinh Lac that night. I was with him, for one thing, and he wouldn't get involved in something like that. Vinh Lac wasn't all that far from where the bombing happened and he got there quick. No, it had to be somebody on the inside. Quy is the culprit. Let me call him right now."

Teague said, "Good. Where do you stand on re-arming and building an organization capable of dealing with the problems?"

"I see no alternative."

"What changed your mind?"

"I'm sick of failures and I'm afraid of what's going to happen if the Stennrides get their way. They'll turn the whole country into an attrition kill zone. If there is a way to stop that from hitting the Delta, the most populous place in the country, I have to do everything I can. I need to bring my team on board and I think they will cooperate."

33

For Teague and company, it was a very long night and afternoon until the reality of the body's arrival the next afternoon.

Xam wanted the funeral the following morning. Acosta agreed to help provide security. Hoa Hao didn't like elaborate funerals, but this one became an exception as the 82-year-old mother of Phu So and his sisters would be attending and dignitaries from the other sects.

Teague was amazed at the combination of mourning mixed with the great fanfare on Hoa Hao Island. The simplicity of the Hoa Hao gave way to some grandeur.

Dozens of junks on the river combined with choppers brought in by Acosta provided security. He was also using sophisticated listening devices on Stennride's compound in case the colonel was going to do something really stupid.

Teague saw much sadness for a warrior greatly admired. The procession was led by the warrior's sister, the brilliant and beautiful Xam.

He hoped Vinh Lac's vision would continue and grow and that she would bring together the leaders of the different groups not only in the Delta but the Yards, Hmong, Pathet Lao and Free Khmer as well.

As the funeral barge inched toward the island, surrounded by what looked like a thousand sampans, junks, and fishing craft, Teague felt an emotion that combined sadness for the man who'd saved him, and the bitterness and anger of not having been in a position to return the favor.

It was the best people in this country who were constantly being killed off by one side or the other. The communists did it consciously and systematically, the Americans did it with blindness and ignorance.

Decked out in reds and yellows and maroons, the boats were packed with peasants, Hoa Hao in their simple clothes, others dressed in their finest, some with old mandarin-like jackets, or western suit coats, anything with a look of formality. The main barge itself had a replica of a peasant's house on top and the casket carrying the body of Vinh Lac lay on a platform on the foredeck.

The wails of mourning women mixed with the almost festive sound of guitars, singers and cymbals.

The men who lined the banks and those who stood in the sampans and junks saluted as the barge carrying Vinh Lac passed.

Per Teague's request, supported by Xam, there was another innovation at this funeral: an honor guard to fire a salute.

People had thrown paper money on board and it fluttered around in the breeze like dry leaves, some notes ending up in the water, drifting about, buffeted in the wake of the endless procession of boats.

Alongside the barge were several junks carrying family and

close relatives of the deceased.

No American or Saigon dignitaries were invited. The cynical game where An Giang Province was always being touted as a very successful pacification project was a joke, as it was always the Hoa Hao who kept it safe.

One of the more influential people present was Ly Minh Hau, who was once a significant Hoa Hao leader. He'd spent four years in French and Diem prisons and had degrees from the Sorbonne and the University of Chicago, where he had taken his doctorate in economics and now represented virtually the only outspoken proponent of out-and-out free market capitalism among Saigon intellectuals.

He prefaced much of his conversation back in his day with the phrase 'as they are doing in Japan,' thus alienating himself from the American establishment, especially in AID, State and MACV—state planning being the 'in' philosophy for developing Third World countries like Vietnam, the foundation of the new American development philosophy. The 'in' philosophy touted as the way to stop the spread of communism was mass, nationwide bureaucratization, something Khiet, one of Ly Minh Hau's big supporters, also railed against.

When Teague saw Xam in black cotton and a maroon headband, he felt great sorrow for her and her mother who stood beside her on the bow of the junk.

Khiet and the monk were in the following boat.

The barge was towed to the shore and the casket removed. Teague took up his position as a pallbearer just behind Khiet.

Nhu Bon was on the other side with the Hoa Hao General Duyet. The two sisters of Huynh Phu So stood beneath umbrellas waiting for the procession to reach the burial plot.

Frank Acosta did show and was on the bow of one of the boats.

Xam acknowledged Teague with just a flicker of a nod. He had to talk to her, and soon. If he was accepted and trusted enough to be a pallbearer, then it was time he entered into the inner council.

The procession wound up the stone path to the cemetery of unmarked graves where Vinh Lac would be buried with other Hoa Hao heroes. Their graves stayed unmarked as a testament to the murder and desecration of bodies by the communists.

The ultimate question in Teague's mind, and one Chandler had made a major point of, was what might have been if American leaders had chosen to support a Buddhist Third Force right from the start given Hoa Hao were the ones who defeated the communists when no one else could? And why not wake up and correct that mistake?

The funeral ended with Teague's recommendation, a nine-gun salute, one shot for each of the Mekong Delta's Nine Dragon rivers.

34

That evening, following the funeral, Teague, Moore and Khiet went with a security detail across the river to a quiet village and met Frank Acosta in a small thatched-roof house. Outside, four security guards working for the CIA officer stood by.

Teague paused for a moment at the door of the small wood-framed house, his fingers touching the rough surface of the door as he knew this was going to be a major moment.

He heard the voices inside suddenly stop. He pushed the screen door open and walked in with Khiet, leaving Moore and the detail with the security guys.

"Very sad funeral," Acosta said. "JK did a good job getting the body here."

"He did," Teague agreed. "Xam appreciates all the efforts that went into making a funeral possible."

Teague sat down across the small room from Acosta. "So, now we have to deal with the big problem. You've talked with your associates about what we want. They in?"

"Yes. We just have to be damn careful about this. I have some people in Cholon talking to the arms dealers and making them the offer that you and Xam proposed. Given the threat, and the pressure from agents, they have no choice. Last thing they want is a battle there, or the loss of the Gold Triangle."

"They won't try and outmaneuver us with Saigon?"

"No. That's a losing proposition for them as well. They are also the biggest source of corrupt money for politicians."

Teague nodded. Finally, Acosta's people were getting into the reality of what they faced. "All right, I'm listening." He was beginning to believe the program had the go-ahead from above.

Acosta said, "With them it's obviously about money, and they have a big desire to get their position back in the Golden Triangle. It has been decided that, considering the gravity of the threat posed to the Delta not just by Colonel Stennride and his growing forces, and the movement of large VC and NVA forces, we don't really have a choice. The only people that can hold are the Cai Dai and Hoa Hao Buddhists. And we are back to our original position that there has to be some new force in this country, one actually willing to fight for it and work to create a functional government. Add the mass influx of goods and money from America and you have a very negative effect on the economy of the villages. Change has to come hard and fast."

"How soon? Xam has a lot of people up in the Cholon that are ready to go."

"It's got to happen now," Acosta said. "One of the big factors is panic over how fast this colonel is moving. The CIA is losing all its major functions in the Delta and is becoming a minor, servant class to the new MACV powers. I agree this might well be our last chance to actually do something. And given the arms dealers in Cholon are sitting on the largest pile of weapons on planet Earth, I think a deal can be made."

"What kind of transportation? Can't be the trucking system—it's not safe. The oil companies pay the VC not to bother their shipments, but becoming part of that would be too complicated and too many questions would be asked. Air isn't workable because it would require transport of fairly large planes, the whole of Air America, and that's not going to happen."

"It will have to be by ship to the Mekong and then offloaded to smaller boats."

"You have a ship available?"

"We do. We need help getting the weapons and loading them without causing problems."

"That's already in place."

"Okay. You'll bring them where they can be offloaded to smaller boats. The Mekong and Bassac Rivers, being international waterways, and having a flag of a foreign country, means a ship is supposed to be off-limits to being boarded and inspected. But, as you well know, that isn't an absolute."

"We'll need plenty of available firepower to stop any attempt."

"The inland waterway is your turf and you are still in contact with some of your former Rivereign Forces, given you're one of their highly respected former members, and have a growing reputation. It will still be tricky loading and moving downriver. We'll overfly and run as much interference and keep you updated as to potential problems."

Teague was more than a bit shocked by how committed and operationally active Acosta had become. The man was really into this.

The idea of a seriously rearmed Hoa Hao, of large numbers of paramilitary available to protect and secure sect activities was what Vinh Lac and Chandler had been fighting for and what the agents had been opposing all along. Now they were seriously reversing course, surrendering to the only reality there was if they wanted to create the political movement Chandler had envisioned.

The war would take on a new dimension, a new reality, and Saigon and the American military machine would have to accept this at some point.

It was at once exciting, exhilarating, and frightening. In a country overrun with military forces, but not a single one popular in the peasant population, this had to become a reality. That change had been happening for a time in the fifties, but Americans had sided with a corrupt Saigon in crushing the Buddhists and trying to replace them by bringing down 'dark age' Catholics from the north to run things. That didn't work out. Vietnam wasn't the Philippines.

When they finished discussing the new arrangements, Acosta said, "And Teague, we're really sorry about what happened. But we have to keep this under control."

"We will. How much power is this colonel getting?"

"We'll find out. He already has some major forces that are completely off the record. The upper crust of the sect leadership, not directly involved in the weapons procurement need to disappear, or hide in place. Your team can be in Saigon as soon as you're ready."

Teague realized that the war-within-the-war was about to become much bigger and more dangerous.

35

After leaving the meeting with Acosta, Teague felt a powerful sense of the possible, that this could happen. But they had to move fast.

Once aboard the Wayward Angel, he and Khiet discussed how this would all take place and what routes to take once they got the ship to the Delta.

They laid out a map of the river system and where the best offloads should happen. How many sampans and junks they could get into play to meet them and take the weapons to different sites. Khiet would work with General Duyet on the distribution.

They headed for Xam's small flotilla of junks so Teague could discuss the plans with her.

As darkness fell, twenty minutes later he boarded Xam's well-guarded boat, nodding as he climbed on board to the security teams on the surrounding junks.

The door to the cabin opened and Xam, in a light blue blouse and black slacks, her hair flowing around her face down onto her shoulders and chest, greeted him with a thin, strained smile.

"Chao," he said.

She stepped back, "Please, come in."

The air in this cabin had the faint, pleasant smell of sandalwood and flowers. Both coffee and tea were in pots on the coffee table. He took the small wicker chair, sitting with the caution of a man under scrutiny. She had obviously prepared for his visit and he hoped that was a very good sign. He felt a bit awkward on this day. This visit to her home on the water after the funeral of Vinh Lac was not easy, but they had much to discuss and little time.

"You talked to the CIA agent?"

"Yes. His people are fully committed now and want this to happen fast." He told her about the agreement, and the need to get her leaders and their squads out into safe places. "This colonel is getting a lot of power and he's going to come after us hard. Long Xuyen may no longer be safe."

She busied herself with pouring coffee for him and tea for herself as he told her what the CIA operatives had done and what he and Khiet had worked out. She was surprised and pleased at how fast this was going to happen.

He accepted the coffee. He felt he was rambling a bit, excited and yet trying to stay within the framework of the tragedy, the horror of losing her brother. On this, the day of his funeral, they were plotting a major campaign and had to be focused on that.

His feelings and thoughts poured out of him like a rampaging stream that has burst its banks. He was doing what he hadn't wanted to do. The Vietnamese were far more reserved, but he had to express himself.

"What happened to your brother is a terrible crime, one that has to be dealt with. I believe, as I know you and Khiet and the agents do, that it was Quy who betrayed Vinh Lac's location."

Xam nodded. "Yes. He and his followers have fled into Cambodia. We will find him and kill him. But first, the re-arming. You have no doubts that your agents are fully committed?"

"I believe they are. They see the writing on the wall."

He saw a bit of positive gleam in her eyes.

They discussed how to get this done. She had a lot of contacts in Saigon and Cholon and it could be done fast.

He told her about the Israeli and other buyers, but that the number of arms and supplies were massive and that the CIA would provide the ship for transport and help with security.

She watched him and listened intently, hardly moving, her teacup in her hands.

"I'm sorry he isn't here to realize the potential we now have. A war without the support and fight of the people is a war without purpose, one that cannot be won. We will do this."

"Yes. It is necessary and what my brother and Chandler were working so hard to bring about."

"Then we should toast to it," he said, holding up his cup and she did the same. He could see that she had softened toward him. "To an idea despised by most intellectuals the world over, that of real freedom." Their cups clinked. "And to the rise of a true Third Force that represents the people."

He sensed that beneath her wariness she now appeared to really connect and trust him.

She said, "The face cream was very helpful."

"Thank you for that. I was beginning to scare people."

She laughed lightly. "Yes. You look much like you once did."

He said, "One thing I can't understand is why, given what has happened, so many Buddhists still like America."

She nodded, brushing back her hair. "America has great virtues, but also, like all people and countries, some vices. But America, as my brother liked to say, is our only beacon in a very dark world."

They went over the plans for going to Saigon. Her teams in Cholon would be ready when they got there.

Then it was time for him to go. He would see her in the morning and they would be in Saigon at dawn. He felt very connected to her and when they reached the door she was so close to him and then reached over and touched his arm and thanked him for all he'd done for her brother and her people.

He was hesitant, wanting to kiss her, but reluctant to make any kind of move. She reached up and put her fingers on some of the scars. "They are healing well."

She stepped back. She ran her hands down her blouse and slacks as if to straighten them. "Goodnight."

"Goodnight." He stepped out, glanced back and she remained in the doorway looking at him. He turned and climbed aboard his boat.

Xam watched the tall, broad-shouldered American go back across the river on one of the small boats to his powerful broad-beamed junk. She hoped he wasn't being used to create a set-up from which the Hoa Hao would be destroyed. She doubted that would happen, but couldn't completely dismiss it as they had been betrayed and nearly destroyed once before by American agents.

She hoped Acosta and his associates in the CIA continued to work with Teague, who was smart and seemed confident and she liked him very much. Maybe, she cautioned herself, a little too much. But he was one of them now and her brother had greatly admired him as much as he had admired Chandler.

With the largest population of the country in the Mekong Delta, a major change in the war was possible. Vietnam had suffered disaster after disaster, occupation after occupation, and things had to change.

36

In the wake of Vinh Lac's death and funeral, Stennride and Chien had expected renewed riots and sabotage in cities across the Delta. And they had teams of PRUs and Viet Rangers and secret police ready.

But that great explosion of violence didn't happen. A silence seemed to fall over the delta. The radical forces slipped into the darkness.

"Are they preparing for a major move?" the colonel asked.

Keller shook his head. "It's very weird. Chien thinks they've gone into the jungles knowing we were going to crush them."

"We need to hunt down that sister of Vinh Lac and Teague. As long as they are out there, it's not over."

Chien had, at Stennride's suggestion, offered big rewards for information on the whereabouts of the rebel leaders. He had forces that had been watching and scouting the rivers and canals and they came up empty.

The strange silence and an absence of political turmoil emerged in the cities where once radical Buddhists were holding debates became itself a worry.

Stennride didn't like that a movement that extended into all the provinces between the Bassac and Mekong, one that was recovering from the death of its biggest leader, had suddenly just vanished, went silent. He agreed with Keller that it meant something really big might be in the works. Some major attack, but from where and aimed at what?

That Teague and Vinh Lac's sister had escaped was bad news, but the following silence across the Delta was disturbing. Something was going on and they had no idea what that was.

Stennride said, "What do we know about this Special Forces Sergeant we ran into and who appears to be with the rebels? They give you anything on him?"

"Apparently, he's been given some kind of special operating status. I've contacted his unit and they suggest he's been reassigned, but to what and where they don't know, or aren't saying. You know how those agency bastards operate. Getting anyone to talk outside their parameters isn't easy. He's worked with the Yards but now he's suddenly with Teague. The CIA is recruiting. These bastards never stop."

"I need to have high-level permission at some point to really crack down on the CIA and their recruits. This can't be allowed to go on."

Stennride paced in his office. He paused and looked out at his chopper landing pad, the small buildings where his recon unit was housed. He wondered if Ferguson's people might be of help. They had boats on all the waterways and if a major move had been made, they'd know.

He stared at the map on the table beside his desk. "We have to find out what these crazies are planning."

The Colonel had lost all interest in the massive movements of the Viet Cong or the NVA. He now had a singular, obsessive focus on former naval officer Michael Teague and his traitorous allegiance to the Buddhist rebels and the insane CIA operatives helping him. Now add the Special Forces Sergeant, and where was that going?

Chandler had been a very sophisticated operative, but Teague was different. In spite of being a hardcore warrior, Teague had never been a real fan of the war, given the articles he wrote at Annapolis based on General MacArthur's warning about ground wars in Asia. It made Stennride wonder why the bastard had bothered to come to Vietnam. "Teague wants to run his own goddamn war. He's dangerous and nuts. And now, because of what he went through with Chien's interrogation, he's all about revenge. We need to find and kill him."

Keller said, "The problem is he's got friends all over the fucking waterways. He's something of a golden boy with the River Forces. They have a lot of boats. He once ran the program with over a hundred of them working all the rivers."

All kinds of wild ideas rolled around in Stennride's mind as he tried to imagine where they were and what these bastards were planning next.

37

Walking toward the Saigon River, Teague followed Moore and Frank Acosta to Cholon's bustling riverfront. Engler had stayed behind on the Bassac with the Wayward Angel and fifteen other junks, including Xam's. They would be waiting at different points for the weapons offload to take them to General Duyet's base camps near the Seven Mountains. If, that is, all went as planned.

Teague watched the women stevedores trudge from the waterfront to the waiting Philco Ford trucks, their neck muscles cable-stiff under the pressure of the fifty-kilo bags perched on their tiny heads, the bundles forcing a corkscrew-like twist to their bodies as they walked. The frail looking yet surprisingly strong women amazed him that creatures so small and spindling could carry such weight without snapping like dry twigs.

Acosta stopped and pointed toward the line of ships waiting out in the middle of the Saigon River for their turn to be loaded or offloaded. "Third one. That's the Pelican's Beak that we've made available. Khiet and Xam are making final arrangements."

It was a small, grey freighter sporting a Liberian Flag.

Acosta said, "We can send the ship right up the Mekong or Bassac. The river police have been warned to stay clear of any and all ships. They aren't allowed to inspect foreign ships anyway, but things aren't what they used to be."

"We're ready to get off-loaded onto smaller craft as soon as we reach the big river," Teague said.

Seagulls drifted and darted over the river and the backed-up ships like small, quick-darting white kites.

Acosta waved his hand over the whole world along the river. "These warehouses and docks are feeding half a dozen armies and who knows how many criminal drug enterprises."

As they approached one of the large warehouses, Acosta pulled a gold medallion out of his shirt and let it hang in the open.

"That a key to entry?" Moore asked.

"Yes. It's a Corsican Crest, the badge of honor, and it will give us access to this arena," Acosta replied.

"It looks like it's worth a lot. Is that solid gold?"

"It is and it's a hell of a lot more valuable than gold." The medallion worked magic in getting responses from the tough looking security men around the warehouse. The man who let them in through a side door had a neck on him like an oil drum.

And there it was, a dreamland arms bazaar. Just like that, they were standing in the all-pervasive smell of oil and paint and all around them in stacks fifteen to thirty feet high, every kind of weapon imaginable, crates and crates of them, many open for inspection and these weapons were brand new.

Acosta went over and talked to two of the men, then came back.

Half a dozen prospective buyers were being escorted up and down aisles looking into crates. Several men passed them. Two sounded like they were probably Israelites and an Asian, and a guy who wore an Aussie hat and had the aura of a mercenary about him was showing off various weapons.

"You're getting a look at not only the world's biggest arms bazaar," Acosta said, "but top of the line, new weapons systems." He picked up a Swedish K automatic pistol.

The guy with the Aussie hat and drum neck answered Moore's questions with a certain quiet disdain. "Laws are four hundred apiece. M-16s are going for about eighty now. The Uzi a bit more. Got lots of 'em. Jeeps we got for two-fifty a month unless you want to out-and-out purchase."

They had uniforms from many different countries, medical supplies, C-rats. Acosta was right. Teague shook his head at the sheer size of the place. They could outfit whole armies. It was pretty amazing. He and Moore once again glanced surreptitiously at each other and shook their heads.

Acosta said, "Moore, you check this stuff out and make your list up and this guy will work out the value. Teague, you come with me, some folks running the show want to meet you."

"Xam and Khiet here?"

"They're negotiating the deal in another building."

"The dealers didn't give you an argument about outfitting the Hoa Hao?"

Acosta shook his head. "No. Pappas and his people at the moment are in the midst of the biggest opium war in the history of this world between the Thais and the Chiu Chau syndicate in the Golden Triangle. It involves KMT divisions, the Laotian and Thai military commands, as well as Burmese and Cambodians and the hill tribes. They would like nothing better than to have a force that can calm that down and not further engage them. They need to make a trade."

"That's really what you're selling? It's not just about the island."

"You're dealing with an organization that needs some help in return. We can offer that, then they can give us what we want."

Acosta led Teague to a back room of the warehouse and introduced him to a collection of men such as Teague had not seen outside of a second-rate crime movie.

Acosta explained, in introducing the Chinese guy, that he was from the Chiu Chau, a region of Southern China which Teague knew was the origin of China's worldwide drug syndicates. The others were mostly French hailing from Marseille, Bangkok, Vientiane, and Phnom Penh. The apparent leader of this mob was the man they needed to get the final agreement from, the Greek, Konar Pappas, a man Acosta said spoke five languages.

Four of the six smoked cigars and the room was choked with acrid smoke.

"So you're the river rat we've been hearing so much about," Konar Pappas said, sizing up Teague like a fighter does to an opponent. There were some inside jokes tossed around that everyone except Teague and the Chinese guy laughed at.

"I've been called that," Teague said. "Most of those who did are dead, but I'm tolerant if there's a good deal to be made."

That brought more laughter and changed the tone in the room.

"You're curious as to who we are, now that it's apparent we know so much about you," Pappas remarked with a cynical man's grin. "I know our friend Frankie here probably didn't tell you much. That's CIA bad manners. That's the difference between them and us—we practice silence with our enemies and they practice it with their friends."

This got a huge response that even the Chinese gangster found something to laugh at, although his laughter was thin, that of an eternal outsider in this company of coarse-skinned long noses.

Pappas said, "I'll use the nickname Gamewarden, if that's acceptable. I've been told that's what they call you down on the rivers."

"I'll accept it."

"The Hoat Vu made us an offer we normally couldn't refuse. That was to hunt you down even in Cambodia and bring your head in on a silver platter. Big money was waved before my nose and promises by these secret police to live carefree. But that didn't guarantee what I really want."

"What is that?" Teague said, settling back casually in his chair like a man with money about to join a big poker game.

Pappas grinned. "Property and passage are the keys to all realms. The Hoa Hao took one of my most important islands away from me and appear to want to become a strong force in the Golden Triangle. They threaten a lot of people we work with and it costs big money."

The cigar jumped up and down when he talked. He had a worn, pitted face, a face that had been savaged by a rough life.

Teague said, "They didn't like over-paying to get across the border every time they moved rice or other products. But we're here to deal so both sides win. The Buddhists don't want a war with you. They have other enemies and you have enough conflict in the Golden Triangle. They are willing to work this out at a price."

For a moment, Pappas stared with wide-eyed incredulity and curiosity at Teague, before saying, "Well, things do change in this world, so how do we set this right? I'm told Vinh Lac's sister has a goddamn army roaming around the streets of Cholon. Last thing any of us needs is a war here, believe me. How will this work for all of us?"

He seemed reasonable. "The Buddhists will get out of the Golden Triangle and off that island for arms. As I said, the real enemy isn't you or your people. It's Saigon."

"I understand. But will it stay that way down the road?"

"The future is anyone's guess. Right now, we're talking about the present. You've worked with the CIA on many levels. They stay out of your business and you stay out of theirs. But now it has to change because the problems are getting worse."

Pappas nodded and said, "Yes, I have worked with them. I've worked with intelligence services all over this world—the OSS to break the Reddock strikes in Marseille, the goddamn French SDECE in cleaning out Saigon, and I helped organize the Binh Xuyen paramilitary. Your people are seeking political revival as it was a decade ago. I'm not opposed to that if they let us go about our business. We need trust based on mutual needs."

Teague said, "Trust is built on fear of what will happen if it breaks down. And, as I said, there is no desire on the part of the Hoa Hao to rule the Golden Triangle."

"Good," Pappas said. "It just so happens that we have more goddamn equipment and weapons then we can even keep track of at the moment." He picked up a folder and looked at the lists. "All right, we'll do this." He glanced at Acosta who had stayed out of the discussion. "I take it you're willing to see this works for both of us."

"Yes. We'll make damn sure it does."

They talked details for the next hour before leaving.

"He, like most of the folks you deal with in your fashion, didn't like your attitude at first," Acosta said as they made their way out of the arms bazaar warehouse, "but he showed real respect at the end. I wouldn't hard ass this crew too much. They've survived the Japs, communists, reformers and fanatics and they're sure as hell going to survive us. The only question you have to worry about is, will you survive them down the road?"

"I'll worry about down the road when I get there."

"It's one hell of a business," Moore said. "But it's organized chaos. The docks and warehouses are full. They're already moving stuff for us out on the docks. Tons of goddamn weapons."

Acosta nodded with a wry smile. "America is the greatest mass production machine on the globe and possesses the most efficient logistical system ever devised, but they're dumping millions of tons of material a month on the slowest, most inefficient and corrupt distribution system ever. Anyone who stands at the juncture of these two systems can siphon off what he wants. The Corsicans stand right there with their buckets out. Every day is like Christmas. They aren't the only ones raking it in."

Ten minutes of listing weapons in the main warehouse got a little intense when Moore got into a loud argument with one of the dealers.

"Crap," Moore stated, tossing one of the rocket launchers back into the crate. "They blow up in your face." He picked up a forty-five. "He says this is part of the shipment—all or nothing. And no way do we need all eighty-one. The only mortar worth a shit in the bush is a fifty-five. You can tell the only fight these jokers ever got into was in a bar."

"Pretty bloody choosy and pretty fucking mouthy aren't you, wise guy?" the drum neck said, in his Aussie accent, his eyes bulging like an angry bulldog.

"You're right on both counts and I haven't yet found the man who can stop me from being either."

"Everybody relax," Teague said. "We're putting in a big order and we'll decide what is in that order." To the big man Moore was arguing with, he said, "You have a problem, take it up with Konar Pappas. We'll decide what we need, and Pappas."

The argument was quickly settled when a man came over and talked to the big neck, who then immediately backed off.

After they finished, they left the warehouse and drove down Tu Do Street to a Chinese restaurant near the Caravelle Hotel to get some food.

"You guys enjoy the food here. It's excellent," Acosta said. "Khiet and Xam will be here soon. I have some work to do. I'll catch up later. We need to be moving downriver well before morning."

A Toyota pulled up across the street and Acosta jogged across and got in and drove off.

They watched the car turn up Le Loi at the Caravelle and disappear. "It's damn hard to trust that partner of his," Moore said.

Teague said, "Acosta will handle him and we wouldn't have gotten this far unless he had the support he needs. But with any operative, you make sure you have a grip on what he wants. This is getting way bigger and moving faster on all sides than I think his mentors anticipated. There under some big stress and losing power everywhere to MACV."

Moore said, "Well, given we're dealing with the drug cartels, major arms syndicates, the Thais, KMT, Burmese, Cambodians and Yards, I'm beginning to think I should have stayed up in the mountains sitting around a fire in a loincloth and getting stoned with the Nungs and Yards."

"I take it you need a couple beers."

"For a start."

38

While Teague and Moore were knocking off some excellent food at the Chinese restaurant with their security detail, Khiet showed up and laid a small hand-drawn map out on the table.

It showed the dock area. Warehouses in question were drawn in black outline and showed the location of interior doors, location of forklifts, ramps in blue and yellow, and security forces.

Khiet said, "The arms we're getting are being crated and we have two guys supervising so we get what's on the lists. The boat crew is still being negotiated with. They'll surrender the ship for adequate getting the hell out of town money."

"Port Authority?" Teague asked.

"It's clear. But we need to get down to the Delta and offload onto smaller boats fast."

So, it was all set then. Christ, Teague thought, this is about to happen. He had fears to be sure, of police gunboats and helicopters trying to sink the ship right in front of the docks. That would trigger a battle with the Hoa Hao, who were now heavily involved in the loading and in security. He hoped that didn't happen and didn't think it would. Nobody would benefit but the VC, who were tightening the noose around Saigon and other cities.

Moore leaned over and studied the map and list of supplies. "Gentlemen, as it goes, we'll be creating a serious little army."

A few minutes later, a man came in and greeted Khiet. "This is Xuan Oanh," Khiet said, introducing the man in a loose white shirt and baggy khaki pants and sandals. Behind him at the door stood two of his men.

Xuan Oanh smiled brightly and shook Teague's hand, then Sergeant Moore's.

When Teague spoke to him in his own language, he looked surprised. They exchanged miseries over the death of Vinh Lac, and then it was time to get to the business at hand.

Khiet said, "Xuan Oanh will command the team that takes over the ship. There are only five men aboard during the night. If they change their minds, they'll have to deal with his men who are Vietnamese SEAL types. He's also a martial arts champion and runs the Tai Kwon Do studio."

"Then I won't argue with him," Teague said.

Xuan Oanh grinned broadly, shook hands once again and said, "You come. Xam would like to speak with you now."

Teague followed him out into a hall of an adjoining building near the restaurant. He was led past a martial arts class in progress. The students in their gias sat ten across and thirty deep in the large vaulted room. The instructor, seated before them with his assistants on either side, had a microphone in his hand.

Teague moved past them and into another room that housed the main altar, where a statue of the Buddha looked down on him in contemplative serenity, fifteen feet high, hands and feet folded together in his lap. It was a massive figure, not fat like many, one shoulder bare and with two elongated ears.

Two women approached the altar in bare feet as custom dictated and placed offerings of red candles and fruit at the Buddha's feet. The platform elevated his figure a good ten feet from the floor.

Teague was led through another door into yet another hall and here he found Xam talking to several monks. Seeing him, she broke off her conversation and the two monks hurried out.

For a moment from a space of about twenty feet she looked beyond radiant in the Vietnamese national female dress, white quons and red ao dai. But to him she would look great in anything.

She motioned for him to follow her into a small, empty office.

Her hands hung at her sides, the fingers folded, her thumbs moving back and forth as the only sign she was in any way disturbed by something, maybe his presence.

Teague said, as matter-of-factly as he could, "Are you going back tonight, or are you going to wait here until it's over?"

"I'm going back with you on the Pelican's Beak," she said. "We have plenty of boats moving from the Bassac and Mekong Rivers that will make pickups. And Mister Acosta will give us protective flyover assistance."

Teague smiled at her use of Mister Acosta and nodded. "Good." He glanced down at the floor for a moment and then looked at her and said, "I think we're going get this done."

That got a very engaging smile from her. She said, "Goodnight. We all need a couple hours sleep. Tomorrow will be a big day."

She gave him a look that he chose to interpret as a promise of a time when eventually things would change. But she had a hold of his arm and didn't let go. He moved just a bit toward her to see what her intent held. Then he kissed her and she was beautifully receptive, but ended it quickly and in spite of a powerful look of affirmation, he still felt the need to apologize. "I'm sorry, I—"

"Please. I don't need you to say sorry. Our cultures are different. Vietnamese are trained from childhood to suppress their personal desires, but I choose differently."

She smiled and he submitted as Vinh Lac said he would.

39

A fog quilt lay heavy in the darkness making the ships on the Saigon River nearly invisible as Teague, Khiet and Moore and three armed Hoa Hao crept between two warehouses and back out on the wharf area. The sky had the busy sound of aircraft moving in and out of Tan Son Nhut.

Teague crouched beside Khiet as Moore went ahead with several Hoa Hao dressed as Saigon military police.

Khiet said quietly, "Di cham lai." He started forward, Teague keeping just off his right flank, touching the wall to help stop himself when the men ahead abruptly halted, then moving again. So far everything had gone smoothly. The boat crew had accepted the offer, having no alternative, and left. The loading was well underway, but they had to get the hell out of Cholon fast.

Khiet stopped and whispered into his walkie-talkie again. He turned to Teague. "Xam is on board." He depressed the button three times, giving the go-ahead to the team at the warehouse.

As Teague followed the point team out in front about twenty yards, Moore, quiet as a big cat, dropped back alongside him and said quietly, "Looks good, boss."

It was crazy and exciting that they were taking massive arms and ammo from warehouses that were run by the world's greatest arms merchants, who were basically a major criminal enterprise. It could end with massive bloodshed very quickly if the operation was betrayed.

A voice slipped through the foggy darkness ahead. Teague worked his fingers along his new Swedish K, checking and rechecking the clip, and the safety. They would be going in through the rear doors. Now was the critical time.

Teague hovered in the dark fog and listened. The seconds went by one klick at a time. An angry gull squawked somewhere. It was one of those moments when everything hung in the balance.

Khiet gave them thumbs-up. They had forty-two minutes before the regular crews would be coming in to work and those there now showed no sign of a problem.

When Teague entered the warehouse, some lights were on and the warehouse jeeps were moving the last crates towards the steel roll-top door.

The crews scampered in quietly and fast, a dozen well-rehearsed teams moving in unison. A dozen flat-bottomed sampans moved back and forth to the ship. Within minutes, a human chain was moving the last crates on board sampans and out to the ship and back through the dark and fog with hardly a sound.

"These sonsabitches can really hustle up a storm when they want to," Moore observed.

"The right incentive apparently can move anybody or anything in this arena," Teague added. He was highly impressed.

He had harbored some immense fears and doubts about the whole operation, but now he was seriously becoming a believer that was possible. They just had to get out and get to the Mekong Delta and he would then become a full believer in the potential of Chandler's dream that was now his and was possibly becoming a reality soon.

This was the first critical step to affect the growth of the power necessary to change the very nature of the war. He was in full rebellion now. He had lost all doubt about his decisions. As he and Chandler and now Acosta absolutely agreed—a war built solely on attrition and body count would never succeed against an ideology in a world like Asia.

The Buddhists in the Mekong Delta offered an answer and nobody in power listened to them. But that could change and fast.

PART FOUR

The Third Force

40

The journey to the Delta was delayed twice for hours as Acosta's flyovers and boats leading the way had to deal with situations where river police were checking sampans and junks.

Finally, they made it out to sea and headed for the Mekong River, but it had cost them a lot of time. Teague and Khiet took turns as pilot of the small craft. With the mass of weapons on board, the ship ran low in the water. Twice a coastal patrol came close and was warned off by the pilots overhead.

In the predawn of the following day, the Pelican's Beak left the sea and ran up the Mekong to a connection by the river between the Mekong and its lower branch, the Bassac. The loading of junks had begun and was moving fast.

In the distance, some bombing was taking place against the movement of communist forces.

Fortunately, Acosta's fast boats ahead of them, and following as well as CIA planes periodically cruising protectively overhead and feeding information about military and police vessels and any indications of VC moments ahead of them. Teague had a lot of friends on the rivers and communications with the Rivereign Forces was good.

Xam was behind him, talking on one of the new, small radio-phones to her people who would be picking up the arms at designated spots as they cruised down to the Bassac River and on toward Cambodia.

Teague walked along the deck. Not a sign of interference so far.

Moore was leaning on the railing. He turned, a wry grin on his face. "Ease up. You act like this is your first job, Commander."

Teague nodded morosely. "It is, of this kind anyway. It's a road I never expected to travel, but now that I'm on it, I never felt so right about my journey as I do now."

"I think we're in full agreement," Moore said. He looked positively confident. They were in the Delta with massive arms that would soon be offloaded and distributed by sampans and junks. "I worked in the mountains helping build an army out of a bunch of ragtag stone worshipers. Back in those days, poppy growing in the triangle was the big cash crop. The CIA supported it because it was the practical thing to do at the time. A lot has changed, but some things not so much."

Teague, watching another boat leave with a load of weapons, said, "One of the things I really like about Hoa Hao Buddhism is they have an ethical base and that's what separates the revolutionary from the mercenary or warlord."

"You get no argument out of me. You're the high priest. Me, I'm just a trooper hoping for the best outcome."

Teague straightened up and yelled, "Heads up!" From their leeward side, a Cessna appeared over the trees, running straight at them as if out of the moon itself. It passed low and dipped its wings and darted out over the treetops.

They watched as the small plane came back up the river from in front of them. A man was hanging out the door and waved his arm and the plane's wings. That meant they were all clear.

A cheer went up again from the Viet crew. Moore grinned at Teague. "You need to become a believer. We are good to go."

Teague gave Moore control and went down into the captain's quarters where one of Khiet's men was listening to radio traffic and Khiet was studying maps of the Delta's river systems.

"We have boats yet to load. They'll take a lot of the load within a twenty-minute reach," Khiet said. "We're on our way. Xam's and your boat are moving up a canal from the Bassac toward us."

They went over the logistics of having to transfer the arms to smaller craft. Half the arms would be transferred on the way, headed down into the jungles near the Seven Mountains where General Duyet had his base camp. Many of the boats on the waterways would be from the fleet of hundreds of junks and sampans operated by the Special Forces, the rest on Hoa Hao and navy boats under Vietnamese commanders sympathetic to the cause. The labyrinths of Vietnamese society would be appreciated by any Byzantine.

Khiet got another update on the movement of boats. "Xam's boat is just down a tributary ahead. She can board and move a load upriver."

Half an hour later, the rising sun painted a shiny glaze on the long stretch of the river, revealing a boat a quarter mile ahead.

Moore said, "We're severing the last strands of the umbilical cord. We will soon belong to no government entity. How's that feel?"

"Exciting and scary as hell," Teague said. "I grew up on a diet of glorious stories out of World War Two, and how history was the steady march of civilization to its final perfection in Main Street USA—and then enter the services thinking I would go off like Lafayette to save the world's oppressed for democracy, only to discover we are killing communists with one hand and feeding the cause that breeds them with the other. Korea was a lesson that apparently taught us nothing."

"That's true, and it's why you and I are here," Moore said.

They stood now on the starboard side, the predawn beginning to spread a glaze across the vast stretch of rivers and waterways and he asked himself point blank about his own intervention, and the answer was simple and obvious. This was now his duty.

Teague said, "Chandler told me that it really changed him when he read 'All Quiet on the Western Front' about how the last great war of attrition, World War I, had ruined a whole generation. He said he didn't want that to be the legacy of this war. I agree with him."

"I won't argue with that," Moore said.

Xam's boat appeared out of a rivulet and not far behind came Engler in the high-speed super junk.

So far, so good, Teague thought. The ship would be empty and dozens of small boats would be heading to sect bases around the western Delta from the Mekong to the Seven Mountains and some all the way into Cambodia to a secret base run by the Free Khmer.

When Xam was on her boat and he and Moore joined Engler and crew on the Wayward Angel, they left the empty ship up the against the river bank, the second phase was well underway.

41

At seven in the morning, Colonel Stennride was working behind his massive teak desk when everything changed.

Keller walked in. The colonel looked up from a map, coffee in one hand and pen in the other. "What now?"

Keller shook his head. "We have bad news from an intel agent in Saigon."

"What kind of bad news?"

"Unbelievable. A major arms dealer in Cholon, guy named Konar Pappas, who happens to run major criminal syndicates in the Golden Triangle—"

"I know who he is."

"Well, he says he was forced to send a massive shipload of arms to the Delta. He wants to talk to you specifically about the problem."

"What the hell are you talking about? Why would he want to talk to me? What shipment? To where? Who is telling you this?"

"I got the call from Major West. He knows the arms dealers and they're saying it might interest us as it's connected to the CIA operations with the Hoa Hao and the American they call Gamewarden."

Stunned, the colonel put pen and coffee down and sat back utterly shocked. "How long ago?"

"The man he talked to wouldn't give much information. This Pappas has an issue he wants our help with. That's why he wants to talk to you. He has contacts all over the goddamn place, so he probably knows more about what's going on here than anyone."

Stennride grabbed his metal cigarette lighter off the desk and started flipping the top back and forth, clink, clink, clink. "Goddammit, get the chopper ready. We're going up and talk to this Greek. Find out where we can meet him."

Stennride couldn't believe this. It was crazy, but if true, it was the worst possible news. "We need to find out what happened, what kind of shipment and where it is by now. This is insane. Goddamn CIA is way out of bounds."

Keller called their pilot. Stennride got hold of Chien, who was in Saigon, and told him to get some security ready for the jaunt into Cholon.

For a while, after the death of Vinh Lac and the abandonment of Western provinces by the radical factions of the Hoa Hao, Stennride had entertained the illusion that higher levels in the CIA might have forced Acosta to back Teague and his people off, end the insanity. That obviously wasn't the case. If it was a serious shipment and those arms reached their destinations in the secret bases in the Delta, it would change everything. It would be a disaster.

Now he once again felt that dark, growing cloud of apprehension. That if true, they may have forced the crime syndicate to surrender arms, and a goddamn ship meant the CIA, rather than backing down, had decided on a major move.

Stennride shook his head in disbelief and shock as he glanced at a map on his desk that featured the river operations with the hundreds of swamp boat runs, and province forces with numbers, special operations alone with dozens of agency controlled areas where New Life Hamlets would soon replace all independent villages.

After making arrangements, Stennride and Keller and a three-man security detail choppered into the new MACV headquarters on Tan Son Nhut and from there took an armored vehicle to a location in Cholon where Chien had set the meeting with the dealer.

Inside a nondescript building, an old Chinese man approached. "Please, you come this way."

Stennride and Keller and security followed the man through a curtained doorway at the rear of the restaurant that smelled heavily of joss sticks and pork.

In an adjoining room, he came face-to-face with the man reputed to be one of the most powerful gangsters in Southeast Asia. Konar Pappas sat alone, drinking from a sparkly glass next to a bottle of red wine and eating some kind of lobster dish. He wiped his mouth with a handkerchief and said, "Food, gentlemen?"

"No, thanks," Stennride said. He glanced around the empty restaurant. Pappas nodded and shooed the papasan and a waiter away with a wave of his hand. "Please, sit."

He opened a box of cigars and pushed them over to Stennride, who refused, but Keller didn't. Stennride went for his Marlboros.

"I hear you have interest in some stolen merchandise," Pappas said in respectable English.

"That's right. I'm hearing a lot of arms have been shipped out of your warehouses that you weren't happy about but weren't given much choice short of war. We need to know who the buyer is and where the shipment headed."

Pappas dunked a piece of lobster in melted butter and while it sat soaking, he said, "They tell me you hunt for this guy they call Gamewarden?"

Stennride said, "Yes."

"He helped the Hoa Hao take my island."

"We'll get that back for you. He's advising a CIA-sponsored Buddhist rebel faction in the Delta. I need to know where he is, how I can get to him. If there's a chance to stop that shipment I need to do it. What did they get?"

Pappas took a drink of his wine, nodded and said, "Enough matches to start a good-sized bonfire." His buttery chin glistened in the light from the candle lantern. "They came with enough force, including CIA threats, to make me submit to their deal. They steal my island, threaten my businesses, and offer to give it back if I give them arms. A war right here if I refused. Nobody ever held me up like that before. I hear about you and your problems with these people, so now I help you, you help me."

"We can do that." Stennride said. "You have connections to all the major operators in the Delta, Cambodia and Laos. You help me against the radical sects and I will help you regain what they took and protect your interests in the Golden Triangle. We're not interested in a conflict with you or your people."

Pappas said, "What they have taken from me is small compared to what will happen if they re-arm and get real power. The ship they stole and put the arms on board is called the Pelican's Beak. Flies Liberian flag."

"How big an arms load?"

"Enough to arm thousands with top of the line weapons, light and heavy."

After leaving Pappas, Stennride called General Paulick at MACV's new steel and stone structure at the corner of Tan San Nhut and arranged an immediate emergency meeting.

He knew this would be a major fight with the general, but one that he had to win. Confirmation of his worst fears made Colonel Stennride very testy and he needed to meet with his superiors and make them understand the problem and his needs.

If the arms had been delivered then the generals had to hand over one of the secret SOG-run bases near the Cambodian border that had hardcore Viet Rangers trained for hunt and kill operations especially in Laos. This situation with the rebels was on the verge of out of control and could lead to real war. He also needed more air power and hardcore Province Recon Units.

Even before returning to the Delta, the ship had to be located and to that end Keller made calls to their operations center and to Chien.

But first, Stennride needed to get permission to carry out a major operation that would begin with the sinking of a ship on international waters.

It was a very big move and he had to meet with General Paulick before heading back. It was time for the General to wake up and fully understand the potential disaster they faced. The little underground war could suddenly become a major above ground conflict.

42

The Colonel met Paulick less than an hour later in a windowless, heavily walled room at MACV headquarters. He gave him the bad news about the arms and the need to find and sink that ship, which river police patrols were searching for.

He got no response for a time as the General digested the news, tapping his fingers on the long table.

Finally, trying to get his mind around this and Stennride knew it was a step the General really didn't want to take, but had no choice as he shook his head in dismay, saying, "Jesus H. Christ. Sinking a ship that has an international flag on an international waterway is not something that could be done without the highest authority. I mean from the very top and it won't happen unless that ship is known to be delivering weapons to the Viet Cong. Even bringing it up would create massive problems with what we are doing and what is going on. And you don't even know if it hasn't already been unloaded."

"We have no choice," Stennride said, keeping as calm and matter-of-fact as he could. "These CIA-backed rebels have to be stopped. They can't be re-armed. This has to be done very fast and in secret. And if it has already been unloaded, I still want it sunk to deliver a message. In the present chaos, with communists on the move everywhere and battles all over the country, this won't ring any alarm bells. A ship taken by VC gets blown out of the water. Not a big deal in the scheme of the present chaos."

Paulick apparently had been warned of what was coming and now gave confirmation he was not a happy camper. He got up and paced like an angry, wounded bear in a cage. He chewed on his cigar. "Damn! How did this happen? You want to sink a goddamn ship flying an international flag and think that will remain a secret! Besides, it's probably already offloaded."

"It will send a message. And all of the offloads from the ship to smaller boats will need to be hunted down. It can have a different look if reported to have been taken over by the Viet Cong. That will cover us. And that's just the start. To prevent an all-out Mekong Delta war, one that could be a really big headache, I need that secret special operations base of yours in the Western Delta near the Cambodian border. Those are hardcore Viets trained by SOG and among the best hunter-killer ops of any Viet units."

"Jesus Christ, Stennride, this is crazy."

"It is. But it can get a hell of a lot crazier if that shipload of arms gets to the jungle camps. It's enough not just to start a real war, one that, once it gets really big, can't be hidden. It will create civil conflict that will undermine everything we are doing. We need to locate that ship and sink it and that'll send a big message to the Buddhist rebels and their CIA mentors. The agency needs to be pushed out everywhere, and that includes the new Phoenix program. And I need the necessary power of ground forces to carry out the mission."

Paulick's expression seemed to pull back, a hard, invisible wall coming up between them.

Stennride said, "We play our hand right, we can keep this away from any wider audience. The CIA sure as hell doesn't want the media to reveal their activities in this."

After he had fully collected himself, Paulick said, "That firebase is for operations into Cambodia and Laos. I can't just deactivate the current command and turn it over to you."

"I think you can, General. Otherwise you're going to have two ugly wars on your hands. Look, I'm not here to pressure you into making a disastrous decision. I'm here to save you from a potential catastrophe."

"You want your own army, for Christ's sake? You've got four Skyraiders to call on."

"This is bigger than four Skyraiders. These CIA-backed Buddhist rebels walked off with enough arms to field a fucking division. You'd better get some aircraft out there. The whole Market Time Task Force, every Coast Guard Cutter, every junk, every available plane better be on this. They get through—"

"Colonel, we sent you down there with a hell of a lot of units available. You were supposed to prevent this sort of thing. I can't turn a base over to you that SOG uses to train Viet hunter-killer teams."

SOG, Studies and Observations Group, was MACV's intel and their knives and Stennride wanted one of those knives. A name that sounded so academic was in fact a major operational hunting force unlike any other and operated in the mountains, especially in Laos.

Stennride, tired of pleading his case, glanced at his watch. "We've got little time. They offload and send to different sites on a hundred sampans and junks, it'll be a goddamn nightmare and

I'm sure that's what they may already be doing. And I want that base activated tonight under my direct command. The Viet commander running things there must accept that or be moved to some other base."

"This is crazy." Paulick plucked his cigar from his mouth. "Why can't we just put one of the Riverine Forces on this? Stop and search all the sampans and ships—"

"General, you know what the name of the Rivereign task force is and that's what they now call Teague? They're on his river system. Nobody in our naval forces will go after him unless forced to and he'll get all kinds of warnings and it'll be a big deal. We're not going to get much help. He might have twice the backing Chandler did."

"Colonel, goddammit, it's not easy to hand over the forces you want. I have to deal with other factors. Under certain emergency conditions, you've been given some extraordinary powers in the past because things got so botched up nobody knew what the hell to do. But there are still chains of command. Things are nuts right here. Why do you think half the goddamn army has been called back to Saigon? And now you want me to hand over the major Delta forces to you. We haven't got to the point yet where we just hand out a unit here and a battalion there to whomever the hell wants one."

The general had a very distressed look on his face and Stennride needed to bring him fully on board. "General, there was a time when the CIA had eight or nine different armies going. Right now, there are fifteen fucking intel agencies here in Saigon, each with his private operations. This is total chaos and has to end. Half the generals in the South Vietnamese army have special battalions in their provinces that answer only to them because they have enemies on all sides. Everybody in this miserable, stinking country has his own little army to protect his province and interests and isn't fighting the big war. And ask yourself a simple question. If a rebellion becomes serious, it will bring a media frenzy and panic and chaos in the provinces and threaten Saigon. If I was a communist commander, it'd be celebration time."

After a long pause, Paulick said, "If I give you that base, and I'll have to push hard on some powerful people, you better goddamn well bring this to an end quick."

Stennride said, "A re-armed Hoa Hao linked up with the Yards, Cao Dai, Hmong and Free Khmer forces, and if they succeed you'll be back in the States washing dishes at a bad restaurant. Imagine ten thousand rebel Buddhists under arms and linked to all these other groups. Get me what I need and I'll deal with this fast."

After another long, intense pause, the general said, "All right, goddammit, but get this done."

Stennride knew that once that base was his, he could ask for a lot more in the way of airpower, some serious rolling thunder, and manpower, and there was nothing the general could do because he would be in way over his head. "If and when I locate that ship, I'll need Phantoms to blow it out of the water."

"Jesus, if something like that ever got out—"

"All eyes are on Khe Sanh, the bombing of the Hanoi-Haiphone region, the Gaithuong military supply base, and new shipyards and the center of Haiphong. Even Hanoi itself was being hit by naval fire and nobody is focused on the Delta."

"That may be, but it can shift quickly if something gets really out of control in the Delta. And you have to realize that the growing number of support bases are sucking out the resources like never before. Soon nine of every ten soldiers will be involved in logistical support making only high-power attacks possible. That's why giving you bases and resources isn't going to be easy."

"I'll handle it so that what happens in the dark stays in the dark. This has to be stopped."

The general shook his head slowly, frowning. This had him by the balls. He had to act. There was no way out of this but to put an end to the resurrection, fast, or it would blow up in their faces.

"Colonel, you win, but you better do this fast and keep it in the dark and get it done. We'll define every action as a response to the VC and NVA."

Colonel Stennride knew that nothing could stop him now. Once he got the base of trained commandoes, he could hit hard. The general was locked in and couldn't back out.

43

The next morning, as a massive search was underway on the Bassac and Mekong Rivers, Colonel Stennride walked out on a narrow promontory a couple miles from where the Mekong River swept out into the South China Sea. His mood was grim.

He didn't curse the CIA because he was well aware that they had created the circumstances that would give him the resources and power he wanted. He had to just play this out without causing any real problems. This could be the career gift that kept on giving if handled right.

The end to the chaos that the Viet sects were causing had to give way, but they and their rogue CIA operatives had to pay the price. This was a war between America and communism. Vietnam was just a temporary battlefield.

The triangular white sails of the junks listed in the breeze and the waves glinted in the white sun on this beautiful, bright day.

He turned as Captain Keller, after jumping from one of the

MKII patrol boats of the 166 Coastal Task Force, trudged up the bank.

For a moment, Stennride felt the past penetrate like a thin live wire—to a time in another war, another enemy, when Stennride was a young intelligence officer in the Pacific, the Solomons, a smaller, more manageable conflict.

When Keller adjusted his sunglasses, Stennride could see his own image reflected in the silver mirrors. "Can't get much out of these slopes," Keller said. "Survival to them is keeping their mouth shut. Getting anything is like trying to open a sardine can with your teeth."

If Teague and company off-loaded the arms to smaller crafts and sent them to camps, then it could all be headed to their destinations by now. "No intelligence here whatsoever?" Stennride asked disgustedly. General Thieu's supposed control of the Viet Navy was suspect.

Stennride watched Chien board another junk. Stennride then panned with the binoculars over the line of fishing boats. A hundred and fifty thousand people lived off the Mekong and Bassac Rivers directly, millions indirectly, a people with no government loyalty, no respect.

With ten thousand vulnerable hamlets under pressure from the Vanderlins of the war, as they built their little paradises for thousands of displaced peasants, the only benefit Stennride saw was that it opened up more room for bombing and herbicides, but the negative was it made it easier for the communists to infiltrate and propagandize.

"Colonel Stennride!"

Stennride and Keller turned to the army intelligence officer who was manning a radio. "We've got a sighting. Definite fix on an abandoned ship up river about four miles. Liberian flag."

"That means she's already unloaded," Keller said.

Stennride and Keller climbed aboard their chopper and after a short ride up the Mekong, they saw the ship below sitting abandoned on the bank of the river partially covered by frond overhang.

Stennride now had to send a big lesson to the river rats, but also to General Paulick and company. "Grey Star one to Searchlight."

A clear voice came back over the headset. "This is Searchlight—go ahead Grey Star One, we read you loud and clear."

"We need to hit a ship that armed VC pirates have taken." He gave the numbers for the coordinates in the form of a series of letters and names that would match the code Searchlight had.

Fifteen minutes later, they saw the Phantoms come sleek and fast across the pale sky like a pair of magnificent hunting hawks. About a mile out, the lead plane slanted and swept down toward the river, pulling up at only a few hundred feet as rockets streaked out of its belly and lanced toward the target, exploding with a bright flash.

That first plane cleared the scene, rising almost straight up and the second swooped down and fired its rockets before also rising in a long sweeping curve across the back of the horizon. The Phantoms came back for bomb runs. Having no anti-aircraft fire to worry about, they took their time and their accuracy was perfect. The small ship floundered in smoke and flames and began sinking.

Stennride thanked the pilots of the Phantoms. One of the fast boats arrived and several PRUs boarded the wreckage of the ship to see what was there. They found nothing of consequence.

Then Stennride informed Paulick of the ship's destruction and that the arms had been offloaded and were now heading for the rebel forces. The rapidly deteriorating situation would give the general no escape or excuse from delivering what Stennride wanted.

Paulick informed him that an emergency meeting was already underway.

"Looks good," the colonel told Keller. "They have no options now."

He was proven right four hours later. The secret former SOG training base was now in his hands, and the elite Viet hunter-killer teams made up of Viet Rangers and Special Forces had accepted the new order of things.

Later that afternoon, Stennride's chopper slid back and forth over the invisible line that separated Cambodia and Laos from Vietnam, and he leaned out and craned to get a look at his secret new fire support base below as they passed over the treetops and came to a clearing. The base had been named Scipio after the great Roman General, Scipio Africanis.

Like all the other American-designed and built prefab fire bases in Vietnam, this one had a 246-foot radius of perimeter wire; at the 131-foot circumference was the bunker line and in the center the observation tower like an oil derrick with a roof, was surrounded by a dozen heavily sandbagged concrete buildings: command post, commo center, administration building, ground surveillance and anti-personnel radar emplacements, infantry bunkers and the Howitzer emplacements. There were also two twin 81mm mortar positions used to fire H&E or illumination during heavy attacks.

The troops here were special hunter-killer teams whose existence was outside the normal order of battle. Powerful, untouched by the quivering hands of impotent bureaucracy, they were the scalpel in the hands of the surgeon.

The chopper settled down near a line of corrugated steel shelters that housed Skyraiders and a dozen Huey choppers.

The base commander, a thin, strac captain came trotting across the tarmac in his tiger fatigues, flanked by his aids. Most of them were carrying SOG's popular High Standard H-D suppressed pistols.

He swaggered up and saluted with all the polish of Fort Bragg's best where he and his men had first been trained. An added feature was that their time at Fort Bragg's training base in the States had included learning some English.

Stennride thought of Trang as the perfect example of what the Americans ought to be producing in the Third World. No hint of corruption in this man. No hint of fear. And disciplined to the will of his advisors as few Vietnamese were. He had been trained in the advanced art of quick reaction, hot pursuit and all the latest advancements in technologically advanced conventional warfare. He was too much for the regular Vietnamese army. He was almost more American than the Americans.

After a quick reviewing ceremony, Stennride followed Trang into the concrete bunker headquarters to look at stats and maps. The captain showed Stennride where the Yard camps were moving to and where the rebel Hoa Hao operated near the Seven Mountains. He showed where the remnants of Madame Ba Cut's forces, another potentially dangerous group, had been located.

After some interruption from his operators, Trang said, "There is a struggle for power between Hoa Hao factions. Maybe soon fight each other. We watch close. We have Eagle's Nest surveillance. I show you."

Stennride loved his new base. He was shown the aerial and ground surveillance they used. In the past month indicating a lot of movement of what appears to be a growing and the rise in conflicts with the sects."

He learned some negative information from Captain Trang. The Yard army, under the command of the rebel Y Bham, was receiving tons of supplies and weapons dropped into the mountains from the air.

The captain stared at the map for a moment, then turned and looked at Stennride with those hard, eager bird-dog eyes. He smiled exuberantly. "Yes, we must hunt them down and kill them."

Finally, Stennride had much of the authority and power he needed to flush out and crush these would-be revolutionaries and get this war back on the right course.

Within hours they were getting sightings from the planes operating out of three bases that were now linking to Stennride's growing forces. If the goddamn CIA and their lost cause wanted a fight, they were going to get a taste of rolling thunder.

44

The last of the arms on board sampans and junks were well on their way to the deepest of Duyet's camps. Teague was conferring with Xam about meeting with the rebel Free Khmer units in the jungles across the border when word came that Quy had been spotted across the border in Cambodia not all that far away.

Teague knew what Xam's reaction would be. She wanted to go get him now, before he became aware of where they were.

The fisherman they were questioning excitedly flailed his arms about as he talked, shifting his weight from one foot to another, his eyes flitting nervously back and forth between the groups of men confronting him.

Teague tilted his bush hat back on his head as Xam asked him how he knew about Quy and his men.

"I had a tear in my net and I went to the hamlet there to have it fixed. I heard these men. Please excuse me—"

"You're doing just fine," Xam said. Teague assured him as

well that he had nothing to fear.

When he spoke to them in their language and with nuanced inflection, it always calmed them. "You went into the village to fix your net?"

The man said they were only about ten kilometers into Cambodia.

Teague glanced around the lagoon. The mid-morning sun had bled the sky of color and the lagoon lay hot and breathlessly still. Half the shipment had been sent on its way to the base camps, but the other half was still there in the narrow holds of sampans and junks.

Acosta had warned them that things were rapidly changing. That communications even from naval ships may well be intercepted. The bombing of the ship was a deliberate message to all the boaters on the rivers. And now they were being threatened by the communists moving ever closer. For the villagers and river dwellers, it was the worst of situations.

Most of the weapons were well spread out on small convoys headed towards the half-dozen base camps, but these two that Quy had meant this had to end very soon. They headed across the border.

Teague feared Quy was working with the secret police and Stennride. They had to get that bastard quickly.

He stared across the banyans and the copses of bamboo and sugarcane at the sky. They had to get on a narrow, jungle-covered waterway real soon.

Not a single sampan had been stopped on the journey except the two junks headed into Cambodia and one of them had been intercepted by Quy and his men.

The Delta was a sieve. Anything could and did pass through it from smugglers to private armies to communist battalions, and all that was required was a little grease.

After the death of Vinh Lac, Teague had never discovered exactly who would end up running the thirteen-member Central Committee. General Duyet commanded all the Hoa Hao rebel elements still holding out from the old days down in the U Minh and the Seven Mountains and thus represented a powerful segment.

Xam was the new element, the sophisticated political theorist and the rightful heir to Vinh Lac's faction. But first they had to deal with the self-appointed opposition leader who had wanted to take over after Vinh Lac's death.

They moved into Cambodia with seven well-armed junks and fifty hardcore soldiers.

"We are getting radio messages from three agents," Khiet said. "Quy appears to have a small but well-armed force not far ahead."

Teague saw in all these political tribal struggles a swamp of problems that Xam and Vinh Lac had wanted to clear out that reached back to the Buddhist Struggle Six Movement to the present.

But the bigger worry was if Quy had support from Stennride. That could compound everything.

Squad commanders from different waterways were ordered by Khiet to come to join the force. They were given assignments, a junk fleet assembled in the lagoon with sapper teams sent out to prepare for battle. The excitement on the river reached a frenetic level by nightfall.

45

As the boats merged from the river and canals, moving deeper into Cambodia, the jungle gloom thickened. Teague stood on the deck of the Wayward Angel, enjoying the rich tropical breeze, but not the devastation of what once were peaceful and very attractive villages.

Xam had sent a boat through canals and rivulets to circle the village where they thought Quy was located. He lacked their level of sophisticated commo and air observations that Acosta's agents brought to the hunt.

One after another, the rest of the boats slipped out through the dark alley of a channel from the river. The moon, now hidden in the clouds and diffused like a light behind curtains, painted the wide smooth latania fronds like unpolished silver.

Moore came out of the cabin of the super junk and said, "Teams are out and clear so far."

Xam was just ahead of them, escorted by three heavily armed

gunboats and beyond the lead boats, sampans had been sent on ahead to spring any traps. Along the way, teams of sappers had been inserted ashore on the far side of the river. They would attempt to maneuver out into a blocking position around the village.

Teague watched one of the Hoa Hao leaning on the gunwale, taping his weapons clips to the side of the gun for quick changes, his face rigid and hard as a bronzed statue. Other soldiers squatted all around the deck, fixing weapons, checking ammo, silent, some in tiger suits, others in the more prevalent black pajamas, hats of all kinds: Aussie, American baseball hats, French floppies, or some with just the Hoa Hao headbands, the long hair and ammo bandoleers draped across their chests, adding to the Apache like effect.

The quiet night ended with a burst of machine gun fire that came from the port bank ahead, tracers leaping out of the blackness and flying toward them like fire arrows.

The boats surged forward. A gunner on the Wayward Angel swung the fifty around and let loose with a long steady answer. Teague hit the throttle and the Wayward Angel sprang forward, her power sending a shudder through her solid body. The nose lifted out of the water and the craft shot over the dark river like a missile. Teague glanced back at the ferocious column of fire from the other boats.

Within seconds, the junks had suppressed the light weapons on the bank. They raced toward the fishing village.

"We lose anybody?" Teague yelled.

Khiet was on the radio to the other boat commanders. Next to him, Sergeant Moore was searching ahead through the tripod mounted AN/TVS-4 Night Observation Device, one of the goodies that came with the weapons. It was one he'd picked out and demanded and it could amplify the faintest bit of light 40,000 times and give an image at 1,300 yards.

"One boat destroyed."

Somebody kicked the casings of the spent cartridges across the deck, their jackets jangling as they reloaded to fire suppression at the jungle.

The rocket teams moved up to its position on the foredeck, jabbering at each other. Everyone was shifting around getting ready, double checking the little things in the muggy air. The boat lanced into the grim void, seeming to fly forward against reason into the dark mouth of combat violence.

Teague stood grimly, peering into the dark grey sky holding his weapon loosely in his hands, his thoughts flying forward just ahead of the boat like a radar to discern how and where the battle would unfold. You had only seconds to get the feel of it, react with the right initial move your instinct handed you, and if you were right, you were the one who came out with the least casualties and called the tune of the other's retreat.

"Gentlemen!" Sergeant Moore yelled, peering through the night scope, "We are about to greet the enemy and welcome him to his final destination."

The fishing village was in the arch of the long turn, and when they hit the curve, the river came alive. Junks along the bank where some fire had come from had exploded into flames from the rockets and grenade launchers.

Xam couldn't be restrained and went directly into the heart of the battle.

Fire control and maneuver tactics quickly vanished. Battle chaos and the madness of warfare took over.

The river danced in a nightmare of explosions and screams, tracers and flames adding to the wild madness of it. The water was alive with men trying to swim towards one bank or the other—many getting machine-gunned in the withering crossfires.

The Wayward Angel ran the gauntlet, turned and started back. It was an insanely agile, fast instrument on these waters. Teague attempted to keep some semblance of control as the boats ran the gauntlet, returning fire at a far greater rate than they were receiving it.

Behind him, Khiet stayed on the open channel, talking calmly into the radio phone, telling the commanders of each squadron of boats—they were in five boat teams—to maintain fire control, attack the most available targets. What he was doing was not directing the course of the fight, which right from the beginning was impossible, but keeping the commanders in touch with each other. Xam would be doing the same.

The shore teams proved themselves as they came at Quy's men from unexpected points and they were gaining the edge.

The Wayward Angel hadn't taken any serious hits and surged through the water with all her normal power. Moore directed the fire from the bow, his big voice shouting in English followed instantly by Khiet's commands in Vietnamese. They had formed a fire team as good as any Teague had ever worked with before.

The battle was in reality a half a dozen different firefights up and down the river at four different concentrations around one of the islands and shore villages.

Ahead, a junk near the south bank had turned upriver and was racing away. The junk was fast, but the Wayward Angel was faster and drawing closer with each second.

The escaping junk fired back at them with a burst of its automatic rifles and the crew of the Wayward Angel returned the fire with machine guns.

Moore, with his shotgun resting on the gunwale, yelled out words of doom for the escaping boat as they ran it down.

When they drew within fifty meters, a rocket from Xam's boat whooshed across the water and hit the junk dead on and blew its back end off. They came on the boat as it sank.

The crew of the Wayward Angel pulled the living from the water. The fourth man they yanked aboard was the man himself. Quy was badly wounded and Moore looked at Teague and shook his head. The man was going to die and would give them no information about who he'd connected with.

The difference in the end was the experience, power and discipline of the men who had once been Vinh Lac's elite boatmen with their ability to maneuver and direct concentrated firepower that more than made up for their inferior numbers.

The main part of the battle had lasted less than half an hour, but skirmishes continued for a time, then silence came over the waterway and villages, the peasants having retreated into the jungle to await the end.

Moore the soldier now transformed into Moore the bac se, with the same intensity, the same massive presence—just a different capacity. The deck was covered with blood, sticky with it and the air stank with it. This first light defused into the jungle.

Many boats on both sides had burned before they sank.

None of Quy's boats had gotten past the blocking forces up or down river, and none of Quy's other groups had made it through to help. They had all vanished into the jungle except three of their prisoners who had been on the boats. They were very happy to rejoin Xam and Khiet.

Xam's boat pulled alongside and she boarded the Wayward Angel, her black cotton blouse soaking wet and clinging to her body, a thirty-eight hanging from her waist. She went up to Quy. In spite of Moore's attempts, the man was dead. Had he lived, it probably wouldn't have been for long given the look on her face.

Xam entered into the Wayward Angel's cabin and conferred with Khiet for a few minutes and then came back out and informed them that Khiet was getting intel that the special operations base across the border had been alerted about the battle.

She turned to Teague, but said nothing, just gave him a powerful look and a slight nod, which he returned. The man who had betrayed her brother was dead. The big question was, did he communicate with other forces?

They had to get out of there.

46

Colonel Stennride and Keller were spending the night and planned on several more days at the new base when they were awakened and informed that something was happening across the Cambodian border.

They went into the war room where half a dozen Viet Special Forces were manning radios.

Stennride said to Captain Trang, "Do we know what this is?"

"Reports coming in suggest a fierce conflict across the Cambodian border. It was thought at first to be a VC skirmish with Free Khmer forces, maybe part of an expanding drug war, but now, from the communication we're picking up from Quy, he's surrounded by his Hoa Hao enemies."

"Where is the information coming from?"

"We have river and ground contacts in the area. The intercepts are solid."

More information came in and now it was obvious the battle

was between Hoa Hao Buddhist factions. Finally, with searches going on all over the river system, they had a location. "Let's saddle up," Stennride said.

Within the hour, choppers from the base leaned against the horizon and banked in the direction of a group of villages in Cambodia just across the border. Stennride peered through night glasses at the river below, twisting out across the paddies and jungles. Black smoke rose from several close-knit villages and the narrow river banks and drifted a thousand feet into the sky before vaporing off.

He studied the terrain and listened to the dispatches over his headset. Keller told him reports coming in confirmed that the retreat was going south and not back across the border, with junks headed down narrow rivulets toward deeper jungle.

"Let's bring a Carthaginian peace to this," Stennride said. He was very unhappy the bastards were escaping, but it was a potential opportunity to end this if he could get them in the open and bring in the Skyraiders to soften things up.

Choppers were bringing in ground forces under Trang's command to finish the job.

He had Keller inform units like the 9th Division in the Western Delta that the VC attacks were being handled.

"They left behind some small units to delay and distract," Keller said, "but Trang believes the main forces are moving into a place controlled by the Free Khmer."

That wasn't good news. "We need some information from the people in the area."

Keller set the chopper down near one of the villages. The prisoners being interviewed by Trang were mostly old men and women.

"Any American bodies found?" Stennride asked.

"No American."

"How many causalities have you taken?"

Trang hesitated. "Very difficult. Jungle. Hai muoi. How you say English?"

"Twenty," Keller said.

"Any Americans involved?"

Trang nodded. "Two Americans. One a black man and the river pirate they call Gamewarden. Also, the woman, Vinh Lac's sister. They escape. But Quy's body has been identified."

Stennride was not happy by the loss of the one Hoa Hao leader who had assisted them. He stared at the debris floating around in the river. "That bastard had a great opportunity to end it all right here," he said with a note of rebuke in his voice. "We need to track them down."

That the main force and the Americans had escaped was not good. And now the bastards were well-armed and had wiped out maybe the only opposition within their ranks. It was a big issue. But this operation was just getting started. There would be no let up until all the rebel forces were wiped out or driven into submission. They were on the verge of all-out war.

This would fast become a nightmare if they vanished into the jungles and mountains. Well-armed, and with major support in the western provinces, and the potential for forming alliances with other rebel forces in Cambodia and Laos put Stennride in a nervous state of mind. But then some good news came in. They had a sighting of fleeing rebel forces a few miles south of a river crossing. "Let's get them."

47

The Hoa Hao units that had destroyed Quy were now trying to make a fast move into the jungles with the help of the Free Khmer forces, yet with so many boats and soldiers, Teague feared they'd be caught in the paddy and village world before they reached the deep jungles across the border in Duyet's jungle camps.

Teague and Xam were the last boats to leave down the narrow canal. They had gotten about five klicks from the battle with Quy when reports came from Acosta that his people were intercepting communications from a base near the border that was now under Colonel Stennride's control and moving into attack mode.

They needed to get into the deep jungle before morning, but they also had to worry about getting ambushed by VC forces.

Xam was alive and Quy was dead and that would end the internal rebellion. The conflict on intercepts already was calling it a drug war and it would be written off by officials in Phnom Penh and Saigon as the ongoing struggle in the Golden Triangle.

That is, unless this conflict broke out in a big way, and out in the open. The colonel would fear that as much as they did.

The threat of daylight looming, they passed fishing villages and pulled up next to Xam at the edge of the inlet.

She said, "We will be very open on a canal for a mile or so ahead."

On the other side of the canal, a fisherman ignoring them twirled his net, bringing it around his head like a lasso until he had built up speed, and then he let it fly, the net spreading in the early morning air, plopping down over a span of water with a thousand-bubble splash.

Already they could hear the children and the women preparing for the day. But there was another sound, familiar but out of place, and he turned and craned his neck in the direction from which it came as the boat surged forward.

They were in a dilemma. Stay for the cover and these villages could be decimated, or take the chance and cross some open paddies.

As their boats moved forward on the narrow waterways, the trees around him fell silent and the birds and monkeys stilled their incessant chatter.

On the water, dozens of families sat on their sampans and their conical hats were tipped skyward as if they feared horror raining down from the skies: heavy ordinance, anti-personnel bombs that hung like goiters, napalm canisters, rockets.

And that fear became a reality when they were out in the open on a canal that cut across the rice fields, but with all the weight and the shallowness of the canal, high speed was not going to happen.

They were about halfway with a quarter mile to go before the security of jungle when a Skyraider appeared. They'd been located. The plane was the perfect jungle warfare bomber precisely because it could come in low and slow and find its targets with an enormous amount of destructive firepower.

They opened up and took the risk to get out of the open stretch of canal into the heavy overhang.

The Skyraider dipped, angled, its wings catching the early rays of the rising sun, and it opened fire with its twenty-millimeter cannons, the bullets strafing through one of the sampans like a rapid-fire sledgehammer, the crew jumping into the water. The other boat crews fired back.

Entire families that had moved out into the rice fields now ran in panic. Women grabbed their children and scattered like frightened geese. A second plane appeared. The first had now banked and its bombs came off and tumbled down, exploding on the banks, a mushroom of black and orange rose in the sky.

They reached the overhang just behind Xam's team. Now they had a chance.

The second Skyraider appeared from the west and dropped ordnance into the trees.

Above were flames and the stink of cordite, soldiers trying to organize.

The napalm exploded in the sixty-foot-high treetops. The speed of the boat outdistanced the fall of the napalm, but it still sent a furious wave of heat over them. Six of the seven junks moved deeper, but slower into the thick jungle overhang through massive copses of bamboo and thick fronds.

But soldiers were heard firing some distance away. Khiet said that Duyet's men were in position and the second plane had left after dropping napalm.

The escape had been successful, having lost only one junk and two men wounded. They were lucky to have gotten far enough that no bringing in of ground troops was likely and they had major jungle ahead through the treelines around canals and villages.

Once they reached the triple canopy, the hunt for them would come to an end.

48

Teague and company moved through copses of papaya and bamboo, down tunnels of black green where early light sliced through like the razor gleam of a prism and the birds screamed and fluttered about in hysteria.

Teague's lungs burned from the acrid smoke and the heat as the bombing continued. His wet clothes dragged at him like grasping hands.

Two Hoa Hao and some Free Khmer shot past like shadows heading toward a small lagoon, one carrying a light machine gun, the other a tripod.

Bombs exploded off to his right and the dapple-leafed trees shook violently, but the jungle here was so thick their presence couldn't be seen by the Skyraider pilots. He slowed, sucking hard on the stifling air, his chest pounding, and joined those who had gathered at a clearing.

They stopped at a clearing. The trees burned and a black

smoke curled into the pale sky.

He turned as a cheer went up on the banks of the river as a Skyraider leaned sideways, trailing a thin tendril of smoke as it passed over the middle of the lagoon, and then dove into the treeline and exploded in a gush of flames.

Teague found Khiet in front of the trees directing the fire. He had machine guns working from three points along the rice field, forming a triangle of fire.

Khiet ran around in the open like a wild man as another plane made its pass; he was screaming orders in an attempt to get the gunners to lead the plane. But they missed this one and the second Skyraider moved on over the treeline.

Teague retraced his steps along the path, looking for Xam. He went into the massive fronds along the bank, pushing through tangles of weed to where the boats were hidden.

They stayed quiet and silent in the deep overhang and waited for hours. They had ambushes set up in case gunboats were sent into the narrow waterway. None showed up.

"Where's Moore?" Teague asked as Khiet reappeared from the trees.

"He's taking care of the wounded."

No ground forces showed and the bombing came to a sudden halt.

They stood near the edge of a narrow canal, a few hidden thatched homes on stilts spread out in the trees along both sides of the water. The ragtag force of free Khmers watched curiously

Teague stared a moment at the body wrapped in the grey sail cloth.

The people living in the area came and fed them glutinous rice balls with fish sauce. They huddled in small silent groups, waiting for the news to come back from the patrols. When it did it was good. The attacks by air were limited and no boat or ground forces were involved.

Teague used his RS-I emergency radio pack to contact Acosta. The radio, one of the most sophisticated the CIA had, put him in direct contact from almost anywhere, including the jungle. The message Teague send was terse and potent: "Watchful Hawk down."

Teague waited a moment, then repeated the code message, followed by the coordinates given in a series of letters that corresponded to a date one hundred years in the future from Teague's birthday.

Acosta would do the appropriate calculation and know exactly where Teague wanted the rendezvous.

A message from Acosta gave them a location to go to that was under control of the Free Khmer and he would meet them there. The rest of the Hoa Hao with Xam and Khiet would continue on to Duyet's base camps just over the border.

Teague met the leader of the ragged Free Khmer force, who shook his hand vigorously and studied Teague with the ingenuous enthusiasm of a man who has happened on a miracle. The only words he knew that resembled something Teague could communicate with were "Ah!" and "Hokay!" He wore combat pants, a black shirt and an old green wool jacket that must have come from the French. But the weapon he cradled across his lap as he squatted in front of Teague was a brand-new carbine.

They rested and waited. Three soldiers arrived through the trees with a small girl in tow. She came hesitantly. The commander barked gruffly at her and she moved forward with all the slow caution of a big-eyed lemur. The commander motioned that he wanted her to speak.

"Please," she said slowly, "my English no good."

"It's very good," Teague said.

The commander, fascinated, jabbered something to her. She stared at him and then turned to Teague. "Beaucoup VC. Come Ho Chi Minh trail. They close. Many thousand. More than they've ever seen before."

Being American, he could see in the naive expressions on their faces that they expected much from the Americans. The Free Khmer were as trapped between their government and the communists as were the Hoa Hao between their government and the communists.

"Maybe," Teague said to the cute, hopeful girl, "one day soon, the Americans will help the Free Khmer."

The little girl smiled broadly and translated this back and the men with her cheered and raised their rifles.

What he did not tell them was it would take a revolution in South Vietnam and a complete reversal of American policy, and that meant a defeat for Westmoreland of such magnitude the policy of attrition could not survive. Would they cheer if they understood American politics and policies? Would they cheer if they knew that those in power had no intention of supporting any group outside of the current military regimes?

But there was nothing to be gained by destroying what little thread of hope existed for these groups. Many oppressed or ignored people were waiting for a miracle.

"One day soon," he repeated. That 'one day soon' might not be as soon as they wanted, if at all.

Now, maybe for the first time since Chandler brought him into this 'Third Force' mission, a sense of the enormity and potential across the whole of Southeast Asia took over his thinking.

But it was critical that they succeed fast with the massive numbers of NVA and VC moving into the Delta. The theory held by many in the military was the communists were leaving the borders to hide out near the cities to avoid the massive bombing campaign. Teague didn't buy into that at all. Something big was in the works, maybe much bigger than anyone anticipated because in a sense, the communists were getting desperate for a major victory.

To Stennride, and those giving him authorization, the Buddhist sects had become a bigger threat than the communists. It was crazy.

Teague hoped that Acosta was getting serious help in dealing with this growing crisis.

The last of their team, Engler, Moore, Khiet and five Hoa Hao left to go back to the river and then south and east to the major camps.

Waiting to be picked up by Acosta, Teague stayed behind with a Free Khmer security force.

49

Teague watched Acosta's chopper drop from a clear sky. Two planes circled protectively above. The chopper settled on the edge of the Cambodian paddy field and the agent exited, his pilot keeping the bird ready to take off.

Acosta looked around and nodded toward the guarding Khmer soldiers, then walked over to Teague. "You lose many?"

"We lost a few, and some wounded. We had them taken downriver to the hospital in Long Xuyen. What's going on?"

"A former associate of John Paul Vann's with a different perspective than his former colleague wants a chat. He's got some serious ideas that might be of help."

"Can Tho?"

"Yes. But you won't have to worry. Nobody is going to touch this guy. He might be something of a pariah in the intel circles, but he's got a lot of friends, including me. He's very connected to the Yards and other mountain tribes. If they get behind the movement, it makes a big difference. Let's find out what he has to offer."

They walked to the chopper. The fields were bright green with the third and final crop of the year of young rice, rice that would be prematurely harvested by the peasants in order to prevent the VC from getting the whole crop.

The layers of duplicity were so thick Teague knew he would probably only discover the truth when the crisis in the top layers reached critical mass, and he had a feeling that time would be soon if it hadn't already arrived.

This former associate of Vann's, who was considered by many to be the last hero left in the American expeditionary force, might have something to offer.

"Why is this guy I'm going to meet no longer working with Vann?"

"Maybe he thinks Vann has submitted to the reality of there never being a Third Force. This guy is far closer to Chandler's vision, and yours."

The Viet pilot flew them to Can Tho in a very circuitous way and landed on the top of a flat-roofed building at the edge of the western part of town.

"Looks good," Acosta said. "No problems."

It felt a little strange being plucked from the jungle and dropped into a city that was increasingly under siege by communists moving in around the city and under internal siege from Saigon with its jails overflowing.

"There's a cyclo waiting and plenty of security. The café is just a block away. I'll be here for a few minutes making some calls."

Teague went down the stairs of the empty building. He pulled his bush hat tight against the brightness of the morning sun as he rode through busy streets to the restaurant. Going along in the cyclo, he witnessed two contradictory actions. The decorations on houses for Tet were everywhere.

But he saw something else, people digging in open places and that meant the residents out in this village area up against the city were preparing for something other than celebration.

He went inside a small, empty, open-air cafe three blocks from the Eaton Compound in Can Tho. The café was protected from grenades by chicken wire. On the rafters, a monkey danced back and forth, looking at Teague with suspicion.

Teague waited. His attention fixed on a Vietnamese boy across the street, a gaunt youth in a white shirt several sizes too large trying to see something in a box. The traffic on this street was light, a few bicycles and cyclos.

John Paul Vann, a hero for many, having fought the bureaucracy as a soldier, lost, resigned and then had come back as a lowly civilian, working his way back up and becoming involved with AID. But even AID was moving into the hands of the military.

Teague had heard a lot about the man, though he suspected much of it was the usual rumor mill product. Vann seemed to be always around at the critical moments. He was the advisor on hand at the Ap Bae disaster in 1963 that had turned what should have been an easy ARVN victory into a disaster. His report to Harkins had been received with ridicule and contempt by the chiefs. The press, siding with Vann, went against MACV. Chandler had known the man, but didn't regard him as having much power in the new struggles.

Across the street a jeep pulled up and an American got out. He crossed the nearly empty street and walked in and said, "I'm Mike Hayes and you're Teague, I presume?"

"Yes?"

The thin, balding man, maybe about fifty, ran his fingers through his sparse blond hair. He came over and shook Teague's hand and sat down, his movements quick like a nervous badger's.

He faced Teague across the table, studying him. He said, "There is a disturbing rumor going around that a friend of Chandler's, an ex-naval officer, got himself killed trying to run guns to a bunch of opium smugglers in Cambodia. Apparently, that rumor isn't true."

"I don't know," Teague said, getting a thin smile from Hayes.

They waited as a mamasan appeared from the back with a couple of well-worn glasses filled big chunks of ice that had unknown spots of yellow and brown refracted in the light. She asked if they wanted water or beer. They declined both and she returned to the back room.

"You knew Chandler well?" Teague asked.

"Yes. His death was a big shock. I supported his view of what had to be done if this war was going to ever make any sense. I'm here to make a suggestion. There are a lot of people who secretly support what you are trying to do. But most don't believe it's possible." He glanced around like someone always expecting trouble.

"But you do?" Teague asked.

Hayes nodded. "Chandler had a lot of secret supporters and I'm one of them. But things are changing so fast the belief that a radical change can happen is diminishing. To stop that retreat, something needs to happen very soon. We know about the success of the massive arms shipment and about MACV's boy Colonel Stennride's failure to stop it. He's serious business and has a lot of support for his mission to bury the Third Force idea once and for all. In the meantime, the VC and NVA now threaten most major cities across the country and that includes the Delta. Yet it might be a hidden opportunity."

"How so?"

"If there is an attack, and we know there will be, and it will very possibly happen during Tet as it happened eight years ago, the city officials need to be convinced that a re-armed Buddhist force will be key to their survival. That could change everything. But survival isn't enough. There has to be a major transformation of how things are done. That means something close to a political revolution that needs to happen very soon, in the coming weeks. If armed Hoa Hao forces protect the cities from the communists, they will have made a very strong impression not only on the people, but on America's strategy. Or lack thereof. But it has to be even bigger than Hoa Hao."

Teague liked everything this man was proposing. "And how do we get such a force built up that fast?"

Hayes said, "It exists. Just needs to be brought together. We've been contacting elements in Laos and Cambodia, as has Frank. You've already seen what the Free Khmer are capable of. But there are thousands of Montagnards, Hmong, Nungs, Khmers and other groups who could give you the power you need and they appear ready. Chandler's dream of a radical change will have died with him unless there is something that can emerge quickly. If a Third Force comes in to save the day, that might be the perfect circumstance that can lead to its emergence. It's the only way to break the paradigms of those who believe that massive American bombing and body count, combined with forced relocation and reeducation of the peasants, isn't going to work in Asia and has to be replaced soon. We're arranging a conference in the mountains. It can happen fast with the right agreements. The coalition is there; it just needs to be put into a workable force very soon or the attacks we believe are inevitable will turn this whole country into a Rolling Thunder kill zone. If it's possible to change the course of this war, it had better happen now because a massive bureaucratic

Quint us Fabius Maximus will consume everything."

Above them in the corner, the monkey watched, its head moving with a tiny sideways tic, as if trying hard to understand the conversation.

Hayes got to his feet. "Acosta will take you to meet the Yards and others. The trip up into the mountains to a new, very secret, difficult to reach Yard encampment must be done very quietly, as it were. The NVA coming down the trails haven't located it and they want to keep it that way. When you get there, work something out. The resources necessary will be made available if you can bring the sect leaders on board. Good luck."

They shook hands again, then he left. Teague felt very good about this meeting. Something much larger than he was aware of was in the works.

Moments later, Acosta walked in. "You ready for a trip to the mountains?"

"I am. This Hayes is, I take it, one of those operatives you never hear about."

"He's as deep dark as they get. Let's go."

They walked outside. Teague looked at the shops and the people, a doe-eyed girl in a doorway, a blind woman being led by a tethered young boy, a flock of delicate schoolgirls in black trousers and white blouses passed by, the pace of the town lazy, subdued under the easy sky, but with the people he saw coming in digging around their houses, he knew they expected something.

The jeep with the driver and Hayes turned at the corner and disappeared. Teague and Acosta headed back to the building where the chopper waited.

"I detected a note of something close to serious alarm in his voice," Teague said.

"That's accurate. The people with him, who support everything we're doing, are apprehensive. That's why this had to happen and fast and before Tet. If it doesn't, all hell will break loose."

50

At 4 a.m. on a clear star-studded night, an unmarked Huey chopper dropped down out of the Laotian sky towards the black mountain forests.

The communists were on a major move down the trails and the last thing Teague and company wanted was to compromise the very secretive and isolated Yard camp, so they decided to follow some SOG operational methods and make it to the camp the hard way to keep from it being discovered.

When the chopper slowed to a hover just above the jungle roof in search of the tiny landing zone, it was time. One of the Viets rode a STABO rig and was let down and then found a place that a landing for the chopper was possible.

They got out quickly and the chopper rose and headed back to Vietnam.

This was the second entry; the first had been a false drop to throw any alert enemy off track, get them hunting in the wrong places.

Reaching the new Montagnard camp, given the conditions on the ground, was a big issue and they took the hard route to avoid revealing its location. They had a hike in front of them.

Teague studied for a moment, the Styro ring on his chest, and then he checked Moore's backpack and that of one of the Yards as he himself was in turn checked.

They moved out immediately, wordlessly into the vast murmuring triple canopy forest. They all wore black, and Teague had smeared black grease on his face. "He's always trying to look as pretty as me," Moore had quipped to the Yards, who thought that was funny as hell.

They all carried rucksacks loaded with ponchos, C-rations, extra socks, foot powder, rope, tape, claymore mines. Teague's pockets were stuffed with maps, a signal mirror, a flare-gun, a pencil, and a can of insect repellent. Each man also carried collapsible water canteens.

They wore luminescent dots on their backs so they could see one another in the dark as they inched along for fifteen minutes, then stopped and listened for ten. In this fashion, they traveled for three hours, twisting and pushing through heavy foliage, until Moore was satisfied they were reasonably safe in case their insertion had been observed.

Then they made a false camp, yet slipped out and slept several hundred meters away, waking after only a few hours of fitful rest and moving out to avoid any communist units who might have surrounded the false camp.

This kind of movement, this cat and mouse game of circling, false camps, moving fifteen minutes and listening ten went on for twenty-six hours before they made their first contact. All communication was by hand signal or whispers.

They were moving along the heavy growth and towering trees

on the east side of a mountain. Winding down through the gorge ahead was a road that cut through the Special Forces encampment at Gia Vue in the Valley of the Wind. Those were hardcore 'White Star' teams that gave the communists a lot of trouble.

"Viet Cong trails," Moore said. Teague took the binoculars and studied the long stretch of mostly hidden road that wound like a brown ribbon through the trees.

They hunkered down and looked at the map with a tiny, hooded flashlight, the Hoa Hao, several Nungs and Yards hovering around them.

Moore said, "This is Ban Me Thuot and here is Bon Sar Pa and up here Ban Don. The Ho Chi Minh trail cuts between the capital at Ban Me Thuot and the Special Forces camps. There are SOG teams working these hills and they've been alerted to the drop. Those boys are some serious dudes. I've gotten a few of their wounded out. Man, it's like they have the most casualties of any group operating anywhere. I don't think they'd be happy that Viets they trained were being used as political weapons against a people who are also great fighters against the communists."

Moore turned and pointed towards the mountains behind them. "The leader of a major force, Y Bham, will be located about twenty-five klicks that way. He will meet us at the Yard camp. He's in a very good spot if it all goes to hell. He can escape deeper into Laos if things break down and from there he can, if he chooses, march on Ban Me Thuot in a day and a half."

After eating some rice cakes, they began the final leg of the journey. They traveled faster now, unable to take the precautions they had on the first day. They were behind schedule, the terrain more rugged than they had anticipated.

Teague slipped twice coming down the underbelly of a ravine and was getting up when he was stopped by Moore's raised hand. Everyone froze. Light filtered through the double canopy jungle in occasional, refracted shots in the otherwise relentless black gloom.

A quick stream hissed by as he sucked in the heavy dank air and felt the weight and the weariness of altitude and the climb. They were all exhausted now. But fear of ambush demanded alertness.

His Rucksack straps dug deep into the sores on his shoulders and even with the possible danger, he remained acutely aware of their bite.

The column halted. No one moved for ten minutes, ears straining against the normal sounds of the jungle, seeking those indicators of human movement: voice, metallic clicks and coughs. Teague instinctively reached for a blade of grass to chew but caught himself. Moore had already warned him that only Americans chew grass and the VC know when Americans are around by signs as seemingly insignificant as that.

It seemed as if Teague stood there an hour before he heard the communists distinctly. It was not the usual three-man VC patrol. They were close, moving fast and they seemed relaxed and confident, talking and laughing.

The leader of the advance Yard team said in stumbling Vietnamese, English mix, that there were thousands of communists on the trails. "I do not know what conditions in the area between the Ho Chi Minh Trail and Ban Me Thuot. My long-range patrols do not reach so far."

Finally, men from the camp linked up and guided them to their destination.

The Montagnard camp hidden in the boulders and trees was revealed only when they were there and it suddenly appeared in the wavering light, a mist that floated over the ground in chunks like large grey jellyfish.

Chinese Nung soldiers were there to greet them. These were the great mountain men and now allies of the Yards. They had come down from the North in the fifties. Some became soldiers of fortune for whoever paid them. Diem had used many of them back in fifty-five to destroy the coalition of Hoa Hao, Cao Dai and Catholics who had beaten the Viet Cong but were a threat to Diem. But these Nungs in the mountains weren't part of that.

They ducked under a shelter as a sudden change in the weather brought a rain squall howling over the mountains. It might be the dry season in Nam, but not so much up here.

The Yard camp was a group of bunkers and longhouses hidden in the massive rocks and trees connected by paths.

The area was so difficult that just clearing a potential landing zone for choppers was underway if big meetings were to happen.

Moore was greeting people with enthusiasm and became the translator for the talks that went on all day as representatives of other mountain groups came in.

Patrols in every direction found that the camp was not in any trouble of being discovered by VC patrols.

Teague and Acosta discussed the situation and the safety issue. The Yards and their compatriots had created a wide perimeter manned by security teams positioned to stop any assault.

A tiny landing zone was ready for choppers. Acosta, with General Lessing's representative, a guy name Costello, came in that afternoon. The chopper that brought them headed back to prepare to bring others.

Acosta promised the Yard leaders to have C-130s, called Blackbirds because they had no insignias, drop supplies and more weapons.

Watching the activity around the camp, Y Bham told Teague he knew Paul Nur. "He Special Commissioner Highlander Affairs. We met in Diem jail. Paul Nur smart man. Decree...Statu

Particulier. Want Americans force Saigon give Yards autonomy."

"Yes, we know him. Very smart."

"You want some Yang Coi."

Moore turned to Teague's questioning look and said, "Yang Coi is the rice spirit and up here it's a spirit you need."

"A little Yang Coi is not a bad idea."

Y Bham said to Moore, "I like friend of you. Yes."

The sky had cleared now and they walked along the ridgeline. The valleys below were deep and green with some of the world's thickest jungles. Above towered the fog-capped Annamese Mountains, the primitive power of nature sweeping out before them in all her majesty, relentless and unchallenged.

Since a good number of mountain tribes were matriarchal with women owning all the land, bringing in a female to the meetings wasn't any problem. Acosta agreed it was time to bring the others.

51

Teague was very excited with the arrival from the Delta of Xam, Khiet and General Duyet. And the various tribal leaders from the Rhade, Jeh, Jarai, Nung and Mnong were very happy to see these powerful Viet rebels.

A second chopper arrived a little later from Saigon just after the Delta chopper left. The landing area was too small for two birds.

This chopper brought in one of Saigon's former mayors and short-term premier, Tran Van Huong, a diminutive, soft-spoken guerrilla leader. This former school teacher had been one of the darlings of the American politicos. Also, there was a representative working with General Lessing.

Once the talks began in the marao communal house, it went very smoothly.

It was obvious Y Bham seemed absolutely fascinated with the young female Hoa Hao leader. He told her that on only two occasions in the past the Vietnamese had proved trustworthy to Yards and helped them in a war, and on both occasions the leaders were female warriors.

Teague sat across from Xam and Duyet and alongside Moore and Y Bham on long benches in the communal house.

General Duyet, in his baggy cotton clothes, and the elegant professor, the one coming from twenty years in the jungles of the U Minh forest, the other from the jungles of Saigon politics and jails, got along very well.

While the talks went on through the afternoon about the possibility of cooperation and joining forces, preparations were being made for a ceremonial feast that would seal an agreement that would bind all major segments of the coalition to a single goal, a uniform set of basic principles, and they would have the means to drastically alter the course of events, not only across Indochina.

The prospect sent shivers through Teague. He glanced at Moore and the Sergeant returned his look as if he too was contemplating exactly the same thing.

"The factions of the South have gathered a dozen times in the past," Tran Van Huong said, "but I think never before have our diverse tribal ambitions been transcended by a common national goal. To forge a new political entity, a true alternative that will lay the foundation for free institutions and real democracy—that is our purpose, our great need. We are the polit—"

He was interrupted by a Yard soldier who barged in, then abruptly stopped when facing so much authority.

Teague feared something was happening. Maybe they'd been discovered by the communists, or Stennride.

The young soldier cleared his throat and gathered his composure. He went over and spoke to Sergeant Moore in a hushed voice.

Moore rose to his feet. "You gentlemen will have to excuse me but I have a house call. A Jeh woman is having a breech."

A sigh of relief came from the room.

After Moore had gone, the talks resumed in the marao and all was going very well until Sergeant Moore returned forty minutes later, his face sweaty and distraught. He dropped down beside Teague, propping his riot gun up against one of the rice wine jars.

The conversation stopped and everyone looked quizzically at Moore, who was fighting to get a cigarette lit.

"The baby okay?" Teague asked.

"Baby is fine. Healthiest little guy you ever saw. The Jeh mother died." Moore looked very disturbed. "Bad breech. She was hemorrhaging like she'd stepped on a landmine."

Teague shook his head. "I'm sorry. That's tough."

Others in the room from the various tribes commiserated when they were told.

Moore took a drag and balanced the cigarette on the edge of the table and blew the smoke out his nostrils. He looked around the room. "I had one of the Hoa Hao I personally trained to help me. When a Jeh woman dies at birth, it's their custom to bury the kid with her so his spirit doesn't wander around causing trouble. Even the fathers accept this. Problem is, word got around to the Hoa Hao security detail and they don't like it. Especially since one of them helped save the kid."

"Who's got the baby?" Xam asked.

"Your soldiers and they say they aren't going to let the Yards bury him."

"That is as it must be," she said.

"Damn!" Acosta muttered. "This can't happen right now. How do we fix this? We got this almost signed, sealed and delivered."

When Teague followed Moore outside, there were a dozen mountain women gathered. One of them was a wizened creature carrying a hood-bladed machete called a mak, her black hair cut in the style of a French cap, her arms encased in metal bracelets. She also wore a cut-off army shirt and saucer-sized circular earrings dangling from her earlobes.

More women emerged from the huts and gathered in the center of the compound. It turned into a bitter debate that now threatened a complete breakdown of relations between the lowlanders and highlanders.

Many of these women had black stained teeth filed to sharp points according to the aesthetic demands of their culture. They were joined by Yard soldiers carrying their weapons.

Teague and Moore were now joined by Frank Acosta and Y Bham.

Moore walked among those in dispute like some great black prophet of old. He wore their ceremonial costume, the loincloth barely reaching his knees, the upper piece embellished with a red square across the chest. On his wrist, he wore three metal bracelets given to him by the three largest tribes. Teague hoped he was the voice everyone would listen to.

The rebel Montagnard flag—blue top with a green bottom and a red middle with three stars—flew outside of half the secret, barely visible structures of this camp.

Teague, also dressed in his ceremonial loincloth, said, "Any ideas?"

"Like Solomon, we could threaten to cut the kid in half and whichever side refused—"

The woman with the wicked looking mak appeared in front of them. Half a dozen other women stood behind her. All around them, tiger-suited Yard soldiers and Nungs looked on.

"You great friend," she said in staggered English. Moore

nodded and spoke in phrases of her language to indicate he was a blood brother, not just friend. "Our custom demands we must have the child," the woman said, Moore translating.

"There will be no need for that," Moore told her, and then in English. "We will find a way."

She stepped aside as the Americans made their way into the communal house to find the answer.

On one side sat the council of leaders with Y Bham in the center. On the other Xam, Nhu Bon and the commander of the Hoa Hao platoon.

Between them on the floor were offerings of food and the large jugs of rice beer, the long drinking straws spouting from them like weeds.

Teague watched with fascination. Xam, in simple black cotton trousers and blouse, her hair tied tight to the back of her head, still failed to hide her beauty as she spoke and Moore quietly translated the argument that was mostly in the language called Austroasiatic of the Degar. It boiled down to how the baby could be kept alive as it was inappropriate to kill a baby that an American soldier had saved.

The Yard leader then turned and discussed it with his council members, then replied, "That is not a question for anyone to decide but us."

Xam stared at him and it was a critical moment. She answered, "In the history of all peoples, all cultures, some customs are abandoned in favor of new ones. The Romans once buried children they did not want. The Americans once practiced slavery—as your good friend Sergeant Moore could tell you. Great cultures abandon such practices and adopt new ones. It is the sign of a great people that they are able to change what is barbaric and adopt what is civilized."

Moore stumbled around a bit in the translation and they

waited until he was finished.

Teague saw in Y Bham's face and others a great quandary. His respect for the virtues of this young woman was obvious for all to see. Yet he, as the leader of the mountain men, had no choice but to refute her no matter what he himself believed in the matter. Teague felt that it was a hopeless situation.

"Maybe someday we will change many of our practices," Y Bham said. "But to do so now, under threat and pressure from lowlanders, would humiliate us."

In the silence that fell between them, Teague interjected through Moore. "Ask the members of the Jeh what is important to them in this matter. That the child be killed, or that it simply no longer be allowed to be with the tribe where its angry spirit would cause much trouble?"

Y Bham listened carefully to the interpretation, and then spoke with the Jeh members before turning back to Moore and Teague. "If the child is not buried, it must be banished from tribal lands. The further away the better."

"If an American were to adopt this baby," Moore said, "and take it to Saigon and later America, and it would never come back to the mountains, would that be favorable to the Jeh?"

After much discussion Y Bham nodded. "They would not want a Vietnamese to take the baby, under these circumstances... But an American chief they find acceptable—an honor."

Teague asked Acosta and Moore to follow him outside to discuss the crisis and how to resolve it.

"Obviously," Teague said, "one of us must take the baby. But it can't be Moore, as he had to deal with these Yards. And it can't be me, as I'm not in a position."

"No way, I'm not adopting the kid, so get that out of your minds."

"Listen, Frank," Teague said, glancing at Moore, "that's what they want. They see you as the great white father and you need to give the baby to some big chief. Only you have the power to take this bad spirit away from here and calm it down and give it a proper home once the boy is out of here."

Moore nodded, adding, "And it's serious. No way are they gonna go on with negotiations. They won't come to any agreements. There won't be any ceremony of alliance without this. It's the only way."

"This is nuts."

"Just for the sake of appearance," Teague said. "Later, in Saigon, you can get your baby a nice home. Give it to an orphanage or whatever."

Acosta sat on an ammo box smoking, sipping coffee and staring at Teague and Moore. He knew he'd been had. The baby, at least for now, was his.

"Real cute," he said with disgust, yet had a sardonic grin at what they'd been able to trap him with.

"Why should life be unremitting gloom? Congratulations, papasan. You can name him after us," Teague suggested.

"Spare me the homily."

Teague and Moore glanced at each other, grinned conspiratorially and started to leave. "By the way, Frank," Moore said, "the ceremonies of allegiance are starting soon and you are now the top guest of honor. We need to get into uniform."

52

The mountain soldiers were framed in the vast panorama of the untamed Annamite Cordillera: the rugged serpentine tail at the end of the 1500-mile Himalayas that sprawled across a good portion of the world. The valleys cut through the mountains like dark green lakes, and above, now that the rain squalls had vanished, the clouds haloed the peaks and marbled the sky. To their backs was Laos, to the east of Vietnam, and to the south lay Cambodia. Whose piece of land they were on now no one knew for sure. It depended on whose map you were looking at.

Stripped of their clothing and wearing loincloths like the Nungs, Teague, Acosta and Moore squatted around a primitive fire on top of a primeval mountain, exchanging food and drink with the slash and burn culture of these people who were now likely allies.

The Nungs were having a drinking contest. Moore said that not only were they the best mountain climbers, they were also the best drinkers. The Hoa Hao, opposed to alcohol and drugs, stayed out of the contest.

A very large, black buffalo stood on the hill under a full moon looking around with innocent animal ignorance of the fate awaiting it, legs stiff as implanted stakes, body held by ropes. He grunted and then started to turn his head, stretching out his neck to see to one side when the man with the knife approached, a thin, brown man in a loincloth carrying a wicked, curved, sharp-looking knife. Behind the doomed creature, the women waited with their cups and clay vessels.

The man slit the buffalo's throat with such a quick move that the animal didn't appear to realize for a moment what happened. He snorted and the snort died quickly, the blood squirted out, a signal to the women to dart forward and gather in the precious liquid before the great animal sank to its knees. The beast stumbled, lunged against the ropes and fell, tongue sliding out of its mouth, jaw slack, eyes turning to glass.

The women, their cups awash in the beast's blood, moved back and the men moved in to build a fire around the animal.

They removed some parts and then cooked the buffalo where it lay. Soon the air wafted with the crackling sizzling burn of skin and meat. The feast began.

It struck Teague, as he watched the ceremonies and participated in them, from the exchanging of bracelets, the sipping of the ceremonial rice wine, the review of the troops that this was one of the great moments in his life, one he would never forget. Very diverse, antagonistic cultures bound by desperation, diplomacy, and the common attitude of rebels.

How bizarre, he thought. He was aware that at this very moment McNamara was building an electronic barrier across the DMZ, as if that would halt infiltration into the south, while at this same moment the heavy canopy covering the hills and valleys hid massive NVA forces on their way south. He wondered just how tragically ludicrous American leadership had become.

In the final rituals, they were surrounded by representatives of the mountain tribes who were squatted with them around the fire passing the food, the pipe and the wine hoses. It seemed like a very good beginning to a real coalition.

As the leaders made short speeches, Teague thought about that the long journey from the more primitive to the more sophisticated was a necessary expression of human genius, yet he felt at the same time a certain loss.

In their simple physical existence and complex mental life, these people retained much of the innocence of historic primitive tribes. And, from Moore's testimony, they were endlessly friendly, and never got into vicious arguments that led to physical assault. "We look down on them because they are so primitive. No science, no economic development, nothing like we have. But in their own fashion they have created a way of living that is at least peaceful and relaxed. So, they have locked themselves in on one hand, but locked a lot of problems out on the other."

"Unfortunately, that looks to be coming to an end," Teague said.

Moore nodded. "It's the rice wine. Be careful or you'll start praying to rocks before morning. Even the women up here start taking on a kind of Madison Avenue look when you're on your second or third jug, but keeping up with the Nungs is impossible. It would kill you."

Acosta took another pull on his rice wine.

Teague glanced over at the women squatted around the fire, full bellied now after the feast, their flat splay-feet pointing out, their arms resting on their knees as they puffed on their pipes. They seemed always to be smoking their pipes, these mountain women. They loved Moore, you could see it in their eyes whenever he was around. Not the kind of love that would make their men jealous, but the same kind of love the men also had for the big Sergeant.

"It'll take ten jugs," Acosta said.

After a short night of plans and decisions and with no sleep for anyone in the group, it was time to go back to Vietnam. Before the first light of the following day, the choppers were coming to get them.

After discussing the success of the gathering with Xam, Teague went over to Acosta, who'd been talking on his radio phone with JK. The news wasn't good.

"We need to move now," Acosta said. "Stennride is widening his search teams and building a serious military strike force. Our choppers are coming in. We'll have aerial protection, but we need to get to the camps."

The first CIA chopper settled on the mountaintop. The troops lined up again to salute a farewell as Y Bham escorted Lessing's representative, Acosta with his baby, and Ly Minh Hau. They would be going straight to Saigon.

Teague, Xam and Moore and three Buddhist leaders boarded the second chopper a few minutes later.

Teague felt Xam's eyes watching him and he turned to her and nodded and wondered what she thought and did she believe this was all going to really happen.

The chopper, dark and unmarked, leaped off the mountain and slid into the metallic red sky, the colors of the sunrise brilliant over the incandescent peaks.

"What do you think?" Moore asked. "Acosta looked very shaky."

"He's getting bad news about the growing threat. We need to get this show rolling."

Below on the hidden jungle trails, the scouts were reporting massive communist forces on the move.

PART FIVE

Rolling Thunder

53

Madame Mang was having a ceremony at one of the New Life Hamlets and wanted Stennride to be there, not just for the ceremony, but to deal with a growing problem. She wanted him there and she wanted a jet flyover as a reminder of who had the real power in the hamlets of the province.

But General Paulick wanted him in Saigon later that day. The disappearing Hoa Hao forces might have been located.

The colonel told Keller they would make a stop at the New Life Hamlet to placate Madame Mang, but then go straight to MACV headquarters for the 4 p.m. meeting.

According to reports from the Mangs and their PRU intel agents, the New Life Hamlets in their province were being infiltrated by Viet Cong who were hiding among the peasants and stealing their food.

To make a big show about strengthening the presence of provincial authority in those hamlets, the Mangs had arranged a dedication ceremony at the latest of the hamlets where they wanted a new Catholic school built.

"The goddamn hamlet needs to be brought into the program," Stennride said. "Moving the peasants from their ancestral homes and putting them in some social scientist's dreamland doesn't build the kind of disciplined loyalty needed unless there is provincial oversight like the Mangs. We need to talk to our paradise builder and get him on board the new world order."

"You're right about that," Keller agreed.

When Keller sat their chopper down on the outskirts of the Really New Life Hamlet, the peasants were already lined up to greet the Mangs when they arrived. Unlike normal villages, these New Life Hamlet houses stood in perfect rows, neat, identical, drab, treeless.

He and Captain Keller exited the chopper as the man Stennride wanted to talk with emerged from beneath a tarpaulin and watched their approach.

"You are here for the ceremony?"

"That's one of the reasons."

"The province chief's convoy will be here soon. And the other reason is?" Vanderlin asked in that deep sarcasm that was the heart and soul of his dislike and disdain for Stennride personally and the military in general.

"Since our last conversation, things haven't improved according to what I'm told." Stennride said. The air of the hamlet was billowed up in shimmering waves from the dust from construction still going on.

"I think they have, actually. What are you being told?"

Stennride really disliked this man. "We have problems and some of it may involve your New Life Hamlets. I'm getting reports that there is significant VC penetration and some resistance by you to the new school."

"I'm not aware of any major infiltration in my villages. There's a lot of movement this time of the year as Tet approaches. This is the time everyone goes to their home villages for the big celebration coming."

The people of the hamlet, sullen under clear skies, stood in long lines down the road all the way to the gate of 'Peace and Prosperity' as they waited dutifully for the arrival of their new province chief and his wife.

"I'm not against the concept of gathering all the peasants in these New Life Hamlets," Stennride said. "I'm against lack of security and knowledge of who the inhabitants are in contact with, who the visitors are. It's great that they have a dispensary, fishery, and civic lessons organized on the principles geared to make them good citizens and supporters, but that support is for the Saigon regime, not any revolutionaries, be they VC or Buddhists. We need to implant more police and government authority inside these populations and you seemed to be resisting that."

In the distance, the wail of the sirens carried, indicating the province chief and his convoy were on their way down the spur road. Village leaders began admonishing the spectators, who had been given small government flags, to get them out of the dust and start waving.

"I have no idea about any VC activities," Vanderlin said. "I'm not resisting anything. I'm doing what I was sent here to do and that is build a better life for these people."

Stennride shook his head. "What you define as a better life and what the peasants who are torn from their ancestral villages think might not be the same. You don't own the new villages and these aren't your people. A better life can only come from victory in that war."

"That's your job. I put my life into what we're doing here,"

Vanderlin said with mounting anger.

"Vandy, I have your records. I know all about your great awakening after reading the travails of the Joad family—the poor under the iron heel of an insensate capitalism in Steinbeck's 'Grapes of Wrath'. But you're in a war, not in California thirty years ago."

"History teaches us some things apart from war," Vanderlin shot back. "The contrast between the camps in that novel—of the clean, decent, humane government camps, versus the camps run by the greedy, California farms is very much what we're dealing with here. I want to improve the lives of the peasants. We have different missions. Yours needs the support of the peasants and I'm trying to make their lives better."

Stennride nodded, saying, "I'm not here to challenge the nobility of your motives, just your blindness to our real enemy. The greatest creator of poverty and misery in the world is communism." He nodded to the tarpaulin. "As the sign says above your headquarters 'The greatest work is to do the greatest good for the greatest number of people.' And I have no doubt that even someone like you, who comes from a family worth millions, that there is some guilt that you wish to purge by being out here."

"Your sarcasm, Colonel, is duly noted. I can't help you and I don't like having Can Loa spies in my villages."

"They aren't your villages."

Vanderlin started to say something, but was cut off by the wail of the sirens as the lead jeep raced under the arch of Peace and Prosperity, past the emblem of clasped hands and into the hamlet.

"I've seen enough of the future for one day," Stennride said. "But you need to cooperate with the Mangs. Don't push too hard if you want to stay here doing your life's work. One of your top Vietnamese pacification chiefs is a member of the Viet Cong...

that at least three in lower echelons are members of the very same secret society..."

"You can't be serious."

"I'm very serious. And so are people above me. You have a good friend in Hurwitz. In fact, some think those articles that condemn the military approach may have been written by you under his name."

"You came out here to fight about some article I didn't write?"

"That isn't what I'm hearing. And the man who co-authored with Hurwitz is named Vogel. They're published in the French La Monde and a Swedish periodical in sociology, among other venues."

"You here to fire me?"

"No. I just want you on board. Hurwitz's convoluted, Orwellian views, defining the government of South Vietnam as a Hitlerian phenomenon, and this war the Spanish Civil War part II, with America as the Nazi Germany of our time isn't something you want to end up connected to. Your buddy Hurwitz is trouble. You need better friends. He's going to get pushed out. Stockholm might be a more auspicious location for him and maybe, if things don't change, for you."

They turned as the convoy entered through the gate. The new province chief got out of the lead jeep, resplendent in his combat fatigues with his metals glistening on his chest, though he'd never been in real combat in his life.

The real warrior, Madame Mang, was magnificent in her white and gold outfit, her elegant coiffure—the latest Parisian style of heavy short waves and sudden troughs—worn like a crown on the head of a queen.

Stennride marveled at her bearing. Few women in this world had a bearing like that, so prideful, natural, full of power and tradition all at once.

Colonel Mang escorted his wife and several dozen dignitaries on a tour of the hamlet. Stennride stayed happily behind, getting the smile he wanted as he waved to her.

The speeches began and it was time to leave. But he waited because he had another element in the welcome. One the Mangs had demanded—a flyover.

It happed a few minutes into the speeches. Two jets passed the treetops half a mile out, coming full bore now, the sound mounting like a great invisible force delivering a serious message.

Nice, Stennride thought.

A few heads turned toward the approaching aircraft, then many. Anxious eyes turned to the podium to see if there was any reason to be afraid.

The sheer fury of the fighter bombers overwhelmed any calm Vanderlin could produce and the people of the hamlet scattered in panic. The jets came a few hundred feet off the ground, wing tip to wing tip, the scream of the engines deafening.

The wind blast ripped off pieces of roof, and shook the tarpaulin like a hurricane. The jets slanted gracefully, powerfully upward, parting and curling out from each other, afterburners on full bore.

The trembling stopped and the air stilled. Those peasants who had gone to the ground now got to their feet and dusted themselves off. Babies cried and children stared after the planes with wide-eyed awe and fear.

"Now that," Stennride said to Keller as he boarded the chopper and watched the jets disappear, "is the proper way to deliver a meaningful message."

Stennride felt very good at the moment. Victory in the Delta would be a first major step in getting this miserable goddamn country under control so they could pursue the war properly by bombing the north back into the Stone Age where they belonged. The beginning of the end of communism would start here.

"Okay, we have to go," Stennride said.

They climbed back into the chopper and headed for Tan Son Nhut and the meeting.

54

When Colonel Stennride and Captain Keller arrived once again for a critical meeting at Tan Son Nhut airfield, they'd had to wait longer than usual for their turn to land. The entire airfield was packed and stacked with incoming and outgoing flights of all types of craft.

Keller stayed with the chopper after they landed. Stennride, carrying a briefcase of documents, was picked up in a jeep by one of General Paulick's men. He hoped things were falling apart, that the meeting was good news and not bad.

They went straight into the side building of MACV headquarters.

The three generals he'd dealt with before were present in the stark back room, all looking very uneasy.

Stennride accepted coffee and then joined them at the long table. The room had little else, not even pictures on the barren brown walls.

Stennride watched Paulick unfold a map of the western Delta, one that included the eastern border regions of Cambodia and Laos.

The general said, "The red circles are where we've located independent rebel forces. We have data from the new ADSIDs seismic devices that were dropped from F-4 Phantoms still doing the job all through the jungles and Seven Mountains. There was also evidence from both high recon and some low-level night scope flights that brought in corroborating information. A linear pattern of ADSIDs could detect troop movement and large encampments and we have a very interesting reading. The VC and NVA don't gather in big groups or move into an area occupied by other units. So, what we think is that those missing Buddhist forces are moving around in the areas circled. Has to be them. When they escaped going south in Cambodia, we think they are gathering in these areas." He tapped the circles.

Stennride was excited. "It's where the old rebel forces were located back in the fifties."

"Colonel, how big is this rebel force getting?" General Mills asked.

"If they bring in other sects, and it appears that is what's going on, they'll be very big and dangerous if they are allowed to go into the cities because of fears of a mass communist attack at Tet, like what happened eight years ago, they'll be impossible to dig out. They have to be taken deadly serious and dealt with soon. They get into power in the cities in the Mekong Delta, it won't be long before Saigon becomes their next target."

General Paulick said, "Tell us what you need to go in and destroy these rebels."

"What I want is operational authority to call in a B-52 Rolling Thunder from time to time when it's available and if a major assault is in play.

"Then I'd like more assistance from the two ARVN divisions that can be available to work from the Cao Long river and create an ambush belt, night and day patrols with at least two hundred platoons of regional forces under my command as well. I need a serious kill zone that extends from A Trung near the border all the way to the South China Sea. That means under extreme circumstances access to major power. If there is a major gathering of force as this map indicates, it has to be taken care of very soon before it spreads into the cities."

"That's a helluva sizable area," Mills said. "It'd be like we're authorizing you to run the whole war down there."

"In a fundamental sense, given the nature of the threat, what you are authorizing me to do is to stop the rise of a force that could undermine the political structure of the country. The radical forces from the mountains to the rice paddies are coming together as never before and we need to hit them hard and soon while they are concentrated or we'll not be able to achieve our goal of bringing the largest population in the country under Saigon's control. The consequences of failure will undermine everything."

"Give us a few minutes to discuss this, Colonel," General Paulick said. "There's more coffee and donuts in the room across the hall."

Stennride went in, but couldn't sit and didn't want donuts or coffee. He paced. The generals now understood the dangers of chasing the enemy around the jungles when another and potentially more dangerous enemy was emerging in the most populous region in Vietnam. He hoped he'd gotten through to them.

They finally called him back in.

"Colonel," General Paulick said, pointing to his map, "We

agree with you. Massive force and relentless attrition is the ultimate answer. Rolling Thunder will be made available when needed. You will have fighters, Skyraiders and a Skikorsky Skycrane, and gunships. But it's all dark force and we don't want reporters sniffing around, so you must stay invisible in your ops and they must all appear to be about hunting and killing VC. We have high expectations that you will handle the elimination of this threat. Additional resources will be available for final cleanup later. You have to be good with that. We're way the hell out on a limb as it is. So, let's get this moving. And we will put maximum pressure on the province authority and city leaders not to let these rebels come in on the illusion that they want to defend the cities. They want to take them over."

"I appreciate everything you gentlemen are doing," Stennride said, happy they were finally on board. "I was sent into the Delta to do a job and now I think it can be done fast with the help of a Skycrane that can bring in a very effective weapon in the marshlands."

General Miller said, "Now get the hell out of here, Colonel, before we change our minds."

That garnered some laughter.

But the colonel wasn't quite finished. "It's essential that no major Delta city allow armed Hoa Hao or their allies to come in on the grounds that they will protect the city from a communist attack when their real goal is to take over those cities. Any kind of pressure from Saigon or MACV to let them know this is unacceptable will be very helpful. Maybe critical. Thank you, gentlemen, for all that you are doing."

Stennride smiled and snapped off an appreciative salute to these generals who were risking their careers.

Paulick went out with Stennride, where a jeep waited to take him to the chopper, saying as they got outside, "You handle this, I suspect you won't be a colonel for very much longer. In fact, there will be an opening for a new general in the Mekong Delta as the one there now is retiring. He has in a sense been retired for some time."

Stennride appreciated hearing this. They shook hands and parted company.

When Stennride boarded the chopper ten minutes later, he gave the good news to Keller. "We're getting everything. And that includes the Skycrane. We know where they are and they will soon know where we are, right in their backyard."

Stennride showed him the map Paulick had given him. "There's a temple here." He circled an area in red and drew an arrow. "It's about fifteen klicks southeast of Long Xuyen. A lot of activity over the past few days and we're getting some information of movements." He drew a curve. "This isn't an area the VC actually avoid precisely because it's Hoa Hao land. We have the target we've been looking for. And there's more good news."

"I don't know if I can handle more good news."

"General Paulick thinks I might be the perfect fit for the entire Mekong Delta. But, in the near future, as General Stennride."

"Are you serious?"

"All it takes is settling these issues in the Mekong Delta. Oh, and I'd have to adjust to calling you Major Keller. That be okay with you?"

"I think I could adjust."

They laughed. It was one of those powerful moments.

55

Teague and Moore and their squad had reached an area where they were now meeting Duyet's forces.

Engler, in a hidden waterway near the Bassac River, kept them updated as he was in contact with six other boats at different points on the rivers and canals that would come in at dawn, bringing people from the major cities for some big meetings.

A major gathering was already in play around Duyet's camps and they were doing everything to protect the arrivals.

Normally the peasants would be well out in the fields and working all over the Delta to get the biggest rice crop of the year in, but the bombing campaigns were so intense they waited until full daylight when the threat receded.

As the peasants began moving into the fields, the Hoa Hao boats brought new colleagues to Duyet's secret base deep in the jungles near the Seven Mountains.

As Teague waited for Duyet and Xam, Moore and Khiet were

busy with some very young recruits who'd been driven out of bombed villages and had decided not to join the VC, but rather the Hoa Hao.

"You gotta remember," Sergeant Moore yelled, his booming voice resonating through the trees, "this baby"—he pointed to the claymore mine being held up for inspection by a tiger suited Hoa Hao guerrilla—"shoots out in one direction."

Khiet translated and brought some laughter.

Watching from the sideline, Teague was thinking these boys were too young, yet they wanted training so they could join the rebel, anti-communist forces.

When General Duyet arrived, he invited them to his command post. His austere face that showed little emotion, except in the eyes when the general was angered or humored. He was rumored to have a great capacity then for either extreme anger or extreme warmth. But Teague had noticed that whenever Duyet dealt with Khiet, his eyes softened and he was suddenly malleable. He treated Khiet more like a favored son then an agent or subordinate commander.

Xam and her team weren't there yet as they were meeting with some village leaders along the canals that drained into the Bassac River.

Over the past year, with the help of Vinh Lac and Kiet, General Duyet had set up a dozen rebel camps stretching from the Cau Mau peninsula at the southern tip of Vietnam to the mountains near Ban Me Thuot. They were all operational now, and they'd accomplished this prodigious feat in areas either dominated by the VC or were heavily contested, which amazed Teague. That the best fighters in South Vietnam were excluded from being a force in the war would end.

And this, the headquarters camp, and the one from which, if it came to that, a major political move would be launched in Can Tho and Vinh Long and beyond. The object was to win politically and not militarily in the Delta, but they had to be ready to survive attacks from both sides of the war. They now had the equivalent of three battalions in the immediate area and another one under recruitment.

The newest recruits, mostly young boys from Catholic and Hoa Hao villages in Bae Lieu Province that had lately come under pressure from the VC and the bombing campaigns, squatted in the dappled light of the forest as the American Special Forces sergeant showed them the various weapons they would learn how to use.

Khiet was seated on a tree stump nearby. He'd become very good at his new role as chief translator and seemed to enjoy it. The recruits watched intently as Moore hooked the wire to the detonator.

"The reason we use an advance tripwire," Moore yelled, "is so the enemy doesn't sneak in and turn these babies around and then sneak back out. Then when the attack comes, you wipe yourselves out." The recruits laughed, but Moore, doing much of the translating along with Khiet admonished them to pay attention.

Teague and General Duyet left and headed to the base camp command bunker. They passed the street mock-up—fifteen miniature stucco buildings a replica of downtown Can Tho. If it came to a war, these were buildings Duyet wanted to take and secure first: government offices, radio station and city jail. He had similar mockups for Soc Trang and Vinh Long.

They paused to watch commandoes and sappers move through the streets on an exercise. "They must know the cities so well they could move through with blindfolds on," Duyet said.

Every team had a backup, every route an alternative. Nothing was being left to chance. Though the CIA was providing safe houses, Duyet, having dealt with the CIA before, was using his own secret houses. And he was expecting a major VC assault across the Delta soon, but a force that the American Colonel Stennride wasn't interested in. His focus was the Hoa Hao.

They left the mock-up and entered the musky underground bunker, a complex of rooms and tunnels linked to other bunkers and making up Duyet's headquarters.

On the large wall map, red pins located every major VC/NVA battalion, division, or brigade—blue showed where the Americans were and yellow the South Vietnamese. As new information came in from the intelligence networks the map was continuously updated.

Duyet tapped a stick pointer on the map. "General Giap lured Westmoreland out to the borders in a series of battles. Here at Song Be, here Loe Ninh—it looks like a major strike at Kontum. But see here, they are moving major elements around Khe Sanh—and Dak To. This actually allowed the VC units to expand and upgrade and getting NVA political and military cadre in their ranks and moving into position around the cities." He stabbed the map in a dozen places. "Now, in a panic, the American forces out along the borders are being rapidly pulled in around Saigon in the event of a major strike. Yet what the world is being told is that everything is just fine."

"Absolutely nothing significant was done to interdict this invasion?" Teague asked.

"Without human intelligence feeding you reliable information on a regular basis," Duyet said, giving off a shrug, "there is no way to determine the truth of anything without direct contact with the people, and supportive agents among the people. That is why it is so easy to manipulate such a great power as Westmoreland's army."

Teague was staring at the map but he was seeing the villages and jungles, the American bases, the towns and cities, mountains and rivers... He was seeing how all the most potent American divisions were bogged down in the static defense of massive military complexes, while the South Vietnamese ARVN, demoted from combat, had been handed responsibility for pacification and the province chief's security—a move comparable to giving over to Al Capone the responsibility for cleaning up the streets of Chicago."

They stood there for a long time just studying the map. Finally, Teague asked, "Will the VC attack during Tet? Supposedly there's some kind of peace accord being created."

Duyet replied, "Any peace accord will be a ruse. The attack will come during Tet, like in nineteen-sixty. We must move into the cities and be there to defend them. Many of Saigon's soldiers and police will be gone, off celebrating Tet at their villages with family. The cities will become indefensible. But first we must survive what might be a massive attack from the new powers in the Delta."

Teague nodded his agreement.

The big meeting was set at a pagoda five klicks away and they left Duyet's headquarters as soon as they got word the other leaders, including Xam, were coming.

56

The core group left Duyet's headquarters and moved along the edges of a swampy jungle and rice paddies to the old temple.

There Teague, Moore, and a dozen other men squatted in the shade of a triangle of palms midway between the river and the temple as they waited for Xam's four-boat flotilla, bringing her and other representatives of the major leaders, to arrive. Engler was part of the escort from the river up the canal.

They were now less than two weeks to Tet and reports of mass communist movements were increasing by the day. They had to get into the cities very soon to prepare for the coming attack. The communists were avoiding getting bogged down in normal attacks and that made it easier for the rebel groups to move around without getting into battles.

The sect leaders from around the Mekong Delta began arriving down the rivers and canals for talks at this temple location. Four of the Yard leaders also were coming in and working to bring in factions from Laos and Cambodia with Acosta's. It was a serious coalition of forces being formed. It had Teague excited, but apprehensive.

The temple had vegetable gardens and rows of lesser buildings along its walls, giving it that same functional self-contained appearance as an old Spanish Church in the New World, except that its arches and pointed cornices betrayed its oriental focus. By Hoa Hao Buddhist standards, it was a little excessive and ornate. A monument to spiritual gaudiness that the Hoa Hao considered a corrupted form of true Buddhism. But it was a very convenient location for the meetings.

A dozen squads under Khiet's command were spread out all the way to the Bassac, protecting the approach of the other incoming leaders.

Near the closest stream where boats would be coming in Teague and a dozen soldiers were ready to deal with any issue that came up. Teague watched another boat pulled to shore under the overhang. He shifted, laying his Swedish K across his knees and propping his back against the base of the palm—the palm had been wrapped in betel vines near the base to keep the rats from going up and these vine twists made Teague uncomfortable, but he tried to ignore them.

Eventually he got up, rested his weapon against his leg and re-seated the clip and studied the area, waiting for the woman he had unlimited admiration for.

Nothing but the quiet of normal jungle sounds, the heat on the grass giving off a strong smell of decay and in the air a faint hint of incense. When he got word Xam was approaching, he waited on the narrow waterway near the temple walls.

When the flotilla of fast junks, led by Engler in the Wayward Angel, appeared in the narrow rivulet, Teague was standing on the bank waiting for her even as he was listening to the radio about the movement of government forces and Riverine force craft on the rivers. This was the final meeting before the movement toward the cities began.

Meetings went on at various parts of the temple all day long as the sun went down and dusk came up heavy, the cicadas and tree frogs loud.

He watched her as she talked to colleagues she had brought in from the different cities. Other boats snuck into the heavy grasses and more Hoa Hao came into the compound.

Xam finally found time to recognize his existence. She came over at one point. "You are hungry?" she asked.

"Always."

She removed the conical hat. "You become like Vietname'. Living is eating, eating is living. We have dinner."

He sat on a cushion on the floor on one side of a low table next to two of her soldiers; the visitors sat at other tables. They ate fish, shrimp, rice, and a vegetable soup and did little talking until they were finished. Moore and Khiet sat at another table, and occasionally spoke. The atmosphere between the leaders of various factions seemed excellent.

Xam told him she was leaving for Can Tho early in the morning. "We will meet with political and some local police leaders to discuss the security problem and see if there is a way to prevent so many troops leaving for the holidays with growing VC units so close."

He feared for her safety, but he knew he had to accept the reality of big risks.

Dark came perceptibly, palpably. Hooded cooking fires dotted the tree line but the temple was kept dark except for the gas lamps in the dining area. A few tents had tiny lights in them and the men moving around cast large shadows against the canvas. Many of the soldiers slept suspended from trees in hammocks covered with mosquito netting.

Teague sat on the low wall around the pond. He turned and there she was staring at him from a doorway. He slipped into a dark hallway with her. Then he followed her into a small room lit by an oil lamp and they embraced and kissed for a brief moment, then she backed away.

"It is very difficult for Vietnamese to understand their role with Americans," Xam said. "We struggle against ourselves. We have only a few groups who possess any vision for Vietnam. We have no political organization that has ever been allowed to grow to maturity. The social and political stress is very difficult. This is maybe the beginning of what needs to rise here and then spread north. We will have an attack in the Tet holidays. That must be prepared for."

Listening to her, he tried to imagine the contradictions the Vietnamese faced, particularly this woman, who was so political and intellectual.

Xam said, "We are in a terrible trap and seeking the right path out, a way to escape our growing dependency on the Americans and becoming the instrument of a new Vietnam. This is the problem Chandler and now you are helping us with. I had a wood carving on the wall above my bed when I was a little girl. It was the image of a young female warrior on a golden elephant. Her name was Triu An and she lived two thousand years ago. She had a very cruel sister-in-law and one day she could no longer stand the oppression. She killed this woman, then fled to the hills. She raised an army and led a revolt against the Chinese occupation forces. She revolted not just against the Chinese, but against Confucianism, against enslavement to family, village, court. I have always admired her. She did not win, but she refused to surrender."

"Is she the one who ended up committing suicide rather than bow to them?"

"Yes. We have many great woman leaders in our past. But most were the wives of men of the court. Our female nobles were equal to our men. But Triu An was different. My image of her is different. A nation free of foreign rulers is not enough. One must be free of oppression within the nation, the community, the family and most importantly, within one's own mind."

A voice informed them that her boat was ready. She took a few steps and then turned and looked at him, her expression strong, but sad. "Soon I will see you again—when we can proclaim a provisional revolutionary government for Vietnam."

"Chao co," he said.

Once again Teague watched her leave. She and others were headed to the cities to meet with those who were working with the rebel sects.

He stood with Moore, Khiet, Engler and a dozen soldiers on the bank. Khiet played with a cigarette and combed his hair with his fingers as he stood nearby watching the convoy twist up the flat ribbon of water, coppery in the sun, the boats slipping into the encircling folds of the hostile jungle, sliding away, until finally they disappeared altogether, they were swallowed up. Teague felt a sense of deep apprehension yet a powerful conviction. Between him and what he and all these rebels and Xam wanted stood the political and military forces on all sides that threatened to destroy them and their dreams.

His great fear was that, given the situation she was going into, he might never see her again.

Moore walked over and talked to some of his men from the mountains, then came back over. "We're getting close now. This is the time when a little luck helps. It's not going to be a picnic.

By the way, your lady looks like a young Madame Ba Cut, one very beautiful and tough woman."

"You've met Madame Ba Cut?"

"I had that privilege when I first went into Laos from Cambodia to meet the tribe leaders. She was being hunted and on the move, but I met her and we escorted her and her security force deep into the Seven Mountains area. Now, if there is a real revolution, she can move troops here and that'll be a major help."

They headed back into the deep jungle south of the Bassac River. General Duyet's main task was preparing his forces to create security for major cities like Can Tho, Vinh Long, Soc Trang and An Binh as the national forces seemed not to be taking the growing VC threat seriously.

Secret meetings were taking place in small villages all along the rivers in the western provinces and now in the major city centers.

Hoa Hao were going in to prepare the acceptance of their forces. A few were smuggling weapons in aboard sampans.

57

Reports coming in to Teague from Acosta's vast intel organization were not good and getting worse. The movements of the sect forces through the jungles and to the base camps had been picked up by new seismic devices. An attack appeared to be imminent. Stennride was moving forces and had acquired Viet Rangers and Special Forces to add to his growing army.

The secret little war was about to explode in the dark jungles south of the Bassac River. They'd been so careful, going completely dark, yet now they'd been discovered.

Teague's boat made a scraping sound as they brushed against the vines and tangle of heavy leaves.

Timing wasn't good as half of Duyet's soldiers had moved out toward three different cities to be ready when called on to go into those cities.

Teague ducked as they slid through a narrow passage where the fat latania fronds completely covered the water. Fifteen minutes later, the boat rammed into the bank.

Five of Khiet's men appeared, grabbing the bow and pulling the craft up out of the water as the men in it were jumping out. Engler and two men stayed behind with the boat.

Communications went out to all the teams to get ready and to alert and move peasants into safe areas.

Teague and Moore trudged on and were joined by dozens of men from the other. They headed through the swampy forest toward rice paddies. When the faint hum of a plane came to them, they all turned and craned skyward, listening. A small Cessna spotter plane came and went.

Moore glanced back at Teague with a shake of his head and a contemptuous look on his face. "Why don't they just send a telegram?"

They tromped to their destination through mud and water, reaching it near the edge of the paddy fields. It was getting light now, a silvery glow seeping into the tops of the trees.

The rice farmers were busy taking in the harvest. Women beat rice stalks against the threshing sheds in a swish slap, swish slap rhythm. On the road, the leather-faced laborers were hauling the rice toward the local mill; already the gleaners picked over the cleared fields like flocks of blackbirds in search of valuable grains.

Peasant women prepared for what was coming and buried rice in earthen jars and now worked through the night under tiny hooded lights that were immediately extinguished under conical hats at the warning of the listeners-for-planes.

Somewhere out in the pre-dawn came the faint sound of choppers with that distinctive thwack, thwack. That was, followed by gunfire from the north.

From far behind them near the hamlet, a soldier began yelling at the people in the fields to run. Other soldiers appeared from nowhere, as if up out of the ground, and began helping these peasants that lived too close to the paddies to leave and get deeper into the treeline and the underground tunnels.

The peasants began to abandon the work in the fields. Families grabbed up their children and were moving deep into the surrounding jungle in a very ordered, practiced retreat of people for whom war was a constant reality.

Duyet's hamlets were very well prepared twenty-four hours a day for attacks from either government forces or Viet Cong, but the forces that protected them had been depleted by the move to the cities and that was not good.

Teague glanced at the emptied fields. He knew that pockets of machine gunners were underground in various points in the jungles around the rice fields in these areas where Duyet operated. Other areas were mined.

Sapper teams would be moving now by boats and on foot to pre-designated locations. The general hadn't survived one of the greatest manhunts in history for nothing. The fields, only moments ago filled, were now empty.

Duyet protected an area that encompassed fifteen villages containing ninety-four hamlets with tens of thousands of peasants and it seemed every single one of them had been working virtually around the clock for the past three days to get this harvest in.

The sappers created ambush belts, concentration points, and a retreat path. More and more information came in from both the CIA and supporters of the movement that a major attack was coming.

Moore pointed out to the fields. "That's where we're going to bury these bastards if they attempt to dump troops in here." He turned to Teague. "I've been waiting for a day like this for a long, long time. I've got some personal getting-even to do."

"Looks like you're about to get your chance," Teague said.

What worried Teague was how they'd been located with

enough conviction that a major assault was underway. The choppers, dark as beetles against the iron-grey morning sky, appeared over the treetops.

The radio man handed Khiet the phone and he listened and then he informed Duyet of the situation. Then came messages from team leaders to the south and west of the base area reporting the appearance of the choppers and overflights of phantoms.

"We're gonna have some nasty fun today," Moore said, actually seeming excited with the tension of a man entering a contest he has prepared most of his life for and felt ready to win. Teague understood.

The wait was over with the arrival of Phantoms unloading their ordnance across the paddies and jungles. The brutal assault shook the tunnels and bunkers but didn't have the needed accuracy or clearance to do any real damage.

This initial assault was followed by powerful Cobra choppers who could come in much closer to lay down their fire and rockets. The counter-fire, per Duyet's orders, was limited, saved for the actual invasion they knew was coming.

The first chopper landed on the corner of the most hard-hit paddy area. The troops came out fast, tumbling on one another, and the chopper was leaping up as the last man fell out. He hit hard and stayed down.

Teague couldn't believe what was happening. Why would they put troops down here? Made no sense until the reason they wanted troops on the ground made its way across the top of the jungle to the north. A chopper appeared with a howitzer hanging from its belly.

Moore dropped down beside Teague. "What the hell, this is not going to be as much fun as I thought. You believe this shit? A Skikorsky Skycrane. Man, I haven't seen one of those babies lately."

The commandoes fanned out on the run, dark figures carrying heavy packs, bogged down so tight with gear in the mud and water of the rice field that several stumbled and fell.

Teague felt a strange contradictory mixture of elation and dread with that ineffable sensation one has in participating in some great violence, yet awed by it even as one loathes the potential consequences.

One of the Hoa Hao turned excitedly. "Dai-uy! You see?"

A gunship darted across the paddies—another sleek, fast, slope-nosed Cobra. Deadly sharks on the hunt.

"When did that bastard get his hands on those killing machines?" Moore asked, expressing the same wonder as the Viet.

A second Cobra reappeared. Teague noted grimly, "The Mad Colonel must have all the pull in the world." The hornet-nosed choppers slid along the treeline, apparently seeing if they could draw fire.

But the superbly disciplined Hoa Hao went back to remaining quiet and waiting for the troops in the field to decide to move.

When about half of the battalion had landed in three different points Duyet sent out the word to open fire.

Teague knelt behind the thick base of a banyan tree, peering out over the root watching the battle develop, firing occasional bursts when a target presented itself. Mortars popped from their tubes, rockets shot from their launchers with a violent swoosh and the M-60 machine guns rattled nervously. Regular forces never came in this fast. They were looking for a quick in and out of the kill. One that wasn't going to happen.

As the chopper with the howitzer hanging from its belly descended, the Cobras laid down massive fire that drove everyone down to whatever cover they had.

The chopper, after depositing the howitzer where the soldiers were, rose but didn't get far as massive fire from Duyet's commandos risked everything to fire at the chopper even as Cobras laid down fire on them. The chopper tilted, then fell and crashed in the paddy.

Teague and Moore and a dozen of Duyet's soldiers moved along the treeline, looking for the best angle to deal with the howitzer, hoping to take it out before it got operational.

58

Circling three thousand feet above the rice paddies and jungles, Colonel Stennride watched the ground forces set up the howitzer. The generals had given him what he needed, a real location filled with the enemy in a very remote area. It was time to deliver a big message.

The chopper that had been shot down would have been a disaster if it hadn't first landed the howitzer.

Stennride loved that he had superbly trained combat forces under his command and generals who finally understood the reality.

He sat in the co-pilot's seat with his map board on his lap. The chopper shuddered as Keller moved from a hover into translational flight.

Stennride switched to Trang's frequency. The young commander's chopper was about a quarter mile ahead out over the center of the battlefield. "Captain, put your howitzer into action."

"Yes, very good. We have the old fox trapped now—we kill him."

Stennride waited for the battle to unfold beneath them as they circled. He stared through his field glasses down at the forest and jungle, the burning houses, and hoped that treasonous bastard Teague was down there and would get blown to hell where he belonged.

The howitzers would drive the rebel forces deeper into the jungle and allow more and more troops to be dropped in. Airpower would prevent the rebels from escaping across the canals and rice fields. The speed and fury of the attack would break down the centralized command and control and turn the battle into a series of skirmishes all along the five-mile dog leg. Stennride was pleased. These bastards were finally going to be trapped and destroyed.

Stennride had equipment from the 9th ARVN Division and soldiers trained at the SOG base and now with the artillery battery in place, this would end fast and furious.

A trio of 105s aimed southward to cover the movements of the Ranger battalions that were on the move now, flanked by unseen PRUs who had been dropped on the edge of the forest. Almost two battalions, a little over a thousand men altogether, were going to rip the false army to sheds. Each piece of the attack had been carefully orchestrated.

"We'll show this little Third Force what the First Force endgame looks like," Stennride said.

Where in this whole miserable country could you find a South Vietnamese force that is properly trained, properly led, and free of debilitating political interference? He was looking at it as they engaged the enemy.

"Take it down to twenty-five hundred. I want to see this up close and personal."

The howitzer fired, the long barrel kicking back, the gunners, looking tiny on the ground, working in furious concert, tossing the empty shells aside, passing up and thrusting home new rounds, pulling the cord. It was a beautiful sight to behold.

Stennride swelled with the moment, tasting an illicit pleasure of surrounding and attacking his enemies, and something few men would ever taste—the command of a military force with no accountability except to him and his locked-in general worked outside their normal perimeters of action to save the goddamn country.

And down here in the rice paddies and jungles, the CIA's last grasp attempt at a revolution was going to be buried. Those bastards and all their secretive little plans, their conspiracies, needed to end right here and now.

He felt a powerful fulfillment, a sense of gratification he hadn't felt in a long time. His heart pumped boldly and he knew the pure joy, the thrill of the beginning of the final push. The sheer beauty of it was beyond description, those angry Cobra gunships buzzing around the treetops, those bull-throated 105s, and now the surge of the line of hardcore soldiers across the open fields—and not a single reporter, or, for that matter, apprehensive general, within a hundred miles. This kind of freedom was beautiful.

Finally, his generals were beginning to understand that they needed a force like his, a big secret force. And they needed to give him even more power and that meant Rolling Thunder. After he got rid of the rebels, the communists would be next and he needed the massive power to blow them into oblivion.

The only regret he felt about this most magnificent moment was that it, along with the entire campaign organized to bring the rogue elephant firmly under control, would sink into anonymity, buried, the silence of the super-secret operations where SOG-P joined SOG. It was not public notoriety or fame, but the teaching element in it that might be lost.

When the real triumphs went unheralded, only the catastrophes involving American and communist forces got press in this war. The irony of super-secret covert operations was precisely no one ever knew about them and this would be no exception.

Colonel Stennride's fantasy was that one day he could stand before the world and tell the hostile forces, the fools and idiots, that all their philosophizing, their love of communism and socialism was a pathetic joke. The expansion across Southeast Asia of Marx ended here in Vietnam. This victory would stay dark and he just had to accept that.

The colonel didn't yet have the power of Rolling Thunder here in the Delta but that would come. And soon would half a million American soldiers on the ground to clean up after the air power did its job. Finally, they would have the means to end this. The war machine that America needed to bomb the North and the Viet Cong back into the Stone Age where they belonged was just gearing up and that attack would push everything forward and fast and that's why the enemy was heading to the cities to hide from mass bombings.

But, first things first. That so much energy and time and resources were being wasted on the goddamn CIA's fantasies and building bases that were sucking up all the resources might well prove a stepping stone to a new all-out war. One where General Stennride would have a very big role and Teague's hero, General MacArthur, would be proven wrong about ground wars in Asia.

The nature of the game had changed. The secret of victory was the gap between technologies. It was all about that critical moment when the communist body count grew so fast the dead couldn't be replaced. That was the ultimate strategy of attrition.

59

Teague watched the tracer's narrow beams of light lance out across the fields, crisscrossing in the dawn's half-light like special effects from War of the Worlds. A chopper dropped more troops and when it pulled up to leave, it was hit and exploded; the troops that had exited jumped for cover as the chopper went down in the paddy.

Mortar rounds fell into the paddies, sending geysers of mud and water into the air. All hell was breaking loose and looked like it could all end here if they didn't find a way to take out that howitzer.

The electronically detonated mines that Duyet had planted were triggered but weren't close enough to the howitzer. The invading troops out in the paddy fields had to know now they had landed in a dangerous place and were eventually going to be cut to pieces.

The Cobra gunships attacked again, hitting the treeline with phosphorous rockets. Twice, Teague and the others in the treeline dove for cover and then popped up again.

Teague and those around him squeezed off steady bursts, trying to lead the choppers. But the Cobras proved elusive and fast targets and they turned again and again in a vain attempt to suppress the firing from the treeline.

Duyet's gunners laid down wilting crossfire and then vanished again only to move positions in order to avoid the Cobra attacks.

When the gunships made another appearance and the howitzer began direct fire, Teague followed Moore and half a dozen others as they moved deeper where there was some underground cover. They squirreled down into a tunnel.

Teague pressed his hands against the wooden support beams and waited until the flashlight revealed where he was moving and then he squirmed forward, his shoulders touching both sides of the walls, his knees scraping hard on the solid packed, cool earth. He pushed into a small underground bunker. Moore came behind him and Teague had to lean back in and help pull the big man through.

"I'd never hack it as a tunnel rat," Moore said.

"They didn't build these for buffalo," Teague countered.

One of the Viets who spoke good English translated and the others laughed and made some jokes.

The ground and walls of the underground tunnel shook with the impact of the bombs.

"A lot of dead men out in that paddy," Moore said.

Teague nodded. There would probably be a lot more soon.

"Maybe they've been told they're bombing VC," Moore said. "Or Stennride and his buddies now run the whole fucking military."

Just as Teague was thinking of going out, the bunker shuddered. "Bastards got us zeroed in," Moore said. "Dropping those babies right down the chute has to be stopped."

Khiet looked angry and grim in the glow of headlamps. He grabbed the radio from the operator and spoke to Duyet, then handed it back and came over to the map table. "Other government troops have been brought in as blocking forces." He marked the spots on the map.

"Damn," Teague said. "This kind of coordination involving ARVN units rarely happens. Never underestimate your adversary. These were elite Viet Special Forces and some Rangers who wore their red berets."

"That one-oh-five is in the perfect spot to bracket us," Teague said.

Dust hung in the bunker air. The shadows of the lamp danced wildly on the wall as the artillery rounds exploded in the trees above, sending a tremor down the tree trunks into the ground.

"We have to get that howitzer out of action and bring down one of those Cobras if we're going to turn this around," Teague said. That a howitzer would be dropped in was unexpected and very bad.

"No way to get to it except through the swamp." Moore replied.

"Bad swamp." Khiet shook his head.

"Give me ten men," Moore said. "We can take five rocket launchers and two mortar tubes. That swamp can't be worse than some of the places I've been. We have to knock that gun out and then get these bastards."

They came back up out of the tunnel and moved to where one of Duyet's squads was hunkered down. The swamp ahead looked dense and no doubt full of nasty creatures. But they had to get that howitzer out of action.

<u>60</u>

The swamp engulfed them and for Teague it was a much different and scarier environment than the mountains of Laos. The bamboo copse around the edge of the swamp was so heavy and thick that in places the trunks of the sixty-foot trees clustered too close to penetrate and they had to go sideways until they found ways through. And there was always the dread of running into the residents of the swamp: cobras, vipers, pythons, gators, and huge scorpions.

Teague pushed against the side of a rough clump of bamboo, stepped over a root and pushed on into the swamp, water up to his knees, the darkness relieved only by the faint hint of light above and the natural phosphorescence of the rotting swamp floor, a kind of greenish glow that gave the place an eeriness and a nearly suffocating stench.

In front of them, the point trooper moved through the water, his weapon held chest high. Teague could feel the big leeches falling on him, brushing them off fast before they could get a hold. And he could hear the whine of the thumbnail-sized mosquitoes around his ears. Nature exacting her revenge.

At places they were reduced to a cautious step at a time, having nothing but a tiny glow strip to indicate where the man in front was.

The bamboo made a creaking, breaking noise that grated on the nerves. They stopped for a moment. In the fermented luminosity, Teague could make out some of the ghost-like soldiers near him. He came up to Moore, who'd stopped and was wiping some of the sweat from his forehead with his curled arm and then pulling his hat back on. He glanced at Teague and shook his head as if to say this was a nasty environment. He no doubt preferred the mountains.

Teague struggled for oxygen in the steamy thick air. His lungs and his legs were tight. He took several deep, slow breaths and held them a moment and let the air out and then pushed forward. He had smelled burned flesh, rotting flesh, the excrement of dying men, but nothing compared to the sulfur stink of this cloying, choking swelter of rotting vegetation.

There was commotion behind him, a moment of intense furious struggle followed by a faint cry, then silence. After a few seconds, he heard men whispering in hushed voices.

Teague waited. Did a snake or gator get somebody? It was a chilling notion.

But they couldn't find whoever was in trouble and they had to keep moving. Teague grabbed a root and pulled himself out of the muck and up onto higher ground, his mud and water-soaked clothes dragging against him as he pushed forward through thick foliage. Vines and limbs ensnared him and he struggled to get free, putting his foot down on a limb in the water, slipped, falling to his knees, getting up and lunging on forward to get out of this mess.

They circled around the paddies through the swamp for another half hour, the exploding rockets and firing of cannons nonstop. It was not far, but they made such lousy time he estimated they hadn't gone more than a few hundred yards.

And then suddenly the light ahead was like they were coming out of a vast, nasty cave.

Now they moved a few yards at a time, stopped, listened, waited, then moved a few more yards. They inched forward, each tree cluster studied, each step careful.

And then, near the edge of the swamp, Teague knew they had finally made it and there would be no preemptive reception. The enemy had seen no reason to worry about anyone trying to get through this miserable swamp to attack them.

Teague and those around him squatted in little groups and began de-leeching, picking over one another like a family of monkeys. The Hoa Hao next to him held up a blood-bloated leech four inches long and fat. It was the biggest one Teague had ever seen. Half a dozen of those babies feeding on you could suck you out like goddamn vampires. Moore shook his head in amazement as the soldier threw the leech aside.

One of the men used a lighter heated knife to de-leech Moore. The sergeant cursed all through the process, calling the soldier every name he could think of, but he was obviously happy to be rid of the leeches.

Teague crawled forward until he could see through a break in the foliage. They had circled much closer to the big gun, but the soldiers had some protection from the paddy banks and they had those Cobras working the treelines and available to destroy any open field attack.

This little battle was stretching out and the longer it lasted, the worse for those attackers as more of Duyet's men from camps not far away would get here to engage. The concept of a fast, brutal strike was failing and that put the invaders in serious trouble.

Duyet's soldiers set the mortar tubes, calibrated them, fed in the rounds, set the LAAWs, and then, when it was all ready, Teague turned first one way, then the other, looking at the expectant faces.

They knew what would happen if they didn't get the entire battery out at once. Stennride's boys would lower the howitzer and fire point blank into the swamp's edge and that would be all she wrote.

Teague raised his arm, paused, and then lowered it, and the attack began.

He listened to the pop, pop and waited. The explosions came on each other's heels, both a little long. The adjustment was made. The next rounds flew skyward. The LAAWs fired and impacted in front and on the side of the battery, great fiery explosions, mud and water blasted twenty feet into the air. The next salvo of mortar rounds landed, one on target, the other short.

It was all very mechanical now, very much a matter of timing and relentless pressure. The invaders were on the verge of being trapped as more of Duyet's units were arriving.

Teague moved beside Moore at the jungle's edge and they watched soldiers at the artillery battery a hundred meters away turning the big gun, cranking it down and swinging it into position. They tore at its anchor and they lifted the base and shifted the howitzer just as two more mortar rounds dropped in on them.

The gunners vanished behind their mud banks and then reappeared a moment later, popping up and down like prairie dogs. Machine gun fire from the tree did not stop them from getting the gun around.

The Hoa Hao lobbed three more rounds of mortars in, but it was to no avail. Soon the enemy was ready to fire, the barrel of the 105 staring right at them.

"Hold your hats, ladies, we're gonna get slapped!" Moore yelled.

Teague sank down behind the tree, his back to the incoming round. The world shook under his feet, his ears and head felt as if the round had gone off inside his skull.

Dazed, he looked over and saw Moore pick himself up slowly, then stumble. Blood covered his left eye and he started to wipe it off.

"Get it out there. Lay it down!" Teague shouted as he made his way to Moore. He heard the single pop of the one tube left. Another rocket snaked out just as the big gun fired again.

The world exploded above them once again.

There were struggling gasps of the men hit, yet no calling for help as these were soldiers protected by the hard shell of their stoic Buddhism.

"Hey, wait!" Teague yelled at Moore.

But Moore didn't listen. He and two other men with him surged out into the paddy field in a crouch.

Teague watched Moore continue forward, his riot gun in one hand, a grenade in the other.

The men with the sergeant tried to give cover fire as he extended his body out further into the paddy. Craning in a half turn like a discus thrower, he hurled the grenade. It sailed into the grey morning sky, seeming to hang for a moment at its apogee, the last object left in the world, and then, turning slowly, methodically end over end, the metal pineapple arced downward, and it was a perfect throw and the blast silenced the gun crew.

A soldier popped up over the mud bank with a weapon and Moore blew the man away with a blast of his riot gun.

Then a Cobra chopper came in low and furious, cannons blazing as gunfire hit the water, ripping toward Moore, who tried to fire but the rage from the machine guns on the Cobra took him down.

Teague and two of the Yards raced to the fallen sergeant, as the others laid down a heavy cover fire.

But on reaching him, Teague knew with a terrible realization that one of the truly great warriors he'd ever met was gone, his lifeless body sinking in the paddy water.

The Cobras reappeared, driving everyone back into the cover of the jungle.

61

After refueling at his new remote base twenty miles north of the battle, Colonel Stennride had a hard time containing his mounting fury that the fighting had spread and was far from finished. Now was when he needed the big bombers and they were the one major force denied him at this moment as they were bombing the hell out of targets in the northern provinces. Time was now the enemy.

Instead of ending in the first hour, the attack had failed to come in fast enough and it was more like walking into a quagmire. It couldn't become a drawn-out battle. His forces were organized for a quick kill, in and out, not a drawn-out battle. He'd been given false info on just how big and organized the rebels were.

As he and Keller flew over the far end of the battlefield, it only got worse when they heard on their radio that the artillery battery had been knocked out and the flanking squads stopped and many killed. They passed over the remains of a temple lying in total ruin. Stennride said angrily, "What are these bastards doing down there. Goddammit, get over there!"

Keller banked and raced over the paddies, turning at the corner of the forest.

Through his powerful field glasses Stennride saw bodies lying in grotesque positions around the guns. It looked like a sandbox of toys and dolls in someone's messy backyard.

Feeling a chill of apprehension in his gut as more bad news came over his headset, Stennride told Keller to pull up and head for the dogleg where the troops were bogged down.

It was degenerating into a nightmare. More rebel forces were arriving and Captain Trang and his units were in big trouble. The rebels appeared to have regrouped and counterattacked with even greater numbers.

Stennride's radio had gone almost totally silent. Was he being interfered with?

He saw that the operation leader, Captain Trang, was now on the ground and running across the rice paddy dike toward the howitzer.

With only a few hours of daylight left, Stennride saw a growing catastrophe as the dying sunlight spilled through the multilayered clouds, turning the paddy fields and the jungle into a wild colored canvas.

With the well-laid plans unraveling, the ground commanders were all radioing for close air support. One platoon to the north was completely cut off. Another was retreating.

The strength of the counterattack had caught them all by surprise. It had come, not from the forest, but from the swamp behind Trang's units, from where a counterattack was never expected.

As they flew over the thick jungle/forest, the triple-layer treetops rising sixty feet in the air flowed by under Stennride's feet, foliage so dense firing into it was a waste of time, he felt the full anxiety of unacceptable failure.

Down there in this dense primeval forest, that bastard Teague and his sect fanatics had proved they had become more of a serious military force then he had assumed.

"We needed the goddamn B-52s rolling some thunder down there," Stennride said angrily, shaking his head in disgust because the goddamn bombers were busy and he was about to lose a major and very important battle.

The gunboats that were supposed to be in place as a blocking force had been attacked on the narrow river that led into the Bassac. Everything was going wrong and the whole operation appeared to be collapsing beneath them.

Stennride was beside himself, feeling sick, struggling to control his rage. He made a call he really didn't want to make. "Task Force Command to River One, over?"

Silence.

"Task Force Command to River One, over? Do you read me?"

Nothing. A little static broken by silence. Stennride stared at the implacable silence, the jungle, the twisting ribbon of water. It could not happen to him. He would not permit it. "Go up river."

The chopper darted above the river with its shadow racing on the tawny surface as Stennride played with the radio, switching from frequency to frequency. His communication was under attack. The fucking CIA.

About half a klick ahead, scattered all over the river, his gunboats were taking heavy fire, the river and rice paddies crisscrossed with tracers.

Stennride watched in hopeless desperation as his forces on the river and the land were getting chewed up. How had they been so deceived by the intel they'd been getting?

Then he was informed that the nine-boat flotilla appeared to have been bushwhacked along the narrowest point of the river.

Four of the boats were burning and half sunk, the others trapped in a withering crossfire of machine guns and rockets from the jungle.

What they faced down there was a revival of the once greatest fighters in the Mekong Delta with the goddamn CIA behind them, and it was worse than he'd seriously entertained. A retreat of his forces toward the canal, where the boats waited that had brought many of them into the battle, was in full swing.

Stennride said, in bitter defeat, "This little exercise looks like it's going to end in disaster. Maybe Trang can pull off a miracle, but that's what it will take." Defeat was unacceptable and the generals had no choice but to give him everything he wanted once they learned just how big the threat was.

And he learned now from the reports coming in that rebel forces from Cambodia and Laos had come in and were part of the fighting. The rebel forces had been greatly underestimated. That was another big problem as the intelligence sources weren't reliable. He had to find out just how big this was.

A retreat was underway. It was over and the rebels had won.

The intel operatives in MACV were useless when it came to understanding what was really going on. They had given the location but not size or anything that he was really dealing with. This little rebel force living in these jungles was in fact a growing and now heavily armed military force.

Failure was unacceptable. He needed to get help from the only people in the Delta who would know what the hell they were really facing. The people who once ran the country and after the loss of their war stayed on in the South to run most of the bigger businesses, hotels and restaurants and the drug trade on the rivers with the Corsican mob.

Stennride needed to go to the ultimate source of real intelligence in the Delta. As much as he didn't like the French, they were the ones who knew what was really happening. He'd heard that many of them were getting out in a big hurry and that wasn't a good sign.

And he knew who among them would be of help, the man who once ran the most powerful operations in the Delta for the French Expeditionary Corps. As the big dog in the deuxieme bureau that once handled the Cao Dai and Hoa Hao, Jean-Paul Vadot, who became one of the most important operatives in the Surete, would know everything that was happening across the Delta. He had to find out if the man was still in the country or had run off to Paris.

62

The reality of Moore's death stunned Teague and everyone in the core team. The sergeant represented the ultimate warrior medic, a man you could depend on under any circumstance.

Overwhelming as it was, they had little time to deal with the dead and wounded as the battle went on intermittently but violently into the evening.

Skirmishes were fought in the forest, in the fields, in two hamlets and on the waterways as the enemy retreated across canals and left the paddies empty. Somewhere the chatter of the 7.62 light machine gun fire tapered off, two short bursts, hesitation, one last quick shot, and then suddenly the jungle grew oddly still; even creatures like the ever-chattering cicadas had been driven to silence.

The light died in the bamboo and areca trees and became too weak now to filter down to the swampy floor. The last assault had been bloody. The enemy had penetrated two places before being repulsed.

Troops were filtering through the trees in long lines, some carrying wounded on their backs, or dragging the dead in ponchos. They would have to be taken care of in the villages and Duyet's camps as there would be no choppers to get them to hospitals.

The ceasefire came with the final withdrawal of the attacking forces. Duyet's men went out to collect their dead and wounded and the peasants came out to help. They would take the dead to where the coffins were already built near the base camps. The wounded would be taken care of in the villages.

The men lit small oil lamps with leaf shades, just enough light to see the ground. Then word came that some of the soldiers were bringing back Sergeant Moore.

The only light now, as the perfume lamps were extinguished, came from the tarpaulin that was acting as a field hospital where those with some medic training were working on the dozens of wounded.

The sapper team staggered in. First came three men, dirty, wet, their clothes torn. Then two more came, carrying a body hanging from a bamboo pole, hands and legs tied like safari porters lugging the day's kill.

Teague fought off the sorrow that threatened to engulf him at the death of so many and especially Moore.

The returning soldiers were covered with swamp slime. They gathered the wounded clinging to the backs of those who could walk as if they had been molded together. These weary soldiers who were unburdened, collapsed in exhaustion to the ground, some too tired to accept the cigarettes being handed around.

Waiting for them to arrive with Moore's body, Teague watched another straggler come in, crutching himself with his rifle, putting one foot forward and then dragging the other. He was also wounded in the face and had a filthy, bloody cloth wrapped across one eye.

Two men finally dragged Moore in on a stretcher made of bamboo limbs. Maybe they had carried the big man through the swamp, but now they had energy enough only to drag him.

Carefully, slowly, they laid the Special Forces soldier's body down. Soldiers began to gather around him, drawn by disbelief. They stared incredulously as children that so massive a force as this man was dead.

Khiet surged forward angrily, ordering the men to back off. He knelt beside Sergeant Moore and gently tried to close the man's eyes. He was very disturbed and one of the men offered him a cigarette. He smoked it in quick jerky puffs. He began to pace but then suddenly stopped and stared at the bodies.

Khiet asked the Hoa Hao soldiers to give the Yards room to deal with the loss of their bac se.

Teague stood by, reflecting how Vinh Lac and Chandler, Moore and so many of these superior fighters were dying at the hands of those who refused see the reality of the war. His anger knew few bounds. The only salvation was taking the Delta.

Then he walked angrily away into the blackness of the night and slowly allowed himself to feel some of what was happening around him. There was a special almost unstated communication he had had with Moore that he could only have with another American. His death was as devastating as that of Chandler and Vinh Lac.

The Yards will miss you, you bastard! Teague thought. The Hoa Hao will miss you too because you were a warrior in the best sense of the word. You never lost sight of what you were fighting for. He thought of how Moore had saved the girl whose hair had been ripped off by the boat propeller. He wondered about Moore's family, for the big man had seldom talked about home.

The thought that really bothered Teague at the moment was that he'd always planned someday in the future to visit Moore and they would sit down and have a beer and just reminisce. That was never going to happen now.

But there was little time to mourn. Word was coming in from Acosta that the Viet Cong and NVA were moving on the major cities. It was time to face the ultimate enemy.

Tet was already being celebrated, soldiers were leaving the cities for their ancestral homes and it was as if nobody in authority was paying any attention except for the defense of Saigon.

No victory out in the jungles and paddies by the Hoa Hao and their allies would lead to victory for what they were fighting for if the cities refused to accept them. But even the politicians in the cities weren't operating on their own. American power was reaching into every corner of their society and pushed them out and made them irrelevant.

More disturbing news came later as night fell. The infiltration by some members of Duyet's agents into the cities for negotiations was not being well received. Defeating Stennride's soldiers out here in the paddies and swamps wouldn't be enough if Xam and the other leaders negotiating in the major cities were not able to get clearance for the armed Hoa Hao and Cai Dai and other sects to come in to protect them from what was looking like a major communist offensive.

63

When Stennride's sources had discovered that Jean-Paul Vadot was leaving, he had Chien stop the plane before takeoff at the Can Tho airfield. They needed some answers and the Frenchman was the one who would have them. As a former senior member of the Surete, the French secret police, he would know how deep and pervasive the threat was.

Stopping the takeover of the cities was now at a critical stage and as Paulick put it, if you weren't strong enough to defeat the body, go for the head. Pressure was being put on the city leaders not to let armed Hoa Hao in, but whether they were listening was an unknown and Stennride had to find out fast.

Now, as he and Keller looked out at the stopped plane, the angry pilot of the arch-tailed Caribou leaned out the window looking for the reason.

Moments later the tail ramp fell with a bang and passengers that had moments before boarded now were forced to deplane and stood around in the harsh sun complaining loudly and indignantly in French and Vietnamese as heavily armed secret police directed them to where they could be watched in a spot with no shade.

Most of the passengers were either French landlords or the wives of Frenchmen. They had that hauteur of people more used to doing the pushing then being pushed, but now they were fleeing before the big Tet celebration. They knew a lot more than American or Viet intel.

Colonel Stennride, Keller beside him, stood at the air tower's second-floor window and watched secret police chief Chien arrive in a jeep, then get out and walk up to one of the French civilians, the very powerful and very rich businessman, Jean-Paul Vadot.

Stennride smiled and tapped his fingers on the window ledge. "That's right," Stennride said, as Vadot was being taken to the entrance to the air tower. "You frogs aren't hopping out of the pond all that easily."

A crack in the wall of silence was needed and now. What little intelligence that dribbled in, whether about the movement of the VC or that of the coup forces, was unreliable. The rivers of information turned to small streams after the defeat of Trang, then to dribbles once the communists began tightening the noose around one city after another.

Vadot, escorted by the secret police, came into the building up to where Stennride waited with Keller.

When Vadot saw who was in the room, his face turned livid.

"Going on vacation, monsieur?" Stennride asked.

"Qu'est-ce que c'est?" Vadot demanded, again glaring at Chien.

"Speak English. This is military business," Stennride snapped.

"My relations with the commissariat de police are excellent."

Vadot shot back. "General Loan—"

"Ils aient!" Chien said angrily, his eyes glaring at Vadot with reptilian flatness. "Voulez-vous porter plainte?"

"I suggest you have a seat," Stennride said, "And let's keep this in English, gentlemen."

Vadot sat down, but not back, leaning forward, as if he didn't expect to be here long.

There was a moment of intense silence.

Stennride said, "You'll talk to us here, and you'll talk to us now, or you don't go on your little trip. When your once powerful frogs turned filthy rich entrepreneurs of other people's wealth and property are suddenly jumping out of the pond, I want to know why."

"Listen, you bastard!" Vadot said, puffing himself up, accenting his swear words in a way that gave them high elegance. "You're making a very big mistake. You will not like the consequences."

"We're worried about consequences somewhat grander than anything you're likely to manufacture," Stennride shot back. "You're attempting to exit with a fortune in valuables, unknown quantities of jade, gold and opium. Major Chien could have you shot, along with some of your countrymen, unless you cooperate. We're in no mood to play games." Stennride's voice trailed off quietly, giving maximum emphasis to the threat, a threat he knew Vadot would take seriously.

"And what is it you wish me to cooperate with?"

"Boxers watch their opponent's eyes," Stennride said. "That's the best way to determine where the punch is coming from, and when. The eyes in this case are the movements of the French community, former overlords. When former rulers turn into runners, there's good reason."

"We lost here"—Vadot fumbled for a cigarette and finally got it lit— "because we lacked the assets, not the method. You have the opposite problem."

"You French lost here, lost in Algeria, lost on the Maginot Line, not for a lack of assets, but for a lack of will and imagination—plus a touch of decadence."

Vadot smiled derisively. "As the great Ortege Y Gasset suggested, no matter how rotten the Europeans, it is a certainty that neither the Americans nor the Russians have the leadership capacity to replace Europeans on the world stage. I feel he will be proven correct."

Stennride tired quickly of the glib repartee. "No nation that has managed to lose three wars in a row deserves respect. You want to leave Vietnam with your hoard of goodies and your beautiful wife, your third, or is she number four? Anyway, you will give us the information we want. Just a very simple bit of information—the time and date of the CIA-sponsored upcoming coup and its primary leaders in the major cities and who in those cities are the radical Hoa Hao supporters and operatives. Also, when the armed Hoa Hao are coming in and in what cities."

"I know nothing of any coup. We are leaving because of the communists, not the CIA. I'm familiar with your activities since coming into the Delta and I don't agree with them."

The sun attacking the windows cut long angles across the room, leaving Vadot's face in two wedges, an eye in each, like a surreal French painting.

Stennride got up and went over to the window. "It's not the VC or your opinions I'm worried about. We have the means now to bomb the VC and the NVA into oblivion. What I'm dealing with is a little cabal being planned by the radical sects and their CIA backers who've been pulling this shit for a decade. And I know that you know who they are and what they're planning. Now it's serious and has to be stopped."

He paused a moment, containing his anger, then said, "Vadot, your friends are standing in the sun under the watch of the police. Your wife is a very pretty woman who is too young for you. So, let's talk about the real threat here in the Delta."

"What you are doing," Vadot said, "besides being stupid and illegal, can become very public. I have powerful friends and I imagine they will hear quickly about this outrage. Even a head as bloated with power as yours, Colonel, has been known to roll on occasion."

Stennride smiled and shook his head as he looked out the window at the women in large hats, some with parasols resting lazily on their shoulders to shade themselves. "We shall see." Many were sitting on luggage. They talked little and moved less. The sun beat relentlessly down on them. They had neither water nor shade.

The colonel turned and said forcefully, threateningly, "I want a list of significant names working the system right now in the major Delta cities and I'll keep you here until I get them."

"I can't do that."

"I'll let you think about it. And that great power of your friends and associates, most of them part of a criminal enterprise that stretches from Saigon to Cambodia, Laos and beyond is coming to an end. If the fanatic Hoa Hao take over, the days of French exploitation of this former colony is fini. And, if things don't go well right here, right now, that end for you and your associates won't be pleasant."

When Vadot had no response, Stennride turned to Chien. "What's that French war song?

Chien intoned, "Chacun son tour . . . aujourd'hui le tien, demain le mien. To each his turn . . . today yours, tomorrow mine."

Stennride went into an adjoining room to get another cup of coffee, giving the Frenchman a few minutes to think about the situation. He'd outlasted his country's colonial defeat and substituted power for wealth. But that was coming to an end.

When he returned ten minutes later, Stennride said, "You have nothing to gain and everything to lose and no one who can protect you at this critical juncture. We will begin taking your friends out one by one for interrogation in a small airless room at the Center. Your wife as well. You are a tough man and one wouldn't expect you to crack very easily. But—"

"You bastard, I will never forget this!" Vadot uttered with a threatening bitterness.

"I would hope not. When are the radicals going to strike?"

This time it was Vadot who walked to the window and stood looking at his people.

Finally, when he turned back to Stennride, he said, "The sect leaders are negotiating with city officials across the Delta. They want to come back into the cities as a major protective armed force. My information is that the leaders aren't in a position to allow that due to pressure from the Americans and Saigon. They may already have the political 'assets' they need to gain a foothold, but that's as far as it goes. At least right now."

"What else?"

"My sources tell me the CIA's private military force is being advised by a former American Riverine commander who is highly respected by naval forces on the rivers, as he is by the Vietnamese peasants."

"How many ARVN Units are involved?"

"I don't know."

"Do the rebels have any force in the cities?"

"Small teams in the major cities working out details. As you well know, many of Saigon's forces here in the Delta are on leave

for Tet. The cities are virtually wide open. And there's a
suggestion that the Viet Cong are offering a peace accord for Tet
to get everyone to relax."

"Is Nguyen Cao Ky involved in some way?" Stennride asked.

"Not that I know. He's used as a diversion. That is all that I
know, Colonel."

"You want to get out of Vietnam with all your friends and
family, you will give me something of substance. I need names,
positions."

It took Vadot a minute to gather himself as he again stared out
the window at his wife and the others in the midday sun. Stennride
nodded to Keller, who handed the Frenchman a notepad and pen.

"Give me names and locations. Those I really have to worry
about. I'm familiar with Duyet and his jungle forces, but I'm
talking about those trying to convince the city leaders to let an
armed Hoa Hao in supposedly to protect from a communist
invasion, when in reality it's a ploy to take over the Delta."

Vadot wrote down some names and handed it back to Keller
and said, "Vinh Lac may be dead, but his sister is a rising force. It
happens all the time in Indochina when things are falling apart,
some strong female shows up. If I tell you where she is at the
moment, and she's very vulnerable, you must let us go
immediately. She can tell you everything, including where this
Teague is."

Stennride looked at the names he'd written down. Then he
nodded, saying, "You have my word. Where is she?" Xam would
be a major asset and they needed to get her fast.

Vadot hesitated, obviously not liking any of this. But his
friends and his wife needed him to cooperate and Vadot knew he
had no power to stop what Stennride might do. He and his
associates and wife would be dealing with the Hoat Vu.

"She is, as far as I know, right here in Can Tho trying to talk leaders into allowing armed sect forces to come in to protect this major city."

"The American ex-naval officer with her?"

"Not that I know."

"What about this peace accord?"

Vadot studied him for a moment. "Anyone who thinks that's real is nuts. The communists will attack during Tet as they did once before eight years ago. Only this time it will be much bigger. Which is why we're getting out. The reality is they are being decimated by American airpower and they need something big to turn this war around. They believe that once in the cities, no one will be able get them out. And while you Americans can bomb the hell out of the jungles and rice paddies and use millions of gallons of herbicides to clean out half the forests, you won't be able to use those powers in the cities. That, Colonel, is a reality you'll have to deal with."

Stennride turned to Major Chien. "Send Vadot and his people on their way. Then find and arrest this Xam woman. But make damn sure she stays alive. I need her as bait to get the others, including Teague."

He turned to Vadot. "We now have some very sophisticated radio intercept equipment and we have plenty of agents operating in and around the Saigon power centers. Don't play games. We're everywhere and that includes France. Go and keep quiet."

After Vadot was taken out to the plane, Stennride informed General Paulick about the situation. Paulick wanted an immediate meeting and wanted it at the colonel's compound.

That meant to Stennride that something big was going on with the generals. He even wondered if because of the disaster in the battle with the CIA dark forces that he might be getting fired.

64

It was General Paulick's first visit to the colonel's new home in the Delta and Stennride met him as he got out of his chopper. "Welcome, General."

Paulick looked around at the security forces in training, the grounds and multiple buildings. "Regular damn fortress, Colonel."

"Better safe than sorry, as they say."

He led the general into his office/war room where Keller was on the radio. He saluted the general and then went into the next room to give them some privacy.

Stennride expected to get bad news and to be somehow castigated for the failure in the jungles and then fired from his position and replaced.

"What the hell happened down there, Colonel? You had one hell of a lot of power at your disposal."

The general knew damn well what happened but apparently wanted to hear it again, up close. "We came up against a coalition of sects much bigger than we expected. Some came out of the mountains, others from the Free Khmer. We lacked ground intelligence sources. Now the sects are negotiating to get into the cities. To get greater insight of what was under the surface, I stopped that plane and had a little conversation with Jean-Paul Vadot. I wanted names and information about the leaders in the cities who might be a problem. They have to be threatened with major retaliation."

Paulick nodded and lit a cigarette. He sat in one of the wicker chairs to the side of Stennride's big desk and moved an ashtray closer.

Stennride waited, very unsure what was coming.

Paulick sat back and said, "You get usable information from Vadot?"

"Yes. We're moving on Vinh Lac's sister and other leaders."

"Good. That little defeat you suffered near the Seven Mountains is actually looking like something of a victory."

"And how is that?"

"Well, panic is a major driving force. The powers at the top finally really listened to me and to some reports. It forced certain serious negotiations with top elements in the CIA and we're reaching all the way to Washington. I think we'll win this battle and that'll put you in a very good position to clean up the mess soon. The idea of a radical takeover of the cities is unacceptable. This is going all the way to the White House. And now they know about this secret dark operation that aims at creating an alternative to Saigon's rule. Never going to be allowed to happen."

Stennride was a bit shocked.

Paulick said, "We're going to put a stop to this from the top. The CIA is facing major heat. There will be no city in the Delta that accepts the armed elements coming in from the jungles. So, you won't have to deal with them. You and Chien are free to go after those trying to negotiate. All the leaders in the cities and provinces understand that there will be no Third Force. Clean it up."

Stennride was beside himself. "We're going to make a move on Vinh Lac's sister and her team. We get them, and it'll go a long way to getting Teague and put us in a really good position. If the CIA backs down it will leave the rebels out in no-man's-land."

"Good. They can surrender or be wiped out. But don't lose any more battles," the general said with a wry grin as he got to his feet. "I have to make a couple stops on my way back. I'll keep you informed. But it looks good. MACV is running this war now, not Saigon or the CIA. The rebels need to know the new reality. The Hoa Hao will not survive re-armed. That's out of the question. Without CIA support, it's over. And if they stay an armed rebel force out in the jungles you'll get your rolling thunder and they'll go down as just another Viet Cong force. Those agents with the CIA who are behind this are being told how this has to end."

Stennride walked the general out to his waiting chopper and thanked him for his help.

When the colonel came back into the office after the general's chopper went airborne, Keller came in to hear the news.

"Let's have a couple beers. We're going to have a little celebration even if it looks a bit premature. The generals have finally fully awakened here and in D.C. They'll put a stop to any re-armed Hoa Hao getting in the cities and they're putting an arm lock on the CIA. This could all end quickly. Anything from Giac on the Xam woman?"

"They know where she is and will grab her when it won't create a major battle that could get her killed."

"Good." Stennride took the offered beer. "They won in the

jungles, but they won't win in the cities and that is where it will count in the end. In fact, as the general admitted, getting our asses kicked was the best thing that could have happened. Now we can do the clean-up and if the Hoa Hao don't agree to surrender their arms, they will get blown off the face of the earth. So maybe our defeat may turn out to be a major victory."

They clinked bottles.

"What if the communists do attack and take the cities?"

"They won't. If they were successful, the cities would end up getting some Rolling Thunder and massive ground troops that are on the way. I was thinking as he landed that we might get the boot and I'd have to open a restaurant in Phoenix."

Keller laughed. "I'm not a bad cook."

65

Until he received an urgent message from JK to meet him that night, the victory over Stennride's forces in the deep jungles and the growth of the coalition had put Frank Acosta in a very positive mood. He felt it was all going to come together and Chandler's dream might just have a real chance of coming to fruition and damn soon. Armed Hoa Hao needed to be in the cities in the next few days.

Acosta was in Saigon dealing with the Jeh baby, making sure that was being handled right. He had no intention of becoming the boy's papa, but he wanted him well cared for and put up for adoption.

After leaving the orphanage, he went to a bar on top of the Caravelle Hotel where he met with three reporters he'd known for years. It was air-conditioned, had a ceiling with soft lights and music and the windows were taped in case of explosions.

"Gentlemen, it's good to see you." He shook hands and the

three of them settled in the corner table.

He was in a very good mood, fully convinced now that Teague and his associates were living up to and even beyond the ambitions of the dream of the emergence of a Third Force.

Acosta always tried to convince his reporter friends that he was working with AID, but did so tongue in cheek. They knew he was a full-on CIA operative actually running clandestine, off the record operations, and they were always looking for some inside material. He'd feed them bits and pieces from time to time to get them expectant and excited as he did now after buying another round of drinks.

Jason Newbury, who'd been a reporter for the New York Times for half his life, said, "Frank, what do you think of this peace accord? Is it going to work?"

"We'll see. Be nice if it did."

Bill Harrison, one of the best writers about the war, said, "My sources tell me something major is in the works. A big and necessary change in how this country is being run. Not another coup, but a real movement with deep roots and it's very powerful."

He loved when they pressed him, begged him. But he wanted them ready for something big. He told them they needed to be prepared and that he'd give them a lot more information soon about something big. "There is a revolution in the works and when it happens, you'll be the first reporters to get the story."

He loved the game of hide-and-seek with these guys.

"Are you talking about Nguyen Cao Ky?" Dennis Easterwood, a freelance photographer asked. "I've heard he is getting very restless."

"I'll let you know very soon, but no, I'm not talking about Ky. He's just another musical chair. Has no roots except those on his head sprouting out of his giant ego."

They laughed but insisted on more.

Acosta looked around, then came back to the journalists. "Keep your eyes on the Mekong Delta. And be ready to go there when the time is right."

Harrison asked point blank, "You talking about the Buddhist sects, the Cao Dai and Hoa Hao?"

He smiled, finished his drink and said, before getting up to leave them, "Let's just say that if things work out, it'll be a very big story. I'll be in contact with you very soon, so don't go anywhere. I have to go see a partner of mine."

After he left the reporters, he went for a walk, cutting down Tu Do street and all its girlie shops and bars and then turned on the Street of Flowers in the midst of a swarm of pre-Tet shoppers.

Acosta loved walking the streets of Saigon in the evenings. But things had changed. The flotsam of the war festered around him on the exhaust fumes, the crowded, darkened streets. He watched the rich ladies at the elegant French shops and coming out of beauty salons and the beggars and porno card sellers, boysons hawking their twelve-year-old sisters for fifty piasters.

When he crossed a main intersection he watched the traffic controller in his little stand, called by Americans 'white mice' because of their white uniforms, busy blowing his whistle at the mad-hatter traffic, at the craziness of the intersections created by insane drivers, revving like they were at the Indy 500 while their endangered fellow citizens leisurely strolled across as if they were in a park.

Acosta thought of North Vietnam's General Giap, defeater of the French, who had once remarked that the death of tens of thousands meant nothing by itself. What mattered was the effect of their death, not the fact of it, and that was why they could throw endless young to their end in pursuit of what was happening at the very moment in in the outpost at Khe Sanh that remained under siege and had become an obsession with Westmoreland and Washington. No matter how many were killed, they just kept coming. That obsession took the eyes off of what was happening around the cities and in the Delta.

Having witnessed Vietnam's seven coups and attempted coups, this might just be the moment he and JK and Chandler and others in various agencies had been waiting for. Coups were about power changes at the top when what was needed was power of revolution rising from the people and it might very well be happening.

Acosta continued down the streets of Saigon and entered the Chinese section overrun with minnow swarms of black-haired, round-faced kids, past restaurant windows with lacquered chickens hanging in them and the sound of sizzling pork, past laundry fluttering from second floor balconies, and barbers cutting hair in the open medium, their mirrors hanging from trees; everywhere the oriental music and oriental singsong lapping over this beehive of celebrations.

JK called him. "Where are you?"

"Be there in a couple minutes." He didn't like the sound of JK's voice.

When Acosta reached the building where JK had his pad, he took the elevator to the third floor and then walked down the hall to the end room. He put his hand under his shirt on his Wather P-38 and moved cautiously toward the door of the old French hotel. He said, "JK?"

"It's open."

Acosta pushed the door open with his foot and kept out of the line of fire.

"Jesus Christ. What are you doing?" JK said, not amused. "You paranoid bastard, think I'm working for SMERSH, or what?"

"Why not?" Acosta said. He glanced at the agent's packed bags, the cleaned-out apartment. Acosta put his weapon down on the table as he sank into the chair and, looking at the packed bags, turned to JK. "What the hell's going on?"

"I'm going to Washington," JK said. "And it looks like this operation is going to hell."

Acosta studied the man skeptically, not easily buying into anything he was saying. He's bailing out, Acosta thought, but why now? "What are you talking about? This operation is ready to roll. We're finally where we need to be."

JK shook his head. "They may be, but it might not matter. Things have changed and changed quickly. We're getting the rug pulled out from under us."

"What the hell are you talking about?"

"They want me in Washington and that's not good."

"Bullshit. This isn't real. I can't believe they'd attempt to stop us at the last goddamn hour."

"Frank, I know you're excited because of what happened in that little battle near the Seven Mountains, but it has triggered panic at the top and in Washington. This victory over Stennride could turn into our defeat. You need to warn Teague that things might unravel very soon. The agency is getting a ton of shit and they're pulling back. I'm talking project termination."

"Jesus Christ, you can't be serious."

"The big boys are worried that there's major flap potential. We're losing all our programs as well. MACV is taking over. Even the Phoenix program will be in their hands before it really gets going."

"This is fucking crazy. I'm not sure I can believe you. How could things go this far, be on the verge of success, and suddenly everybody gets cold feet."

JK studied him intently. "You aren't hearing me. The CIA is being reduced to a sideshow. It's over. I've been talking to the top dogs. I'm getting out. We're done. This goddamn colonel is the golden boy and his screw up in the jungle is turning out to be the best thing that could have happened to him because it panicked the generals all the way to D.C. I'm also hearing he had a plane held in Can Tho so he could have a pleasant conversation with Jean-Paul Vadot about who is in the cities doing the negotiating. It's over."

Acosta was stunned and outraged. "This is insane. We have a goddamn Third Force ready to go. They're ready, goddammit. They can't just leave them out to hang."

"I'm as devastated as you are. But the insurgency needed already happened. We're talking now about big-time war coming down the pike. You see what's happening here with the communist threatening Saigon and Westy pulling all those troops back from the border? They're going to rename Saigon Panic City. I'm getting the hell out and you need to really think about what you want to do. It's over."

"I can't believe this. Just like that. All the work, the deaths, the organization."

JK toyed with lighting a cigarette. "It's what Chandler feared might happen just as it did in the fifties. I'm tired and my true believer days are over. You have to figure out what you want to do. We lost thousands of American soldiers last year and many more are going to die with MACV and Westmoreland totally committed to the current policy. It's over for us."

Acosta was stunned and enraged. He was so caught off guard it was a shock he couldn't process. "We can't just abandon what we've created. A lot of people have died to make this possible. How can we just abandon them?"

"That's the nature of the beast. Chandler is dead, and now, unfortunately, so is his dream. You've seen this kind of thing many times. A course is followed and then suddenly changed. It's what these bastards do. Teague and his people won the battle, but that may cost them the war. Instead of backing off, Stennride's supporters are going to go all-out to bury this. I would get hold of Teague and let him know the situation. It boils down to disarming once again."

This was insane. Not yet again. "Jesus Christ. After all we went through. All they did to make this possible. They won't accept this. It can't happen."

"It did. If they know where the main rebel camps are, and if the cities won't let them in, it might be over very fast and not pleasant. What happened in that little battle has some generals who hate our operations really pissed off and nervous. They had a lot of power and decided to use it. There is right now absolutely no support anywhere for the rise of a Third Force. Those days are over. It evaporated practically overnight. Everything is changing and fast. If it works the way I think it will, the only way the sect rebels are going to survive are those who once again agree to disarm. If, that is, Vietnam survives what's coming. Look, it's crazy and the whole fucking war is getting crazier every day."

Frank Acosta struggled to absorb this madness, this betrayal. His anger was overflowing throughout his system. He wondered just what JK's role was in what now looked like an unacceptable, ignominious capitulation.

After a long silence between them, JK said, "Colonel Stennride and Major Chien may know who is in the cities negotiating. They'll be hunted down and arrested or killed. This is coming from French intel. You best get that information to the leaders and fast and get them out of harm's way."

"Are we that big of fools that this shit happens over and over and all the dedicated geniuses get nervous and pull the rug out from under us and reverse course? Is there never going to be a time when this becomes unacceptable, a time when these bureaucratic bastards finally grow a pair?"

"I don't know. But I do know that time hasn't arrived."

"This is insane," Acosta said.

JK nodded and said, "There are even some fools up top who actually think this peace accord might be a step toward real peace. The reason for it is simply that the communists don't want Saigon to cancel the Tet leaves, they want the soldiers to go to their homes and villages to celebrate. And there will be a full agreement for this idiotic peace accord. And here's another kicker—Rolling Thunder will be fully opened to hit the Transbassac and that means it'll get ugly. You need to warn Teague and let him know exactly what's going on so he can warn the rebel commanders. They are not going to be allowed into the cities and if they hang around outside, they'll end up in the same bomb runs that will be going after the Viet Cong and NVA. This war is about to become full-on nasty."

Acosta was beyond stunned. He had to talk to some others operatives. He had to make damn sure this was real. The idea of having to deliver this kind of news was sickening. It was a full-on betrayal. And delivering the news to the coalition of rebel sect forces was not something he wanted to do. But if what JK was telling him was true, he'd have no other choice.

At the moment, Acosta hated everyone in the establishment on both sides of the aisle, MACV and CIA and their masters in Washington.

66

As his junk and two others slipped down through a tight waterway toward the Bassac River as darkness threatened, Teague's attempts to contact his CIA mentors at this critical time went unanswered for fifteen hours. What the hell was going on?

But when he finally got the call-back from Acosta, it was shocking. He had to have the message repeated. Not only did Acosta say they were losing support from the agency, but that no city was welcoming armed sects partly because of the peace accord but mostly because of threats and pressure from MACV and Saigon.

Khiet made some calls and things weren't looking good.

Just like that. It was unbelievable. Acosta was making deep probes and would let them know exactly how bad things were. If high-level support was disappearing, it would be a massive betrayal much like what had happened before.

They waited for twenty-four hours, getting only occasional messages from Acosta saying that contact with those in the cities had to be restricted in case the radio traffic was being monitored.

Teague stared at the river they were about to cross. The last thing Xam and Duyet would even consider was going in by force if not invited. That would trigger a major confrontation and it would be a gift to the communist forces. But if they were denied acceptance, it would leave them in a disastrous position.

When Acosta came back to him with confirmation, it was not good. "We've had the rug pulled out once again and it is very serious. If the forces under Duyet don't comply, they will face massive air power. And you need to get Xam and the others who are already in Can Tho, Soc Trang and other cities out and out fast."

"How did this happen?"

"I don't know. Maybe there's something behind this Tet Peace Accord nobody is talking about. In any event, the Hoa Hao once again have to agree to disarm. It's insane, but it's going to happen one way or another."

That the Hoa Hao's only chances of survival was to once again surrender their arms, and after all that had been done to form a real alternative that included the Cao Dai, Free Khmer and Yards was so shocking and unexpected it was very hard to process. A massive betrayal from on high after all that had been accomplished!

Across the Delta, armed Hoa Hao were waiting for permission to move from the jungles and forests and into the cities to protect them from the expected mass attacks. It was considered an opportune moment. Instead it was all falling apart because MACV was taking over the entire war and the CIA had capitulated.

Stennride may have lost in the rice paddies, but he had won in the higher echelons of power. Why? What the hell happened?

Teague couldn't believe it was over just like that and he wasn't sure he could accept it.

"You don't look happy," Engler said, as he steered the junk through the heavy foliage. They talked with Khiet about the mess and none of them could grasp the reality in any way that made sense.

Khiet had to do what he loathed doing, and that was informing Duyet and other commanders that the resistance to entering the cities was no longer backed by the CIA, who'd surrendered to the military.

Meanwhile there was no contact with Xam in Can Tho, nothing about where she was in the city, or who she was meeting with.

The rebel Hoa Hao camps that were deep in the U Minh forest had left behind empty coffins as was custom. These were standing end-to-end waiting for those who would make it. Vietnamese normally built their coffins about twenty years before they expected to die. Now it looked like they'd be using them much earlier if they didn't back down.

Absorbing this sudden collapse of support when they had reached a position of real strength was a blow that Teague simply didn't know how to engage, to process. It was a betrayal on a level and at a time he had a very hard time accepting, as did the other commanders. Nobody would handle this easily. All that had gone into re-arming and reorganizing the sects and their allies was just being thrown overboard.

Khiet learned that Duyet had begun ordering his troops and the aligned forces to back off and retreat back into the jungles and mountains and wait for a better time, leaving the cities to fend for themselves except for the small detachments that had already gone into the cities to prepare for larger forces.

Now it came down to getting the negotiating teams in the

cities out. And for Teague that centered on Xam.

The junks continued slowly and carefully toward Can Tho, but decided not to get in too close as they still had no word from Xam or her small team and needed to be sure they had an exit plan once they made contact.

Teague and Khiet and a team of a dozen soldiers left the boat and would go in on foot. Engler and his three-man crew would take the boats to secure locations to wait for them to get Xam. The trailing junks headed for more secure locations.

They moved along the river and then inland near a village on foot.

With the aid of the stars, and the distant light of street lamps in the town itself, he could see the villages that surrounded Can Tho clearly outlined and the celebrations going on nonstop.

It was late and the clouds kept shifting so the moon was one minute blotted out and the next pouring a deadly light down on them. The news from their contacts in the cities was that communists were moving in tighter and tighter with each lost hour and they were practically shoulder to shoulder with some of the VC units now. Yet the celebrations went on.

This is very wrong, insane, Teague thought as he pressed his face against the dry hard weeds and clay along the canal bank, smelling the richness of the clay. He checked the thin film of tape that covered the muzzle to assure himself it had not been penetrated by dirt. Seconds lengthened into minutes, and the sense of time blurred with the surroundings until everything melted into a timeless tension.

He tried not to think about the disaster. His focus was on getting Xam out of the city before the communists hit.

Khiet had communication with friends and relatives in the outskirts of Can Tho and they had safe houses that the squad could stay in as they worked out where Xam and her people were and how to get them out.

The time it had taken to orchestrate the strategic withdrawal had lost them time and now the situation had changed drastically. A battalion of VC lay out there to their right and another to their left and they knew not what awaited dead ahead.

Teague and Khiet huddled over a map of Can Tho. Khiet ran his fingers over the route. "Once we get Xam and her team out we'll go across here and cut between Ap Due and the village center here. This is Cai Be."

It was time to go in, find her and get her out. That's all that mattered now and Teague was scared she might be in serious jeopardy. He pushed back his shock and anger and focused on getting into Can Tho.

67

In the early darkness, Teague, Khiet and a dozen Hoa Hao soldiers slipped down narrow trails and across the dikes of the rice fields to the villages on the western edge of Can Tho.

They were moving through the rice paddies west of the city when suddenly the clouds shifted, exposing them, bathing them in the shrill, pale moon and starlight and they weren't alone.

The communists were about fifty yards away, moving obliquely across their path from one tree line to the next.

Instinctively, Teague hunched down so his American height wouldn't betray him.

Both the Hoa Hao and the VC columns froze. If they continued they would have crossed each other's path dead center in the rice paddies.

The communists hesitated. Voices filtered across the dry fields. A light breeze from the south-westerly winds made it easy to hear them. Teague tensed. It could get ugly fast.

The VC commander wanted to know who their unit was.

They were both in a very bad position. It was obvious that the VC commander had no desire to get bogged down here, but at the same time either he or somebody else had screwed up. No ARVN forces would normally be out here at night, let alone during Tet.

Without hesitation, Khiet answered that he was the commander of a special sapper unit connected to the VC 309th Main Force.

The VC platoon was about twice the size of Khiet's and they seemed to be carrying some heavy equipment. Teague couldn't make out what it was, but it looked like they were pulling recoilless rifles on carts.

The VC commander had to choose. If he didn't believe Khiet, he could fake belief and pass in hopes of getting into a better position, or he could open fire now, which put him in a slightly worse situation then the Hoa Hao. It was a simple enough choice and he had to make it quickly, but he hesitated. A battle here would end their operation, win or lose.

"Tien len! Tien len!" Khiet shouted angrily.

Still the VC commander hesitated. Then said he wanted to see Khiet's orders. "Di ra. Cho xem chung minh—" He never finished.

A hush fell over the paddy field. The barely audible sound of a small plane fell on them.

The VC commander shouted to his men to move.

The Hoa Hao waited, crouching down. The plane dropped a flare and the burst of hard orange light. Teague quickly covered one eye to protect his night vision.

The pilot must be shitting himself, Teague thought. Probably so excited he couldn't think straight as he struggled to radio the coordinates and if anybody's awake, soon artillery shells would start dropping in a matter of minutes. Then Khiet, listening to radio traffic, said "Puff coming. We're gonna get hit."

A C-47 'Puff the Magic Dragon' with three powerful mini-guns that could pump out massive rounds per minute was coming toward them like a fury-driven sky dragon.

The VC unit scrambled back toward the treeline to the right, so Khiet waved his men forward. It would have been quicker to retreat, but it would put them with the communists. They were double-timing now, not easy in rice paddies on narrow dikes.

Then from somewhere over the treeline behind them, a shell exploded. The Forward Air Control would walk the shells in and they had to get the hell out of there and into the treeline. And the Magic Dragon was going after the communists, giving them a break.

"Mau len!" Khiet yelled. They were all moving as fast as they could across the paddy dikes.

Teague felt the ground shake from the next shell and the third one right on its heels was close, the shrapnel singing in the air. He was now only twenty yards from the tree when an artillery shell landed in the paddy field behind him. A shower of mud knocked him to the ground. Stunned, the wind knocked out of him, he struggled for breath.

He pushed himself to his knees, shook his head to clear it, then groped drunk-like for his weapon. He found it. He stood up.

A body lay over the dike wall like someone's discarded jacket. He saw pieces of another man in the rice stalk stubble. Several wounded crawled up the bank and Teague ran over and grabbed one of them and hoisted the man up on his shoulder like a sack of grain and took off again for the jungle twenty meters ahead.

They had to be out of the paddies and into cover before the serious bombers showed up. Hopefully, when that happened, they would be concentrating on the fleeing communists.

Only when they had gotten far enough into the trees and the outskirts of a village that no more rounds were dropping near them did they stop. Teague put the wounded man down.

Khiet selected three men to stay behind and help the two wounded and bury the dead man in a shallow grave to be retrieved later.

They moved forward for another half an hour and almost had their second run-in with a communist unit, avoiding it only by hiding under the outgrowth along the bank in water up to their chests as VC sampans loaded with troops passed.

Teague was so close to one of the boats he could clearly see the faces of the communist soldiers.

Maybe we'll end up walking in together, he thought ruefully. That was a very real possibility and a very dark joke.

The city was wide open. They moved in along a canal and then into one of the many villages that made up the outskirts of Can Tho.

They split up in small groups and headed for designated safe houses in another village that was closer to the center of a city that had something coming they were little prepared for.

Khiet was in contact with his agents and family. They waited for a cousin of his who would take them to one of the safe houses. When he arrived a short time later, he told them that Xam had been negotiating with local authorities but they had no more contact.

"She was at the headquarters of the Central Committee but that was the last I know. There are many Hoat Vu in town and she might have been arrested by them."

They followed the man to a thatched-roof house where they changed to clean, dry clothes they each carried in their backpacks. Then they followed the agent out of the dense thatched-roofed hamlet and slipped out under the arch and into the town proper.

The streets swarmed with celebrating people, a young couple sitting on the curb, on the balconies above the shops whole families gathered like flocks of birds, on the sidewalks, in the stoops, on bicycles, Vespas, Solexes, and cyclos; the entire city seemed to be out. Firecrackers popped and laughter drifted among the buildings. A parade turned the corner ahead and went down the street.

From constant updates from Acosta and his sources, those VC they'd nearly run into were headed here and were just one of hundreds of units all over the country moving toward all the major cities.

It was now all about survival and getting Xam out. The prisons in Can Tho were filled with thousands of prisoners and he hoped Xam wasn't among them, but now feared she might be.

He still couldn't believe that anybody had bought into the idea of a peace accord, but they obviously had and the celebrations were in full swing and Tet was less than twenty-four hours away.

They went back to the safe house as Khiet's people widened their search for information about Xam.

PART SIX

The Tet Offensive

68

Early on the evening leading to the first day of Tet, Khiet's agent had cyclos waiting to take them to the Committee Headquarters in the center of town to meet a policeman who might give them the information they sought about Xam's team.

The crowds filled the streets with singing, laughing, parading. The peace that Saigon and the communists had agreed to for the Tet holiday seemed for many of the citizens to be working.

The policeman didn't show and at midnight, the milling crowds began to celebrate Tet with firecrackers that, according to Khiet, drive off the celestial dog.

In front of many houses stood thirty-foot high Cay Neu Tet poles with pieces of red paper on top symbolizing the eight-fold path of the Buddha and small squares of woven bamboo with bits of colored glass that tinkled in the breeze. The air was strong with the pleasurable smell of flowers: narcissus, apricot, yellow bong mai blossoms on this most important day of the year. Tet was seen across the country as everyone's birthday.

The four cyclos U-turned and headed toward Due Boulevard. Two partying Americans jumped out of their way and swore mildly at them. The sound of their voices melted into that of the firecrackers and music of the celebration that reverberated through the streets in a dwindling, sporadic manner. It was two-thirty in the morning.

But Teague soon picked up a different sound that he knew wasn't firecrackers as most celebrants appeared to have thought as little changed on the streets. "That's AK!"

The next sound was the muffled blast of grenades exploding no more than a block or two away. The sham that was the peace accord had accomplished the goal the communists sought and now they were attacking full force.

As the reality hit and chaos ensued, panic spread.

In the front cyclo, Khiet leaned out, motioning to them and was shouting something when suddenly the driver of Teague's cyclo was hit and the motorcycle driven cart was careening wildly, twisted and jack-knifed, throwing Teague out, flipping Khiet and the driver off as it crashed on its side and bounced against the wall of the bakery.

Khiet darted back, shouting to the men in the other cyclos. Automatic weapons drove them into an alley and then a grenade went off in a blinding flash. Teague was stunned for a moment. Gunfire seemed to be coming from all directions.

The driver had been killed by a bullet in the head. He lay sprawled in his blood on the sidewalk.

Somewhere in the black tunnel ahead, a door opened and the sparkle of rapid fire jumped at them. A man fell hard with a grunt. Teague tripped over him but regained his balance.

Another grenade went off, the percussion of it in the narrow walls a thousand times exaggerated. Teague felt stings in his arm and leg as if he'd walked into a hornet's nest.

They pushed a door open and went into the dark shattered interior of a shop. They heard family members yelling at each other from an adjoining room.

They went through another door and half a dozen people shied away, cowering against the walls.

"Get us to the roof!" Khiet demanded.

The young boy came forward and pointed to the stairs and then led them up.

Teague turned just as the man behind him whirled and shot a VC coming through the side door, firing as he came. He went down and there was more firing in the darkness of the hall. Teague and Khiet both laid down heavy fire and the attack stopped.

When he turned, he saw through a haze of smoke a cowering family.

Teague whirled and followed Khiet up the steps.

A young boy, eyes filled with terror, ran down yelling for his parents.

Teague and the others ran across the roof of the first building, snaking their way in a low profile as across the city in the midst of the chaotic racket of rocket and machine gun fire. They crossed three buildings before they were forced to hide between some flower pots.

They had hoped to descend into the basketball court at the Chinese school, but this was an obvious mistake. It appeared to be the staging area for a large Viet Cong unit.

They huddled between the big flower pots and watched as the communists took control of the streets. They lay there for what seemed at least an hour and then they saw a C-130, its mini guns raining a hailstorm of red and yellow streaks on the river. It flew in a slow circle, pouring down bullets at a rate that covered the area of two football fields with a bullet striking every two inches and it was moving toward them with all the deadly splendor of a firestorm.

Half a block away, the hotel where American support staff and clerks were housed was hit with violent explosions and part of the building collapsed.

They scrambled to get out of there and were going over the side of the two-story building down to a catwalk when a series of explosions shook the building violently. Teague fell, then abruptly slammed to a stop, then fell again, hitting hard.

He sensed he'd blacked out for a moment. He sat there waiting for his head to clear.

He whispered. "Khiet?" There was no reply.

Teague got a sense of his position. He was tangled in the catwalk, the catwalk suspended over a small courtyard. It was pitch black. He pulled himself free and grabbed a section of the wall, the concrete jagged-edged against his hand.

All around there was yelling and shooting. He pulled himself up and saw Khiet sitting in the middle of half a room looking dazed. He was perched precariously on the edge of a gaping hole. The whole building was gutted and stank of cordite. They were alone.

Khiet called down for his men and someone below answered with an automatic weapon and Teague yanked him back away from the hole and they scurried into an adjacent room as the communists below yelled back and forth.

Teague and Khiet made their way back out onto a roof and crossed to another building.

They could see the street through a break in the wall as a jeep-load of triumphant communists passed by.

But they learned from other parts of the city and the gunboat radio traffic that the ARVN and some Americans with them were giving the VC a major battle in the center and northern parts of the city. Those ARVN units and police still in the city were putting up a serious fight.

Later, as morning hinted, VC soldiers controlling this part of the city started bringing people in from the house searches. Then went around with bull horns and gave orders. People were to report according to their categories. There were several levels of poor, then a middle category of shopkeepers and cycle drivers, and the richer merchants, government officials and counter-revolutionaries.

Then Teague witnessed three executions that took place in the schoolyard just across the street, but could do nothing to stop them as it would jeopardize everyone hidden in the building where he was.

The men were blindfolded, forced to kneel and a political cadre read charges of their various crimes against the people and collaboration with the enemy. Then the cadre walked up behind the first one. He pulled out his revolver and placed it at the base of the man's skull and fired. The man slumped forward until his head hit the macadam of the courtyard, then he fell on his side.

The cadre shot the next two men and then refilled his revolver, made some marks on his clipboard and walked away. About fifteen minutes later, the bodies were dragged off.

The whole time he watched this, Teague had been waiting for them to bring Xam out to execute her and he saved what ammo he had for that moment. When they didn't, he could only hope that she was alive and possibly being protected by police, or in their custody.

From reports Khiet was getting, Can Tho was the hardest hit of the Delta cities. Half of Can Tho was under VC control, but that the ARVN soldiers, with the SEALS and Special Forces, were still holding their own and beginning a pushback in some areas that the communists weren't apparently expecting. They had taken some government buildings, but now were back out fighting in the main square and the river front.

VC control of large parts of the city meant this was going to be a long, drawnout battle. Teague and Khiet talked about where to go to find protection, food and water.

Had Duyet's armed units been allowed to come in, this fight would have been over quickly and a lot of people would have been saved.

69

In parts of the normally peaceful city with its wide French-designed boulevards, the Viet Cong were searching the buildings methodically, one at a time, forcing Teague and the others to keep moving.

They found safe havens for periods of time that turned into days and nights and just scrounging for food and water became a problem in the midst of the fighting. But the people they would come in contact with would provide them with rice cakes and water. The streets were now empty and the siege was tightening

Finally, they reached the river dike on the west edge of the city and camped with some ARVN troops, police and some Americans, most of them clerks experiencing their first combat.

The battle in this and other cities went on and on for days and then a week, and a second and it felt interminable. The once beautiful city was taking a beating. Getting to a safe place that could allow them the necessities was the top priority at the moment.

Teague was in radio contact with the gunboats out on the Bassac and to let them know their location and find out what was happening.

He couldn't give them coordinates to hit certain areas where he knew the VC were heavily congregated because of the population they might be holding. This wasn't going to be done by massive firepower from air or the river, it was going to be done hand-to-hand, building to building, and it was the worst kind of combat. Jungle fighting had moved into a city with people hiding everywhere.

He had learned from Engler, who'd taken the high powered fast boat to a Riverine base so it wouldn't be attacked and destroyed, that the VC were failing across the country to take and hold cities.

The gunboats on the river did fire their cannons occasionally into the city. They would have accuracy given them with aerial flyovers, but that wasn't going to win the battle and they were forced to be careful not to kill civilians.

The VC had apparently been busy cutting holes in the buildings and they moved freely without having to use the streets so the fire did little more than destroy the tops of buildings and litter the streets with debris.

From their hiding place, they overheard a hot argument between a VC cadre and an NVA political officer brake out just below them. The NVA officer was outraged that the population of the town had not come out to greet and support their liberators. He was equally upset that pockets of ARVN, police and regional force soldiers, rather than surrendering, were fighting the VC tenaciously. The arguers moved on.

"When it is dark, we go," Khiet said.

They were only a block and a half from one of the larger buildings in the center of the city.

Moving slowly and carefully, they made their way to where the Central Committee often met. Around midnight, they huddled near the entrance. There was a rancid smell. Above, a gunship passed over and moments later they heard massive firing at some target.

The squad hugged the wall until it calmed, and then they ran to the next building and moved along the sidewalk, skirting the rubble. They sprinted across the courtyard and the door opened and they lunged inside.

There were families hiding there and they had water and some rice which they shared, and in return they provided protection.

Finally, Khiet received some information from a police officer who was slightly wounded and wanting to escape the city that Xam was last seen near the police station where she'd met with city authorities and the odds were that the police had her. The question was, did she survive and if so, was she with the local police or the Hoat Vu secret police?

A man came in and talked to Khiet, who relayed the message that an ARVN Ranger Battalion was on its way. They were led by an agent to a place that had held local police, and half a dozen Americans with the 13th Aviation Battalion. There they could get food and water being dropped in by choppers. And it was a bit of an R&R, a place to rest and recuperate.

The take-back of the city was getting underway.

70

Colonel Stennride had a heavy security team to protect his compound. A big portion of the province's ARVN soldiers were doing the same for the Mangs. But with the exception of some sporadic rockets hitting the compounds neither had been struck by any ground attacks. The communists wanted the cities and from there, they assumed the rest of the country would fall.

He now had enough information about the country-wide offensive to realize how close the communists had come, especially in the cities outside the Delta. Had some communist commanders in I Corps and II Corps not jumped the gun, and had the communists thrown everything they had into it, and had Westmoreland not shifted twelve battalions back in around Saigon, the war might well be over. America would follow the French and Japanese.

What Stennride found to be amazing was not just that the attack on the major cities was so massive and country-wide, but that not a single city had completely fallen. In several of the bigger cities, the communists had taken up residence as if they were going to be staying. Instead they were being pushed out everywhere, including Can Tho, the hardest hit in the Delta. The great uprising that was expected in support of the communists never materialized.

When Keller came into the office at the end of the second week of the battles, he said, "Good news. Vadot proved right. The secret police in Can Tho grabbed and held the Xam woman. She'd been hiding with the help of a local police official, but now Chien has her and wants to know what you want to do with her."

Stennride was shocked that she was still alive and they had her. It gave him an idea. "Protect her and hold her in place. This damn Tet offensive is starting to wind down. Xam could be very helpful in resolving our problem."

Stennride had Keller mark on the plastic map on the table where they had her. The captain traced a line in grease pencil on the map from the military compounds to the river, and on all sides of the line and the compound, and all through the city there were little red flags, circles and X marks—and a very few blue flags marking friendly forces.

"Any sign of Teague?"

"From what we can find out, he may be inside the city and fighting alongside some Americans and ARVN. Lot of communication with Rivereign forces about where to hit. There may be some Hoa Hao with him, but the major units retreated into the jungle before Tet when the cities wouldn't agree to their coming in."

Stennride nodded. The fluorescent light trembled under the impact of another incoming rocket. Dust dropped from the cracked ceiling. Still bitter over the defeat his forces had suffered before the Tet attack, he wanted the VC to get the hell out so he could finish his primary mission to destroy the radical elements. But he had an idea how this might be done without having to go to war.

"We need to contact the CIA operative Frank Acosta. Soon as this offensive is beaten back, we'll need to act fast to prevent the sects from making any moves. We need to put an end to this madness once and for all." Since the CIA had already pulled the plug on the rebels it was time to bring this to a conclusion.

There was no doubt now that the countrywide failure of the communists and the solid defense not only of Americans but the Vietnamese had changed everything. The political aftereffect was going to be big.

Keller said, "We have locations for the names on the blacklist in the major cities that Vadot gave us. The Hoat Vu teams are ready to go after them when the last VC are pushed out."

Stennride said, "Chien will have to hold them back. It'll be better if we can make a deal they feel somewhat comfortable with. I don't think it serves us to go after them. Then the units in the jungle will declare war and the fight could become endless. There's another possible way to solve this. Frank Acosta. Just make sure that Xam is protected. She'll be a key to getting to Teague. Then get hold of Acosta. It's time to work something out. What little support there was for some Third Force is dead. Now it's all-out war between America and the communists. If the Hoa Hao want to survive it'll be by disarming and rejoining society as they did in the fifties. That's the way we need to end this."

"What do you want him to do, come here?"

"Yes. We need to work this out."

When the call came from the CIA operative an hour later, Keller said, "He's back in Saigon being protected by El Presidente Thieu, who actually thought at first the VC attack was a Ky coup.

Nobody was ready for it. It gets better. It seems our renegade Teague has been trying to get hold of Acosta. He's been on his transmitter every couple of hours and that gave us his location."

"Can Tho?"

"Yes. He's trying to get to Xam. He's holed up with some of his friends on the western side of town. There's still some sporadic fighting going on, but the VC are beginning to leave."

"Tell Acosta we're ready to put an end to this. I want him to get his ass down here to discuss the way we might just work this out and save a hell of a lot of lives. It starts with Teague and Xam."

"You want Acosta here right now?"

"Yes. I want to see the look of capitulation up close and personal in his eyes. Make sure he understands this is about finding a way to save lives by disarming the rebels and getting Teague and Xam the hell out of Vietnam. I'm sick of this. It has to end."

"You really think those rebels will give up arms once again?"

"Without support, they won't have a choice. They know what'll happen if they don't."

71

Frank Acosta had no choice. If the colonel had a way to end this without an ongoing conflict and mass bloodshed, then he had to find out what the bastard wanted to do.

He made the direct call. "What do you want from me?"

"Help in saving a lot of people," Stennride said. "Teague is in Can Tho and we know exactly where he and his associates are. And the Hoat Vu have Vinh Lac's sister, Xam. Since the CIA has abandoned the idea of a Third Force, it's over. Teague has to agree to come to terms. Then leave the country. I need you to come to my compound so we can work it out. Get hold of Teague and let him know the circumstances. We're going to end this peacefully. Will you work with me to end this without a bloodbath?"

Acosta hesitated for a moment, before saying, "Yes." He had no choice. Chandler's dream was dead and now it was a matter of shutting it down without a bloody mess.

After the call, Acosta immediately made arrangements to fly to the colonel's compound.

That the secret police had Xam and were close to getting Teague alarmed him. Acosta had to try and save them. They in turn would try and convince the rest of the sect forces that it was, once again, over. It might not work, but they had to try.

The Tet Offensive was the final nail in the coffin of the dream of a populist, political revival. Now it wasn't about politics, it was about all-out war.

He radioed Teague and told him to sit tight and do nothing. He'd get back to him about Xam and the situation after visiting Stennride. He didn't wait for any further conversation. He was sickened, devastated and felt a sense of self-disgust but had to put it aside and get this finished.

Two hours after the call from Stennride, Acosta's chopper circled at high altitude and then dropped down into the landing zone of the colonel's heavily walled and armed compound, a visit Acosta never imagined he'd be forced to make. As usual, he suffered from a bit of his usual paranoia about what was waiting for him.

He exited the chopper, leaving the pilot with the bird. He was met by Captain Keller, who escorted him into the main building and down a hall and into Stennride's office.

"Excellent French bean," Stennride said, pointing to the coffee pot.

Acosta accepted a cup and then sat down for what he knew was going to be a miserable, humiliating surrender. A moment worse than he ever imagined.

"Saigon going to live to see another day?" Stennride asked with that derisive tone of his.

"Looks that way. I take it Fourth Corps will as well."

"It's hanging on quite well."

"Coming in we flew over some New Life Hamlets that looked to be wiped out. Your boy Vanderlin survive?"

"He's more your boy than mine. Never liked or trusted the bastard. He's here in one of the buildings where some of my troops are barracked. I think he had a nervous breakdown. The price of modern war gone wrong is hard on the sensitive mind. I take it you agreed to come down to talk because you have something to offer?"

Acosta sipped his coffee, which turned out to be very good, and said, "I've been in touch with my colleague who is back in D.C. and has been talking to Langley and our associates in the administration. It's now going your way, a full-on military war between America and the communists. Westmoreland will get everything he needs short of nukes. Hundreds of thousands of young, inexperienced new troops are coming in. I came to this goddamn place an idealist and it's not easy for me to give up the dreams and become a cynical realist, but that's where it is."

"Idealism in war," Stennride said, "doesn't long survive. You've been in touch with Teague?"

"Yes."

"Does he and that Xam woman have any authority to bring the Buddhist rebels back under control and disarm them once the VC are pushed out?"

"That I don't know. But Teague is very well connected to all the major leaders. Xam's survival and freedom may have a lot to do with how this ends. She's a major figure. If there is an agreement, I'm sure part of it will be a guarantee the Buddhist rebels won't be hunted down and prosecuted if they agree once again to give up the arms and the resistance. If not, you'll be fighting two wars for a long time."

"We don't want to waste resources fighting a war with the

radical Buddhists, one they can never win. So, let's get Teague on board and find a way to put an end to this."

"What will this 'end' look like?" Acosta asked.

"I think the best solution is that you'll escort the rebel sect leaders out of this country and those soldiers that stay behind have to disarm just like they did in the fifties. They'll survive and not be hunted down if they are willing to accept returning to their previous status. I'll talk that over with Teague. At the moment, he's trapped and I want him brought here. The city is clearing out so I think you can get him from the roof of a building. You will get an escort to suppress any interference."

Acosta hated to have to agree to any of this, but he saw no alternative. After all that had been done, the deaths and an actual victory over this colonel's forces, it was very hard to swallow a defeat when they'd come so close only to be shut down at the last minute. And he was the one that the colonel wanted to engineer the humiliating endgame.

"You ready to end this?" Stennride asked.

"Yes."

The colonel nodded. "Good, let's do this."

Acosta was glad that Chandler didn't have to witness this ignominious end to the dream he had tried to recreate by resurrecting the coalition of Hoa Hao, Cao Dai and Catholic militia that had cleared the Delta of Communists in 1954 only to be betrayed and crushed by Saigon with the support of American agents. And now it was happening once again.

72

Teague suffered the choking air. It had a heavy cordite stink infiltrated with rotten food and the nauseating stench of the wounded. Black flies the size of beetles buzzed around the squalor, looking for open wounds to light on.

The walls were lined with wounded men waiting for a way to get to the medical help. The floor was littered with the debris from endless days and nights of fighting: shell casings, broken ammo boxes, bloodied bandage strips, c-ration cans. City combat was the worst, especially when it trapped a population of children, women and older people.

The doors were now open on the main floor and the healthy men began to help the wounded and take them to the small medical facility that was again open, others to a medical boat on the river.

The Tet celebration of everyone's birthday had turned into a massive funeral for a stillborn revolution and a disaster for all the lies about how successful this great war of attrition was.

For Teague, it all changed with the call from Frank Acosta, who was with Colonel Stennride. "He's willing to end this without a bloodbath. Xam is alive and at the police station. She'll be released in Cambodia if you agree to let me pick you up and bring you here to work out how to end this. I can be on the rooftop of the building where you are in about fifteen minutes. You okay with that?"

Teague said, "I have any options?"

"No."

"Okay. What police have her?"

"I'm not really sure. You can send somebody over there with radio communication. She'll be protected and getting her and other leaders out is what we're working on."

Teague was relieved to hear that Xam was still alive, but knew they'd kill her if something wasn't done fast. He had to accept whatever deal the mad colonel offered if it guaranteed to get her out and not compromise her people.

After the call, Teague discussed the changing situation with Khiet, who agreed and left for the police station with two of his men, both cousins.

Teague went to the roof of the building to wait for Acosta and guide him in. Smoke from a dozen fires blackened the sky. Buildings lay in rubble in the streets. Palm trees had been blown to pieces and their remains were scattered among the ruins. The cloying stench of urban warfare heavy in the air.

The chaos and carnage had lasted weeks. Teague and the men with him had been reduced to living in squalor, food deprivation and struggling just to get water.

Now that the communist rocket teams, grenadiers, sappers, and snipers had left, or had been killed, civilians were coming out of their hiding places and entering the streets.

Some Americans appeared and headed for the docks, their clothes dirty and disheveled, shirts hanging out, unshaven faces, some still in their party clothes from the Tet celebrations.

It struck Teague as he watched them leave that they represented something very strange and sad. Dominant paradigms determine events. The American military and intel had failed to see the true nature of this war. The vision through the smoke and the ruins rose before him in stunning clarity. Failure of vision is itself a dominant paradigm, one that leads to disaster.

The communists had their own delusions in those first hours and days, apparently expecting to take the city and use the building where he now stood as a major staging area. They had not expected the fight they got. After many days of bitter, bloody struggle they gave up trying to take the center of the city and put their resources elsewhere. And then the city began to reassert itself and now was virtually free of major gunfire. It represented a great potential that probably would never be used.

Already many VC units were heading into the jungles. From Khe Sanh to Saigon to the Delta, it was coming to a close. He saw no way the Hoa Hao rebels could win without CIA help and an acceptance by MACV of a political resurrection that would threaten Thieu's government. That everything depended on decisions at the top was the way of this war and those decisions had no room for the average Vietnamese.

He saw Khiet and two of his men go up the street and then turn toward police headquarters.

Across the street a dog was digging at a body trapped under an overturned bus and in a sick way represented the bleak, dark disaster.

The sun was at its perigee, almost directly overhead and Teague wore the bill of his bush hat tight over his sunglasses.

He stood on the roof and watched armored cars and Viet

Rangers moving down the main street. Out on the piece of the river, a troop-filled Tango boat reached the docks. Further down river was a Monitor battleship. Overhead were Navy Sea Hawk choppers, and coming from the west was an army 'dust off' medevac chopper.

Twenty minutes later, a chopper appeared and he talked it in toward the building roof. He still couldn't absorb and digest the stunning reality that it was really over, that this colonel had become the chosen one.

73

When Teague followed Acosta into Stennride's office in the heavily guarded compound, the colonel didn't acknowledge him for a minute. He finally looked up from some paperwork, a sober yet triumphant expression on his face, saying, "I appreciate your coming. Coffee is fresh."

Acosta, a very defeated and depressed look on his face, poured himself a coffee and then sat down.

"No, I'm good," Teague said, as he sat down in one of the wicker chairs at the opposite end of a table from Acosta. "Where's Xam?" He waited, assessing his enemy, this man who represented the brutal opposition to the rise of Buddhist peasants to legitimate power.

"Xam and her inner circle, the ones who've survived, will be released in Cambodia once we come to an understanding. We have a lot to discuss. You'll be in contact with Khiet, who will be with her."

Stennride sat back in his leather chair behind a massive teak desk and studied Teague for a moment, then said, "We want to repatriate the various rebel factions and put an end to these disastrous 'black projects'. Your friends will again be unarmed as they were before the CIA radicals got into this. The war no longer has any room for internal political struggles. It's now one-dimensional. And it's going to get really nasty and we're going to win it, not with the sects or, for that matter, with the ARVN. It'll be an all-out American war with massive force."

The colonel pointed to a large photo on the wall to his right. "That's the infamous Iron Triangle fire. I keep that as a reminder of how wrong things can go. General Westmoreland wanted to eliminate a threat close to Saigon. The VC had been using it as a sanctuary for decades with a vast tunnel complex. The Triangle was covered with jungle, laced with swamps and streams. Search and destroy sweeps in there produced nothing but trouble. It's machete country. Two steps and whack, whack."

Jesus, Teague thought, this bastard is now a professor. This is a class and we're his students.

Stennride took a sip of coffee and fixed a gaze on Teague, as if waiting for some kind of comment. When Teague didn't respond, the colonel continued, "So one night, this advisor, an American captain who had seen whole regiments swallowed up in that forty-square mile jungle, yet won nothing but casualties, voiced his opinion so strongly he ended up getting an invitation to dine with Westy and family. The general thought the war would be over soon and he had his family there. After dinner, when Westy's wife had taken the kids to bed, this captain unveiled his idea to burn the whole fucking place down and be done with it!"

Stennride turned again to the huge photo on the wall behind him, saying, "At the beginning of the dry season, umpteen million gallons of defoliant was dropped to kill off the top cover. That let the sun in to bake the place dry until it was like a California hill in August. Then they sent cargo planes over and had them drop gasoline and oil all over the place. I mean they rained fuel down on that tinder-box until it was saturated."

Teague glanced at Acosta, who looked bitter and depressed as the lecture continued.

"They sent some planes over with loudspeakers to tell the residents, who were in hell, to get the hell out. Some residents elected to stay put. In came the attack planes with incendiary bombs and napalm. The Iron Triangle exploded. The firestorm had heat that could have melted Mars had it gone on long enough. But you know what happened? Something of a shock. That firestorm triggered what they call an atmospheric confluence in the humid air above the Iron Triangle and son-of-a-bitch started to rain and then it poured. And it put the goddamn fire out. Westmoreland's people, shocked, learned from the mistake. They figured out how to control a fire, how to properly use napalm and bombs correctly. Learning from mistakes is the key to victory."

Now Teague figured the colonel was getting to the point he wanted make, and the threat it contained.

Stennride took another sip from his coffee, put the cup down and studied them for a moment, before saying, "The secret to winning this war isn't winning hearts and minds. That's the illusion of fools. The secret to victory in this war, with its jungles, swamps and mountains, is massive, but very tactical bombing that crushes the enemy. That's step one. Step two is half a million American soldiers taking these bastards to the cleaners in every nook and cranny and tunnel in this miserable country. Rolling Thunder from the air, combined with rolling iron on the ground."

He paused, waited, got no questions, so continued. "The point is, we learn from failure and change course. There's absolutely no room for a Third Force in this country. The peasants aren't capable of self-governance. And pacification, those New Life Hamlets, have accomplished nothing. In fact, instead of winning hearts and minds by taking the peasants away from their ancestral villages, it just alienates them and makes them much more recruitable by the VC. It all comes down to building the biggest, nastiest killing machine on the planet to defeat a relentless, brutal enemy. Teague, you need to convey the reality to all your friends. Those who aren't willing to disarm are better off getting out of Vietnam. My offer to you is to open up the way out for those who want to leave, and in the process, we'll free Thi Xam and the others. It's over and now just has to be properly cleaned up."

Teague looked at Acosta, but didn't get a reaction. There was no point to make, no argument. Insane as it was, the colonel, with the help of the massive Tet attacks, had won the battle without a fight. And the people who were the greatest fighters were locked out and would end up once again being disarmed and irrelevant.

Stennride said, "Those who might want to continue the fight need to understand they have no allies. No Chandlers, Acostas, or you, to lend support. And what will happen to their base camps is going to be a lot different than what they're used to. Imagine a firestorm where some of your rebels are located if they refused to give up their arms. It will suck the oxygen out of their jungle strongholds like a slow-motion hydrogen bomb, incinerating everything in its path from three directions. Of course, it will be authorized to go down on the books as destroying VC encampments, but we know the reality. When coordinated bombings are hit by winds, it becomes a moving wall of flame leaping canals and rivers and just keeps moving. B-fifty-two strikes are going to create walls of flame and end to any further Viet Cong or rebel strikes in those areas, Seven Mountains and around the deepest jungles."

He paused, and then said to Teague, "You and Vinh Lac's

sister might consider London or Paris. I hear they are pretty decent this time of year, even if a bit chilly."

Teague ignored the sarcasm. He had no doubt about the reality. He turned to Acosta. "You need to deal with the disarming of those who stay behind. Let Duyet's forces understand that there is no longer any chance of building that peasant-based movement. It's survival now and if there is change later down the road, they have to be around to be part of that."

When Acosta nodded his agreement, Teague turned back to Stennride and said, "How is the exit going to be handled?" Much as he despised the man, and distrusted him, he had no choice but take him seriously.

The colonel said, "We'll send in helicopters to get you and your friends out across the border today. There will be no welcome back. Everything is going to change and change fast." Then, looking at Acosta, he added, "The Phoenix Program is no longer a CIA-run operation and will be moved into high gear, along with the bombing campaigns and the introduction of massive American forces. The days when some Green Berets could be dropped into the mountains to create a revolutionary force are long gone, gentlemen. What's coming is the necessary state of total war. Teague, Frank will send you your discharge papers. We don't need your services in 'Nam anymore. The communist dream of conquering Indochina and then the world stops here."

Stennride stood up. "It's time to go. Acosta will drop you across the border. And Teague, it's a new reality. General MacArthur was wrong because he didn't foresee the kind of power we have available."

"Whether he was right or wrong has yet to be determined," Teague said.

"It will be, and sooner than people think. And your war-within-the-war, as far as the media and the world is concerned, never happened. For the sake of the security and safety of those you're leaving behind, it needs to stay buried in the dark. Understood?"

Teague glanced at the photo of the fire, and then he nodded. "Understood."

He followed Acosta out of the building to the chopper pad. The whole compound looked more like a fort and there were armed personnel all over the place. Mostly Viet Special Forces.

After Teague and Acosta boarded the chopper, Colonel Stennride sat back down and reflected on the element inside the CIA who had caused so many problems, yet he appreciated that they were also responsible precisely because of those problems for giving him the kind of power he had and needed.

Keller came in and sat down.

"General Stennride has a nice ring to it, don't you think, our soon-to-be major?"

"I do. And Major Keller is pretty damn good as well."

It was very difficult for him to grasp the reality of the mindset of these dreamers, especially somebody like Teague who had been the young naval officer with endless potential had he not been sucked into fantasyland by Chandler.

Stennride found it so far out of his wheelhouse it mystified him. How does someone like Teague go so very wrong for a vision that could never have been? How had Chandler and Acosta and their colleagues succeeded in getting to someone like him to the point where he was willing to undermine the entire war effort on behalf of their stupid delusions? That the Viets were incapable of creating a democracy was so obvious he didn't understand the blindness to the reality.

For Stennride, that was the big and maybe unanswerable question of this war. He glanced out the window and watched the chopper lift off and head west toward Cambodia.

Now, maybe this war could be fought properly. They didn't need the goddamn hopeless Vietnamese. All they needed was massive, unrelenting force and that would come with half a million American soldiers on the ground and massive air power. In Stennride's mind there was no other road to victory. The entire country, including the North, had to be targeted hard and relentlessly.

"Success might well mean turning the whole of Vietnam and much of Laos into a kill-zone with a body count that can't be replaced. I don't see any other way."

"I agree," Keller said. "And I don't think you'll get any argument from MACV or Westy." Then he added, "General."

74

Escorted by two phantom jets, the Huey chopper with Teague, Acosta and the pilot darted up the river toward the border with Cambodia.

It was all happening so fast and was so surreal, but what the end might have in store was yet to be determined and Teague felt the full anxiety of the possibilities.

Once they were across the border, coming back wouldn't happen unless he was betrayed. Then it would be much better if they killed him. It was like climbing a steep mountain that took everything out of you and when you think you're near the top, an avalanche takes you and everything you dreamed of down hard.

Explosions from below, probably from VC ammo dumps, sent shock waves up through the air and knocked the chopper around like a dingy in a rough sea.

Teague thought about Colonel Stennride's great confidence that a war could be won without the participation of its most anti-communist citizens, the people who lived here, whose history was here and who had defeated the Viet Minh in the Delta. Massive airpower and half a million ground forces run by Americans was, in Teague's mind, utter insanity. What kind of victory would destroying the country in order to save it be?

The real battle wasn't against an army, it was against an ideology and defeating an ideology comes from possessing a stronger, competing ideology and that wasn't in play. In his mind, that was the real problem.

They skirted over the plumes of smoke above a stretch of an expanding inferno. By agreeing to this final solution, was he bringing the leadership, including Xam, to a nasty final destination?

He saw the boats on the Mekong; one of them was his super junk piloted by Engler. The other boats were filled with refugees from a lost cause. They were heading into Cambodia and an unknown future, one that might be very short and nasty.

The chopper finally settled on a clearing upriver where a small group of people waited on the bank. Teague and Acosta exited and bowed under the rotors. He looked for Xam and Khiet and didn't see either of them on the boats and along the banks where refugees were gathered.

"Don't worry," Acosta said, coming up beside him. He was now on his radio. Then he turned to Teague. "They're coming now."

Teague studied the sky, hoping this all went as it was supposed to. Part of him would not be shocked if the decision had been made to take them all out.

A chopper appeared in the distance. It would either be bringing Xam and Khiet, or rockets and their ignominious end.

The chopper slipped over the trees and river and then slanted toward them. It would either coming in firing or settle into a landing.

They waited in silence along with the others. When the chopper began its descent toward the opening and settled not far away, Teague was still unable to relax until he saw Khiet get out and then Xam.

The chopper rose and left, its breeze snapping her black pantaloons as she walked toward them. His reaction had his heart pounding. Was this real, true?

Acosta said, "It's too bad this didn't work out. It's the way of things in Indochina. That article you wrote about ground wars in this part of the world had some sound advice. But who the hell takes sound advice anymore?"

As he started to walk away toward his chopper, Acosta suddenly stopped and turned back, saying, "Teague, you and Xam remind me of a great line from one of Scott Fitzgerald's books. Maybe The Great Gatsby, but I'm not sure. It was about the romance: 'They slipped briskly into an intimacy from which they never recovered.' Good luck, my friend."

As Acosta passed Xam and Khiet, he nodded to them and then boarded his waiting chopper. It rose quickly and slanted off toward Vietnam.

She was about thirty meters away. Their eyes locked. The great painful emptiness in Teague of the failure slipped away as he was filled with the sight of her. Xam had lost so many who were important to her and so many who were important to the cause, as had he.

"Chao co," Teague said quietly, stepping toward her.

"Chao ong," she replied.

Teague hated that the war for her and the Buddhists was now lost. But the war, terrible as it was, did give him the woman he loved and for that he was grateful.

And yes, as her brother had warned, she would rule him and it was a submission from which he never wanted to recover.

As they were about to get on the waiting boat and leave for Phnom Penh and beyond, Teague took a last, sad glance back in the direction of Vietnam, at a war that was in violation of everything that should have been learned from the Korean War. Instead they were turning the entire country into a kill zone in a strategy of attrition that depended on nothing but body count. It seemed too insane to believe. Yet that was the sad truth.

The End

An online review of this book on the site where you purchased it would be much appreciated. Thanks for taking the time!

About The Author

Richter Watkins is the bestselling author of crime thrillers including the Murder Option series and the Cool series. He grew up in Williamsport, PA where he played his share of little league baseball, and was the captain of his golf team. He is a Vietnam Veteran, attended the University of Miami, and San Jose State where he received a degree in Sociology. He later continued his education and received an MFA from the American Film Institute for screenwriting. He shares his life with romance author, Mary Leo. He is currently working on his next exciting novel.

www.richterwatkins.com
www.facebook.com/richterwatkins

Other Books By The Author

The Cool Series
Book One: Cool Heat
Book Two: Cool Hit
Book Three: Cool Hunt
Book Four: Cool Hell

Murder Option Series
Book One: Murder Option 1
Book Two: Murder Option 2
Book Three: Murder Option 3
Book Four: Murder Option 4

Single Title Books
The Girl On The Golden Elephant
(A Post Vietnam War Thriller)

Betting On Death

Other Works
America On Suicide Watch

Books Written As Terry Watkins
The Big Burn
Stacked Deck

WITHDRAWN FROM
COLLECTION

Made in the USA
Monee, IL
08 January 2020

20014634R00240